Ken MacLeod graduated with a BSc in Zoology from Glasgow University in 1976. Following research in bio-mechanics at Brunel University, he worked in a variety of manual and clerical jobs whilst completing an M.Phil thesis. He previously worked as a computer analyst/programmer in Edinburgh, but is now a full-time writer. He is the author of four novels, the first of which, *The Star Fraction*, was runner-up for the Arthur C. Clarke Award. He lives in West Lothian with his wife and children.

THE CASSINI DIVISION

Ken MacLeod

An *Orbit* Book

First published in Great Britain by Orbit 1998
This edition published by Orbit 1999

Copyright © Ken MacLeod 1998

The moral right of the author has been asserted.

A CIP catalogue record for this book is
available from the British Library.

ISBN 1 85723 730 7

Typeset by Deltatype Ltd
Printed and bound in Great Britain by
Clays Ltd, St Ives plc

Orbit
A Division of
Little, Brown and Company (UK)
Brettenham House
Lancaster Place
London WC2E 7EN

To Mairi Ann Cullen

Thanks to Carol, Sharon and Michael; to John Jarrold and Mic Cheetham; to Iain Banks and Svein Olav Nyberg; to Andy McKillop, Jo Tapsell, Paul Barnett and Kate Farquhar-Thompson.

Thanks also to Tim Holman for editorial work at Orbit; to David Angus for pointing me to the map of Callisto; and to the socialists, for the Earth.

Man is a living personality, whose welfare and purpose is embodied within himself, who has between himself and the world nothing but his needs as a mediator, who owes no allegiance to any law whatever from the moment that it contravenes his needs. The moral duty of an individual never exceeds his interests. The only thing which exceeds those interests is the *material power* of the generality over the individuality.

Joseph Dietzgen, *The Nature of Human Brain-Work*

Contents

1 LOOKING BACKWARD   1
2 AFTER LONDON   18
3 NEWS FROM NOWHERE   40
4 THE STATE OF THE ART   64
5 THE COMING RACE   88
6 VALHALLA   107
7 THE IRON HEEL   119
8 CITY OF THE LIVING DEAD   152
9 A MODERN UTOPIA   183
10 IN THE DAYS OF THE COMET   203
11 LOOKING FORWARD   232

I

Looking Backward

THERE ARE, still, still photographs of the woman who gate-crashed the party on the observation deck of the Casa Azores, one evening in the early summer of 2303. They show her absurdly young – about twenty, less than a tenth of her real age – and tall; muscles built-up by induction isotonics and not dragged down by gravity; hair a black nebula; dark skin, epicanthic eyelids, a flattish nose, and thin lips whose grin is showing broad white teeth. She carries in her right hand a litre bottle of carbon-copy Lagrange 2046. Her left hand is at her shoulder, and on its crooked forefinger is slung a bolero jacket the colour of old gold, matching a gown whose almost circular skirt's hem is swinging about her ankles as she strides in. What looks like a small monkey is perched on her right, bare, shoulder.

Something flashed. I blinked away annular afterimages, and glared at a young man clad in cobalt-blue pyjamas who lowered a boxy apparatus of lenses and reflectors with a brief apologetic smile as he ducked away into the crowd. Apart from him, my arrival had gone unnoticed. Although the deck was a good hundred metres square, it didn't have room for everybody who was invited, let alone everybody who'd turned up. The natural progress of the evening, with people hitting off and drifting away to more private surroundings, would ease the pressure, but not yet.

There was room enough, however, for a variety of activities: close dancing, huddled eating, sprawled drinking, intense talking; and for a surprising number of children to scamper among them all. Cunningly focused sound systems kept each cluster of revellers relatively content with, and compact in, their particular ambience. The local fashions seemed to fit the party, loose and fluid but close to the body: women in saris or shifts, men in pyjama-suits or serious-looking togas and tabards. The predominant colours were the basic sea-silk tones of blue, green, red, and white. My own outfit, though distinctive, didn't seem out of place.

The centre of the deck was taken up by the ten-metre-wide pillar of the building's air shaft. Somewhere in one of the groups around it, talking above the faint white noise of the falling air, would be the couple whose presence was the occasion for the party – the people I'd come to speak to, if only for a moment. There was no point in pushing through the crowd – like anyone here who really wanted to, I'd reach them eventually by always making sure I was headed in their direction.

I made my way to a drinks table, put down my bottle and picked up a glass of Mare Imbrium white. The first sip let me know that it was, aptly enough, very dry. My slight grimace met a knowing smile. It came from the man in blue, who'd somehow managed to appear in front of me.

'Aren't you used to it?'

So he knew, or had guessed, whence I came. I made a show of inspecting him, over a second sip. He was, unlike me, genuinely young. Not bad-looking, in the Angloslav way, with dirty-blonde tousled hair and pink, shaved face; broad cheekbones, blue eyes. Almost as tall as me – taller, if I took my shoes off. His curious device hung on a strap around his neck.

'Comet vodka's more to my taste,' I said. I handed the glass into the monkey-thing's small black paws and stuck out my hand. 'Ellen May Ngwethu. Pleased to meet you, neighbour.'

'Stephan Vrij,' he said, shaking hands. 'Likewise.'

He watched as the drink was returned.

'Smart monkey,' he said.

'That's right,' I replied, unhelpfully. Smart spacesuit, was the truth of it, but people down here tended to get edgy around that sort of stuff.

'Well,' he went on, 'I'm on the block committee, and tonight I'm supposed to welcome the uninvited and the unexpected.'

'Ah, thanks. And to flash bright lights at them?'

'It's a camera,' he said, hefting it. 'I made it myself.'

It was the first time I'd seen a camera visible to the naked eye. My interest in this wasn't *entirely* feigned in order to divert any questions about myself, but after a few minutes of his explaining about celluloid film and focal lengths he seemed unsurprised that my glazed-over gaze was wandering. He smiled and said:

'Well, enjoy yourself, Ellen. I see some other new arrivals.'

'See you around.' I watched him thread his way back towards the doors. So my picture would turn up in the building's newspaper, and a hundred thousand people would see it. Fame. But not such as to worry about. This was the middle of the Atlantic, and the middle of nowhere.

The Casa Azores was (is? unlikely – I'll stick to the past tense, though the pangs are sharp) on Graciosa, a small island in an archipelago in the North Atlantic, which is (probably, even now) an ocean on Earth. It was so far from anywhere that, even from its kilometre-high observation deck, you couldn't observe its neighbouring islands. The sea and sky views might be impressive, but right now all the huge windows showed was reflected light from within. The lift from which I'd made my entrance was at the edge, and I had to get to the central area within the next few hours, sometime after the crowd had thinned but before everyone was too exhausted to think.

I drained the glass, picked up a bottle of good Sungrazer Stolichnya, gave the monkey a clutch of stemmed goblets to hold in its little fingers, and set out to work the party.

'Nanotech's all right in *itself*,' a small and very intense artist was explaining. 'I mean, you can *see* atoms, right? Heck, with the bucky waldoes you can *feel* them, move them about and stick them together. It's mechanical linkages all the way up to your fingers. And to your screen, for that matter. But all that electronic quantum stuff is, like, *spooky* . . .'

She had other listeners. I moved on.

'You're from space? Oh, great. I work with the people in the orbitals. We do zaps. Say you've got a replicator outbreak somewhere, natural or nano, like it makes a difference ... *anyway*, before the zap we all sorta wander around the evac zone, one, to check there's nobody there and, two, just to soak up and record anything that might get lost. You don't get much time, you're in an isolation suit that has to be flashed off you before you come out, for obvious reasons – takes most of your body hair with it, too – but even so, you can see and feel and hear a lot, and for hours or days, depending on how fast the outbreak's spreading, there's nobody else around for tens of kilometres. You know, just about every one I've done, I've picked up a species that wasn't in the bank. Genus, sometimes. Not known to science, as they say. Ran out of girlfriends to name them after, had to start on my actual *relatives*. And then you come out, and you sit around with the goggles and watch the zap. I mean, I like to see the flash, it's the next best thing to watching a nuke go off.'

The ecologist stopped and took another deep hit on the hookah. I waved away his offer of a toke. He sighed.

'The times when there's nobody around but you ... You just gotta love that wilderness experience.'

I had reached halfway across to the centre of the room. I wanted to offer the stoned scientist a shot of vodka, but the monkey had, in a moment of abstraction, devoured my last spare glass. The man didn't mind. He assured me he'd remember my name, and that some beetle or bug or bacterium would, one day, be named in my honour. I realised that I couldn't remember his name. Or perhaps he hadn't told me, or perhaps ... a certain amount of passive smoking was going on around here. I thanked him, and moved on.

'And don't *do* things like that,' I murmured. 'It's conspicuous.' A cold paw teased my ear, and a faint, buzzing voice said:

'We're low on silicates.'

I scratched the little pseudo-beast in response, and hoped no one had noticed my lips move. I felt a sudden pang of hunger and a need for a head-clearing dose of coffee, and stopped at the nearest buffet table. A woman wearing a plain, stained white apron over a gorgeous green sari ladled me a hot plate of limpets in tomato sauce. (All real, if it matters. I guess it must: my mouth waters at the memory, even now.) I decided on a glass of white wine. There were empty chairs around, so I sat. The woman sat, too, at the other side of the table, and chatted with me as I ate.

'I've just spoken to our special guests,' she said. She had an unusual accent. 'Such interesting people. An artificial woman, and a man from the stars! And back from the dead, in a sense.' She looked at me sharply. 'Perhaps you'll have met them before, being from space yourself?'

I smiled at her. 'How come everyone knows I'm from space?'

'Your dress, neighbour,' she said. 'Gold is a space thing, isn't it? It isn't one of our colours.'

'Of course,' I said. For a moment I'd thought she'd guessed it was a spacesuit. After she'd spoken, after I'd had a minute to observe how she moved, the subtle way her face cast its expressions, it was obvious that she was well into her second century. There would be no fooling her. She looked right back at me, her eyes shining like the pins in her piled-up black hair.

'Gold is such a useful metal,' she said. 'You know, Lenin thought we'd use it for urinals . . .'

I laughed. 'Not his only mistake!'

Her reply was a degree or two cooler that her first remarks. 'He didn't make many, and those he did were the opposite of . . . what's usually held against him. He thought too highly of people, as individuals and in the mass. Anyway,' she went on, complacently, 'some of us still think highly of *him*.'

I'd placed her accent now. 'In South Africa?' They were a notoriously conservative lot. Some of them were virtually Communists.

'Why, yes, neighbour!' She smiled. 'And you're from ... now don't tell me . . . not near-Earth; not Lagrange . . . and you're no Loony or Martian, that's for sure.' She frowned, watching as I lifted my glass, looking past me at, perhaps, her memory of how I'd walked up to the table. Weighing and measuring my reflexes. 'Yes!' She clapped her hands. 'You're a Callistan girl, aren't you? And that means . . .'

Her eyes widened a fraction, her brows rose.

'Yes,' I said quietly. 'The Cassini Division. And yes, I've seen your guests before.' I winked, ever so slightly, and made a tiny downward movement with my fingers as I reached across the table for a piece of bread. Not one in a hundred would have as much as noticed the gesture. She understood it, and smiled, and talked about other things.

The Cassini Division . . . In astronomy, the Cassini Division is a dark band in the rings of Saturn. In the astronautics of the Heliocene Epoch, the Cassini Division was the proud name – originally given in jest – of a dark band indeed, a military force in the ring of Jupiter. You know about the ring of Jupiter – but to us it was more than a remarkable product of planetary engineering, it was a standing reminder of the power of our enemies. It was our Guantanamo, our Berlin Wall. (Look them up. Earth history. There are files.)

The Cassini Division was the Solar Union's front-line force, our collective fist in the enemy's face. In our classless society it was the closest thing to an élite; in our anarchy, the nearest we came to a state; in our commonwealth, it held the greatest share of riches. Its recruits chose themselves, and not many could meet a standard of that rigour. In terms of sheer fire power the Division could have flattened all the states Earth ever knew, and still had enough left over for a bit of target practice to occupy the afternoon. The resources it controlled could have bought everything on Earth, in the age when that world was owned – and it still stood ready for the exchange, to give as good as it got, to pit our human might against the puny wrath of gods.

In other words . . . the Division was there to kick post-human ass. And we did.

(And yes. I'm still proud of it.)

The South African woman might have had unsound views about Vladimir Ilyich, but she turned out to be one of the 'old comrades'. Although the International had long since dissolved into the Union, its former members maintained their contacts, their veterans' freemasonry. I'd never really approved of this, but it helped me here. She introduced me to one of her friends, who introduced me to another, and so on. By an unspoken agreement they passed me along their chain of acquaintance, moving me through the crowd a lot faster than I'd managed on my own. Only half-an-hour after I'd finished my coffee, I found myself among a small cluster of people, at the focus of which were the party's special guests: the artificial woman, and the man who had come back from the stars, and from the dead. Even five years after their arrival, they could still pull a crowd – all the more so because they seldom did, preferring to wander around and talk to people they happened to meet.

The artificial woman was called Meg. She didn't look artificial right now, and indeed her body – cloned from that of some long-dead Malaysian-American porn actress, I understand – was in some respects more natural than mine. Only her personality was artificial.

It was a human personality in every way we'd ever been able to observe, but it was – she'd always insisted – running on top of a genuine artificial intelligence.

In which case the small, pretty woman standing a couple of yards away from me, elegantly smoking a tobacco cigarette, with her black hair hanging to her waist, and wearing a long black silk-satin shift and (unless my eyes deceived me) *absolutely nothing else*, was the only autonomous AI on Earth. A troubling thought, and it had troubled me ever since I'd met her.

The autonomous AI hadn't noticed me yet. She was looking at her companion, Jonathan Wilde, the man who had come back. Wilde, as usual, was holding forth; as usual, waving his hands; as usual, smoking tobacco, a vile habit that seemed hardwired into him and Meg both. He was a tall man, sharp-featured, hook-nosed, loud-voiced. His accent had changed, but still rang strangely in my ears.

'– never actually *met* him,' he was saying, 'but I did see him on television, and read some of what he put out during the Fall Revolution. I must say it's a surprise to find him still remembered.' He paused, flashing a quick, rueful smile. 'Especially since I'm forgotten!'

People around him laughed. It was one of Wilde's standing jokes that the ideas he – or rather, the human being of which he was a copy – had espoused back in the twenty-first century were now of interest only to antiquarians, and that his name was only a footnote in the history of the Space Movement. In some odd way, this very obscurity flattered his vanity.

As he stood there grinning he saw me. He stared at me, as if momentarily confused. Meg turned and saw me and gave me a welcoming smile. Wilde nodded slightly, and returned to his discourse. I didn't know whether to feel slighted or relieved. As the first person he'd seen on his emergence from the wormhole, I had some importance in Wilde's life ... but I didn't want him introducing me as such, and thus letting everyone present know where I was from.

Meg stepped over and caught my hands.

'It's good to see you again, Ellen.'

'Yeah, you too,' I said, and meant it. Her personality might be synthetic, but its appeal was genuine. I'd sometimes wondered what she saw in Wilde, whose fabled charm had never worked on me.

'What brings you here?' Meg asked.

'You don't make yourselves easy to find,' I said lightly. 'So I thought I'd take the opportunity.'

Meg smiled. 'You're a busy woman, Ellen. You want something.'

'Oh, you know,' I said. 'Perhaps we can talk about it later?'

She was looking up at me, a small frown on her smooth brow. 'Of course,' she said. 'Things should quiet down, soon.'

I laughed. 'You mean, like when Wilde's spoken to everybody?'

'Something like that.' She drew me to a nearby seat, just outside the huddle, and I sat down with her. 'This is all a bit exhausting,' she said absently. She stroked one bare foot with the other, and stubbed out her cigarette. The monkey hopped from my shoulder and clutched the edge of the ashtray, its big eyes entreating me. I shook my head at it. It bared its teeth, then turned away from me and let Meg play with it.

Wilde's voice, carrying:

'– this whole thing: turning his sayings into a scripture, and him into a martyred prophet – it's almost the only irrationality you people have left! I think he would have *laughed*!' And with that Wilde's laugh boomed, and those around him joined in, hesitantly. The conversation broke up over the next few minutes, and Wilde ambled over and sat down beside me. The three of us were perched as if on a log in an eddied swirl. Around us people partied on; now and again someone would drift over, see no response signalled, and turn away. Some left, but most hung around, tactfully out of earshot.

We exchanged greetings and then Wilde leaned away from me and sat shoulder-to-shoulder with Meg.

'Well, Ellen,' he said. 'You got us where you want us.' He lit a cigarette and accepted a shot of vodka. He looked down at his glass. 'This has already had several other drinks in it,' he observed. 'Nice thing about vodka, of course, is it doesn't matter. Any taste is an improvement. I'm drunk already. So if there's anything you forgot to ask us, in the debriefing –'

'Interrogation.' I always hated the old statist euphemisms.

'– go right ahead. Now's your chance.' He swayed farther back and looked at me with a defiant grin.

'You know what I want, Wilde,' I said heavily. I was a bit drunk myself, and more than a little tired. Gravity gets you down (and space sucks, but that's life). 'Don't ask me to spell it out.'

He leaned forward. I could smell the smoke and spirits on his breath.

'Oh, I know better than that,' he said. 'The same old question. Well, it's the same old answer: no. There is no way, no fucking *way* I'm going to give *you people* what you are so carefully not asking for.'

'Why not?'

Always the same question, which always got the same answer:

'I won't let you lot get your hands on the place.'

I felt my fists clench at my sides, and slowly relaxed them.

'We don't *want* the wretched place!'

'Hah!' said Wilde, with open disbelief. 'Whatever. It won't be me who gives you the means to take it.'

It would have to be somebody else who did, then, I thought. I kept my voice steady, and quiet.

'Not even to fight the Outwarders?'

'You don't need it to fight the Outwarders.'

'Isn't that for us to judge?'

Wilde nodded. 'Sure. You make your judgements, and I'll make mine.'

I wanted to shake the answer out of him. I would have had no compunction about it. As far as I was concerned, he wasn't a human being, just a clever copy of one.

I also, paradoxically, wished I *could* regard him as a fellow human, as a neighbour. This just served to increase my frustration. If I could have taken Wilde into my confidence, and let him know just how how bad, how fast, things were going, he might very well have agreed to tell me all I needed to know. But the Division trusted him even less than he trusted us. Telling him the full truth might trigger things far, far worse. Wilde and Meg had both been in the hands of the enemy, were quite literally products of the enemy, and even now we weren't one hundred per cent confident that they were – or were only – what they claimed, and seemed, to be. I thought for a moment of what it might be like if we ever had to treat them as an outbreak and hit them with an orbital zap. There would be no warning, no evacuation, no last-minute work for the ecologists.

The monkey-thing bounded from Meg's lap to mine. I let it scurry up my arm and nestle on my shoulder, and smoothed out the lap of my skirt. I looked up.

'That's fine,' I said. 'It's up to you.' I shrugged, the false animal's false fur brushing my cheek. 'You do what seems best.' I stood up and smiled at them both.

For a moment Wilde looked nonplussed. I hoped he'd be so thrown off balance by my lack of persistence that he would change his mind. But the ploy didn't work. I would have to go for the second option: more difficult, more perilous and, if anything, less likely to succeed.

'Goodbye,' I said. 'See you around.'

In hell, probably.

I leaned over the guardrail around the roof of the Casa Azores and looked down. The ground was a thousand metres below. I felt no vertigo. I've climbed taller trees. There were lights along the beach, bobbing boats in front of the beach, then a breakwater; and beyond that, blue-green fields of algae, fish-farms and kelp plantations and ocean thermal-energy converters, all the way to the horizon. Airships – whether on night-work or recreation I didn't know – drifted like silvery bubbles above them. The building itself, although in the middle of all this thermal power, drew its electricity from a different source. Technically the whole structure was a Carson Tower, powered by cooled air from the top falling down a central shaft and turning turbines on the way.

It was cold on the roof. I turned away from the downward view, wrapped the bolero jacket around my shoulders, and looked at the sky. Once my irises had adjusted, I could see Jupiter, among the clutter of orbital factories, mirrors, lightsails, satellites, and habitats. With binoculars, I could have seen Callisto, Io, Europa – and the ring. It was as good a symbol as any of the forces we were up against.

Our enemies, by some process which even after two centuries was, as we say, *not well understood*, had disintegrated Jupiter's largest moon, Ganymede, to leave that ring of hurrying debris and worrying machinery. And – originally within the ring, but now well outside it – was something even more impressive and threatening: a sixteen-hundred-metre-wide gap in space-time, a wormhole gate to the stars.

Two centuries ago, the Outwarders – people like ourselves, who scant years earlier had been arguing politics with us in the sweaty confines of primitive space habitats – had become very much not like us: post-human, and superhuman. Men Like Gods, like. The Ring was their work, as was the Gate.

After these triumphs, nemesis. Their fast minds hit some limit in processing-speed, or attained enlightenment, or perhaps simply wandered. Most of them distintegrated, others drifted into the Jovian atmosphere, where they re-established some kind of contact with reality.

Their only contact with us, a few years later, was a burst of radio-borne information viruses which failed to take over, but managed to crash, every computer in the Solar System. The dark twenty-second century settled down like drizzle.

Humanity struggled through the Fall, the Green Death, and the Crash, and came out of the dark century with a deep disapproval of the capitalist system (which brought the Fall), for the Greens (who brought the Death), and for the Outwarders (who brought the Crash, and whose viral programs still radiated, making electronic computation and communication hazardous at best).

The capitalist system was abolished, the Greens became extinct, and the Outwarders –

The Outwarders had still to be dealt with.

I checked that I was alone on the roof. The chill, fluted funnels of the Carson process sighed in their endless breath, their beaded condensation quivering into driblets. I moved around in their shadow, and sighted on, not low-looming Jupiter, but the Moon. I squatted, spreading the dress carelessly, and reached up and scratched the monkey's head and whispered in its ear.

The monkey began to melt into the jacket's shoulder, and then dress and jacket together flowed like mercury, and reshaped themselves into a ten-foot-wide dish aerial within which I crouched, my head covered by a fine net that spun itself up from where the collar had been. A needle-thin rod grew swiftly to the aerial's focus. Threads of wire spooled out across the deck, seeking power sources, finding one in seconds. The transformed smart-suit hummed around me.

'It's still no,' I said. 'Going for the second option.'

'Tight-beam message sent,' said the suit. 'Acknowledged by Lagrange relay.'

And that was that. The recipients of the message would know what I meant by 'the second option'. Nobody else would. My mission was confined to more than radio silence; the whole reason I'd come here myself was that we couldn't even trust word-of-mouth. The narrow-beamed radio message would be picked up and passed on by laser, which had the advantage that the Jovians could neither interfere with nor overhear it. It would be bounced to our ship, the *Terrible Beauty*, which was at this moment on the other side of the Earth, and sent on to the Division's base on Callisto. There would be a bare acknowledgement from Callisto, in a matter of hours. I was not going to wait around for it, not like this. I stood up and told the suit to resume its previous shape. When the dress was restored I gave it an unnecessary but celebratory twirl, and spun straight into somebody's arms. As I stumbled back a pace I saw that I'd bumped into Stephan Vrij, the photographer.

We stood looking at each other for a moment.

'The things you see when you don't have your camera,' I said.

'I didn't follow you,' he said awkwardly. 'I was just looking around. Last part of my job for the evening. It's amazing the crazy things people do up here, after a party.'

'Can you forget this?' I asked.

'OK,' he said. He looked away.

'Then I'll promise to forget you.' I reached out and caught his hand. 'Come on. I've had a lot of drinks, and you've had none, right?'

'Yes,' he said, looking a bit puzzled as I tugged at his hand and set off determinedly towards the elevator shaft. I grinned down at him.

'What better way to start the night?'

'You have a point there,' he said.

'Well, no,' I said, 'I rather hope *you* . . .'

Laughing, we went to his room.

When you are among another people, or another people is among you, and you lust after their strange flesh, go you and take your pleasure in them, and have sons and daughters by them, and your people shall live long upon the lands and your children shall fill the skies.

So it is written in the Books of Jordan, anyway. *Genetics*, chapter 3, verse 8.

I woke in a comfortable, if disorderly, bed. Stephan Vrij snored peacefully beside me. We were both naked, and I was under a quilt. I drew the quilt over him and he rolled over in his sleep.

From the angle of the light through the window, it was mid-morning on another fine day. The room was made of something that looked and smelled like pine, but it had never been cut into planks then hammered or glued together (which some people on Earth still do, as I later discovered, and not all of them because they have to but because they can afford the time to indulge such fads). Instead, it had been grown on-site, the walls and floor curving into each other, utility cables emerging like vines from the knotholes. Glossy monochrome pictures – of people, landscapes, seascapes – were stuck to the walls. They looked detailed and precise, just like photographs, apart from the lack of colour. Scattered about, on the low chairs and table or on the floor, was a rather embarrassing quantity and diversity of lingerie. Evidently I had been showing off, or the smart-suit had. My memories of the night were hazy, and warm.

I lay there a few minutes, smiling to myself and hoping I'd got pregnant. Doing so just before a war seemed perverse – it's traditionally done afterwards – but this war would be over before the pregnancy was noticeable. If we won, I might not be back on Earth for a long time, and we needed all the genes we could get. If we lost . . . but defeat wasn't worth thinking about.

I rolled out of bed and gathered the bits and pieces and set them to work reassembling themselves into hiking gear, apart from the one or two items that would be serviceable as underwear. Not that I actually needed underwear in a smart-matter spacesuit, but they were very nice. So, in their own way, were the shorts and socks, boots and rucksack that came together on the floor. The suit always did have good taste.

The apartment was pretty basic and standard, and the functional logic of it was familiar, so I had no difficulty in finding the makings of breakfast. I brought the breakfast through to Stephan, and we ate it, and made love for a final time. Stephan took some photographs of me, and I promised again to forget him, and we said goodbye.

I suppose he has forgotten me, by now, but I like to think that someone still has the photographs.

Down at ground level it was hot. The sun was high in the sky, enormous, so bright I could see it with my eyes closed and so hot it hurt my skin. Even the air was hot. It's one of the things they don't tell you about, like gravity.

Between the base of the tower and the beach were some low buildings. Stores and warehouses of equipment for use by people working in the blue-greens or playing on the beach, refreshment stalls, eating-houses, and so on. I wandered along the shore road, looking for the tourist place.

Naked small children ran about, yelling, racing from the tower to the beach and back. Somewhat older children lolled in shade and listened to adults or adolescents as they talked earnestly in front of a flip-chart or above a machine. Now and again a child would join one of these groups; now and again a child would rise, nod politely to the teacher, and wander off to do something else.

Two such children were minding the tourist place when I found it. The store was easy enough to spot, a rough construction of sea-crete and plastic and what looked like driftwood, but was probably scrap synthetic wood. I told myself it must be more solid than it looked, as I ducked under the sea-silk awning and stood blinking in the cool, dim interior.

Inside, the walls were lined with sagging shelves, which were piled with everything a tourist might need. Old tin boxes of gold and silver coins, new plastic boxes of bullets, firearms oiled and racked, hats, scarves, boots. From the ceiling hung a wide range of casual clothing: loose sundresses, seal-fur suits, tee shirts and towelling robes. There seemed to be more possible destinations than the number of possible tourists. I was alone in the store, apart from a boy and a girl sitting on the counter with a chessboard between them.

The boy looked up. 'Hi,' he said. He waved his hand. 'Help yourself. If you want something that isn't there, let us know.' He smiled absently then returned to frowning over the chessboard.

I dug through clinking piles of dollars, roubles, marks, pounds, and yen to make up sixty grams of gold and a hundred of silver, in the smallest coins I could find. From the weapons rack I selected a .45 automatic and a dozen clips of ammunition. Food and other consumables I could get anywhere, and the suit had produced better boots, socks, etc. than anything here. But I couldn't pass up the chance of an amazing penknife with a red handle marked with an inlaid steel cross within a shield. It had two blades and a lot of ingenious tools. I was sure I'd find a use for most of them.

I said goodbye to the children, promised to pass on anything I didn't use (with a mental reservation about the knife), and stepped out again into the sunlight. After a few seconds I went back inside and picked up a pair of sunglasses. The girl's laughter followed me out.

Now that I didn't have to screw up my eyes to look up, it was easy to work out the location of the airport from the paths of the airships and microlights and helicopters. I followed the coast road for a couple of miles until I reached it. I got several offers of lifts on the way, but I declined them all. Despite the heat, and the gravity, and the moments of disorientation when some conservative part of my brain decided the horizon just *could not* be that far away, I had to get used to walking in the open on the surface of this planet; and soon, to my surprise, I found that I enjoyed it. The sea breeze carried the homely scent of blue-green fields, the distant converters shimmered and hummed, the nearby waters within the artificial reef sparkled, and on them swimmers and boating-parties filled the air with joyous cries.

The airport was on a spit of land that extended a few hundred yards, traversing the reef-barrier. Airships wallowed at mooring masts, 'copters and microlights buzzed between them. High overhead, the diamond-fibre flying-wings used for serious lifting strained at their cables like gigantic kites. I had arrived on one, from the Guiné spaceport, and it looked as if I'd have to leave on one. The thought of an airship passage was appealing, but it would take too long. I didn't know how much time I had to spare, but the final deadline, the Impact Event, was less than three weeks away. Whatever I did had to be done before that.

Just before the airport perimeter fence I turned and looked back at the Casa Azores. From here it was possible to see it, if not take it all in. A hundred and fifty metres square at the base, tapering in its kilometre height to a hundred at the top. The sides looked oddly natural, covered by climbing plants and hanging gardens, pocked by glider-ports, and by window-bays which shone like ice. Built and maintained by quadrillions of organically engineered nanomachines, it was almost as remarkable as a tree, and a good deal more efficient. The way of life that it and the surrounding aquaculture sustained was not mine, but it was one I was happy to protect. Plenty of interesting work, and plenty of interesting leisure; adventure if you wanted it, ease if you preferred that. Indefinitely extended youth and health. Anything that you couldn't get for the asking you could, with some feasible commitment of time and trouble, nanofacture for yourself.

The paucity of broadcast media, and the difficulties of real-time communication, were the only losses from the world before the Fall and the Crash. We had tried to make it an opportunity. All the entertainment and knowledge to be found among thirty billion people was (eventually) available on pipe, and live action provided by the steady, casual arrival and departure of entertainers and researchers and lecturers. The absence of artificial celebrity meant the endless presence of surprise.

Throughout the Inner System – Earth, near-Earth, Lagrange, Luna, Mars, and the Belt – variants of this same way of life went on. Cultures and languages were more diverse than ever, but the system that underpinned them was the same everywhere. In floating cities, in artificial mountains stepped like ziggurats, in towers like this or taller, in towns below the ground, in huge orbital habitats, in sunlit pressure domes, in caves of ice, most people had settled into this lifestyle: simple, self-sufficient, low-impact, and ecologically sound.

It was sustainable materially and psychologically, a climax community of the human species, the natural environment of a conscious animal, which that conscious animal, after so much time and trouble, had at last made for itself. We called it the Heliocene Epoch. It seemed like a moment in the sun, but there was no reason, in principle, why it couldn't outlast the sun, and spread to all the suns of the sky.

With our solar mirrors we controlled the polar caps. The glaciations and mass extinctions that had marked the Pleistocene were over; the next ice age, long overdue, would never come. With our space-based lasers and nukes, we could shield the earth from asteroid impacts. We could bring back lost species from the DNA in museum exhibits. Soon, any century now, we would control the Milankovitch cycle. We were secure.

No wonder they had so few tourists here: who would want to leave a place like this? I sighed, with a small shiver, and turned to the airport gate.

2

After London

I GOT MY airship journey, after all. The flying-wing route took me as far as Bristol, a city that was still a port for Atlantic traffic, though no longer for trade. The old city with its docks had been fairly well preserved, but the quays where sugar (exchanged for, and grown by, slaves) had once been landed now sustained only recreational craft. The new town was in the fashionable Aztec-pyramid style, with a projecting air-jetty about halfway up. We landed there at one p.m., having left Graciosa at eleven. I was lucky to catch the day's second flight to London. It left at around one-thirty in the afternoon, and would reach Alexandra Port about six. This is the sort of thing that happens when you travel inside an atmosphere.

Weather, of course, is another. I stepped out of the lift and on to the roof, to find large drops of water falling from the grey sky, on to me. I dug out of my rucksack a hooded cape – all part of the suit, naturally – and put it on. With the hood to keep water out of my eyes, it was easier to see where I was. The roof had the size and appearance of a small park – apart from the hills in the distance and the curious visual effects the rain made, it could have been under a municipal dome anywhere. I walked across the grass, past dripping trees and bushes, to where a small and gaily coloured dirigible was moored to a central pylon. Other people were also making their way over, a couple of dozen in all when we'd climbed the spiral staircase and crossed the gangway to the airship's gondola. My fellow passengers were dressed similarly to me, but most carried rather more equipment. From overheard conversations as we shook out our wet overclothes and took our seats, I gathered that most of them were – at least to themselves – serious eco-tourists, earnestly studying natural history or urban archaeology. But few had resisted the temptation to bring a rod or a rifle. The hunting and fishing in London was reputed to be excellent.

The seating was arranged in a manner more like a room than a vehicle, but I had no difficulty getting a seat by a window. The airship cast off on schedule, rising through the low cloud and then passing beyond it. After staring out the window for half-an-hour at deciduous woodland interrupted only by old roads and new buildings, I got up and wandered around asking people what refreshments they wanted, then went to the galley and prepared them.

While the coffee was brewing I was joined by a woman who introduced herself as Suze. She was small, brown-haired, hazel-eyed, dark-skinned. Very English. I figured her for being about her apparent age.

'Did you know,' she said as we poured coffee into mugs and tea into cups, 'that in the old system, there were people who did this as a full-time occupation?'

'Did what?'

'Serve refreshments on aircraft.'

I knew this perfectly well.

'Really?' I said. 'Why? Did they . . . enjoy it or something?'

'No,' she said earnestly, 'they did it because it was a way of getting what they needed to live on.'

I waved a hand at the rack of sandwiches. 'You mean this was all they had to eat?'

'No, no, it was because –'

She laughed suddenly. 'You're winding me up, aren't you?'

'Yes,' I admitted. I started pouring the coffee. 'Let's see if we can do the job better than the wage slaves, shall we?'

When we'd finished serving lunch to the other passengers we took our own trays. I saw that she, like myself, was making to sit alone, so I asked her to join me. We talked as we ate.

It wasn't polite to ask neighbours what they were doing, where they were going, and so on. You had to work around to it, and not pry if they didn't open up.

'Why did you tell me that thing about the old system?' I asked.

'At the moment,' Suze said, 'I'm a sociologist.'

I dragged up the unfamiliar word from old memories.

'Someone who studies society?'

She nodded. 'Yes, but there's not much to study any more!'

'How d'you mean?'

'Look around you.' She waved a hand. 'These days, you want to investigate society, and what do you find?'

It was a rhetorical question, but I really wanted to know her answer.

'Well,' she went on, 'it's all so *obvious*, so transparent. We all know how things work from the age of about five or so. You go and try to find out, and somebody will just *tell* you! And it'll be true, there are no secrets, nothing going on behind the scenes. Because there are no *scenes*, know what I mean?'

'Yes, of course,' I said, thinking *Ha! Little do you know, girl!* 'So what society do you study, if not our own?'

'I study the old system,' Suze said, 'and I do learn interesting things. Sometimes I just can't help telling people about them. And anyway, it's a way of getting people to talk.'

I snorted. 'Yeah, it's a great line,' I said. 'Almost anything you're doing, you can say to someone, "Did – you – know – that under the wages system, some people had to do this every day or *starve to death*?"'

She laughed at my mock-shocked tone and saucer eyes. For the next few minutes we vied to suggest some activity to which the statement didn't apply, and found our resources of ribaldry and gruesomeness inadequate to the task.

'All the same,' she said when we'd given up, 'it is fascinating in a way.' She shot me a glance, as if unsure whether to go on. 'Capitalism had a sort of . . . elegance about it. The trouble is, well, the old people, uh, no offence, aren't very good at explaining it, because they hate it so much, and the old books . . .' She sighed and shrugged. 'They just don't make *sense*. They have all these equations in them, like real science, but you look at the assumptions and you think, hey, wait a minute, that can't be right, so how *did* it work? *Anyway*,' she went on, more firmly, 'it's the only interesting sociological question left.' She looked out of the window, then leaned forward and spoke quietly. 'That's why I go to London,' she confided. 'To talk to people outside the Union.'

Then she leaned back, and looked at me as if defying me to be shocked, unsure that she hadn't misjudged my broad-mindedness. I didn't need to feign my response – I was pleased, and interested.

We had, of course, a network of agents and contacts in the London area, and the old comrades could always be counted on – but my mission was too secret even for them. Nobody knew I was coming, or what I was looking for, although that information-leakage couldn't be delayed much longer. I had expected to have to rely on hastily learned, and possibily outdated, background.

Now I had the possibility of a guide. This could be a stroke of luck! Or something else entirely, if I wanted to be paranoid about it. Her earlier comments about there being no secrets were too transparent to be some kind of double bluff; if she were involved in any secrets herself (other than her – to some – distasteful interests) she would hardly have brought the subject up. And anyway, she was too young . . .

I studied her face, and tried to hide my second thoughts, my second-guessing of myself. You lose the knack for conspiracy, over the decades and centuries. The Division was not the Union, true enough, but even our politics had weathered and softened into non-lethality, like a rusty artillery piece in a mossy emplacement – all our destructive power was directed outwards.

I decided that, whether her presence was fortuitous, or the outcome of one of those hidden forces whose existence she'd so naively denied, I couldn't lose. If she was innocent, then I'd gain some valuable contacts and information – if not, the only way to find out was by playing along.

So I said: 'Hmm, that's interesting. Do you know many non-cooperators?' (That was the polite term; the others included 'parasites', 'scabs', 'scum', and – spoken with a sneer and a pretend spit – 'bankers'.) It was considered all right to exchange coins with them for their odd handicrafts and eccentric nanofactures, and to employ them as guides – but most people shrank from any closer contact, as if the non-cos carried some invisible skin disease.

'A few,' she said, looking relieved. 'I'm studying, you know, trade patterns in the Thames Valley.'

'Trade patterns?'

'Most people think the non-cos live by scrounging stuff from the Union, but that's just a prejudice.' She grimaced; she was still talking in a low voice, as if not wanting the other passengers to overhear. 'Actually they're pretty self-sufficient. They make things and swap them among themselves, using little metal weights for indirect swaps. That's why whenever they offer to do things for tourists, they only do it for metal weights.' Suze laughed. 'There I go again. I'm sure you know all this.'

'Well, in theory,' I admitted, 'but it'll be interesting to see how it works in practice. The fact is, I'm going to London to find – a certain person.' I thought about risks. I'd be making inquiries after this guy as soon as we landed, among all kinds of people. No matter how discreet I was about it, word would get around. There seemed to be no harm in starting now. 'His name is Isambard Kingdom Malley.'

'He's *alive*?' Suze sounded incredulous. 'In London?' Comprehension dawned on her face.

'Yes,' I said. 'He's a non-co.'

Isambard Kingdom Malley was, or had been, a physicist. He worked out the Theory of Everything. The final equations. When I was as young as I look, there was a fashion for tee shirts with the Malley equations on them. TOE shirts, we called them. The equations, at least, were elegant.

Malley was born in 2039, so he was six years old at the time of the Fall Revolution. His theory was born in the early 2060s, in the brief surge of new technologies and research advances that marked the period when the US/UN empire had fallen, but the barbarians had not yet won. His last paper was the modest classic *Space-time manipulation with non-exotic matter*, Malley, I K, Phys. Rev. D 128 (10), 3182 (2080). It established the theoretical possibility of the quantum-chaotic wormhole and the vacuum-fluctuation virtual-mass drive. Its celebrated 'Appendix II: Engineering Considerations' pointed out some practical problems with constructing the Gate and the Drive, notably that it would require about a billion times as much computational power as was currently available.

A week after the article's publication, the journal was shut down by the gang in charge of its local fragment of the Former United States, for 'un-Scriptural physical speculation', 'blasphemy', and (according to some sources) 'witchcraft'. There's a certain elegiac aptness in the thought that the paper which pointed the road to the stars was published in what turned out to be the journal's final issue: the West was still soaring when it fell.

Thirteen years later, the Outwarders built the wormhole gate and torched off their interstellar probe, reaching for the end of space and time. That it never did reach the expected end – that it was, in fact, still going strong, still transmitting almost incomprehensible data from an unimaginable futurity – refuted Malley's Theory of Everything, which had been based on the hitherto impregnable Standard Model finite-universe cosmology. But Malley's was still the only theory we had. It fitted all the data, except the irrefragable fact of the probe. Within the limits of our engineering, the theory still worked. Nobody had come up with anything to replace it. (This was a sore point with me. I sometimes thought it reflected badly on our society: perhaps, after all, it does take some fundamental social insecurity to sharpen the wits of genius. Perhaps we had no more chance of developing further fundamental physics than the Pacific Islanders had of developing the steam engine. Or – I hoped – it could just be that a Newton, an Einstein or a Malley doesn't come along very often.)

I suspected that Malley would have been an Outwarder himself, but he never made it to space. America's last launch sites were already being stormed by mobs who thought rockets damaged the ozone layer, or made holes in the crystal spheres of the firmament. He fled America for Japan, and then quixotically returned to England at the time of the Green Death, where he worked to the best of his growing ability and dwindling resources as a medicine man, dealing out antibiotics and antigeriatrics to superstitious settlers and nostalgic refugees, administering the telomere hack to frightened adolescents who understood it, if at all, as yet another rite-of-passage ordeal. We knew he'd survived the century of barbarism, and that he'd registered to vote in the elections that formally abolished capitalism and established the Solar Union. Evidently he'd voted against the social revolution, because in the subsequent century of the world commonwealth he had retreated to the wilds of London, a stubborn non-cooperator.

We badly needed his cooperation now.

Malley was apparently following the Epicurean injunction to 'live unknown'. Suze had never heard so much as a rumour of him.

'Would you like me to come with you, at least part of the way?' she suggested. 'I could help you find your way around, and you could – well, to be honest there are places I'd rather not go on my own.'

'Yes, I'd like that very much,' I said. 'That's real neighbourly of you, Suze.'

She gave me a full-beam smile and asked, 'How do you expect to track him down? Do you have any idea where he is? And why do you want to talk to him, anyway? If you don't mind me asking.'

I scratched my ear and looked out of the window. We were again above some low cloud, and through its dazzling white a town rose on our left. 'Swindon tower,' Suze remarked. Ahead of us the airship's shadow raced like a rippling fluke across the contours of the clouds. I looked back at Suze.

'No, I don't mind you asking,' I said. 'I'll tell you the answers once we have a bit more privacy. And then, it'll be up to you whether you want to come along with me or not.'

'That's OK,' she said.

'Tell me what you've found out about London,' I said, and she did. By the time she had finished, we were almost there. We looked out at woodlands and marshes, ruins and the traces of streets and arterial roads, at the junctions of which smoke drifted up from the chimneys of huddled settlements. Suze began excitedly pointing out landmarks: Heathrow airport, its hexagram of runways only visible from the air, like the sigil of some ancient cult addressed to gods in the sky; the Thames Flood Barrier far to the east, a lonely line of silver dots in the Thames flood plain; Hyde Park with its historic Speaker's Corner, where the Memorial to the Unknown Socialist rose a hundred metres above the trees, gazing in the disdain of victory at the fallen or falling towers of the City; and, as the airship turned and began to drift lower, our destination, the proud pylons of Alexandra Port.

The sight of Alexandra Port set the hairs of my nape prickling. It had been one of the early centres of the space movement which was the common ancestor of the Outwarders and ourselves; there were people alive today whose journey into space had begun in its crowded concourses, waiting for the airship connection to the launch sites of Guiné and Khazakhstan. Its mooring masts were their Statue of Liberty, their Ellis Island.

Or their Botany Bay. My fingernails were digging into my palms. I turned away and prepared to disembark.

The airship settled, its motors humming as they steadied its position, just above the terminal's flat roof. A wheeled stairway rolled up to the exit and we all trooped down. Two or three people working on maintenance boarded the dirigible and began checking it over; although its automated systems were more than adequate to the task, there's something about aviation which keeps the habit of human supervision alive.

From the terminal's roof we could see an almost panoramic view of London, its rolling hills hazy with woodsmoke. The trees were interrupted here and there by towers whose steel and concrete had survived two centuries of neglect, and by broad corridors around ancient roadways. To the east the Lee Water broadened out to the Hackney marshes and the distant gleam of the Thames. On the nearby hills to the west the ruins of the old brick buildings and streets were still, barely, visible as crumbling walls and cracked slabs among the trees.

It was a common misconception – one which, to be honest, none of us had ever found it politic to publicly correct, though the facts were there for anyone who cared to look – that the Green Death was a single plague, the result of a virus genetically engineered by some Green faction in a fit of Malthusian overkill. More sober epidemiology has revealed that it was several diseases, probably natural, all of which hit at the same time and which were spread by soldiers, refugees and settlers. The disorder, and the weakening of the social immune-systems of medicine and science, were indeed partly the responsibility of the Green gangs and their many allies and precursors, going back through a century or more of irrationalism and anti-humanism. Indeed, the panicky abandonment of the cities as plague-centres was itself, in part, the outcome of that way of thinking, and it probably led to more deaths than the diseases ever did. So, while the Greens weren't quite as responsible as folk once thought for the billions of deaths, I find it hard to reproach anyone for the so-called 'excesses' after the liberation. (The execution figures were inflated by over-enthusiastic local committees, anyway. It wasn't more than a hundred thousand, worldwide. Tops. Honestly.)

The long-term effect of the Green Death wasn't on the size of the population – which bounced back sharply after the social revolution, and was now coming along very nicely, thank you – but on its distribution. Most of the old metropoles remained empty, long after they became perfectly safe to live in. They were happily left, quite appropriately, to those who rejected the new society and preferred some version of the old.

The countryside, too, was reverting to the wild, as agriculture was replaced by aquaculture, hydroponics, and artificial photosynthesis. It was less frequently ceded to the non-cos than the old cities, however, because of its recreational value to people from the dense arcologies of the Union.

Alexandra Port itself had changed little, because it had never been abandoned to the ravages of nature or man. In the Green Death it had been a conduit for refugees going out and relief flowing in, and even in the West's century of collapse it had been maintained by the earthbound remnant of the Space Movement, its boundaries guarded, its personnel supplied from outside, a garrison in the midst of desolation.

It was all just like in the old pictures, I thought as we descended to the concourse: the People's Palace, retro-styled even when it was new, back in the twentieth century, and the newer, twenty-first-century terminal buildings and workshops sprawling across the crown of the hill under the high pylons. The only evidence of modern technology I could see was the escalator down which we rode and its continuation in the walkway which carried us to the exit. Their seamless flow of plastic – not nanotech, just clever – would have baffled the complex's early engineers.

We walked over to the People's Palace, now a guesthouse as well as a home for the people working in the port. I looked at the sun, and at my watch.

'Shall we stay here for the night?' I suggested. 'Go on our travels in the morning?'

Suze nodded. 'Yeah, it's too late to go travelling,' she said. 'I do know some places to sleep in London, but they're strictly something you do for the experience.' We checked at the board in the foyer and found there were plenty of vacancies; most of our fellow tourists apparently preferred the dubious glamour and adventure of finding accommodation in one of London's native inns or shooting lodges. We selected a double room in the west wing, and took our stuff up. There was a small stove, coffee, and other supplies in the room, and an invitation to the evening meal and/or later social activities. While Suze was showering, I asked the suit to make an unobtrusive sweep of the room. It found nothing, apart from the expected wildlife and the standard cleany-crawlies. There were definitely none of the other kind of bugs – not that I seriously expected any, but it was routine, like the airship inspection.

Suze stepped out of the shower just as the suit's agent was reporting back.

'Oh!' she said. 'A pet mouse. How sweet!'

'Grrr,' said the suit, but I'm sure all Suze heard was a squeak. I took a shower myself, and emerged to find that Suze had brewed some coffee and dressed for dinner.

'Thanks,' I said, taking the coffee. 'Nice dress.'

Suze looked down at it smugly. 'Fortuny pleats, they're called,' she said. 'You can just ball it up in a rucksack, and when you shake it out it still looks great.'

'Ah,' I said, 'I have something to show you.'

I climbed back into my clothes, which were still sweaty and crumpled from travelling. They all added up to only part of the suit – the rest being the mouse, and the rucksack with its contents – but there was still enough for it to do the Cinderella trick, and mimic net and lace from an archived memory of debutante froth. I twirled, and grinned at Suze's open mouth.

'Smart-matter spacesuit,' I explained, sitting down and patting its bouffant skirts. Suze was still goggle-eyed.

'You're from space?'

'Yes,' I said. 'The Cassini Division, in fact.'

'Wow!' Suze's amazed look turned to an awed, and slightly guilty, excitement which I'd encountered before. In a world of abundance, of peace and security, the Division was the biggest focus for the dangerous appeal of danger, the sexy thrill of violence. There were those who despised and feared it for that very reason, and those who – sometimes secretly, even from themselves – loved it. Suze, it seemed, was among the latter.

'That's why I want to talk to Malley,' I said.

'About the wormhole?' Sharp girl.

'Yes. We want him to show us how to get through it. To New Mars.'

'Start our *own* settlement?'

I shook my head firmly. 'We don't need another lot of deserts!'

Something – some sudden light in her eyes – told me her secret answer: we do, we do! Not everybody would feel that way, but I knew that enough did for Wilde to have seen that look all the many times he told his tales. No wonder he had the crazy notion that if we could go through, we'd colonize the place.

'So why do we need to go through?' Suze asked. 'Why now?'

'We need to go through,' I said carefully, 'because there's a chance that the people on the other side of the wormhole are tinkering about with the same entities that the Outwarders became – the Jovians – on this side. We're going to go through, and stop them, with whatever it takes.' (This was true, as far as it went, which was not very far.) Suze sat back in one of the armchairs and looked at me, shaking her head.

'Why don't people *know* about this? Why haven't we been told?'

'We're not keeping it exactly secret,' I said. 'It's just that we've released the information in scientific reports and so on, rather than making a big splash of it. So far, everybody who's managed to figure out what's going on must have agreed with us that there's no need to panic.'

'That may be right,' she said indignantly, 'but there is a need to discuss it! You can't just go and *do* something like that, without any, any –'

'Authorization? Actually, we *can*, in the sense that nobody could stop us. We wouldn't want to do that, because we – that is, the Division – would fall apart if we ever went against the Union, because we'd have a strong and well-armed minority who *didn't* want to go against the Union. But as a matter of fact, we do have authorization. We're mandated to protect the Inner System from outside threats, and if a possible post-human invasion coming out of the wormhole isn't one, I don't know what is.'

Suze still looked troubled. 'What about the New Martians?' she asked. 'I don't see them going along with it.'

I laughed. 'If they're still people . . . they're just a bunch of non-cos. And we know how to deal with *them*.'

Suze shot me an odd glance, and seemed about to speak, but whatever was on her mind, she thought better of it.

'Well,' she said brightly, 'enough of this. Let's go and grab ourselves some aircraftmen.'

Dinner was in the great hall, with one of the daily planning-meetings before it (we sat it out in the bar) and a dance afterwards. The hall, a former exhibition centre, was decorated with murals depicting episodes from London's history: the Plague, the Fire, the Blitz, the Death; the battles of Cable Street, Lewisham, Trafalgar Square, Norlonto; the horrors of life under the Greens (one particularly imaginative panel showed some persecuted rationalist tied to a tree and left to die of starvation and dehydration, gloating Green savages dancing around and a woman loyally lurking in nearby bushes, recording the words of the black gospel he croaked from his parched mouth); the joy and vengeance of liberation, cheering crowds welcoming the Sino-Soviet troops (the Sheenisov, as everybody still calls them) and stringing up Green chiefs and witchdoctors from their own sacred trees; the tense balloting of the social revolution. Uplifting stuff.

The other decoration in the hall, that of its occupants, was more attractive. Costume on Earth tends to follow local traditions and techniques; here, it was a native style, picked up (as we later noticed) from the non-cos: cotton, with lots of dyes and embroidery. Some of the clothes worn after work were far more beautiful than ours, but at least our party frocks marked us out as visitors. We had no lack of attention, and we did, indeed, pull an aircraftman each.

Early the next morning we made our separate ways back to the room in which neither of us had spent the night, gathered up our gear, and had breakfast in the main hall. In the daylight the murals looked lurid and naive rather than heroic. The sunlight through the roof panels was bright and warm. Suze spread out a map.

'Well,' she said, 'where are we going today?'

'Our friend currently lives in Ealing Forest,' I said. 'I have a kind of address for him. He hangs out in some non-co technical college, and he's known to scour the markets for old books and gear.'

'Easy,' said Suze. 'We drive down the main path to Camden Market, stash the car at the Union depot, then take a boat up the canal to the North Circular –' her finger jabbed at a trail marked on the map, then traced it to another thin line '– then down into Ealing.'

'You sure the canal's quickest?'

Suze nodded briskly. 'The roads are kept up by the non-cos, and they're just what you'd expect. The waterways are ours. Everything from the dredging to the lock-keeping is done by Union machines.'

'Why?'

She shrugged. 'It's the least obtrusive way of keeping a presence. And if we ever need to increase it, the canals have the great advantage of going round the back, especially with hovercraft.'

'Hmm,' I said. 'I wonder if we could get away with borrowing a hovercraft.'

'Too noisy. The tourists don't like it, and it makes the locals expect trouble.'

At the car-pool we selected a rugged, low-slung buggy with wheels that could, according to the spec, cope with any pothole or tree root in London. The controls were standard, but I didn't yet trust my reflexes in this gravity, so Suze took the wheel. We drove down the long, curving road to the southern exit, through a crowd of importunate people (for me, a new and alarming experience; for Suze: 'Just beggars and pedlars; you'll get used to it'), up and over a hill, and down into the wild woods.

The vehicle's compact electric engine was quiet. As we drove slowly along the muddy trackways, in the shade of tall oaks and elms dripping with the previous night's rain, we could hear constant birdsong, the occasional howl of a wolf or bark of a fox, and the far-off, uncanny whooping laugh of gibbons. Kestrels hovered high above the forest paths. Wood pigeons clattered among the trees, and now and again the vivid flash of a parakeet passed before our startled eyes. Every so often a small deer would bound on to the path, take one look at us and sprint away, its thudding hooves unexpectedly loud.

Most of the ruins on either side were covered with ivy, its green cables silently and slowly dragging the crumbled brickwork back into the earth. Some of the walls, however, bore the marks of recent repair, with clay and wattle or bricks cannibalized from other ruins making good the gaps, and the roofs – usually a floor or two lower than the originals – beamed and thatched. There were clearings where entire villages had been built from recycled materials, with not a trace of the original buildings left standing. We got used to treating rising smoke ahead as a signal to slow down and watch out for scuttling chickens, ambling pigs, barking dogs and racing, yelling children. The interest of the adults varied from covert and sullen to open and servile, the latter type frantically drawing our attention to wares that were depicted or described on garish signboards.

I put to Suze a question that had occurred to me from comparing old political maps with the current geographical ones: that the present communities might be remnants of the ancient, with Christian fundamentalists flourishing here, anarchic tribes around Alexandra Port, usurers still haunting the leaning towers down by the river, Muslims to the east and Hindus to the west . . . but she disabused me of this fanciful notion. The vast migrations of the Death and the dark century had literally walked over the great city, leaving of its former fractious cultures not a trace.

The human traffic on the path increased as, over the next hour, we approached Camden Market. There were few powered vehicles, and horse-drawn ones were only a little more frequent. Pedestrians generally walked in groups: gay parties of tourists with rucksacks and rifles, who waved and greeted us as we passed; and serious squads of non-cos, tramping with heavy loads on their backs, or on overburdened animals, or on similarly overloaded carts. The non-cos usually spared us no more than a calculating glance or a canny smile.

Camden Lock Market, a vast, trampled clearing at the intersection of several roads and a major canal, had the look of a place which the trees – and their worshippers – had never conquered. Like Alexandra Port, but for economic rather than strategic reasons, it had remained alive and functioning through all the disasters that had befallen the city. In physical extent it was actually larger than it had been in the twenty-first century, because some of London's other traditional markets, in the East, were now six feet under the Thames estuary at low tide.

Our first stop was the Union depot, a stockaded area on the edge of the market. Inside the casually guarded gate were a low garage, a warehouse, and a rest-and-recreation building. Suze gave the last a disparaging glance.

'For wimps,' she remarked. 'What's the point of coming here if you're not willing to mix?'

After we'd garaged the vehicle, hoisted our packs, holstered our pistols and wandered around for a few minutes, I began to see exactly what the point was. The place was guaranteed to give most Union people a severe culture shock. To me it looked like utter chaos, and sounded – to use words whose roots lie in ancient experiences of similar situations – like a barbarous babel.

The market consisted of: long fenced-off areas packed with sad-eyed beasts; marble tables running with the blood, piled with the flesh of beasts; fish swimming in glass tanks or flopping on slabs; canopied wooden tables stacked with pottery, weaponry, books, machinery, clothes, textiles, herbs, drugs, antiquities, foodstuffs; racks from which coats swayed and dresses fluttered in the warm breeze.

Each of the stalls and tables had behind it someone whose full-time occupation was minding it, watching over it, talking to anybody on the other side of the table and passing wares over and taking money back. The sellers and the buyers filled the air with the sound of their dickering, bickering, joking, teasing, offering, refusing; and with the recorded music which every stall-holder, and most of their customers, discordantly inflicted on everybody else, played at an unsociable volume from portable devices which were aptly called loudspeakers.

Then there were the smells: of the animals and their dung and their slaughter, of the people and their sweat and the scents which failed to disguise it, of smoked herbal drugs which were, I began to suspect, not a recreation here but a necessity.

I stopped in front of a stall on which dried leaves of tobacco and hemp were laid out in labelled bundles, neatly sorted into open-topped boxes. The woman behind the stall was prettily dressed in an embroidered cotton blouse and a printed cotton long skirt, gathered at the waist with a drawstring. It was hard to work out her age – like many of the adult non-cos, she seemed to combine the detached watchfulness of age with the innocent selfishness of youth, and, on top of that, her cosmetics made a baffling mask: her cheeks reddened, the rest of her face whitened, eyes darkened and lips flushed, as if she'd been awake all night and was now in a state of sexual arousal. But she had an attractive smile.

'Suze,' I said, nudging, 'could we – ?'

Suze grinned and nodded, then, when I reached into the pocket of my rucksack, frowned and shook her head.

'I'll do it,' she murmured.

She looked up at the woman behind the table, and fingered a leaf labelled 'Kent Ganja'.

'How much you got on this?'

'Best stuff, lady,' the woman said. 'Two grams gold, five grams silver an ounce.'

(That's what I later worked out she said. At the time her strange singsong went into my ears as: 'Besstuff laidy, two gramzgold five gramzsilveranahnce.')

Suze recoiled. 'Fackinell!' she said. 'Thassexpensiv init?' (I still haven't figured that one; I'll leave it as it sounded.)

'Nah,' said the woman. 'From cross the riveh, thatiz. Transport's fackin criminal. You won't get cheaper anywhere.'

She waved around at the rest of the market. 'Try 't an' see f' y'selves. You'll be back.'

'Not likely,' said Suze, taking me by the elbow and firmly steering me away. We'd gone only a few steps when the woman called out: 'Awright, I'll give you a special, just to try it aht. Frow in paypas, too.'

Back we went and the bargain, after a few more verbal exchanges, was concluded. To my surprise both the woman and Suze were smiling at each other, both apparently satisfied with an outcome which they had each insisted would, if repeated too often, reduce one or the other to complete wretchedness.

We sat down at a table a few yards away and ordered coffee and bread rolls stuffed with cooked meat which had almost certainly not been grown from blue-greens. I'm not sentimental about beasts, but I tried not to think about it too much – marine molluscs are one thing, vertebrates are something else. When we'd finished eating Suze built a small joint of tobacco and hemp, lit it and passed it to me after a few appreciative puffs.

'Good stuff,' she said.

I tested and confirmed this. 'Yes,' I said. 'Just like the woman said it was. But won't she . . . dislike you for the way you made her accept such a small amount of silver for it?'

Suze guffawed. 'She got a very good price – an acceptable amount of silver – for it. She's happy with the silver, and we're happy with the hemp. Oh, thanks.'

I looked at her as she drew on it again. 'So you were both lying?'

'No, of course not,' Suze chuckled. 'It's a convention. Like bluffing in a strategy game.'

'But why did you bother to go through it? Why didn't you just give her what she asked in the first place? I mean . . .' I shrugged, having enough nous to understand that saying out loud how much metal we had on us might not be a good idea.

'Ah,' said Suze. 'That's an interesting point. In theory, OK, all the Union tourists here could bring as much, uh, negotiables as they could carry, and buy anything they wanted. All that would happen is that the amount the locals expected for their goods would go up, and everybody would be worse off all round. That's one of the things that get explained to first-timers. It used to be called inflation when there were states.' She frowned. 'Sort of, except they used pretend money –'

I cut her off hastily, not wanting to get my head around yet another complication (*pretend* money? Say *what*?).

'OK, but if the woman had stuck with her first offer, what – oh! I see. You'd have gone to another stall.'

Suze grinned, passing back the joint. 'Make an economist of you yet.'

'Hah! Hard to believe, now, that the whole world was once run like this.'

Suze nodded soberly. 'This, and various combinations of this and pushing people around. Weird.'

We got up to leave, and were recalled by an indignant yell from the food-stall minder.

'Sorree!' Suze said to him, blushing as she passed him a silver coin. 'Keep the change.'

It took her even longer to explain to me about that: the custom of a price that wasn't a price, on top of the price; a sum that was never asked for, but whose omission was always resented. We wandered on towards the stalls of books and machines. The smoke, and the coffee and food, had shifted my brain chemistry in the way I'd hoped. They were helping me to adjust to what was going on around me, but I still let Suze do the talking.

She browsed the bookstalls and machine shops and nanotech tanks, making the occasional small purchase and apparently idle inquiries after Malley. Sometimes she used his full name, sometimes she just wondered aloud if anyone had heard of 'the scientist' or 'the old doc'. Most of the sellers seemed to know her by sight, and gave her less of a hard bargain than some other Union tourists were getting. At the last stall she picked up and leafed through an obsolete textbook of physics which she'd dug up from one of the plastic boxes at the foot of the stall.

'I wish I knew someone who could explain this to me,' she said, casually handing the book to the seller. He was plump, even for a non-co, pink-skinned, and wrapped in a curious multicoloured patchwork coat that made him look like some tubby wizard. He glanced at the book; his eyes narrowed and his grip suddenly tightened. He pulled the book back.

'Sorry, miss,' he said. 'Not for sale.'

Suze gave him her best innocent-tourist look.

'Oh? That's a shame. Why not?'

'I've been asked to save anything by this bloke Wheeler for the professor.'

'Sure,' said Suze. 'Professor Malley, isn't it?' She seemed to forget the matter, leaning forward and pouncing on a copy of the rare *Home Workshop Nanotech* (Loompanics, 2052). 'Hey, look at this!' She passed it to me and looked again at the stall-holder, eyebrows raised.

'Yeah, Malley,' he said. 'He comes by now and again. Ain't seen him for a few weeks, though.'

'He's still running a school down Ealing way, ain't he?'

'That's right,' said the stall-holder. His accent blended in with the local speech, but his diction was clearer, at least to me. Suze glanced at the price pencilled on the book's inside cover, and passed the man a gold coin, without her customary haggling. He seemed to take this as a payment for a little more than the book (I was beginning to grasp how these people's minds worked, I thought smugly) and went on:

'Funny you should be asking after him.' He scratched the stubble on his upper chin. 'Couple of your lot –' he coughed '– uh, Union members were through the other day, looking for him.'

I felt a jolt of surprise.

'Yes, he's quite famous really,' Suze responded lightly. 'I'm sure lots of people want to talk to him. I wonder if they're anyone I know?'

He shrugged. 'Hard to say, you people all – what I mean is, they were two blokes, right, about your age – real age – and about her height.' He indicated me. 'Tall, dark, but not – uh, more sort of Indian-looking than you ladies, if you know what I mean.'

'Did you notice,' I asked carefully, 'anything unusual in the way they moved?'

His face brightened. 'Yeah! That's it! Something about them bothered me. Couldn't put me finger on it. But one of them had a funny way of hanging on to the edge of the table, like what you're doing now –' I let go and straightened up, self-consciously '– and they both had a way of dropping things. Books they'd picked up.' He took a pencil from behind his ear and demonstrated, mimicking someone absently putting the pencil down a foot above the table, then turning back and looking for it where it wasn't. We all laughed.

'I think I know who they are,' I smiled. 'When exactly did you say they were here?'

'Must've been Sunday,' the man said. 'Weekend market. Today's midweek.'

Today was – I had to think for a moment – Wednesday. I nodded and smiled. 'Thanks very much.'

'Be seeing you,' the stall-holder said.

'Cheers, Tommy,' Suze said, and we left, Suze intent on the old book she'd bought, pointing out to me its appallingly accurate instructions for building nanotech replicators using only a primitive computer, a scanning tunnelling electron microscope made out of television parts, and a few chemicals likely to be found under the kitchen sink in which the results could be 'safely isolated' according to the book's demonically irresponsible author, one Dr Frank N. Stein (probably a pseudonym, Suze told me solemnly).

' "Sold for informational purposes only",' she said, incredulously quoting the publisher's disclaimer. 'You know, the stuff in this book is *still* dangerous! You could start your very own outbreak with it!'

'Just as well you've got it out of the non-cos' hot little hands,' I said.

She glanced at me. 'Hmm,' she said. 'That's a point. Never thought of that.'

We had reached the end of one of the aisles of stalls. I walked on, until we'd reached the edge of the clearing. Suze followed me into the shade of one of the tall trees. We sat down on springy beech mast and gazed back at the ever-busier market.

'Well,' I said, letting out a long sigh, 'I had no idea they still made 'em like you, Suze. That was brilliant. You could be like one of those guys from the old days, a spy or a detective or whatever.'

'Ah, thanks.' Suze picked up a dried kernel and began picking at it with her fingernails. 'I suppose I am in a way. An investigator.' She shot me an awkward, almost embarrassed look, and I wondered, not for the first time, what social pressures – as undetectable to her, perhaps, as the pressure of the air she breathed – bore down on her from the society she wasn't investigating: her own. 'So there are other people looking for Malley.'

'Yes,' I said. 'And none that I know, I'll tell you that.'

'Perhaps they really are just students, keen on talking to a great physicist,' Suze said in a flat tone. 'What was that about the way they moved?'

'Spacers,' I said. 'Classic low-gee reflexes. Lagrangers or Loonies, if you ask me. Not from the Division, as far as I know.'

'But would you know?'

'I reckon so.'

Suze cocked an eyebrow at me. 'I know about need-to-know,' she said. She looked down again, then up. 'From books.'

I took this as a reproof, and had a momentary impulse to tell her everything. But I resisted it.

'That book dealer,' I said. 'You called him Tommy. You know him?'

'Chatted to him a couple of times,' she said. 'He's – he's ex-Union.'

'Really? Well, that explains the way he talks.'

Suze laughed. 'We're all so conscious of our superiority, aren't we?'

'I suppose so.' Well, we were superior. I'd never considered the matter. 'Why should anyone leave the Union?'

'I've asked him that,' Suze said. 'Couldn't get any answer out of him that made sense.' It sounded like an admission of personal failure. 'He didn't get on with neighbours, that's how he put it.'

'With thirty billion to choose from? I'm surprised he can get on with anybody.'

'I don't think he meant any particular neighbours.'

I grimaced. 'Weird. Anyway, it's his business.'

'That's *exactly* how he put it!'

I stared up at the sun-dappled leaves. A squirrel bounded along a low branch, looked at me and began scolding, just like my conscience.

'It's almost noon,' I said. 'I think I'd best be on my way.'

Suze's face fell. 'You don't want me to come along?'

I leaned over and squeezed her hand. 'You've helped me a lot, Suze. But . . . I really think it wouldn't be fair to get you further into this. It could be more dangerous than you expect.'

She expostulated further, to no avail; but with outward cheerfulness led me to the canal-boat dock, and said goodbye to me with an unexpected and more than neighbourly embrace.

I borrowed a small inflatable with an electric outboard. It could make five kilometres an hour, and even with the inevitable delays in locks, would only take a couple of hours to get me to the Union station at the intersection of the Grand Union Canal and the trail known as the North Circular.

The canal, under the oak and beech and overhanging willow that crowded its banks, was often dark. The towpath had not been maintained, so the only traffic was self-powered: the slowly chugging barges of non-co traders and travellers, the silently skimming launches, skiffs, and kayaks of Union trippers. Dredgers and other maintenance-robots went about their work, shiny metal crabs glimpsed crawling along the bottom or clambering on the banks. Shoals of minnows and sticklebacks lifted their noses to the surface, spotting the water like brief, local flurries of rain; herons and kingfishers took aim in response. Where the stone or brickwork bank was crumbled to the waterline, deer and wallabies looked up as I passed. The bridges were mostly recent, wooden; all but a few of the old stone bridges had long since collapsed, and their remains had been hauled from the water and dumped in unceremonious heaps at each side.

I settled back in the dinghy's air-cushioning, the tiller under one elbow, and relaxed my muscles while letting my mind freewheel, gradually overcoming the lingering effect of the joint. From the collar of my shirt I allowed a tendril of the suit to creep up my neck, over my jaw and cheek and around the back of my eyeball, where it patched into my optic nerve. It would be noticed by anyone closer than a few feet away, and probably recognized, but to anyone further away would look like a strange, hair-thin scar. For the moment I left it to maintain my position on a representation of the map, which with a deliberate wink I could view in front of my eyes like an after-image. Minute by minute the tiny bead of my real-time Global Position moved along the kinked and curved wire of the scaled-down canal.

I watched it all, and worried. Two men from space were after Malley, and they had three days' start on me. One of the more minor things I hadn't told Suze was that there was a faction – no, that was putting it too strongly – a school of thought in the Division (and, more widely, among the space settlers outside it, and even on Earth) which wanted to negotiate with the Outwarders, if such a thing were possible. As if! The very thought of attempting to negotiate with entities who could use any communication to corrupt your brain as easily as hacking a computer made me feel cold and sick. If the men looking for Malley were part of this group – appeasers, we called them – then we could be in the worst kind of trouble.

And there was no way I could call for help, without increasing whatever danger I was in.

The boat's engine had a bit more speed in it, for emergencies; I leaned forward, and pushed down hard on the stick. I reached the Union station a quarter of an hour earlier than I'd estimated. I deflated the boat, picked up another gas-cylinder for it, and packed it in another borrowed buggy. Then it was a matter of driving southward, picking my way carefully among upheaved concrete slabs and fallen trees.

Traffic was slow on the North Circular.

3

News From Nowhere

Gunnery's going ballistic. The alarms set bulkheads drumming, periodontal ligaments resonating: my whole jaw aches as I slam into my seat. I bounce back, then it grabs me and hugs me in. Suit goes rigid for a second (*I can't move!*), everything goes black for a second (*we'll get that bug out of the next release or somebody DIES!*), then the optical fibres cut in and the joints articulate and my fingers are tapping the armrest pads and I'm in charge.

'Shut that noise!'

My teeth and ears sing with relief. I'm looking straight ahead. The Gate is sixty-odd miles away, right in the sights, as always, and the number of invading ships or projectile comets or Lovecraftian unspeakables heading straight at us is, count 'em, *none*.

'If this is another bodging drill I'll –'

'THIS IS NOT A DRILL,' says the ship. Its voice drops as the magnification racks up; lenses zoom, cameras click. 'Look.'

It's tiny. The graticule reading shows, what? 24 *inches* across. In starboard Fire Control, somebody laughs. My first thought is *welcome back, Pioneer 10!* It is, indeed, like some early space probe: body like a spider's, brain like a gnat's; but (second thought) *not one of ours*. It matches none of the spacecraft designs humans have ever built (I know them all, like the faces of old friends) and the apparently solid instrumentation of the thing is (*click, click*) suddenly, blatantly, nanotech stuff. Fractal depths of smart-matter come into focus as the zoom increases and the probe continues to drift towards us: surfaces flowing, crawling –

I hit the cut-out and the view dwindles to a speck. There wasn't enough definition to implement a Langford visual hack (*but you would think that, wouldn't you?*) and I set the micro-scale babbages skittering across print-out and they report back in seconds that it's clear. No nasty viruses have impacted our retinae, raced up our optic nerves and taken over our minds (*but they would say that, wouldn't they?*) and paranoia beckons –

Enough. Ignore your feelings. Trust the computers.

(And yes, I *know* the Langford hack is just a viral meme in its own right, replicating down the centuries like an old joke, wasting resources every time we act on the insignificant off chance that if someone could think of it, somehow it could be done. What kind of twisted mind *starts* these things?)

There are two dozen ships in the wing this watch, and since just before the alert (all of ninety seconds ago) every ship-to-ship radio has been shut down and physically unplugged: total radio silence is the ships' first reflex, even before they warn their crews. Decades of nothing coming through but the odd rock, decades of drills for every imaginable (and then some) contingency. Everybody in the Division has to do it, the stints come round regular as orbits, and every time it's drilled into you that if something does happen, you're on your own.

We're all right behind you. But when you're up against the superhuman, the orders run in reverse: the first is *sauve qui peut*, the second is 'havoc', the third is 'no quarter' . . . you get the picture. Our swords are permanently notched.

Thinking for myself is what I'm here for. At this moment the glorious possibility of First Contact is clamouring with the alarming thought that this thing originates with our long-departed – or ever-present – enemies. The little probe has closed its distance by ten miles, and seems to be decelerating: its puffs of reaction-mass volatiles another piece of evidence that it isn't some long-lost voyager.

'Hailing it,' I say, and key out a standard all-bands interrogative and a single radar sweep. To my surprise there's an immediate response. The babbages chatter for a second and then my suit's interpreters spell out the message:

'Cometary mining vessel NK slash eight-seven-one out of Ship City to unidentified, please respond, over.'

I don't take it in; my mind's still full of clutter about this craft's being (since it's obviously not the enemy coming back and telling us resistance is useless, etc.) a genuine alien space probe. To my lasting embarrassment, the only thing I can think of (but did I think?) is to hit the video transmission and say, my voice squeaky with astonishment:

'Speak *Angloslav*, robot?'

More computer chatter, then a human voice:

'English?'

'Yes, English,' I babble happily, still speaking falsetto, still hearing space opera, 'you pick it up from old transmissions, yes? Language has changed –'

At that point the video input starts up, the image grainy through anti-virus snow. It's the face of an old, old man. He's had the telomere hack, and some fairly primitive rejuvenation, but that's it. The significance of all the machine has said dawns on me. This is no alien emissary, but something almost as strange: the digital ghost of an escaped prisoner, one of the Outwarders' bondsmen who, two centuries ago, had fled their orbital work camp for whatever lay beyond the Gate.

'Much has changed,' I tell it.

Remembering my first encounter with what turned out to be the replicated minds of Wilde and Meg could still make my ears burn, as I found when the recollection came to me while I drove down a relatively clear stretch of the trail, just north of Ealing Forest.

I knew roughly who or what he was straight away. He had no idea who we were, and was surprised when we told him. I don't think he believed us. Partially overcoming our mutual suspicions took hours of talk, followed by almost direct physical contact before Wilde and Meg would accept that we were human. Even after we had taken the stored cells they'd brought with them (kept like a lucky charm through all their robotic adventures) and re-grown bodies for the pair of them, and transferred their minds to the new brains, I could never bring myself to think of them as human. Their tale of what had happened to them did nothing to reduce my unease.

Wilde told us that the human and ex-human labourers had hacked a path through a spun-off 'daughter wormhole' to a just-about-habitable world they called New Mars. The uploaded ones had turned themselves back into humans, and were 'now' (thousands of light years away, and thousands of years in the future) turning New Mars into a new Earth, in a rather cavalier terraforming process which exploited the local system's large complement of comets.

Society on New Mars was what Wilde called a free market anarchy. To us, it sounded more like a multiple mutual tyranny. The most powerful person in it was our oldest surviving enemy – a man called David Reid, the original owner of the forced-labour company. He had in his possession copies of the stored mind-states of the Outwarders, and was open to the argument that it would be safe to reboot them Real Soon Now.

Imagine our delight.

I brought the buggy to a halt beside a six-foot-high hawthorn hedge, a sort of natural barbed-wire entanglement, just a few paces before the gap in that hedge containing the gate of Ealing Technical College. I turned off the engine, and sat back for a moment, stretching and relaxing muscles that had tensed in the long and alert drive here, and looked around. The College was a mid-twenty-first-century building whose steel, concrete and glass had been built for blast. Its squat, three-storey bulk had survived the machinery of a more insidious destruction a lot better than the score or so of older buildings in the clearing that surrounded it. These had long since been reprocessed into low dwellings with all the usual accompaniments of non-co post-urban life, children and dogs and pigs and shit.

It was about four in the afternoon. The shadows of the forest's hundred-foot oaks and elms covered a good quarter of the clearing. A hundred yards away, on the edge of the forest, smoke rose from behind a small shed from which the ringing of repeatedly struck metal could be heard; a low-tech version of a forge, I guessed, wondering idly what it was called. The few adults about treated me with more than usual non-cooperation, pointedly ignoring my presence and sharply tugging away any children who didn't. I left the rucksack in the back – like a fierce dog, it could look after itself – but made sure my holstered pistol was obvious as I walked to the gate.

The gate, of stout creosoted wood, was on a latch, evidently designed to keep out any animal less intelligent than a dog. I closed it behind me and strolled up ten yards of flagstoned path to the main entrance. To left and right of the path were vegetable gardens, with plots marked out in stretched string and lettered labels. A young man, kneeling on an old sack and poking at the soil, looked up at me incuriously.

On the concrete slab above the double doors some original name had been chiselled off, and the new one carved in, with much embellishment of leaves, hammers, sickles, and glassware to mask this necessary vandalism. The windows on the ground floor were little more than slots; on the other floors they were a more normal size. Glancing up, I saw that several of them had been cracked, in a time so distant that some green algae or moss had settled there and spread along the zigzag flaws. Tough glass. The walls themselves, of course, were covered with ivy.

I pushed at the door, which swung open to admit me to a broad foyer with stone stairs ascending to left and right, and a wide U-shaped wooden barrier in the middle, behind which a young man sat, smoking a pipe and reading a book. No one else was about, though a murmur of voices and the sounds of machinery carried from other parts of the building. There was a strong smell of non-mineral oil, presumably used for lubrication rather than cookery. Lighting was provided by the doorway, the stairwells, and a very bright tube above where the man sat. ('I've never met a non-co yet,' Suze had told me, 'who was too proud to generate electricity, or too poor to steal it.')

As the door swung back behind me, the man glanced up, laid down his pipe casually and kept his hand where it was, behind the sill of the desk. He eyed me warily as I walked up. He had a thin face and narrow beard, and was wearing a homespun cotton shirt.

'Good afternoon, lady,' he said.

'Good afternoon, man,' I replied with equal formality. 'I wonder if I could speak to Dr Malley?'

He bristled. 'I'm afraid not,' he said. The muscles of his right arm tensed.

'If he's busy, I'll wait,' I said, glancing around as though looking for a seat.

'It ain't that,' he said. 'Waiting wouldn't do no good. Dr Malley says he don't want to see no more of you people.'

'Any more of what people?'

He looked away, looked back defiantly.

'Space people.'

Ah.

'Listen, young man,' I said. 'I've come a long way to see Dr Malley. Even longer than you think. And I'm not going to be stopped by you, or even by whatever laughable weapon you have your hand on. Using these things fast takes practice, and I have a couple hundred years' head start.'

Sheepishly, he withdrew his hand.

'And now,' I said politely, 'I'd thank you to take me to see him.'

I sauntered behind his sullen walk, all the way up two flights of stairs and along a dim-lit corridor to a room on whose brass nameplate showed (among more curlicued foliage, within which the roman capitals lurked like ruins) the name of Dr I. K. Malley.

'Knock and enter,' I said quietly, and he did. I followed him into a small office with a wide window whose evidently thick and old plate glass distorted the outside view. Wooden shelving along the walls bowed under the weight of books and papers, which also partly covered the floor. The room smelled of old paper, worn carpet, pipe-smoke, whisky, and sweat. It had two chairs, one of them behind the desk, which was edge-on to the window. Hunched in it, looking up at us, was a man whose apparent age must have stabilized about thirty, but who had not touched an antigeriatric for at least a hundred years. His hair and stubbly beard were white, his skin dark and lined, his eyes grey, cold as a Martian winter.

'I thought I *told* –' he began. Then he looked at me and waved a hand with weary resignation. 'It's all right,' he said in a dull voice. 'It wouldn't do any good, anyway. They'll just keep coming.' There was a half-empty bottle of whisky on the desk, and a full glass.

The young man went reluctantly out, scowling in response to my farewell smile. Malley turned to me and motioned to the room's other seat, a worn leather armchair by the window. I told him my name and held out my hand. He looked slightly surprised, and stood up and shook it. His grip felt like an old leather glove fitted closely over a metal hand. He was tall, but stooped, and he wore an open-necked check cotton shirt and twill trousers. All his clothes seemed too wide for his girth and too short for his limbs. He folded himself back into his seat and leaned his elbows on the desk.

'So what do you bastards want now?' he said without preamble or apology. He took a sip of his drink, and hooded his eyes.

I shrugged and spread my hands. 'Dr Malley,' I said, 'I must tell

45

you I have very little idea what you're talking about. I'm here on behalf of the Cassini Division of the Solar Defence Group, and I assure you that no one else has been sent to see you.'

Malley fiddled with the bowl of his pipe. His fingers were stubby, their tips ingrained with grey ash and yellow tar.

'Day before yesterday,' he said, 'a couple of chaps turned up out of the blue, and told me they were from space defence. Said they were checking out rumours that I was dabbling in AI work. Total bollocks, of course. I just teach the local farm boys basic electronics. Any bright sparks that turn up, I throw a bit of Feynman and Hawking at them.' His eyes flashed conspiratorially. 'And a bit of Malley. The few who make any sense of it invariably fuck off and join the Union, no matter what I say.' He unzipped a leather pouch and began filling the bowl, hands working automatically as he gazed sadly out of the window. 'You could say I've been lowering the average intelligence in these parts – a crime in my book, but not, I guess, in yours.'

He snorted a laugh. I smiled encouragingly; not that I quite understood what he was saying word for word, but I got his drift.

'So,' he went on, lighting up his mixture with an antique Zippo, 'it was a bit of a surprise to be leaned on by two of your heavies, leaving me with subtle warnings about dire consequences. The words "outbreak" and, I think, "red-hot smoking crater" happened to crop up in the conversation. Just like the good old days under the Yanks. No black suits with bulges at the shoulder, but otherwise, *plus ça change*.'

This, I have to say, gave me pause. There was no *law* against dabbling with artificial intelligence (or against anything else, for that matter). There was not even a Union rule against it. For anything not covered by Union rules (just about everything) we'd settled on the iron rule: 'Do What You Can Get Away With.' But touching off an outbreak – of artificial intelligence, disease, nano-assemblers, or any other kind of replicator – was something you couldn't get away with. Your neighbours would ostracize you, or boycott you, and if one of the essential amenities they chose not to supply turned out to be, e.g., your next breath, why then that was something that – when the matter reached the agenda of a neighbourhood moot – *they* would get away with.

And at worst, if an outbreak actually began to spread, the Inner

System's own space defence forces would apply the orbital zap. I had never heard of them coming down and threatening people before the fact. It seemed rather illiberal.

'Excess of zeal,' I said, partly thinking aloud, partly bluffing. 'I'll have it looked into. But I assure you the Division has nothing to do with it. We have a rather different proposition to put to you.'

'Yes,' he sighed, 'I'm sure you do. Hard-cop, soft-cop, and all that.'

Could it be? The thought that someone else in the Division, or in the wider Solar Defence apparatus, might be playing games with my mission was so enraging that for a moment, fortunately, I was speechless. After a second or two I gathered my thoughts, and calmed down: I might be out of practice at conspiracy, but not at self-control. I shrugged.

'I know nothing of that,' I said.

'So what do you want me to do?'

'Dr Malley,' I said, smiling, 'do you know what the people on the other side of the wormhole, the people Wilde told us about, call it? They call it the Malley Mile.'

'I've seen the tapes,' Malley said dryly. 'Flattering, isn't it?'

I had hoped so. Time to lay on some more.

'We find ourselves,' I said carefully, 'in a position where we urgently need to understand the wormhole. And on our own, we can't. There's only one person who can help us, and that is you. Would you like to come with me to Jupiter, and do some real physics?'

Malley was taking a sip of whisky as I said this, and he snorted so hard it went up the back of his nose. He spluttered, coughed, then leaned back and laughed.

'So it's come to this! Thirty billion people in your utopia, and you have to come to me! You people really disappoint!'

I smiled. 'I know what you mean, Dr Malley. And I think what we want to do may change all that, in the long run. The Division is not the Union. That's all I want to say, for now.'

He rested his chin on a cat's-cradle of fingers and looked at me.

'Hmm,' he said. 'Interesting. That used to be called the Wolff gambit.'

I raised my eyebrows; he shrugged. 'Look it up.' (I never did.)

'Anyway,' he went on, 'you're too late.' He refilled his tumbler, and raised it to me in an ironic toast:

'Here's to the scientific genius of Isambard Kingdom Malley.' He knocked it back and slammed the tumbler down. 'And here's what has long since pissed it away. This, advancing age, and corrupting youth.'

'No!' I stood up. 'You're wrong! Those are symptoms. Your real problem is this: you worked out the most beautiful and successful physical theory a human being ever developed, and then super-human beings went right ahead, used it, applied it, took it to the limits and *disproved it*! And you have never gotten over the suspicion that, to go beyond your theory, you'd have to go beyond your human limitations. And now, you can't even do that!'

'Precisely,' he said. He refilled the tumbler, again. 'Thanks to you people!'

'Us?' I said, stung by the injustice of this accusation.

'Yes, you – with your armlock on space development and on computer work, your endless cold war with the Jovians. The Cassini Division has a very cushy number out there, while the rest of the human population gets fobbed off with a sort of static comfort. Restricted without their noticing, rationed without knowing what they're missing. The rations are generous, I'll give you that, but basically what you so grandly call the Solar Union is the civilian hinterland of a war economy.'

This was beyond arguing about.

'Think what you like,' I said. 'But why not come and see for yourself?'

Malley took out a penknife, unfolded a yellowed steel spike and began poking about in the bowl of his pipe. I looked away. There was a scrape of flint and the now-familiar smell of burning dried weed refreshed itself in the room.

'It's tempting,' Malley acknowledged. 'To be honest, I'd love to see the gate – the Malley Mile, ha-ha! – up close. I'd be delighted to find a way through it to the world Wilde described, which sounds so much more interesting than this one.' (I almost jumped – I hadn't even raised the matter of navigating the wormhole, which was what we really wanted him to do.) 'But like I said, it's a waste of time. I can't handle the math any more. It's a young man's game, and the young man who was Malley is no more.'

He really was sounding dangerously close to maudlin. I sat down again, and leaned across the desk and looked earnestly into his somewhat bloodshot eyes.

'Age and alcoholism,' I said, 'are curable. As you well know. A couple of treatments and you'll feel better than you can remember, better than you can now even *imagine*. You'll have access to the biggest computers the Division has, the best instruments, decades of observations. All we want you to do is show us the way to New Mars. If you do that, you can do whatever else you can get away with, just like the rest of us.'

Malley leaned back, sucking on his pipe. I'd never noticed before the horrible bubbling sound the tar and spittle make in the things.

'It's a deal,' he said.

It took me a moment to work out that this meant he agreed.

'You mean, we have a plan?'

'Yes!' Malley chuckled. 'Indeed we do. We have a plan.'

My plan, at this point, was to retrace my route to Alexandra Port, and get the next airship connection to a flying-wing flight to Guiné, and the next laser-launcher to rendezvous with the *Terrible Beauty*, the fusion clipper on which I'd arrived, which was currently parked in low Earth orbit. On the way – a recent update – I intended to show or describe to Malley some of the features of Union society, from which he'd so carefully exiled himself these past one hundred years: the gigantic Babbage engines churning through their Leontiev material-balance matrices, the sea-farms, the miles-high skyscrapers, the miles-deep caves, the (almost deserted) great hall of the Central Planning Board with its golden statue of Mises . . .

Alas for plans.

'Isn't there anyone you want to say goodbye to?'

Malley was stuffing books, instruments and stashes of tobacco into an overnight bag with every indication of being ready to leave there and then. He gave me a wintry smile.

'What do you think?'

'You're not in a close relationship?'

'No doubt the village whore will miss me.'

I blushed and looked out the window; changed the subject.

'Why's this place built like a fortress, anyway?'

Malley coughed at dust stirred up by his rummaging.

'Police station. The windows do open, by the way. I understand this was so that prisoners could dive out of them.'

Not entirely sure what he meant (or, perhaps, not wanting to believe I understood) I fiddled with a lock and latch. The window swung open, and I leaned out to inhale a breath of uncontaminated air. After my first long sigh of relief I looked across at the nodding treetops, the lowering sun, and down –

In front of the college was a crowd of about fifty people, mostly adult, and all clutching some kind of weapon: rifles, shotguns, even – like peasants out of an old horror movie – pitchforks. Some were crowded around the gate, others formed a wide semicircle around the buggy, above which the rucksack part of my suit had transformed itself into a hornet-cloud of buzzing defence-motes.

I must have said something to draw Malley's attention. He stuck his head out the window beside me.

'Oh, shit!' he said.

'Is this the doing of that nice young man in reception?'

'Probably,' said Malley.

'Why?'

He turned to me and frowned. 'You really don't get it, do you? People live here because they *don't like* you guys! And they don't want you taking me away.'

'You can tell them you're going because you want to!'

He retracted his head. 'I can try.'

The people around the vehicle were backing off from the futile and painful task of attempting anything against the defence swarm. They moved through the crowd at the gate and, being apparently more adventurous spirits, began to lead them to the main door. Someone looked up and saw me. Yells rose and the move towards the door became a surge.

They'd be up the stairs in about a minute.

'Suit!' I screamed, tapping instructions on to my cuff. The swarm above the buggy circled once then made a beeline for me, and as I ducked back inside they crowded over me and reformed. The whole of my outfit flowed and reshaped into its basic spacesuit form. The suit went rigid, everything went black (two releases on, and that one-second bug was *still* not fixed) and then became clear and mobile again.

Malley stared open-mouthed as my clothes changed into seamless matt black close-fitting armour, with a faceless black ball for a helmet and massively over-muscled shoulders.

'Nanotech spacesuit,' I explained impatiently. 'Out on the window-sill, now!'

He hesitated, then heard the sound of running feet in the corridor. He grabbed his bag and clambered out, half-sitting under the swung-up window. I followed him on to the ledge and wrapped my arms around him. 'Hang on,' I told him unnecessarily.

'Rope,' I requested, and jumped. From the shoulders of the suit a couple of cables extended, one end grabbing the window-ledge by pure adhesion, the other lowering us rapidly to the ground. We landed gently. I looked around. The crowd's vanguard were looking down at us from the window as the cables snaked back into the suit, the crowd's stragglers were standing around between the gate and the doorway, looking at us with expressions that I still remember with somewhat malicious satisfaction.

Malley was tottering on his feet beside me, wheyfaced. He'd vomited over the suit; already it was thirstily absorbing the organics. I picked Malley up, like an actor in a Killer Robot outfit carrying off an actress in a Torn And Revealing outfit, and bounded to the buggy. The crowd scattered around me. I set Malley down in the passenger seat and hopped into the driver's seat.

I had underestimated the crowd. They were not some panicked mob, but a peasant village, watching what they saw as the suborning or abduction of a well-liked and much-needed teacher. Those who'd gone up the stairs were streaming back down, and those who hadn't were closing around the buggy. Students, young men mostly, added to the numbers pouring out of the college doorway. They made no threatening approaches, giving it a good few yards' clearance, but they formed an increasingly solid mass around us. I looked out at a wall of people dressed in their colourful wools and cottons, their broad leather belts; at their competently held, though crude, weapons, their smooth and hostile faces.

Well, at least they should see my face. 'Scroll helmet,' I murmured, and the globe around my head opened at the top, the aperture widening, then narrowing, as the smart-matter flowed back into the temporary ring-seal resting on my collarbones. I turned to Malley before anyone could react and said:

'Could you please explain things to them?'

Malley shrugged. His hands were quivering. He wiped the back of one hand across his mouth and stood up, gripping the rim of the buggy's windshield.

'Hey, friends!' he called out. 'Listen to me! Thanks for your concern, but everything's all right. I'm going away for a short while with this woman from the . . . outside. I'm going of my own free will. So please don't worry! Let us through, please.'

The tallest and toughest-looking man in sight shouldered his way to the front and stood right in our way.

'I'm sorry, Dr Malley,' he said. 'But we ain't sure you *are* going of your own free will. Those space-folks, those *socialists*, they can do things to your brain so's you *think* you're doing what you want, but you're doing what *they* want, see?'

'Not *that* old lie,' I muttered under my breath. I should have guessed that the non-co dominant ideology could only be a full-blown paranoid delusional system.

'I'm sure they can,' Malley said. He'd recovered some of his poise. 'But I very much doubt that they can do it in half an hour.'

The tall guy looked nonplussed for all of two seconds.

'Well then,' he said with implacable logic, 'she must've threatened you. That they'd zap the village, or some'ing. It's all right, Dr Malley, you tell us! We ain't scared of them!'

'I assure you –' Malley began, but I knew it was of no use. Argument would get us nowhere. I couldn't credibly threaten Malley, and if it came to threatening the crowd my pistol (now inside my suit, and pressing painfully against my hip) was no match for their guns. Whether the suit could recreate the helmet in time to protect me from a shot was an experiment I didn't care to try.

'Scroll helmet up,' I whispered, and turned on the engine. In the moment of blackness I reached up and caught Malley's shoulder.

'Get right down!' I yelled, pulling hard. With the other hand I caught the wheel. I groped with my foot for the control pedal and pushed it down. The buggy leapt forward and as the view cleared I saw the man in front of us hurl himself out of the way at the last possible second. The others did likewise, scattering like skittles. And then we were through, careening down the village street in a flurry of chickens and a shower of stones. One or two shots were fired, but they whizzed overhead – I doubted that they were seriously aimed to hit. The only people between us and the end of the village were more interested in getting out of our way than in stopping us. But one of them, glimpsed as we hurtled past, was holding a rectangular chunk of plastic with a yard-long thin rod poking up from it. He held it with one end at his mouth and the other at his ear, and was speaking rapidly into it.

I had a nasty suspicion that this was a radio.

'I told you I taught them electronics,' Malley said a few minutes later, as we bounced along yet another forest track, heading in completely the wrong direction for any return to Alexandra Port.

'How irresponsible can you get!' I yelled. 'Radios can pick up viruses, you know that.'

'Yeah, and melt in your hand – so what!'

'What about *mind* viruses? Have you thought about that?'

'Of course I have,' Malley said, struggling to get the seatbelt on. 'They're just a fancy term for ideas you don't like.'

'Ideas *who* don't like?'

'You lot,' Malley said, waving his hand around his head. 'The Union. The Division. It's just censorship.'

I laughed so hard that the buggy swung dangerously as I steered around a log. 'Sure, like taking what you want is rationing!'

'Exactly my point,' Malley said, with unaccountable triumph.

I sighed. 'Dr Malley, I have great admiration for you and all you've accomplished, and I can even see you've been doing good to these people, but I respectfully suggest that you're a bit out of touch, or maybe misinformed –'

'Hah!'

'– and you'll see things differently once you get out to the Division.'

'No doubt,' Malley chuckled, wheezing. 'No doubt I will.'

The map – still patched to my eye – showed that we were nearing Gunnersmere, one of the first fens of the Thames Estuary. The village of Under Flyover was marked as a straggle of houses along the shore. Ahead, I could already see the trees thinning, oak and beech being replaced by alder and birch.

'What do you think they were using the radio for?' I asked.

Malley gave me an evil grin. 'Oh, warning ahead, probably.'

'Skies above, man!' I applied the brake gently and we slithered to a halt in a spray of leaf mould and beechnuts. Suddenly our surroundings seemed very quiet, apart from sinister cracklings under the trees, and deserted, apart from flitting shapes in the long shadows. 'You mean we're heading straight into an *ambush*?'

'*You* are,' Malley said calmly. 'I would have stopped you any minute now, but I was waiting to see how long it'd take before you realized you needed my local knowledge to get you out of this.'

I took a deep breath. 'OK, Dr Malley. I need your local knowledge. That, or a rescue chopper.'

'Maybe both. First things first. Let's get this buggy off the road, preferably somewhere not too obvious. There's a bit of exposed roadway a couple of hundred metres ahead, and some ruins alongside. Tracks shouldn't be too conspicuous, especially in poor light.'

I restarted the engine and let the vehicle roll forward quietly to the area Malley had indicated, where the chances of wind and weather had laid bare the cracked tarmac. I sought out a ruin whose approach wasn't itself covered with plants or plant remains, and found one with a battered concrete ramp leading to the gap where its doors had been. Within a minute or two we had the buggy stashed inside a rectangle of crumbled wall, within which nettles, willow-herb and hemp grew to a height of over six feet. I looked down at the former contents of the rucksack, scattered forlornly in the rear well of the buggy. I changed the suit into a rucksack and a dappled black-and-green jumpsuit, then repacked, with the weighty addition of the deflated boat, its electric outboard engine and fuel cell, and the spare gas cylinder.

'That's one possible way out,' Malley acknowledged.

'Now what?' I asked.

'Do you have any way of contacting the nearest Union outpost?'

Outpost, indeed. 'Not directly,' I said. 'I could contact them via my ship. It'll be above the horizon in about –' I blinked up the watch floating in my left eye, and checked '– fifteen minutes. But I'd really rather not do that, or send out some general distress –'

At that moment I heard a rhythmic thudding along the trail in the direction from which we'd come.

'What's that?'

'Galloping horse,' Malley said. 'Get down!'

We ducked behind the wall. I drew my pistol, wishing as I did so that I'd known of the properties of nettles before changing my suit: my hands were coming up in a nasty rash. The thudding sound got closer, then slowed and changed to a clatter as the horse encountered the stretch of paving. As it drew level I peered out through the stems of weeds.

A young woman was sitting on the back of the strange, huge beast, holding on and controlling it by an arrangement of leather straps and metal footrests. She was riding quite slowly now, looking from side to side. Her clothes were filthy, as were the sides of the horse, and a trickle of blood was drying below a bruise on her temple. As she turned to the right, almost facing me, I recognized her.

'Suze!' I called, standing up.

She jumped and the horse shied and whinnied, then she tugged on the straps she held and said something, and the beast settled. Malley, with a grunt and a glower, straightened up and followed more slowly as I skipped over the tumbled brickwork and down to the path.

'Are you all right, Ellen?' She looked past me at Malley, and her eyes widened. 'Is that –?'

'The great man himself, yes,' I said. 'But Suze, what about you? What happened?' Not that it was hard to guess.

'I followed you,' she said. 'I know you didn't want me to come, but –'

'It was a kind thought,' I said.

'Well.' She smiled down at us, uncertainly. 'I took a barge up the canal and borrowed Bonnie here.' She patted the horse's neck. 'I've ridden her before, and she's much better on the forest paths than a buggy, you know. When I rode into the village back there the locals saw I was Union, and some sort of riot started, all yelling and running. They pelted me with stones and, uh, shit. I didn't know what was going on, so I just put my head down and dug in my heels. And here I am.'

Here you are. Another innocent to look after.

'Anybody follow you?'

She shook her head. 'What about you?' she asked.

I introduced her to Malley and outlined our plight.

'Oh!' she said, peering anxiously around. 'You mean there might be people out looking for us right now?'

'Yes,' I said. 'Over to you, Dr Malley.'

'Call me Sam,' he said, possibly irritated by Suze's star-struck glances at him. 'Everybody does. Short for Isambard. Right. Suze, can you put a call through to Alexandra Port, arrange a chopper pick-up?'

'Yes, of course, Doc – Sam.'

'OK.' He closed his eyes and pinched his forehead with thumb and forefinger, looking as tired as I felt. 'You do that, ask them to be ready for take off in about an hour. We make our way through the trees to the east of the path, around the back of the village, hide out by the shore, and then no doubt Ellen here will be able to give them our exact coordinates from her magic suit's gee-pals link, right?'

I nodded.

'Okay,' said Malley. 'Suze, you're going to have to say goodbye to the horse, I'm afraid, but I assure you the locals won't maltreat her.'

Suze removed the horse's harness and sent her cantering away southward with an affectionate slap on the rump. Then she unclipped a narrow-band transmitter from her belt, tuned it to the nearest communications satellite relay, and called up Alexandra Port. She frowned and shook her head.

'Message got through, but there's no acknowledgement.'

Malley shrugged. 'Try again when we get there.'

He turned, and Suze and I followed him under the trees to the east of the path. The way through the trees, bearing generally rightward, was much harder than one might expect. They were old woods, so the canopy was high and thick enough to choke off most undergrowth. However, the ruins underneath the deceptive layers of leaf mould more than made up for this lack. We banged our shins on hidden blocks, plunged knee-deep into hidden pits. What appeared to be a dead branch could turn out to be a disconcertingly solid and sharp prong of rusted metal. Malley persisted in staying in the denser part of the wood, and walked its treacherous footing with confidence, carrying his overnight bag like somebody heading for a transport terminal. We concentrated on avoiding injury and struggled silently – or at least inarticulately – along behind him.

After about half an hour of this Malley began to bear a little further right and we shortly emerged in a more open area of long grass dotted with bushes and low trees. The water was about a hundred yards away and at this point was almost two miles across. A mile to our left was Under Flyover with its surrounding fields and gardens. Only a few pillars remained of the structure which had given it its name.

Spread out across the fields was a line of people with dogs, working their way systematically towards where we were and communicating with other people, no doubt out of sight in the forest, with their hand-held radios. We crouched down and Suze tried again to raise Alexandra Port.

'Nothing,' she said. 'I don't understand this. It's like they're deliberately ignoring us!'

'Could this be policy?' I asked her. 'Is it something to do with the ruckus we – I – caused back in that village? Like, if you stir up the non-cos, you're on your own?'

She shook her head fiercely. 'No way. You'd have some explaining to do, but we always pull our own people out. Hey, we even help non-cos if they ask for it.'

Malley grunted. 'Huh, usually those who least deserve it – village hooligans or thieves.'

Suze was agreeing with him and the searchers were getting closer.

'Enough,' I said. 'Here's what we're going to do.'

What we did was run hell-for-leather down to the shore. I tore through the long grass, not bothering to hide or dodge, slid down banks, felt my feet grit on gravel, and pulled the inflation cord of the boat. Putting the gas cylinder and the motor in place was the only preparation we'd made.

The dinghy *whoomphed* into shape in about five seconds, even as I was throwing it forward onto the water. Suze came panting, Malley puffing, behind me and we all splashed through the shallows and pushed the boat out until the water was knee-deep, then clambered in. It all took less than a minute, which was more than enough time for yells and yaps to break out. By the time the first of our pursuers had reached the water's edge I had the engine started and we were about ten yards out. A couple of men waded in after us and a dog plunged in and bravely paddled in our wake.

I looked back. They were gaining on us, but as the water got deeper the advantage changed. By the time the water became too deep to wade, we were beyond their reach. Somebody whistled, and the dog too turned back. By now six people had gathered on the bank, and as we turned and headed downriver I noticed that one of them was speaking into a radio.

'What do you think he's up to?' I asked Malley. For answer, Malley pointed back along the shore, to Under Flyover's long wooden jetty. Four men were just visible, running along the quay. They scrambled down a ladder and into a boat. With the four of them working two pairs of oars, it pulled away from the quay and gave us chase.

'They haven't a chance,' Malley said, just before two of the men shipped their oars and raised a mast, then a sail.

'Looks like they do,' said Suze.

With the sail up their rate of closing on us increased visibly, though I figured it would take them at least half an hour. I steered a course away from the shore, hoping to pick up the main current and gain some much-needed speed.

'What *is* this?' I demanded of Malley. 'This is crazy. They must know you want to come along with us, you could have got away easily back there if you didn't. They can't all believe that story about me brainwashing you, or whatever. So why are they still chasing us?'

He shrugged. 'I don't know. I'm more surprised that your lot haven't responded to our call.'

Not quite my lot, but he was right. It was most disconcerting. I looked around. The sunlight was by now at a quite acute angle, and the scene – the sheet of water over which we moved, the wooded banks curving to the left ahead of us – would in other circumstances have been idyllic. Waterfowl swam or skimmed the widened river, and its surface was otherwise marred by only a few small craft . . .

'What about those other boats?' I asked Suze. 'Surely some of them are Union visitors?'

'Yes, but it's hard to say which – ah!'

She pointed downriver to a tiny vee of white spray. 'We're saved! That's a Union patrol boat!' Carried away by excitement, she began waving her arms and shouting, although the boat – a hydrofoil, I now saw – was still a couple of miles off. She desisted after a moment and stripped off her shirt and began waving that.

'What does a patrol boat have to do?' I asked.

'River rescue, mostly,' said Malley.

'And maintaining a presence, as they say,' Suze remarked, flapping her shirt and all but standing up.

'Do they ever interfere with non-cos?'

Malley scowled and shook his head. 'Maybe they should – the Thames boatmen are inclined to take what the traffic will bear. Daylight robbery.'

I didn't understand this, but Suze gave it an appreciative laugh.

The hydrofoil's course shifted a fraction. 'They've seen us,' I said. I looked over my shoulder. The men in the boat were working the sail again, tacking off in a different direction. Within a few minutes the hydrofoil – a thirty-foot launch, painted white, its ensign the Union's starry plough – had cut back its engine and dropped into the water, and circled behind us and hove to alongside. The woman at the wheel waved to us and called out: 'Hi! You having trouble with those people?'

'Yes!' I yelled. 'Thanks for coming to help.'

'That's fine,' she said. 'Where are you going?'

I thought for a moment. 'Alexandra Port – but the mouth of the Lee would be fine, if you want to give us a lift.'

'Sure. No problem. Come aboard.' She threw us a rope, and we pulled the wallowing dinghy in to a small ladder at the side of her boat. First Malley, then Suze, then I climbed in, and I used a boathook to haul the dinghy up after me. The woman, who introduced herself as Carla, had long blonde hair and a suntanned face and a smile that showed crooked teeth. Her yellow jumpsuit had a small patch with her name and 'River Patrol' stitched on it.

'Did you pick up a call?' Suze asked. 'We tried to hail Alexandra Port.'

Carla shook her head. She motioned us into the cabin in front of the cockpit, and re-started the engine. 'Make yourselves comfortable,' she yelled. 'Tell me about what happened when I've got this thing on course.'

The boat picked up speed, the foils dug into the water and we lifted off. Malley lit his pipe, Suze settled to gazing out of the window, and I stood beside Carla and told her a conveniently edited version of what had gone on. She was as baffled by the non-response as we were. We crossed Gunnersmere, Hammersea, Southwater and had just reached the City Basin when Carla remarked: 'There's a lot of non-co boats on the river this evening . . .'

I had noticed the boats, but not having any basis for comparison hadn't known it was unusual. Rowing boats, sailboats, skiffs, steam-launches, smoke-trailing woodburners, and barges were visible all across the pool, their courses at first uncoordinated, and then – as I looked again and again – obviously converging. On us.

Carla noticed it a few seconds after I did. She frowned and tried her communications equipment. The microwave laser pinged off whatever satellite it was tuned to, but no response came back. The boats were still at a distance – a few hundred yards all around – but were slowly surrounding us. Suze and Malley came out of the cabin and we watched in silent puzzlement and growing dismay.

'This is too much,' I said. 'No more miss nice girl. Carla, please take *fast* evasive action before they block us off completely.'

She grinned and gave me the thumbs-up and pulled out the throttle. The boat shot forward, then began a curving course towards the City towers, which gleamed gold and bronze in the low sun, like drunken, armoured Goliaths wading out to meet some aquatic David. Between them and us were a couple of non-co craft: a four-man rowing boat, perhaps similar to the one that had first followed us, which skittered across the water like a surface-tension bug; and a much slower, heavier wood-fired puffer that chugged with shocking determination across our bows. Carla touched the wheel, once to left, once to right. The rowing boat was swamped, and I glimpsed white faces from the steam boat's decks as we hurtled past its stern with yards to spare. Then we were in among the leaning, looming towers, our reflection speeding and flashing in their glassy flanks.

I stepped carefully to the rear deck and squatted down and flowed the suit into its dish aerial form, and sent an urgent call to the *Terrible Beauty*.

The others were clinging to any available handhold, and looking at me in bemusement as I stood up with the reconstituted clothes climbing back over my skin.

'Twenty minutes,' I said. Our wake set waves crossing and recrossing the geometric spaces of the boxed canyons. The non-cos' vessels prowled about the flooded buildings but kept well back.

'Until what happens?' Carla asked.

I grinned, suddenly cocksure again, already back in my own world, already far above this one, with its conspiracies of non-cooperators, its unresponsive rescue services, its general principle of leaving far too much to a natural world and a prehistoric humanity that pounced on any moment of weakness.

'Watch the sky,' I told them. '*Terrible Beauty*'s coming down.'

It was Malley who spotted it first, a new and brighter evening star low in the glare of the sunset. Although it was coming down, it seemed to climb, as it moved away from the horizon and towards us. Twice it seemed to flare, and broader secondary flashes drifted away. Then, closer, it really did flare, with a thunder that tumbled down to us through miles of air, and that was as suddenly replaced by the screaming whistle of the aerobraking flues. Plumes of superheated air founted from its surface, then the third and final parachute was deployed, a half-mile-wide canopy of monolayer carbon filament on which the huge ship floated like the seed beneath a thistledown.

'Head for mid-channel,' I told Carla. She complied, barely able to take her gaze away from the descending ship. The harrassing boats fled from its encroaching shadow in a widening circle of accelerating haste. We nosed out from among the towers and set a course to meet it, as if in perverse defiance of the surrounding panic.

'Oh, oh!' cried Suze. 'It's beautiful – terrible beauty all right!'

Its surfaces glowing like a lantern, curved like a shell, intricate like a vase; its shape like the paradoxical egg of an alien, avian species that lived in higher dimensions; its sound like a choir of angry angels or a host of adoring devils, the *Terrible Beauty* released its drogue, which flitted out of sight above the towers and trees, and no doubt made more than one fortune for whoever found it; fired its attitude jets and its final retro-flare, sending roiling clouds of steam across the water towards us, and settled at last on the riverbed of the pool of London.

'That,' said Malley, 'is the most *shocking* waste of delta-vee I have *ever* seen.'

Carla looked at me sidelong. I nodded: 'Full ahead.' The hydrofoil surged across the few hundred yards that separated us from the improbable object on the river. As we drew closer the water hissed and bubbled, and the foils failed to support our craft. Carla moved a control lever and the hull sank back; skilfully she adjusted our speed until we came almost to a halt beneath the spaceship's curving overhang. Around us, the silvery bellies of killed or stunned fishes flashed in the churning water. Some of them had undoubtedly been cooked alive; I found myself hoping that the intake valves – already open and gulping in water, thirsty to replace the squandered reaction-mass – would filter some of them off to the commissary. It was probable: like many of the Division's mechanisms, the ship had a sensitive nose – and a ravenous appetite – for usable organics.

About fifty feet above us, at the *Terrible Beauty*'s widest diameter, a hatch unlidded and a face peered down at us: Tony Girard, currently the security officer on the ship.

'Hi, Ellen!' he shouted. 'Sending a ladder down.'

I caught the plastic ladder as it reached the boat, and turned to Malley. 'After you.'

Malley grinned at me, all cynicism gone from his face. He looked like a small boy about to go on a carnival ride. He picked up his bag, looped its longest strap across the back of his neck and under his armpits, and set off up the ladder.

'Carla,' I said, 'we'll obviously wait till you're well clear before we lift, but will you be all right?'

She made a performance of shading her eyes and looking around the now almost deserted stretch of river. 'I'll be fine,' she said. 'There's a Union station at the mouth of the Lee. I'll find out there why nobody answered your call – or mine, and why there weren't any other patrol boats around to help.' Her expression darkened. '*Somebody*'s gonna have some hard questions to answer.'

'Contact us when they do,' I said, scribbling a note of our call sign and passing it to her, along with the money I'd taken from Graciosa. 'And thanks for everything. Anybody gives you trouble, you just give us a call.' I jerked my thumb at the ship, and she smiled – grateful for the moral support, but probably not taking my promise seriously. This is a mistake people make about the Division, but each person only makes it once. I smiled, half to myself, and grasped Suze's shoulder.

'You were great,' I said. 'You helped me a lot, and it was real neighbourly of you to come after us.'

'Even if it wasn't necessary!' Suze laughed. 'Forget goodbyes,

Ellen. I'm coming with you.' She put her hand on one of the steps of the ladder.

'What? You can't –'

'I can,' she said confidently. 'Anybody in the Union can join the Division if there's a ship available to take them, and –' she patted the hull '– here it is.'

She was right. It was a rule, but in practice it was only applied by experienced spacers from the Inner System defences joining the Division as a natural progression, and by members of various administrative committees coming out to exercise what they supposed was democratic oversight. We had long experience in dissuading starry-eyed youngsters from Earth, but ultimately we could only dissuade, and – if the new volunteer turned out to be useless – gently disillusion them with some really boring tasks.

'But Suze!' I expostulated. 'You've got a job to do here. Something's up among the non-cos – all this radio communication, nobody knew *that* was going on. You'd do better to use what you know to help the Union find out –'

She held up her free hand. 'No,' she said. 'I'm useless for that now. The non-cos saw me with you, and we've seen how fast word can spread. They won't trust me any more, and they'd be right! And if you're really going to – where you said – I wouldn't miss that chance for anything. I'm coming.'

And with that she turned away and climbed swiftly up the ladder. I watched her almost halfway, then looked at Carla. She had an ironic smirk, as if to say, *you'll have trouble with that one*. The only response I could think of was to shrug and spread my hands.

'That's life,' I said, shaking my head, and then followed my new comrade up the ladder and into the ship.

4

The State of the Art

THE SOUND of that hatch sealing behind me was the most welcome I'd heard for some time. Tony Girard caught me by the forearms, and then let himself be swept into a hug.

'It's great to be back!' I said when I'd let go of him and he'd stood aside, red-faced, as we stepped out of the airlock. The inner hatch closed behind us and we heard a brief, muffled surge as the airlock filled with water. The deck thrummed under my feet, the curving walls of the narrow corridor enclosed me, the familiar shipboard smells of metal and plastic and blue-green, of endlessly recycled air and water and organics, filled my grateful nostrils. 'That was a brilliant landing, I must say.'

'Great to have you back,' Tony said. 'Especially with such success.'

I turned the sides of my mouth downward. 'Wilde would've been better. He *knows* the way –'

'And who's to say it still works? We'll get more out of Malley in the long run. You did fine.'

'Hope you're right. Have to dry him out and give his brain a reboot first.'

Tony laughed. 'Two tabs from the medical bay. I've pulled worse cases out of brawls in Aldringrad.' He motioned me to precede him along the radial corridor. 'Who's the little sweetie?'

'Calls herself Suze,' I told him. 'Don't know her other names. She's just volunteered. I met her by chance, and she's been helpful. She's a sociologist –'

'A what?' I glanced back at him. He rolled his eyes up, then down. 'Oh, right, I see.' He blinked hard, shutting off his suit's encyclopaedia.

'Check her out,' I advised. 'She's nice, but –' I spread my fingers and waggled my hand where he could see it over my shoulder.

'Gotcha,' he said. 'You had some trouble with the locals?'

'Minor trouble,' I said. 'No tissue damage to anyone – but something serious is going on. Malley was leaned on by a couple of guys who claimed to be from the Inner System's space defence, and the descriptions of them check out, low-gee reflexes and all that. Hinted that he was a potential source of an outbreak. He denies it, but what he's actually been doing is teaching electronics to the non-cos – no harm in that, but the grubby sods are using radios.'

'Mind viruses could have been the worry.'

'Possible,' I said. 'Or maybe the appeasers have picked up some hint of what we're up to. The local Union rep is looking into it, she'll be in touch.'

'I'll keep an ear out,' Tony said. We'd reached the internal doorway to the mid deck. 'Oh, and Ellen . . .'

'Yes?' I paused, my hand on the plate, and looked back at him. He eyed me up and down and mimed disapproval. 'You can't face the rest of the crew dressed like *that*.'

'Oh.' I looked down at my torn jumpsuit, stained webbing, scratched boots; thumbed the straps of my backpack. 'I suppose not.'

I put down the bits of hardware I'd accumulated and hesitated before transforming the suit. In the natural human environment of free fall or low-gee most of us went for some permutation of closely fitting and lightly floating; but we weren't going to enjoy that comfortable condition for some time, and I'd need some padding. I selected the appropriate parameters, and let the suit come up with something to match them. I found myself in a bulky, quilted one-piece with the arms and legs sealed at the wide cuffs to skintight gloves and socks. It had a thrown-back anorak hood which could quickly convert to a helmet in an emergency. Deep pockets were on the front of each thigh. The whole thing was presumably modelled on its race memory of a Project Apollo spacesuit, except that it was rendered in pale pink satin quilting, and embellished with a deep pink satin sash and lot of lace, ribbons and bows, all pink.

The suit has its little moods, sometimes.

'Oh, very dignified,' Tony said. 'You look like somebody's great, great grandmother in a bed jacket.'

So that was what was on its mind. There were several layers of clothing underneath; from the feel of them, the suit had elaborated further on the maternal-boudoir theme. Perhaps it had registered that I was pregnant, even though I hadn't asked it to check. It was quite touching, in a way.

'I *am* somebody's great, great grandmother,' I reminded Tony, as I gathered up the pistol, ammo, and clasp knife. He looked at the last with covetous interest.

'A Swiss Army knife!' he said. 'Can I have that?'

'No,' I said, pocketing it. 'You can have the gun, though. I think our new recruits will expect it of the security officer.'

'Yeah,' he said as I pushed the plate and the door slid open. 'I just don't think they'll expect that suit of the skipper.'

The mid deck is the control area on a fusion clipper. Circular, fifty feet across and fifteen feet high, it's shielded from the engine by the main water tanks, and from external radiation by shells of water between the outer and inner hull. It looks and feels like a greenhouse, warm and slightly humid, with illumination provided by water-filtered sunlight and electric lamps; the instrumentation and cabling intertwined with the hydroponics and the inevitable coiled tubes of transparent plastic through which the algae circulate. In a sunstorm the whole company – usually up to sixty, counting crew and passengers – can crowd into it, but most of the time it's occupied only by the active crew. On this trip there were no passengers, so we were all there.

My wonderful team, my gang. Tony Girard beside me, my security expert, whose conspiratorial skills went back to the old faction fights in Lagrange. Jaime Andrades, the navigator, who joked that his talents came from his Portuguese ancestry, but who was a pure-black survivor of the famously disastrous Angolan moon colony. Boris Grobovski, the gunner, who'd spent his first century of adulthood with the Sino–Soviet mobile artillery, in their slow but inexorable advance from Vladivostok to Lisbon, spreading democracy from sea to shining sea. Andrea Gromova, the pilot, who had started out, before the Fall, boosting antique Energias crammed with bonded labourers from the privatized gulags to the asteroid mining camps, then gone over to the revolution in the battle of New South Yorkshire. Lu Yeng, the computer specialist; at seventy, she was the youngest, born on Callisto. Her parents had come there in the initial negotiations between the Union and the Division. The intensity of her experience with neutralizing Outwarder viruses more than made up for her relative youth, although in political terms she was a bit naive, retaining an odd reverence for Kim Nok-Yung, Shin Se-Ha and other finders of the true knowledge.

None of the crew so much as raised an eyebrow at my suit when Tony and I strode out on to the mid deck. Eccentricity is policy. Suze and Malley were sitting together on the edge of an acceleration couch, and they had some difficulty not laughing out loud. I gave them a withering glance, and grinned and waved at the other crew members, who were spread out around the circle of a dozen or so acceleration couches.

'Thanks, everybody,' I said. 'That was an excellent landing. Congratulations to Jaime and Andrea.' The navigator and pilot waved back. I walked straight over to the nearest acceleration couch and lay down. Tony settled in another couch, hauled down a boom-borne instrument resembling a television screen with handlebars, and began scanning.

'Tony,' I asked after a minute, 'are there any people within a mile of us?'

He kept twisting the bars for a few seconds.

'Nah,' he said. 'None on the water, for sure, and any who're too deep in the trees for me to pick up should be safe enough.'

'Sound the alarm anyway,' I said.

The internal alarms on a fighter-bomber are cacophonous. The external alarms on a fusion-clipper about to lift from a planet are calculated to wake the dead and send them running anywhere out of its range. We only heard it faintly ourselves, but it still set our teeth on edge. I let it sound for ten minutes while we went through the final checklist: everybody strapped in, water-intake valves closed, fusion lasers powered up, flight path clear . . .

'OK, comrades,' I said, 'let's lift.'

Andrea eased out the fusion regulator, and the ship rose, slowly at first, shuddering from nose to tail.

'Fifty feet,' Andrea intoned. 'One hundred, hundred and fifty, two hundred . . .'

'At two thousand feet, go for the burn,' I said.

'Eat proton death, Canary Wharf!' said Suze.

'Hey, come on,' I said. 'A few broken windows.'

Ten seconds later Andrea pulled out the regulator all the way, and a succession of invisible people started an unkind experiment to find out how many could lie on top of me. By the time we reached orbit, they'd piled up seven deep.

The drive shut off, and they all went away. I unbuckled and let myself drift for a moment, enjoying the sensation while it lasted. 'Everybody all right?' I called out. Everybody was.

'Okay,' I said, 'don't get too happy in free fall. We're going to pick up some ice, and then we're boosting all the way at one gee.'

'Thank god for that,' said Malley, who was clinging to his couch as if he were afraid of falling off. Suze had the silent, pale look of someone who is determined not to think about being sick. Several crew members made mutinous moaning noises.

'Shut up, you lot,' I said. 'I've been in one gee for three days, while you've all been loafing about in orbit. You can live with it for another ten days.'

'But we've *already* lived with it for ten days,' grumbled Andrea. 'On the way in.'

Malley rolled on his couch and looked over at me. 'So you'll have been in one gee for all of twenty-three days? I wonder how the human frame can stand it.'

'It can't,' I said, launching myself over to float above him. 'Hence — many of the ills that flesh is heir to. Which reminds me.'

I grabbed a boom and pushed myself over to the medical bay and clicked out three surgeries.

'Just swallow these,' I told him on my return. He clutched the colour-coded capsules and looked at them suspiciously.

'What'll they do?'

'One's to stop your addictions – you'll still enjoy a drink or a smoke, but you won't need them – one to rejuvenate you – circulation, muscle tone, skin and so on – and one to burnish up your synapses.' I grinned at his suspicious look. 'Just the hardware – the software's still down to you. No commie brainwashing involved, honest.'

'I guess I have to trust you sometimes,' he said wryly, and placed the surgeries in his mouth and swallowed hard. 'All I feel right now is I could do with a drink.'

'Better wait until we're under acceleration,' I said. 'Squirting from bulbs ain't much fun.'

Suze observed this with dull interest.

'I don't suppose,' she asked plaintively, 'you have anything for space sickness?'

'I'm afraid not,' I said. 'You just have to get used to it.' I refrained from adding the bit about the first six months being the worst.

Suze fixed her gaze on something above her and nodded, her lips set in a thin line. I felt sorry for her, but at the same time a little amused that she'd come up with the same request as every other newbie we'd ever lifted. A cure for motion sickness, indeed! What did they expect from medical nanotechnology – miracles?

'What's with the imperial units?' Malley asked, as we watched and listened to Andrea guiding us in to dock with the ice tanker.

'You'll hear arguments about human scale and intuition and convenience and so forth,' I explained, 'but the older and coarser characters in space will sum it up in two words: fucking NASA. Most of the space settlements were built with ex-NASA stock or to NASA spec way back in the early days, and ever since then it's been too much trouble to change. We're locked into it.'

'Yeah,' said Andrea. 'Which is why we are now two point five seven miles from a hundred thousand metric tons of ice. You've just gotta love the consistency of it all.'

'Mind you,' Malley chuckled, his teeth clenched on an unlit pipe, 'I suppose I should be grateful. The Malley One Point Five Eight Kilometres just wouldn't have the same ring to it.'

Even Suze managed a laugh, though she was still looking a bit green. The thought of the mess she could at any moment make impelled me to seek out a couple of suits. I hauled them over and thrust one each to Malley and Suze.

'What do I do with this?' Suze asked, drifting away with her arms wrapped around a twenty-pound, eighteen-inch ball of rubbery glop.

'Just let it get to know you,' I told her. It was already flowing around her waist and across her midriff. 'It'll take the form of a set of basic fatigues and backpack in the first instance, and it'll show you how to vary that if you want. It can mimic almost any texture and external appearance you specify.' I waved a satin-gloved hand, pink lace flurrying around my forearm. 'If you don't specify the details, expect surprises! But no matter how frivolous it may look, it reacts to vacuum before you can blink. If you go outside, or if we have, uh, a *sudden loss of cabin pressure*, it snaps into a spacesuit. Grab an oxy bottle if you can, but if necessary it can work on a closed-loop basis indefinitely.'

'What about the clothes we've got on?' Malley asked.

'They will be assimilated,' I assured him. 'The suit can reprocess just about anything.'

Suze looked around, rather wildly, as the smart-matter crawled up her arms.

'What about going to the toilet?' she said.

'There's a place called the head, over there – oh, you mean if you're outside in the suit?'

'Yes.'

'Like I said,' I reiterated patiently, 'the suit can reprocess just about anything.'

At this point she gave the suit an opportunity to demonstrate this ability and several others, including that of catching projectile droplets. I left them to it.

An hour later we had replaced the reaction-mass and fuel used up in the *Terrible Beauty*'s unscheduled planetary surface excursion, and were accelerating at a steady one gravity in a more-or-less straight line across the plane of the ecliptic to Jupiter – or rather, to where Jupiter would be in ten days' time. After five days, we'd turn off the engine, swing the ship around, and decelerate at one gravity the rest of the way. This, as anyone will tell you, is not the most fuel-efficient way to get around. Most of the transport in the Solar System hardly used any fuel at all, and was pretty fast even so; with a big enough light sail you can get from Earth orbit to Mars orbit in weeks, Jupiter in months. We had no compunction about using fusion-clippers, on the minority of journeys for which we didn't have weeks or months to play with.

(As it happens, fuel efficiency, or even reaction-mass, wasn't the limiting factor. With the laser-fusion drive and the practically inexhaustible amounts of ice available, we could have used clippers for everything. The limiting factor was the availability of ships.)

The return to weight made Malley and Suze a lot more cheerful, and the rest of us a little less. We made our way down the stairwell from the command deck to the commissary. It was a slightly smaller room, also circular, with several small tables and one big round table, more than adequate for all of us. In the centre of that table was the serving lift, and at each setting was a menu mat. I sat down with Malley on one side and Suze on the other.

'You can dial up quite a wide range of foods and drinks,' I explained, 'but for obvious reasons anything made with boiling water is a speciality of the house.' I scrolled the menu. 'May I recommend the Thames salmon, freshly caught?'

Most of us made the same choice, tapping the appropriate lines on the menu, and the steaming, almond-flaked dishes rose from the centre of the table and were passed eagerly around. Now that it had the template, the kitchen could carbon-copy 'freshly caught' Thames salmon till the drive went out, but the real thing did have a thrill. It's subjective, but as Malley (slightly drunk on Tranquilitatis 2296, and high on the first buzz from the swallowed surgeries) tried to tell us, value was all subjective anyway. He seemed to think he was making a point, and we politely deferred to this misconception.

We finished eating and shoved the plates back into the middle. The lift silently sank away with them. Malley fished in his pocket (his suit had based its initial form on what he'd been wearing, and had a quaint tweedy appearance) and pulled out his pipe and tobacco.

'Is it OK to smoke on the ship?' he asked.

'Sure,' I said. 'We're sitting sixty feet above a fusion torch, man. Fire is the least of our worries.' I hoped he'd give it a rest when the addiction passed, though. Various comrades unthinkingly wrinkled their noses, until someone tapped a command on their mat to increase the ventilation.

By the time we reached the coffee I had introduced everybody: Andrea, Jaime, Boris, Tony and Yeng. Suze looked at me when I'd finished and said: 'But Ellen – who are you?'

We all laughed. 'Ellen May Ngwethu,' I said. 'I was born in 2041, in a Lagrange space settlement, so I'm almost as old as Malley – I mean, Sam! Fought in the initial split between the Earth Tendency and the Outwarders, and on Earth during the dark century. I worked on Earth Defence for a long time, then moved out to Jupiter. I've been in the Cassini Division for the past, let me see, seventy-odd years, and right now I'm on the Division's Command Committee, and I'm the liaison on the Jovian Anomaly Research Committee. That's a non-military, scientific body which is responsible to the Solar Council and has the next-to-final say in what the Division gets up to. The Solar Council has the final say.' I smiled around the table. 'In theory. In practice, the Division docs what it pleases.'

Suze looked slightly shocked, Malley smug.

'I know the theory,' Malley said. 'In theory, everyone does what they damn well please. "The free development of each is the condition of the war of all against all", or some such nonsense.'

Yeng frowned at this comment; Malley turned up his hands. 'Screw the politics – I gather from what you've just said, Ellen May Ngwethu, that you are what in a more openly hierarchical arrangement would be called a member of the General Staff. A top military officer and politician. So – what the fuck are you doing getting your hands dirty, rolling about in the mud on the kulak reservation, all just to lift an old physicist?'

'Good question,' I said. Malley looked me in the eye and began fiddling with his pipe; I wished I had something equally distracting with which to occupy my hands. 'One part of the answer is that we don't work the way you think – our committees may look like a hierarchy if you draw them out on a schematic, but that's all. It genuinely isn't some kind of concealed top-down structure. So if the Command Committee wants certain kinds of job done, it doesn't have some poor minion down below to send off and do it. We're elected to do a job, and I was the best for this one.

'The other part of the answer is that we need to keep what we're doing secret. Apart from the Division's Command Committee, the only people who know that we're planning an assault through the wormhole are those of us on this ship.' I looked around. 'We're it, we're the team, and you're in! If you don't like what we're doing, you're both free to pull out, but not to leave the Division's space until it's all over.'

Malley and Suze both looked troubled and about to speak. Suze said it first: 'But who are you keeping all this a secret *from*?'

'From the Jovians,' Tony said.

'But – but –' Malley was almost stuttering, as his synapses

misfired with excited articulation. 'The Jovians, the Outwarders, they're, they're just mad, they're trapped in their own virtual realities!'

I glanced around the team, and caught minute nods and shrugs.

'Not any more,' I said. 'But it's a long story, and we've all had a long day. Tomorrow for that. Let me show you around the ship.'

One thing that distinguishes a fusion–clipper from most space-craft is that its internal layout has a definite 'up' and 'down'; and because this one was only carrying the crew there was plenty of room in which to show Malley and Suze around. After dinner I used my remaining energy to climb up and down stairways all over the ship and explain all that could be explained.

The fusion–clipper's hull is like a somewhat pear-shaped egg, two hundred feet long and seventy across at its widest diameter, which is occupied by the commissary and the command deck. The narrow end tapers to the jet, and contains the fusion torch, the main water tanks, and the life-support systems. Above, or forward, from the command deck are the sleeping–quarters – cramped, but festooned with climbing plants and recycling tubes (hard to distinguish, in practice) which give it a more open feel. Above that, clustered around the big glass eye of the heat shield, are the active-defence laser cannon, for dealing with any wandering space junk which (at the sort of velocities a fusion–clipper can reach) *all* has to be dealt with.

Our tour ended in the sleeping gallery which, typically for this class of ship, was deliberately designed to resemble a cliff-face of caves overlooking the central air well, whose bottom was the transparent mid deck roof and whose top was the transparent forward heat shield, through which a a distorted but distinct pattern of stars could be seen. The erratic, silent flaring of incoming dust and meteoroids, vaporized by the reflex lasers of the ship's active-defence system, provided a soothing analogue of the shooting stars in a natural sky.

Malley leaned over a guardrail and looked up and down.

'Why the recyling plant?' he asked. 'The journey times are days or weeks. Why not just carry supplies?'

'Not all the journeys are so short, and they don't all end at ports,' I said.

'Hmm,' he said. 'Colonizing.'

'Well,' I shrugged, 'there's the Kuiper Belt, and the Oort.'

'And New Mars?' Suze asked mischievously.

'We plan ahead,' I agreed. They both laughed.

Malley stretched and yawned. 'You were right,' he said. 'Time for bed. Now where did I leave my bag?'

I retrieved their luggage, such as it was, then showed them their cabins and crawled into mine. With just enough room to stand up and to lie down in, its rounded walls veined with translucent tubes ferrying swirling swarms of engineered noctilucent protozoa, it was like an undersea cave, with the sand-coloured foam rectangle of the bed its only furnishing. I let the outer garment of the spacesuit change into a thick quilt and pillow; and discovered that for the inner layers the suit had extended its range of textures to fluffy knitted wool and brushed silk tricot, and its range of colours to ecru, beige, and several shades of peach. It was all very cosy. I unfastened a few bows, pulled the quilt over my head, and went to sleep.

'You want to live in a dream world!' I accuse.

I'm clinging by my left big toe to a hole in an angled aluminium bracket, floating at right angles to the kid I'm arguing with, and squirting jets of hash beer into my mouth from a nozzled plastic bottle that once contained something quite different (whose taste lingers) in the crowded recreation-deck (or, inevitably: 'wreck-deck') of an Earth Defence battlesat abandoned to squatters and orbital decay and it's 2062 and I just know it can't be, and I'm dreaming. So the accusation doesn't carry much conviction.

The kid is about nineteen and must be a recent arrival: he's fat, and nobody gets – or stays – fat in free fall (it's that great weight-loss diet we have). His face, dotted with more eruptions than Io, calls to mind all the pizzas he must've stuffed in it. His eyes tend to bulge: the modern equivalent of pebble lenses, due to several corrective cornea ops for reading-induced myopia. Disdaining the hops and hemp as unhealthy, he's sucking some vile cocktail of smart drugs, spiked with euphorics. He knows everything.

'You're the dreamer,' he says. He waves a hand at the window, thirty feet away on the other side of the wreck-deck. Through the mass of drifting drinkers, through clouds of smoke and stray droplets, the image of a brick-red surface crawls past. Madagascar, I'd know it anywhere. 'You're still stuck in commie altruism. You want to help people who're beyond help. They're doomed. "Earth – the Third World", ha-ha. Time to grow up and get with the programme, Ellen. Time to move it out. There's a big universe out there.'

'My point exactly.' I gesture, too, at what's now the Indian Ocean. 'And Earth is part of it. You want to live in a virtual reality.'

'Not entirely.' He smiles, showing bad teeth. 'We'll pay a lot of attention to the outside – we'll have to, if we're gonna turn all that dumb mass into smart-matter. Matter that thinks, and dreams. A world of wonders, where you can be anything you like, not what chance and your genes have made you.'

'I don't want to turn the universe into a big computer running virtual realities,' I tell him. 'And don't call me a "commie altruist", by the way. It's just ordinary human concern. I just don't like to see people suffer, so it would be very *unselfish* of me to ignore ten billion people blundering into the dark.'

'You won't have to see them suffer,' he tells me, with insufferable assurance. 'You can just *edit them out*. Anyway, their problems are *their* problem. Why make them yours?'

'Because I care about them, and if that sounds altruistic, just think of it this way: I'm selfish enough to want to be, oh, the princess of the Galaxy! OK – at a pinch, I'd be happy just to live forever in a Galactic Empire. I *personally want* to see a universe crowded with people having a good time.'

I wave expansively at the wreck-deck, to illustrate.

'People!' He snorts. 'Where's your ambition? We can do better than that.'

'You want to be machines.' I knock back a shot of the drink. 'I don't.'

He shrugs. 'If you want to live in space, you're better off as a machine than as a bag of sea water. The human body's design spec is: a spacesuit for a fish. Machines are at home in the universe.'

I give him a grin so wide and delighted that he thinks I like him, and I come back with a quote from a dated dystopia that had a huge resonance for me when I was a kid: *This Perfect Day* by Ira Levin. (Not that we were in any danger of that perfect day, or any other, but the book spoke to me.)

' "Machines are at home in the universe. People are aliens." '

He's still smiling back, still thinks I'm agreeing. The hash beer drives me to stoned and pissed elaboration: 'Strangers in a strange land. Marx was wrong – we aren't alienated *from* our humanity, alienation *is* humanity. We're always capable of stepping back and looking at what we're doing, from the outside as it were – we have an outside, *inside*, and it's as infinite as space. No Turing test can come close, no matter how good it is at faking an organism. Machines calculate; people count. Machines have programs; people have purposes.' I stop and stare at him and take another shot of beer. 'So there.'

'People are machines too,' he says. 'And machines will have all we have, once we've transferred our minds to them.'

'That's what you call it. Stripping your brain away layer by layer and modelling it on a computer is what I call *dying*.'

'It's transcending,' he says. He slaps his chest, almost setting himself spinning. '*This* is dying. "The meat is murder." '

'Yeah,' I say cruelly. 'If I had *your* body, I'd want to be something else.'

He doesn't take this as the crushing put-down it's intended to be. 'Yes,' he says, still smiling. 'When I upload, I might model my virtual body on yours.'

My attention is distracted by the television screen at the end of the bar, where my parents' faces have appeared, talking to me in a language I don't understand, smiling, reassuring. Their twitching, dead-but-galvanized bodies are drifting in front of the screen, attached by pipes that are sucking up their brains. 'Goodbye, Ellen,' they're saying, 'goodbye. See you in ten thousand years.'

Furious, I turn back to the kid, but he's already changed, from slob to blob, a paramecium shape buzzing with fractal cilia, a patch of which snows to pixels and freezes to a face – my face.

'I like your body,' he says.

'In your dreams!' I yell at him. 'In your dreams!'

And I wake.

The quilt cuddles me, the pillow drinks my tears.

'Hush,' it soothes. 'Everything will be all right.'

The following morning I got up at about 1100 hours, ship time (which, conveniently for those of us who'd boarded yesterday, was the same as GMT), and made my way to the mid deck. Rather to my embarrassment, I was the last to arrive, and the rest of the team had honoured the occasion by setting their suits to various approximations of nattily masculine militarism. Andrea and Boris were entertaining Suze and Malley with a demonstration of the active-defence system, which although automated, could be overridden to provide a spectacular shoot-'em-up game with (mostly tiny, but fast) meteoroids as targets. The others were amusing themselves in less productive ways.

I grunted a good-morning to all of them and had a solitary and thoughtful breakfast in the commissary, chasing the wisps of disturbed dream away with strong coffee. I took my third mug with me back up the stairs and sat down on a couch.

'OK comrades,' I said. 'We're in session. Yeng, would you like to chair?'

She nodded, pushing away her goggles and nanotech tank, and clapped her hands. 'Come *on*, guys. Turn the aiming-computers back on and come over here.'

Andrea, Boris, Malley and Suze dragged themselves away from the manual fire controls and settled down on the ends of couches. I got a shy smile from Suze, a cocky grin from Malley. The surgeries' work, though by no means complete, had transformed his appearance overnight: straightening his stance, smoothing the skin on his face, wiping the wrinkles from around his eyes.

'Your little pills have certainly done something for my reflexes,' he said. Boris spread his hand and made a rocking motion: 'Considering what you started with . . .' The two men laughed; I hoped it indicated, at however tentative a level, the beginning of friendship.

'Suze, Sam,' I began, 'the rest of us all know what I'm going to tell you, but each of us may be able to answer different questions, so . . .'

I worked the long, low seat's controls, raising the central overhead cluster of instrumentation and lowering a boom on which was suspended a holographic projection apparatus. Tendrils snaked out from my gloves into the system's interface. The electric lamps turned off, and I keyed up a football-sized image of Jupiter, softly glowing. I set it spinning with exaggerated speed in the light from the outside, under the refracted, multiply-distorted images of the real stars above us.

'A brief history of the Jovian system,' I said. 'Let's start with how it was before the Outwarders got underway with Project Jove.' The four Galilean moons shuttled around it, the Great Red Spot turned with the planet's coloured bands. 'Here's the first indication that something big was going on, which we noticed in 2090. Real archive tape from the Farside Observatory.'

Ganymede disintegrated – not exploding, not flying apart, just separating into millions of bits which, on this time-lapsed view, immediately spread out to form a ring.

We'd all seen it before – it's the Zapruder film of astronautics: the most widely known image, and the most thoroughly studied and argued-over sequence of photographs, in the history of space exploration. The technician who recorded it had a sense of humour as well as a sense of history, and I played the audio tape of his (alleged) first reaction: 'Oh my stars, it's full of gods!'

Small polite laughs all round. 'OK,' I said, 'we've all heard it. But he was right. And we *still* don't know how they did it, even in principle. Sam Malley proved the concept of the Gate and the Drive, and nanotech and uploading were all understood well in advance – essentially as far back as the nineteen-eighties. But shattering the biggest moon in the solar system came as, um, a bit of a shock.'

The most frightening moment of my life, to be exact. I nodded to Tony, who took up that side of the story.

'We all,' he said, 'couldn't help remembering that the Outwarders had announced their intention of turning everything except the stars into smart-matter, starting with the smaller asteroids and working their way up, all the way to what they called "Jupiter-sized brains". They had a saying: "If it isn't running programs and it isn't fusing atoms, it's just bending space." So we were all rather concerned when we saw that.' He gave us a thin smile. 'Especially those of us who lived on the Moon.'

Malley looked up from doodling something on a pad he'd conjured from the knee of his suit. 'There may be ways of deriving the, uh, *planet-wrecker* from the same schema as the Gate,' he said. 'I've given it some thought over the years, but I've never taken it far. I'll work on it.'

'Good,' I said, smiling as warmly as I could. 'Well, on to the Gate.' I ran the tape forward again, focusing in on the ring and magnifying the view to what had been the limits of our telescopic resolution back in the twenty-nineties. A complex cat's-cradle of girders rapidly took shape, a three-dimensional web of black threads just inside the ring. At the same time the face of Jupiter was transformed, its bands fractured by crosscurrents. I cut to close-ups of the structure.

'These shots are from files retrieved from a construction robot by the so-called artificial woman, Meg, who was Jonathan Wilde's companion in that robot body,' I explained. 'The black struts are – prosaically enough – polycarbon I-beams, though they have complex internal machinery. The small robots you see rocketing about and apparently working on the structure are the bonded labour force, each of them with a copied human mind running on its onboard computer.' I paused, compressed my lips for a moment and took a deep breath, then continued. 'Now *that* –' I froze the frame, then let it run on – 'is a very different kind of upload. It's what we called a "super-organism" and what the ex-human workers on the project called a "macro". It's a smart-matter object, a constellation of trillions of nanomachines, and one of many. Each of them contains literally millions of minds, mostly replicated – and enhanced – descendants of the original Outwarders. Wilde refers to them as "the fast folk", and the term has caught on, because it's apt: their minds are thinking and experiencing at least a thousand times faster than ours.'

We all sat and stared at the macro, a nightmarishly gigantic and multicoloured amoeboid shape, its fractal surfaces seething, its pseudopodia bulging and retracting as it oozed around the girders. Its size dwarfed the tiny, tinny-looking robots of its pressed servants.

'You've never shown these close-ups to people on Earth,' Suze accused. I nodded briskly.

'That's right,' I said. 'We've kept them to ourselves, for now. All anybody in the Inner System has seen is the fuzzy blobs that showed up in some pictures we got at the time from a spy probe before it was detected and destroyed.'

'Very democratic of you,' said Malley. 'Didn't want to cause panic, is that it?'

'Not exactly,' said Tony, leaning forward. 'If you're like me, Dr Malley, I'm sure you're feeling a reaction of unease or even dread, which is objectively rather hard to justify. We ourselves find it difficult to explain, and suspect it may be deliberately induced by some subtle effect of the surface patterns. If that's the case it was presumably intended to overawe the labour force. Tests on our own personnel have shown that this response might readily translate into a desire for precipitate action against the present-day descendants of these entities. That's a pressure we'd prefer to avoid.'

For the moment, I thought. I went on quickly, showing the subsequent stages of the construction project in fast-forward. The structure suddenly divided, a smaller, circular section detaching itself. The Jovian surface swirled, its equator dotted with what looked like waterspouts which soared in curving trajectories to the ring. A hairline circle around the ring glowed white-hot. The newly separated structure seemed to fold in on itself, and there, hanging like a film of soap in a ring, was the Gate itself: a mile-wide circle of stretched space, its edge shimmering with all the colours of the spectrum.

'The Malley Mile,' I said. Malley gave us all an ironic bow. 'If you watch closely you'll see the moment where it divides into two just-overlapping circles, the two sides of the wormhole. There. The small dark object at the centre is the Outwarders' ship, or probe, which . . .'

A line of light stabbed at a tangent from the glowing line around the great ring, straight for the centre of the Gate.

'. . . goes away.' Everybody blinked; everybody drew breath, even those who'd watched this scene a hundred times. 'Taking one side of the wormhole with it. Observe how the plasma jet apparently just *stops* when it reaches the Gate. There can be not the slightest doubt that the jet is passing from the local region of space-time into – somewhere else. But in case anybody's wondering, we did manage to track the probe for the first few minutes.' The grainy images flashed up, showing a streak of light and a blurry dot. 'As you can see, there's the plasma jet, coming apparently out of nowhere and crossing a few hundred yards of space to the probe, where it's transformed into kinetic energy via what we presume is, ah, a Malley virtual-mass drive. We calculate that the probe reached almost the speed of light in a month. After that, things get complicated, because both sides of the wormhole are in the same reference frame.'

Suze was looking puzzled. I smiled at Malley. 'Sam, over to you.'

Malley shrugged. 'To simplify drastically ... it's not really correct to refer to "both sides" of the wormhole. The ship is travelling at some arbitrarily close approximation to the speed of light, and therefore experiences relativistic time dilation – time runs slower on the ship than it does back home. The truly paradoxical feature of the wormhole is that both ends are in the same place. So anything passing through one end of the wormhole arrives at the other end in ship time, which after, say, a year, could be hundreds of light years away, and hundreds of years in the future. With continued acceleration, the probe reaches the edge of the observable universe in thirty shipboard years. So, thirty years from launch, anybody passing through the wormhole arrives instantly at the same location. It is, if you like, a time machine to the future.'

Suze grinned around at us. 'If you say so.'

I laughed. 'Meanwhile, if that's the word, quite a lot had been going on around Jupiter.'

The planet's surface was mottled, the sites of the still-soaring tornadoes expanding into new variants of the Great Red Spot. I pulled up time-lapsed shots from the records recovered from Meg's AI mind. The macros changed as we watched, their original feverish internal activity speeding up, then slowing to a stop. A few of them seemed to crystallize, and drifted off towards the Jovian atmosphere. The rest visibly shrivelled, rotting to skeletal shapes like the veins of dead leaves.

A new shape burst on the scene, crashing through the dead macros and their vast construction site like a stone through cobwebs. The viewpoint zoomed towards it, revealing a long, jury-rigged assembly of spacecraft and habitats, spinning crazily on its axis and following a precarious course along the line of the plasma jet. And then the viewpoint was evidently *on* the cobbled-together ship, the hot white line strobing past. The shot ended in a burst of blue light.

'Cherenkov radiation,' I said. 'They went through the wormhole – well, through a side-branch of it, a daughter wormhole – and, as we know, found a new home. Now we'll leave them for the moment, and pull back to see what happened on this side.' I switched to the telescope view: the fountains of gas, and the jet that they had fed, ceased.

'We're not sure,' I said, 'whether that was planned, the probe having reached some point where it could continue to accelerate without further input from base; or whether it was a result of the disaster that you saw unfolding there, or whether indeed it was a response to the escape of the labour force on that remarkable excuse for a starship.'

Suze was grinning from ear to ear.

'It was quite a feat, that escape,' she said.

'It sure was,' said Andrea. 'I still shudder every time I look at it.'

'Why didn't they just head for home, for the Inner System?' Malley asked.

I shrugged, hiding a moment of pain. 'Partly because, ironically enough, they didn't have the supplies for such a long journey in, uh, *real space* – it would have taken them years to get back to the nearest human settlement in *that* thing, and partly because their leaders – it wasn't exactly a democratic setup, being an orbital labour camp – had decided they wanted to go to the stars.'

'Also,' Tony added, 'I suspect the post-humans systematically misled them about what was going on in the Inner System. Wilde certainly thought we jammed their communications, which is more or less the opposite of the truth.'

'OK,' Malley said.

'Right,' I went on. 'The next thing that happened, about a year later, was the beginning of a flood of disruptive radio-borne computer viruses from somewhere inside the Jovian atmosphere. It took us a long time to recover, and even longer to get out there ourselves. Within five years, however, our telescopes were picking up something with which most of you are by now so familiar that it's hard to imagine how awesome it seemed at the time.' I laughed briefly. 'There must be kids today who think this appearance of Jupiter is *natural*.'

The planet's image blurred, the orange banding known since Cassini himself dissolving briefly into chaos, then settling into the new configuration it had shown for the past couple of centuries: vast hexagonal upwellings, like Bernoulli convection cells in boiling water.

'As you can see, they were able to affect their environment – deliberately or not, we can't say. Bear in mind the speed the original post-humans worked at – if it was maintained, the entities we now call the Jovians must have done that over five or six thousand subjective years, so it could have been just a by-product of their activity. Every five years or so, these cells collapse and reform, and the radio output changes. We think this represents the repeated rise and fall of post-human cultures in virtual realities, though for all we know they could just as well have degenerated to pre-human levels of intelligence, and all this might have no more significance than the work of coral polyps or bees. The viral messages themselves could be simply a defensive reflex, the equivalent of a squid's cloud of ink or a plant's insecticides.'

Yeng raised her hand, exercising her chairperson's right to interrupt. 'That wouldn't make it any less dangerous,' she pointed out. 'Biological diseases aren't intelligent either, but they can still threaten us, and the computer viruses which something out there is generating are definitely a threat.'

I nodded emphatically. 'Yes . . . which is why our communications are such a bind, and why our most important computers are such lumbering monsters, and *all* our computers, right down to the nano scale, are mechanical. But that's only part of it. Now and again there's some kind of attempt at launching things out of the atmosphere. These attempts have increased over time. Which is where we come in.'

What followed was basically a propaganda video for the Cassini Division, showing the constant vigilance of the orbital fleets patrolling just outside the Jovian atmosphere, zapping anything larger than a grain of sand that looked like heading the wrong way; and the long watch on the Gate. A voice-over carefully explained that the latter wasn't the complete waste of time that it might seem, because we also spooled in the data sent back from the probe, which constantly deepened our knowledge of the far future of the universe. Malley shared with me a sceptical smile.

I paused the video. 'All this is now, sadly, out of date,' I said. 'Because something new has happened.' I bookmarked the place for later use and brought on some new footage.

'This is recent,' I said. 'The last couple of months. We haven't, uh, put it on general release yet.'

The huge upwellings died away, as they had two-score times in the past. When they were renewed, clusters of bubbles appeared within them, bobbing into visibility and then sinking back. Each time they returned to the surface, the clusters had expanded and proliferated, linked up by long and (on this scale) thin black lines. I maxed the res, showing dark shapes shuttling within these black lines, moving in both directions.

'Oh, shit,' said Malley.

'Quite,' I said, running overflight scans. 'It does definitely look like some kind of stable, organized form of life, with habitats, technology, transport. So far, that's the best detail we've got. Perhaps most significant of all, there are narrow-cast beam messages passed between these clusters. We haven't yet interpreted them, but they sure look like intelligent communication. There's every possibility that what we're seeing is evidence that the Jovians have finally got out of the recurrent traps of their inherited virtual realities, and have emerged as a new species. They are developing and changing fast – we're getting traces of flight paths through the atmosphere, and the speed and frequency of these flights are increasing by the week.'

'Wow,' said Suze. 'Aliens!'

'No,' I said. 'Post-humans – a superhuman, post-Singularity form of life, that may be as far above us as we are above the ants. Or will be, Real Soon Now.'

I looked around the circle. Malley and Suze seemed puzzled, but not worried; my crew were united in grim resolution.

'Is this why you're so keen to get through the wormhole?' Suze asked. 'So we can – you can – escape, if necessary?'

'That's part of it,' I admitted. 'And part of it is as I said to you – we don't know what's going on on the *other* side. If it's anything like this, we want to know.'

'There is something else,' Boris said. 'Something you should know.' He nodded to me; I ran the standard spiel at the place where I'd stopped. It showed off our distant expeditions in the Kuiper Belt using lasers and tactical nukes to topple cometary orbits in towards the Inner System, sending them swinging around Jupiter and on to Mars or the Belt.

I stopped it and brought up the lights. We all sat back and looked at Malley and Suze. All of us, I suppose, felt as tense as I did; we had decided, in long debates on our journey to Earth, that Malley (or Wilde, if we'd got him on board) would have to know the full story, because it would be impossible to conceal it from him once he started work on the wormhole problem, and he was unlikely to take kindly to being duped.

Malley's mouth opened, then closed. He swallowed hard and spoke.

'You're not serious,' he said. 'You can't be – are you telling us you're going to actually set up a cometary bombardment and destroy the new Jovians?'

'Yes,' I said. 'That's exactly what we're going to do. As soon as we saw this new development, we set things in motion – literally – out in the Kuiper Belt. It took a lot of work, but it's ready now. We've set up a train of massive comets, and they're due to arrive in less than three weeks. We'll give them a nudge at the last moment, and there'll be a succession of impacts all around the planet. It should work – the new Jovians seem more vulnerable than whatever is making the upwellings. Those bubbles you see are just that, bubbles in the atmosphere. Most of their technology seems to be based on manipulation of electromagnetic fields, gas flows, and large-scale chemical reactions. We are going to direct a stream of fast, heavy comet nuclei into the Jovian atmosphere, hit them with a force greater than a million nuclear wars, and wipe them out for good.'

'But we don't even know if they're hostile!' Suze protested. 'Have you tried to contact them?'

'Of course not,' Yeng said. 'They're still churning out the same old viruses. If we deliberately opened communication with them, who knows but they'd send even more destructive viruses back?'

'You must be able to build in safeguards,' Malley said. He rattled his unlit pipe between his teeth. 'I don't see the justification.'

'They're capable of supplanting us,' Tony said. 'At least, there's a strong chance that they are. They present a threat to us just by existing. Isn't that justification enough?'

Suze and Malley both shook their heads. 'It's a bad thing to do,' Suze said. 'We could learn from them. We could persuade them to stop the virus broadcasts. They might not be able to harm us. They might not even be aware we exist!'

'Here's hoping,' said Andrea. 'That way, they have no chance to fight back.'

We all laughed, except Suze and Malley.

'What about the morality of it?' Malley asked.

Most of us shrugged or smiled. Yeng frowned. 'Morality?' she said uncertainly. 'What's that?'

Some of us smiled; Malley barked a laugh.

'It's an ideology,' Suze said. 'People used to think that there was a very powerful intelligence that controlled the universe, and that it told them what to do. Later they found out there was no intelligence controlling the universe, but for about a century or so after that they thought the *universe* told them what to do. Some of them had doubts about that, but they thought that if people didn't believe it they would start raping and killing and hurting each other.' She grimaced. 'I've never understood why they thought that, because some people were raping and killing and hurting other people all the time anyway. The reason most people weren't doing that is because they didn't want to in the first place, or because they knew they couldn't get away with it. We know now that if we want other people to stop doing bad things we have to *make* them stop and *not* let them get away with it. Which is why we have the Union!' she concluded triumphantly, a little out of breath, but evidently pleased that her arcane studies had made some contribution.

'OK,' said Yeng, 'I understand. It was something people believed before they had the true knowledge?'

'That's right!' I said. 'Exactly. So, Sam, you were saying?'

Malley glowered at me. Then his expression relaxed and he shrugged. 'All right,' he said. 'If that's the way you see it, fine. I think all this "Do What Thou Wilt Shall Be The Whole Of The Law" crap is as satanic as the man who first said it, but let that pass.'

I nodded. It was easy enough to let that pass, because it made no kind of sense to me.

'So to put it in your terms,' Malley went on, 'I don't think it would be to our advantage to destroy the Jovians. They are a form of intelligent life, presumably they're sentient, and disrespect for sentience is a dangerous thing. A bad precedent. And secondly, as Suze pointed out, we could benefit from some kind of peaceful interaction with them, if that's at all possible.'

I stared at him, somewhat shaken. I had known he was old, and had been a non-cooperator most of his life, but for a genius he seemed remarkably obtuse.

'First of all,' I said, 'you're right about sentience. We do have to respect it, each and every one of us, if only for our own peace of mind. But only humans are sentient. Those things out there are just jumped-up computer programs! They may give the appearance of sentience, but if they do, it'll be a protective coloration. You can have a deep, meaningful conversation with your suit – hey, you can have a sexual relationship with it, if that's your thing – but nobody thinks *suits* are sentient. It's just something that suits have evolved, by a kind of natural selection, in order to get along with humans. The Jovians, if we communicate with them, will no doubt seem sensitive, but they can no more feel than the eye-spots on a butterfly's wing can see.'

Malley tilted his head back and roared with laughter.

'And you people sneer at ideology!' he spluttered, when he'd calmed down a bit. 'That's the most airtight piece of dogmatic, closed-loop thinking I've ever heard! You really mean to say that no robots, no uploads, no artificial intelligences are truly sentient and worthy of our concern?'

'Absolutely,' I said. 'It's self-evident.'

'And even if you were right, what's the *advantage* to you, or us, or anybody, in crushing those "butterflies' wings", blind though they may be? Eh?'

'Let me explain,' I said patiently. 'There are no signs of intelligent life anywhere else in the universe. The Outwarder probe has gone a long way, and none of the data coming back from it has shown a smidgin of a trace of a signal. We're alone, apart from the Jovians. If they are superior to us, no matter how friendly they seem to be, we'll always be at their mercy. I will not live at the mercy of anyone or anything. This our best, last, and only chance to have the universe to ourselves, and we're going to take it.'

Malley stood up and looked around at all of us, not angry, not impatient; a bit sad, as though some of the aging damage he was beginning to slough off had settled back on him.

'Not with my help, you're not,' he said.

5

The Coming Race

MALLEY STALKED over to the stairwell and went down to the commissary. Suze rose, looked at me anxiously, shrugged and followed him.

'Meeting's over,' Yeng said. She glanced around, unsure how to take what had happened, then decided to look on the bright side. 'Time we all had some lunch.'

Lunch was usually a relaxed occasion. This one wasn't. We hung around the smaller tables in the commissary in ones and twos. Suze was with Malley on one side of the room, I with Tony on the other. All the talking was in low voices.

'Think we've blown it?' Tony asked.

I shrugged. 'Callisto's buzzing with talk about the bombardment. We couldn't have kept it from him, not without isolation that would've made him suspicious and – non-cooperative!'

Tony stroked his beard, and looked searchingly at me. 'Suppose we're wrong,' he said softly. 'When I think about what we're proposing to do – well, between you and me, Ellen, I sometimes have qualms about it myself. Suppose the Jovians *aren't* flatlines, suppose they really are conscious, just like you and me but far better, with a deeper and richer inner life. After all, they may have naturally evolved away from the earlier Jovians, and they're no longer some kind of new releases of the old mad uploads, but a new species, a new flesh. Wouldn't that make the impact event like, say, some troop of chimps using rocks to beat out the brains of the first humans?'

I fought down my dismayed surprise at this incipient flinch, this *line wobble* as the old comrades would say, coming from – of all people – my security officer and oldest ally. I fought down my indignation. If Tony had qualms, then certainly others would, too, and he was doing me a favour by expressing them.

'All the more reason to do it,' I said, clapping his shoulder fraternally. 'Look where not doing it got the chimps.'

We understood each other perfectly. In our two hundred years of acquaintance, we had never had a sexual relationship (not counting quick drunk fucks, of course). He just wasn't my type, nor I his. But in every other way we knew each other quite intimately. Not that we agreed on everything, at least not at once, but we knew how to get agreement or agree to differ. We knew how each other's minds worked.

I knew what was going on in Tony's, right now. Although he intellectually accepted the true knowledge, he had never been *taken* by it – unlike me, to whom it had struck home with the force of a revelation.

The true knowledge ... the phrase is an English translation of a Korean expression meaning 'modern enlightenment'. Its originators, a group of Japanese and Korean 'contract employees' (inaccurate Korean translation, this time, of the English term 'bonded labourers') had acquired their modern enlightenment from battered, ancient editions of the works of Stirner, Nietzsche, Marx, Engels, Dietzgen, Darwin, and Spencer, which made up the entire philosophical content of their labour-camp library. (Twentieth-century philosophy and science had been excluded by their employers as decadent or subversive – I forget which.) With staggering diligence, they had taken these works – which they ironically treated as the last word in modern thought – and synthesized from them, and from their own bitter experiences, the first socialist philosophy based on totally pessimistic and cynical conclusions about human nature.

Life is a process of breaking down and using other matter, and if need be, other life. Therefore, life is aggression, and successful life is successful aggression. Life is the scum of matter, and people are the scum of life. There is nothing but matter, forces, space and time, which together make power. Nothing matters, except what matters to you. Might makes right, and power makes freedom. You are free to do whatever is in your power, and if you want to survive and thrive you had better do whatever is in your interests. If your interests conflict with those of others, let the others pit their power against yours, everyone for theirselves. If your interests coincide with those of others, let them work together with you, and against the rest. We are what we we eat, and *we* eat *everything*.

All that you really value, and the goodness and truth and beauty of life, have their roots in this apparently barren soil.

This is the true knowledge.

On this rock we had built our church. We had founded our idealism on the most nihilistic implications of science, our socialism on crass self-interest, our peace on our capacity for mutual destruction, and our liberty on determinism. We had replaced morality with convention, bravery with safety, frugality with plenty, philosophy with science, stoicism with anaesthetics and piety with immortality. The universal acid of the true knowledge had burned away a world of words, and exposed a universe of things.

Things we could use.

'It's the Rapture for nerds!'

Now that's a breath of fresh air, I think, and turn to see who's come up with this well aimed sneer at the Singularity. It's a guy bumping alongside me, a slender man with straight black hair gelled to a quiff, a sharp beard modelled on Lenin's, a slim gentle face and darting dark eyes. He's enjoying the laughter he's spread on our side, the discomfited smiles on the other.

It's 2065 and we're back in the wreck-deck, but the recreation area is now much expanded, as is the space station, which has just been boosted to a higher orbit. We are here to celebrate that work's completion. There must be hundreds of people here. To begin with we were one big crowd, but as the arguments have gone on we have, almost literally, drifted apart. We have polarized to opposite sides of the deck.

The arguments have been going on for years, but we've always worked together. The two sides, of which those here are a small sample, are loosely based on two waves of space settlement. The first lot had peaked in the twenty-forties, and consisted of pioneer settlers and the forces in Earth Defence who'd gone over to the Fall Revolution. The second lot had come up in the late twenty-fifties, and early twenty-sixties, and were the product of a quite different process: a deliberate abandonment of Earth by technicians, engineers and scientists – and the desperate rich – who had developed an increasingly advanced technology and launch capability in increasingly isolated and beleaguered enclaves. They'd shot their bolt in the catastrophically botched and counter-productive 'Space Movement coup' of 2059.

They still have stuff coming up, though, and all along they've been using bonded labourers – criminals making restitution, mostly, and political and military prisoners from the losing side in the Fall Revolution and subsequent conflicts – to build and defend their infrastructure, in space and on the ground. To us, this seems little better than slavery, not to mention a sneaky undercutting of the Space Movement's traditional private-enterprise or voluntary-labour ethos. To them, it's payback for the long years of repression before the Revolution, and for their continuing harassment by the fragmented governments and frantic peoples of Earth.

Understandably, they have no interest in using the now-enormous and self-sufficient space presence to aid those from whose ignorant wrath they've barely escaped. We, from the first wave of idealistic or avaricious colonists, are convinced that aiding Earth is exactly the way to overcome that ignorant wrath.

We call ourselves: the first settlers, the Earth tendency, the beautiful people, the star warriors.

We call the others: the others, the outsiders, the nerds, the new lot.

The others call us: the Earth-Tenders, the greenies, the commies, the mundanes, the dirt-farmers, the Space Family Robinson.

The others call themselves: the Outwarders, the Singularity Gang, the Futurists, the post-humans.

Their dream is the Singularity. Ours is the Galactic Empire, or the Federation, or whatever. It makes them laugh.

And right now we're laughing at them, or at least the dozens of people within earshot of this man's gibe are laughing at a roughly equal and opposite group of Outwarders.

'That stuff is just *stupid*,' he goes on. 'I can't understand how anybody ever fell for the idea that a computer model of the brain is the same as the brain. Talk about mechanical materialism! It's about becoming a machine, it's death, and wanting it is *sick*.'

'You wouldn't say that if you knew you were about to die,' says the nearest Outwarder, a young man (but we all look young, now) who doesn't match our favourite nerd stereotype because he's eschewed the coke-and-pizza diet for a different Outwarder vice: body building. He floats, tanned and oiled and naked, in a slow-spinning lotus posture, doing something dynamic and clever with the squirted stream of his drink. 'We already have back-ups of people who got killed guarding Canaveral, you know that?'

He catches a wobbling sphere of liquid in his lips, and swallows it, his next rotation bringing up a questioning smile.

'And you're going to run them?' I ask.

'Sure,' he tells us. 'As soon as we have a few bugs out of the virtual-environment software.'

The man beside me laughs. 'So your slave soldiers get promised paradise when they die! Stay with that idea, guys, it worked for Mohammed.'

This second religious allusion leads the oiled man to ask, challengingly, 'Have you ever read anything on the strong-AI resurrectionist position? Even something classic, like *The Physics of Immortality*?'

'Nah,' says the bearded man. 'Life's too short!'

The Outwarder stops his rotation with a perfectly-timed toss of his empty drink-bulb, and looks coldly at my sniggering face.

'Here's a thought from it,' he says. 'Brief enough for you: refusing to accept intelligent robots as *people* is equivalent to racism.'

'So?' says the man at my side. 'So I'm a racist. A *human* racist.'

'Fine by me,' I chip in, knowing that the Outwarder is playing the racism card with my dark skin in mind. He scowls at me.

'Here's another – claiming that human selves can't be imp-lemented on computers is tantamount to accepting death, for everybody, forever. Is that so fine by you?'

'I can live with it,' I say. The man beside me gives an appreciative chuckle, and adds:

'If you allow us to live.'

The Outwarder smiles, looks around at the jostle of his fellows, then back at us.

'Of course we'll allow you to live,' he says. 'On wildlife reserves, like the other interesting animals. Some of us may prefer to think of you as pets. Sentimental post-humans will no doubt campaign for "human rights" – it'll be one of those fluffy causes, like old-growth forests and spotted owls. Wouldn't it be much better to join us, and be as gods?'

Something twists inside me. Everything is suddenly clear. I have what I later understand as the beginning of the true knowledge.

'We *are* as gods!' I snarl. '*We* are the top predator here. *You* can become machines if you like, but then you'll be dead, and we'll be alive, and we'll *treat* you as machines. If we can't use you, we'll smash you up!'

'If you can,' he says.

I look straight back at him. 'If we can.'

He makes a dismissive gesture, and turns away.

The man beside me performs a mid-air somersault, and floats before me, grinning, arms spread. He seems to think he's just given me a fly-past salute.

'That was good,' he says.

'Hey, I liked what you said,' I tell him. ' "The Rapture for nerds." '

We laugh like it's an old, shared joke, and introduce ourselves. His name is Tony Girard, and he's on the space station's management board, responsible for keeping an eye on the Outwarder component of its inhabitants. The liaison is important – the just-completed boosting of the station has been done with the new rocket engines, which look like they've been injection-moulded from diamond, and are nanofactured by the Outwarders. But he can't help getting into arguments with them.

'They say we're evil,' he says. 'I tell them we are.'

'But we're not!' I protest.

'Not from our point of view. We are from theirs. Reactionaries, counter-*evo*lutionaries, pulling back from the next stage in human development.'

'Yeah – extinction!'

I think about being evil. To them, I realize, we are indeed bad and harmful, but – and the thought catches my breath – we are not bad and harmful to *ourselves*, and that is all that matters, *to us*. So as long as we are actually achieving our own good, it doesn't matter how evil we are to our enemies. Our Federation will be, to them, the evil empire, the domain of dark lords; and I will be a dark lady in it.

Humanity is indeed evil, from any non-human point of view. I hug my human wickedness in a shiver of delight.

I tell Tony some of this, and he nods.

'It's very liberating,' he says. 'Wearing the black hats.' He draws, spins and cocks an imaginary six-gun. (Like all of us, he has a real one on his hip.) 'Saves you a lot of soul-searching. As long as you avoid hitting your own side, you're doing the right thing.'

'Perhaps we're the Indians. The natives.'

Tony likes this. 'That's right,' he says. 'Doomed but brave. A drag on the wheels of progress. Shooting arrows at the iron horses of Manifest Destiny.'

'They are such mechanists,' I say.

'Yeah,' he says. 'That's why I like to wind them up.'

I laugh so much I find myself clinging to him, and later that day-cycle we have the first ever of our quick drunk fucks.

I smiled at Tony, perhaps more warmly than usual, and stood up and caught Yeng's eye, then flicked a glance to the table where Malley and Suze were sitting head-to-head. Yeng nodded. We each picked up our trays and wandered over.

'Mind if we sit down?'

Malley looked up, looked at Suze. 'Not at all,' he said.

I sat down beside Malley, and Yeng slipped on to the bench beside Suze and flashed her a quick smile. Suze looked down at her plate, then up.

'Sam and I have a question for you,' said Suze. 'I'm Union, he's non-co, and it turns out we both have the same question. Independently.'

'OK,' I said.

'Would you be willing to at least *try* to contact the Jovians, before destroying them? Would you at least try to come to some arrangement?'

The idea of contact with the Jovians made my skin crawl; but I also felt its attractions. The danger appealed to my recklessness, my hatred of the Jovians fuelled my curiosity about what they were really like, and, above all, we needed Malley's cooperation to get through the Malley Mile. That was the bottom line.

Yeng looked about to speak. My look signalled her to be quiet.

'We'd consider it,' I said. 'I can't speak for the Division, of course, but I wouldn't say it's ruled out. Why?'

'I'd feel a lot happier about working with you,' Malley said, 'if I knew for sure the Jovians really were a threat to us. A clear and present danger. And opening communication with them is the only way to find out.'

Suze nodded agreement. 'When the folks back home find out what you're doing, which they will – and you *are* going to let them know before the event, aren't you? – I think *they'd* like to know for sure, as well. It would be a rotten shame to wipe out things – even if they *are* just things – that could help us, and that could turn out to be the only friends we have in the whole universe. Like, what if they are gods, but gods on *our* side?'

So Suze was an appeaser, I thought sadly. I wondered again if she'd somehow been sent to spy on me, and dismissed the thought, again.

'All right,' I said. 'We'll do it.'

'How?' asked Malley.

'Shortly after we get back,' I said, 'a fleet of remote probes is due to begin descent into the Jovian atmosphere – essentially to spy, to get a clearer and closer view of what the comets are going to hit. Their telemetry – radio, radar, laser – could easily be adapted for a first stab at communication. I'll put as strong a case as I can for doing it, and you and Suze can argue for it too, if you think that'll help.'

Yeng's eyes flashed surprise; disagreement scored her brow.

'It's dangerous!' she said.

'Sure it is,' I said. 'But if anyone can build the firewalls, it's you. There must be contingency plans somewhere, hardware and software designs, right?'

She nodded reluctantly. 'Good guess.'

It was more than a guess, but Yeng didn't need to know that I knew more than I needed to know.

'So go to it,' I said. 'Let's make some good use of our nine days.' I turned to Malley. 'And you'll help us with the wormhole?'

'If you do as you say, yes.' He picked up his pipe and ran its stem across his upper lip, inhaling gently through his nose, then put it down. 'I'll start work on it now – I mean, I can hardly help thinking about it. When we arrive I'll use all the research facilities you've promised me, and *if* you lot show some indication of having made a sincere attempt to avoid . . . war, because that's what it is, then I'll share my results with you.'

'It's a deal,' I told him. Malley nodded; Suze smiled back at me; Yeng looked vaguely puzzled. 'We have a plan,' I added, for her benefit.

'I have a lot of plans,' Yeng said. 'This is great! Such a challenge!' She grinned at me, her sweet, small face lighting up. 'Don't you worry, Ellen May, you'll have the best protection possible.'

She jumped up and almost ran up the spiral stair, so eager was she to start work on her anti-virus software design.

'What did she mean?' Malley asked. 'Why should it be you who opens communication?'

I knocked back my now-cold coffee. 'Same reason I went to get you,' I said. 'If somebody proposes and pushes some daft, dangerous idea, it's only fair that they should have the fun of trying it out.'

Malley gave me an odd look. 'You must get through a lot of leading cadre that way.'

'We don't have "leading cadre",' said Suze.

'In the Division, we do,' I said. 'Only we don't lead from behind.' Suze looked so concerned that I had to relent.

'We do take back-ups,' I assured her.

Back-ups were controversial. After I'd left Malley talking to Andrea about the available recorded observations of the wormhole gate, and left Suze talking to Tony about *her* interests and observations, I sat and drank more coffee and worried about back-ups.

There were several methods, in principle, of taking back-ups: non-invasive scanning techniques for the living, smart-matter infusions for the dying or newly dead. The end result of all of them was a stored snapshot of the brain's state, down to the last neuron and synapse. This state could be replicated in a 'blank' brain, usually but not necessarily that of a forced-grown clone of the original. The Outwarders had perfected this process long ago, back in the twenty-fifties, and we'd learned it from them. They'd subsequently perfected the far trickier task of 'running' the copied mind, advancing the recorded brain-state from its final instant to the next instant, and the next . . . whether in control of a robot body, or in a virtual environment, or in some combination of both. This they called uploading, and this we did not do. It required the cooperation of autonomous artificial intelligence, and it had a logic of its own which led – unless interrupted by main force – to the Singularity, the Rapture of the nerds as Tony had called it.

Because: once the mind was out of the meat, once it was running in silicon rather than carbon, and surrounded with artificial intelligences that could give it every assistance, there was nothing to stop its running a thousand times faster, and expanding its capabilities – its available knowledge, its sensorium, its memory storage and access – just by *plugging more stuff in*. The uploaded mind could be upgraded, and every upgrade made the next more feasible, and quicker to implement. That way led to runaway artificial intelligence excursion: Singularity.

The Outwarders had regarded this as no bad thing, and the supplanting of humanity as long overdue. We, the ones who'd intended, for whatever reason, to remain human, might even have been convinced. The haunting thought that uploads had no thoughts, no souls; that they were flatlines, mindless emulations of the mind, that subjectivity was (as the finder Shin Se-Ha had wryly said) 'an emergent property of carbon', might have come to seem absurd even to us; were it not for the fact that the supposed superhumans had almost all, to all appearances, gone mad; and the exceptions, the survivors of Project Jove who became the Jovians, had gone bad.

Bad for us, anyway.

The experience, and the long, low-level conflict that followed, had hardened our first quibbles and quarrels with the Outwarders (way back when they'd been of the same flesh as ourselves) into a theory which – as Malley had pointed out – was embarrassingly like an ideology: machines don't think, they calculate; only people count; uploads are flatlines, and copies are not originals.

Which, for anyone contemplating taking a back-up, was a disturbing thought. For anyone who woke up to find that they *were* a copy taken from a back-up, it was even more disturbing.

So I had been told; and soon enough, if my proposed encounter with the new Jovian entities went badly, I would know for myself. Or rather . . . somebody else would, somebody just like me, with my name, my face, my memories, including my memory of thinking this very thought. I wished her well.

Up on the command deck Malley was sitting in an acceleration couch with its back tilted up to make a seat. Yeng sat in a similarly adjusted couch several yards away. In front of each of them was a computer interface screen of a type standard throughout the Union and the Division. It was made of two sheets of thin, tough glass, about three feet by two, with a quarter-inch thick layer of multicoloured liquid between them. The multicoloured liquid was nothing but clear water swarming with nanomachines, which scurried about and held up fine particles in various colours, according to instructions transmitted by chemical and electrical impulses, thus forming the graphics, the moving pictures, and the text.

Malley's screen was blank except for a scrolling block of text. His fingers moved along the pad angled at the base of the screen. I couldn't distinguish whether he was writing or reading, or whether the symbols on the screen were our data or his calculations. His pipe jutted from the corner of his mouth, and small puffs of smoke rose from it every few seconds, each puff drifting gently upwards until the current from the ventilation whipped it away. I knew better than to talk to him, and I doubt he would have talked back.

Yeng, however, looked up at me and seemed eager to discuss what she was doing. She shifted on her seat and motioned to me to sit down. There was plenty of room, though I took up more of it than Yeng did.

One of the advantages that this kind of computer had over the old-fashioned, and dangerously vulnerable, electronic computer was that it doubled as an engineering workshop and biochemical laboratory. You could physically isolate a little box – a fixel, it was called – on the screen, and set up an entire nanofacturing complex. It might be too small to see, but it was a small matter to get the rest of the screen to display what was going on.

The screen I was looking at displayed a line along the top, and a dozen or so columns. Yeng pointed. 'Latest variant of their radio transmission,' she said. 'Signal lasts ten seconds. I'm testing it against an array of input devices – radio, television, radar receiver, mechanical computers of various sizes that might pick it up accidentally – even human visual pigments. Running.'

The message was played, in a silent and invisible pulse represented by a wavefront advancing from the line at the top of the screen to the top of the array of columns. All the devices handled it – or completely failed to react to it – except one, whose column started flashing. Yeng cleared the rest and enlarged that view. Trapped in the circuits of a miniaturized version of our standard radar input, the signal had set up a standing-wave pattern which, as soon as Yeng connected the radar with a clutch of nanocomputers, duly propagated into them and burnt them out.

'Nasty,' I said. 'They're hacking babbages now. That's new.'

Yeng smiled. 'Indeed, but I think I can see a way to neutralize it.' She tagged the message, and moved on to a fixel containing a complex organic molecule, large numbers of which had recently been detected escaping from the Jovian atmosphere. That molecule turned out to have the interesting property of jamming the gears of one of our hull-maintenance nanobots.

'Hmm,' said Yeng, sucking the end of a strand of her long blue-black hair. 'Must have picked on something of ours that drifted the other way. Unless the meshing is accidental, which seems unlikely.' She called up a 3-D model of the gearing mechanism. 'Hmm,' she said again. I decided it was time to leave her alone.

'Messages for you,' Yeng said.

It was the morning of the fourth day out. We had settled into a routine. There wasn't much for the crew to do, apart from reading, watching moving pictures, looking out at the stars, playing games or music and trying to seduce Suze into the constant slow dance of our convoluted relationships. Malley was now engrossed in studying recorded observations of the wormhole Gate, gazing for hours at the strange images, then departing to stare at a sheet of paper which was, very gradually, filling up with pencilled equations. Yeng was working her way through decades of predesigned anti-viral software, updating the programs, throwing them into battle with trapped Outwarder viruses (some of them computer viruses, some of them almost literally biological viruses, molecular engines of destruction) and breeding from the survivors. (And *that* Darwinian process had to be watched, too – for what better way to infiltrate a system than to subtly direct, through manipulating the virus attacks, the evolution of its anti-infiltration software?)

She'd just taken a break to check our mailbox. The few unavoidable real-time communications, mostly on arrival and departure, were handled more directly, through the comms rig – though even there the defensive barriers had to be active. The mailbox was for less-urgent or personal messages, and each of them went through a cryptographic quarantine whose processing kept billions of nanotech babbages busy for seconds on end. She passed me a small vial containing a culture of nanomachines on which the incoming laser communications had been recorded and decrypted.

My suit ate it, and played the messages over my eyes.

'You are in deep trouble, Ellen May Ngwethu,' the first message began, without preliminary. The face of Sylvester Tatsuro, current chairman of the Command Committee, frowned upon me. 'The Research Committee has just passed a vote of no confidence in you, so you're no longer our liaison with the social admin. They've asked us to divert a clipper to Lagrange to pick up a representative of the Solar Council, no less, who will be heading out here to investigate personally what's been going on. There's a lot of concern about our possible intentions.' He allowed himself a brief smile. 'Which no one outside the Division knows yet. Our self-discipline has held the line, *so far*. But the Earth Defence bodies are indulging their usual jealous pique towards us, and arousing all kinds of suspicions. Fortunately they have the wrong end of the stick entirely, in that they're hinting that we've become appeasers! Apparently your clumsy extraction of Malley has caused something of a sensation, and various people who saw you talking to Wilde have been speculating in public. Naturally, the genuine appeasers are making a big thing of this, suggesting that we've seen sense at last and are about to open contact with the Jovians. I've put out a communiqué saying that's the last thing we'll consider, and that our vigilance remains as high as ever.' Another quick smile. 'I didn't see my way clear yet to point out that we're on a *higher* alert than ever. And just to wrap up, Ellen, all this talk has aroused interest in Jupiter, and one or two astronomers on Farside have been jolted out of their routine rut and are looking closely at the planet for the first time in decades. They've already noticed some . . . oddities.

'You have, in short, stirred up a hornets' nest. We're all giving you covering fire, of course, but when you arrive you'll have some explaining to do. I don't expect any reply to this message, by the way. Be seeing you, comrade.'

There was a pause of perhaps a second before the image closed down. In that moment, Tatsuro's head inclined in what could have been a nod, his eyelid flickered in what could have been a wink.

Weeks ago, we had come to a private agreement on what to do, if the worst came to the worst: Plan B. It was something we dared not talk about; even thinking about it made me uneasy. But whatever my mistakes, Tatsuro needed me to carry it out. He would defend me against accusations – give, as he'd said, covering fire.

That I still had his confidence was the only comfort I could draw. The rest of the message left me uncomfortable and indignant. I held off from allowing myself any further reaction and let the suit play the next message.

It was from Carla, of the Thames river patrol. The view was of her sitting in a small room, with screens and papers lying around.

'Message to Ellen May Ngwethu on the *Terrible Beauty*,' she began, awkwardly. 'Uh, Ellen, I shouldn't really be telling you this, but hey, you seemed pretty sound. I've found out why you didn't get a response to your calls for assistance from Alexandra Port. There were a couple of neighbours from Earth Defence around there just about the same time, warning about some radio communications going on among the non-cos, and the possibility of Jovian viruses leaking through. Well, we all saw that the non-cos were using radios, and it turns out that Alexandra Port and the river patrol and so on had all had an emergency shut-down when all that radio babble started, just in case.

'The Earth Defence chaps have been talking to our committee, and it seems they were investigating that man you picked up, Dr Malley. They were waiting to see what he would do, and I have to say they were not best pleased when *Terrible Beauty* suddenly swooped down and carried him off. They're kicking up a bit of a stink about it, and it's all over the discussion tubes back here.'

She stopped and sighed. 'To tell you the truth, Ellen, they're saying Malley and the Division have been in cahoots for some time, and that all those radios the non-cos were using so carelessly were encouraged by Malley – and yourselves – as part of some scheme to try out the effects of people picking up Jovian communications –

testing them on the poor non-cos, rather than on our own people. You can imagine what a fuss that's causing.'

I could, all right.

'Well,' Carla concluded, 'I'll have to leave it at that. I'm sure it's all some big misunderstanding, so it's over to you now. All the best.' She gave a rather forced smile and I saw her hand reaching forward to switch the recorder off.

Yeng's concerned face came into view as the virtual image faded out. 'Are you all right?'

'I'm fine,' I said, standing up.

'It's not any . . . personal bad news, is it?'

I smiled and put my arm around her shoulders. 'No, Yeng, it's nothing like that. Just a little political problem, is all.'

After a watchful moment she turned back to her screen. I stood looking at her back, and at the equally oblivious Malley, for a few seconds, then I sought out Tony. He was lounging on one of the side benches in the commissary, reading a book – I could see his eyes saccade, scanning the invisible page. He blinked it away as he heard my approaching steps, and raised his eyebrows. By way of reply I inclined my head slightly towards the corner table, where Boris was talking to Suze, over a rapidly emptying bottle of ice-clouded vodka and a couple of glasses. He was matching her sips with gulps.

Tony gave me a small nod, flashed five fingers and returned to his book. I picked up a coffee and climbed up the stairwell, past the command deck to the sleeping gallery, and into my room. Five minutes later, as signalled, Tony followed. He tapped on the hatch and ducked in, and sat down in front of me on the spread quilt of my outer suit.

'Still going for the mumsy look, I see,' he remarked. 'Mmm, I don't know if I can contain my lust.'

'You'd better,' I said. 'There's something under all this that seems to be containing *me* –'

'Oh, stop it . . . anyway, Ellen, I don't suppose you asked me here to tear it off you, so . . .'

He listened to my summary of the two messages. Then he lay back and stared up at the ceiling, his hands clasped behind his head.

'I think we've been set up,' he said. 'The Earth Defence . . . comrades . . . are probably trying to muscle in on our patch. *They* don't think we're going for appeasement, no way, nor that we're doing *human experiments* on the non-cos. They think we have some kind of plan to win the war while nobody's looking, take all the credit, declare the Solar System up for grabs, and grab a big chunk of it ourselves.'

I stared at him. 'Earth Defence think *we* are tooling up for a . . . what, a counter-revolution? Dissolving the Solar Union? That's crazy.'

'It's part of their job to worry about that sort of thing,' Tony said.

'All right, I'll take your judgement on that one. But what I most want to ask you –'

'Yes?'

'– is what you've found out about our little sweetie.'

'Ah, modesty forbids,' Tony said gallantly. 'But apart from that: she's basically just a nice girl. She's grown up in the Union, and she can't really imagine anything different. Because all the conflicts she's ever actually been in *have* been settled by discussion, literally around a table.'

He sighed. 'Passionate global debates about what species to bring back this year. It's a bit . . . disorienting, talking to someone so young. It's been a long time since I gave anyone the third degree, and I wasn't giving her anything like that –'

He smiled, looking somewhere else.

'Notwithstanding any screams you may have heard.'

'Do lay off. You think she's clear?'

'Yes. I'd say she's just a nice, normal girl who doesn't know how tough life can be. The youth of today, eh?'

'There is one thing she's . . . hard about,' I said. 'She wants the virus blanketing to stop. She wants expansion.'

'She told you that?'

'No,' I said. 'I guessed.'

'Well, you guessed right. She told me she's really excited about New Mars.'

'So is Sam Malley,' I said. 'And he did tell me that. Maybe if what Suze really wants, deep down, is an end to the standoff, then –'

'She might be winnable on our way of ending it, if it comes to that?'

'Yes. And she might have an influence on how Malley sees it, especially if – well, they do have a lot in common.'

Tony stared at me, the bioluminescence sending bands of light down his face. 'You are incorrigible, Ellen.'

I shrugged. 'I must admit he's looking and smelling better every day –'

'You really do owe me one if I lose Suze's sweet young body to that old reactionary.'

'If you insist.'

'Anyway,' he added a minute later, 'we can't have the gang thinking we're having a secretive discussion, or something.'

'No,' I agreed, trying to find the release-spot for the most impenetrable of the suit's inner layers. 'People might talk.'

That evening I sought out Suze after dinner, and settled down with her in a corner.

'Interesting conversation with Boris?'

Her glance shone. 'He's amazing! An actual Sheenisov veteran! I've never met one of them before. It's like . . . history talking to you.'

'Well,' I said, 'it isn't always reliable history. Boris's memories may have got a bit screwed up along the way.'

(This was the charitable interpretation.)

'What! No tribes of folks with two heads? No yetis? No lost legions of reanimated US/UN casualties?' She smiled.

'I'm afraid not. Not as he describes them, anyway. There *were* weird things on the steppe and in the European forests, and hallucinogen weapons were among them. That, we know for sure, so we can't be too sure about the rest.'

'Yeah, I know,' Suze said, sounding regretful. 'Anyway.' She peered at me from under her brow. 'You didn't come to talk about the battle of democracy. You came to talk about the battle that's coming up.'

'That's true,' I admitted. 'I'm sorry to be so –'

'It's all right,' Suze said. 'I've had these conversations in the past. You say something *way* out of line, and nothing will happen except folks will argue, maybe, but sure as nature you'll find one of the old comrades dropping by for a friendly chat to put you straight.'

'I'm not one of the old comrades!'

'Oh, but you are,' Suze said. 'I'd know that look anywhere. Tolerance that comes from total confidence that you're right.'

I had to smile and nod and shrug to this, because I knew that look myself; even if I'd never recognized it in the mirror.

'OK, Suze, the fact is – we *have* to win. They've been plaguing us, we've been zapping them, for centuries. Nobody has ever said we shouldn't be doing it. This is just . . . finishing the job.'

Suze looked troubled. 'Yes, but it's so final! Everything will change.'

I nodded briskly. 'That's right. But if we don't, everything will change, but for the worse. This way, things will change for the better. We'll be able to expand properly at last. And we have to. Have you *seen* how many kids people are having?'

Suze smiled wryly. 'Yeah. But what you're proposing reminds me of . . . things I've read about, from the old time. *Lebensraum*. Manifest Destiny. All that.'

I almost regretted coming (almost) clean with her and Malley. But this kind of argument would have to be had, and soon, with everybody. When the Solar Council representative arrived, he or she would not be fooled, and would tell everybody. Then the water would hit the fuel-rods in a big way.

'It isn't like that, Suze,' I said. 'Honestly. The Outwarders – the Jovians aren't people. They're nothing like people. They're just smart computer viruses, and this is our chance to wipe the disk for good. And if we don't take that chance –' I hesitated here, because this was the core of the Division's morale, our Central Dogma, and it didn't go over well with folk who'd led more sheltered lives '– they'll destroy us, or use us, as soon as *they* get the chance. It's them or us.'

Suze looked thoughtful. 'OK, I can see that,' she said. 'I try to imagine my mind being taken over, like happened to the old computers back in the Crash, and –' She shuddered. 'I'd do anything to prevent that. I'd rather die.'

'Good on you,' I said. 'But it won't come to that, because we'd rather *kill*.'

'But you'll try to talk first? As you promised?'

And as our own chairman had almost promised we wouldn't.

'Of course,' I said.

Our conversation moved on to less weighty subjects, and when we parted after a few drinks I was fairly sure that the tried and tested technique of the friendly chat from one of the old comrades still had a lot to be said for it.

6

Valhalla

'I T'S FUNNY,' Suze said. 'I always imagined Jupiter from Callisto would fill half the sky, and that everything else would be dark.'

'You're getting blasé, girl,' I told her. 'Jupiter's more than a million miles away, and it still looks big enough to me.'

It was 08.48 GMT on the tenth day. We were in a low orbit around Callisto, its surface of cratered ice with its characteristic appearance of pellet-struck glass. Valhalla's bull's-eye shock-rings slid by below us, giant Jove rose above the horizon in front of us. On both bodies the works of mind were evident: the honeycomb upwellings of the Jovian hive, still monstrous to my eyes after two centuries; on Callisto the bright green-and-gold bubbles of the equatorial crater villages, the dark towers of the defence-lasers, the long white lines of the mass-driver tracks along which blocks of ice were hurtled into space. Callisto has four times more water in its icy crust than Earth has in all its oceans; slingshot around Jupiter, those blocks of ice were sent on slow transfer orbits to the Inner System – the water we'd picked up in Earth orbit had come all the way from here, and it was *still* worth doing; far more efficient than hauling water up Earth's deep gravity-well or scraping frost from Luna's polar shadows.

Between this outermost of Jupiter's major moons and the planet itself was the ring: the near edge showing at this angle and distance as unbelievably sparse lights, which, as the eye took in the longer view, combined to form what seemed a solid crescent band of white. The sun was still recognizably the sun, but its light was just bright enough to look like broad daylight, not so bright it dazzled and burned; much more natural than it looks from Earth.

'Everybody strap in!' yelled Andrea. 'Braking in two minutes!'

We launched ourselves away from the wide CCTV screen and

towards the couches. I strapped in and reached out for the still-floundering Suze, and pushed her gently to her place. She wallowed, grabbed, and turned. Malley had stayed strapped in throughout our minutes in free fall. His eyelids were closed tight, their compression forming the only wrinkles in his rejuvenated face. He and Suze were now on a par, physiologically, but his reflexes, the habits and expectations of his nervous system, remained those of a man who'd lived two hundred and sixty years in the same one gravity. Suze, with less to unlearn, was adapting quicker.

'Braking burn in ten, nine, eight . . .'

There was no real need for a countdown, but Andrea too had old habits. The deceleration this time was shorter and less severe than the acceleration from Earth. *Terrible Beauty* came down and settled into its landing cradle like a well-caught egg. The silence left by the sudden absence of the unheard note of the drive was filled with ominous creaking noises.

'Water melts under the torch,' I told Suze and Malley. 'That's it refreezing. The cradle we're resting on has legs that go deep into the ice, so we're quite safe.'

We all stood up and grinned at each other and bounced around a bit in the low gravity, shouting and caromming off each other and generally acting as if a weight had just been taken off us, which it had. Suze and Malley stared at us and made cautious, experimental little hops.

'It's good to be home,' I said, passing out air-tanks like bottles of champagne. I clapped mine to the front of my suit and the suit's surface flowed around it.

'That's all there is to it?' Malley asked.

I nodded, guiding them through the equally rapid and simple processes of making the suits vacuum-ready. My own suit absorbed some of its more exuberant embellishments as it shrank to fit. I could feel the inner layers flowing away from their nightwear images to a more functional chin-to-toe insulating one-piece. I pulled the hood over my head and murmured, 'Helmet up.'

'You look very funny,' Suze said. She looked around. 'I guess we all do.'

'It's practical,' I said. 'The colours make you more visible out on the surface. In accidents and emergencies, that can save your life.'

'Yeah,' said Malley, gesturing at his magenta carapace. 'You wouldn't want to be seen dead in it.'

We made our way to the airlock and went through in pairs to a lift-platform cranked up by the landing cradle. I took Suze through with me and as we waited for the others she gazed around at the landing-field. We were a hundred feet above the surface, and had a good view of miles of flat and dirty ice, dozens of gantries and landing cradles, scores of crawling vehicles, and hundreds of people in their bright suits, looking from this height like an anomalous species of idiosyncratic, multicoloured ants. One of Valhalla's ring-walls marked the horizon. Ice-blocks from a distant mass-driver soared overhead like meteors going the wrong way at a rate of about one a minute.

I felt, as always on returning here, a sense of homecoming, literally light-headed at being safely back and only minutes away from the warm human tumult of the ice-caverns, and an absurd gratitude to the godless, mindless forces that had placed this precious oasis of water so conveniently within the reach of man. The first wave of space-settlers had a saying, something between a litany and a running joke, which went: 'If God had meant us to go into space, he'd have given us the Moon; if he'd meant us to terraform, he'd have given us Mars; if he'd meant us to mine asteroids, he'd have given us the Belt; if he'd meant us to colonize, he'd have given us Callisto.' And so on. The details, and the name and gender of the deity allegedly responsible varied, but the message was the same. There were even attempts to reformulate it in more philosophically correct terms, as a special case of the anthropic principle, but they always struck me as rather forced.

If there was, as almost everybody now thought, no God, then all one could honestly say was that the human race was just unbelievably lucky. There had to be some winner of the cosmic lottery, some species which every chance event, from the passing of the dinosaurs to the coming of the ice, had worked to bring about, and then to light the fire of reason; and on whose birth as a space-going people the configuration of the planets had been favourable, and the stars themselves had smiled: the true horoscope of our real destiny, infinitely greater than anything imagined in the petty prognostications of astrology.

Other life was certain: the Solar System was dusty with organics, and on extra-solar planets our best telescopes could see the biospheres; Wilde's reported New Mars had multicellular organisms, fossil beds and coal. Other minds there might be; but the great silence of the sky spoke with an unanswerable unanimity. Whatever triumphs these other minds had attained, radio communication and space travel were not among them. The stars were ours alone.

I looked out over the busy, cluttered, cheerful scene of the landing field, watching as a covered walkway to the nearest tunnel mouth rolled itself out towards us. Two by two the others joined me, leaning on the platform's guardrail, silent in their own thoughts. My helmet's newly built laser-link buzzed.

'This is a bleak place,' said Suze.

We travelled from the landing field by descending elevator and rapid tunnel-train to the Division HQ at Valhalla base, six miles from the field and a mile under the ice. The elevator's descent was for much of the way a free fall, with only a gradual deceleration at the lower end. The tunnel-train, likewise, was able to coast for most of its journey on blades like skates, running in channels of perpetually melted and refrozen ice. On the way, Malley asked about ice-quakes; I told him Callisto was the most stable of the major moons. He didn't look reassured. All those recent-looking craters can give the wrong impression.

The Division HQ was a warren of tunnels and chambers lined with a spray-on insulation which smelled faintly of tar and which was coloured according to a scheme so complex that it had been abandoned as soon as it was implemented. We stood outside the inner door of the main airlock while our helmets scrolled down. The air was cool, carrying more of the smell of humans and machines, and less of plants and recyclers, than that of the ship. The distant vibration of air-pumps could be heard, and felt through the floor.

Ahead of us a hundred yards of bright-lit yellow corridor extended to a junction with a blue corridor. Along that corridor people passed every few seconds, in the familiar low-gee stride known as the 'lunar lope'. To allow for the upper part of the lope's trajectory, the corridor roofs were never lower than about nine feet high.

'No guards?' Malley asked. 'No reception?'

'We don't –' began Suze; was stopped by Malley's gesture and smile.

'OK, OK.'

The crew members were all changing their suits into low-gee styles. Suze let her suit revert to the default fatigues and pack. I went for blue fake-leather trousers and top, a crinkly transparent blouson, and a shoulder-bag. Malley surprised me, and possibly himself, with a Medieval-scholar ensemble of leggings, breeches, tunic and cloak with a lot of black fur.

I led the way along the corridor, turned left, then along until the blue changed to a red-and-white tiling, looked at the hand-lettered sign tacked to the wall, turned right at the next junction and stopped at the door of the newly hacked emergency meeting-room. Here, at least, there was a guard, a man in heavy armour, armed with a couple of pistols and a light machine gun. He recognized me and nodded.

'We're expected,' I said.

I knocked and went in. Expected we might be, but those present were busy at their tasks, and it took a few minutes before a meeting could be convened around the table that occupied the first section of the big room. It was a long table, eighteen feet by six, and it had about twenty chairs around it. The part of the room it occupied was tacky with fresh insulation. Behind it was a display screen and a cluster of terminals, and behind that a bank of medium-scale babbages whose gentle clicking and whirring filled any silences. About a dozen people were working among them, looking somewhat harassed: as members of the Command Committee, principles notwithstanding, they didn't have much recent experience of such low-level tasks. The far end of the room abutted on raw ice, and dozens of robots were working at extending the room, melting the ice face, draining off the water, filtering out the organics, uncoiling cables and power lines into freshly melted ducts and applying insulation behind the advancing front of their activity. Beneath the insulation, the new stuff in the walls would eventually freeze into place.

Sylvester Tatsuro was the first to look up from the babbage which he was laboriously programming and come over to greet us. He was a small and stocky man, with receding black hair which he'd never bothered to replace, and narrow dark eyes. He was wearing a sort of belted robe in green fur. His sleeves were studded with display-units, and he had a small control bank hung from a strap around his neck.

He shook hands with Malley, nodded at Suze, and turned to me.

'Why is she here?'

'I want her here,' I said. 'Voice but not vote, obviously. I met her by chance, but she's been helpful, and I think she has a point of view which may be useful for us to hear.'

Tatsuro shrugged. 'She's your responsibility,' he said. 'If you wish to retain her as an adviser, that's fine.'

'I've joined the Division,' Suze said.

'Welcome, comrade,' said Tatsuro. 'But on this committee, you're strictly an adviser. You may leave whenever you wish, but no unauthorized communication outside the Division is permitted. Any such will be noticed at once, and action taken.' He smiled briefly. 'I sound like a cop from the old time reading your rights – but I'm sure you understand why this rule is necessary.'

'Of course, neighbour,' Suze said. 'I understand. I feel very proud to be here.'

'Good,' said Tatsuro, smiling with every appearance of sincerity. 'As to the rest of your gang –' he added, speaking to me.

'My crew stays,' I said.

After a moment of eye-lock, he nodded.

'What's going on here?' Malley asked, indicating the far end of the room.

Tatsuro glanced around. 'We're setting up the information filters for the return data from the probes that are due to enter the Jovian atmosphere in a few hours,' he said. 'Naturally most of the detailed processing will be done by our scientific teams, but we get the first look. The first chance to make sure there are no mind-viruses present.' He smiled thinly. 'One of the privileges of our position.'

'Spoken like a good socialist,' said Malley.

Tatsuro responded with a half-smile and a shrug, as if he didn't want to argue, and rapped loudly on the table.

'Gather round, comrades,' he called out gruffly. 'That stuff can wait.'

One by one the other committee members left off what they were doing and made their way to the table. I indicated to the other crew members that they should spread out among the committee rather than sit in a group, and I myself sat down between Malley and Suze, with Tatsuro at right angles to me, not across. I was not going to give him even the slight advantage of sitting opposite me, if he wanted to make this a confrontation over my actions back on Earth.

It seemed he didn't. The first item on the agenda was, of course, us; but the committee – all familiar faces, some old friends – listened to my summary account with only a few questions. It was when I mentioned my agreement with Malley that the frowning and muttering began.

'Contact hasn't been in any way considered,' said Tatsuro. 'It implicitly changes the basis on which we're acting. It re-opens questions which were settled long ago.'

'Circumstances have changed,' I said. 'I have little confidence in getting anywhere with the Jovians, but if it's what Dr Malley here needs to convince him to share his work with us, I'm more than willing to try.'

Tatsuro shook his head. 'It's far too dangerous. We can't afford to lose you, Ellen, and we can't let some *negotiation* lose us time.'

'We can continue preparations for the impact event,' I said. 'Contact, if it should happen, need not get in the way. If there are negotiations, I imagine they can be complete before the impact event, and in time to avert it if they're successful. If there are post-human minds down there, one thing we know is they'd think fast. And as for the danger, well – is it any worse than making direct observations?'

'If I may?' Yeng said. Nods around the table. 'It is worse, Ellen – with communication you necessarily open yourself more than with observation, and give more away. But I've strengthened the firewalls, and this –' she waved at the back of the room '– has obviously been set up to filter incoming observations, and to isolate them.'

'Correct,' growled Tatsuro.

'So between them,' Yeng went on, 'it should be more than enough. But I recommend a back-up, just in case.'

We argued for about an hour, but finally it was agreed. And once we'd come to agreement – a consensus, in fact; there wasn't even the need for a vote – those of us directly involved went straight to work, while the meeting went on.

Yeng applied the back-up process – the equipment was to hand, because whoever had drawn the short straw, or volunteered, to handle the close-up observations would have needed one anyway. It took forty minutes, every second of which were, for me, deeply unpleasant: it starts with a tendril up a nostril, and ends with a painkiller for the worst headache you can imagine, a real migraine and *petit mal* combined, with thunder in your ears and a dirty yellow lightning in your eyes, as the pain flips over into synaesthesia.

And then it fades, to a dull relief. I stood looking at the cubic inch of smart-matter in my hand, within which my soul was stored, until the tiny block was absorbed seamlessly into the suit, vanishing like a cheap trick: nothing up my sleeve.

'Takes it out of you,' Yeng observed sympathetically; then we both saw the ambiguity, and laughed. I felt better, and stood up. The Command Committee had moved on to discussing the forthcoming visit from the Solar Council delegate. As usual in the Division, they were quite capable of focusing on one thing at a time, and leaving those who were implementing a previous decision to get on with it.

During my backing-up ordeal the television screen had been moved to one side, and Malley was using it to observe the Gate up close and in real-time. The Gate's outline was clearer now than on the old recordings, because over several decades we'd cautiously attached an array of instruments and rockets around its circumference. The instruments we used for observation, the rockets to shift its location, gradually boosting it from low Jupiter orbit to its present position among the outer moons. The current image on the screen came from a fighter among the usual swarm that stood watch.

Where the television screen had been was now a smaller screen showing incoming Mission Control data about, rather than from, the shower of probes currently converging on the planet; and a control deck and wraparound helmet, for the privileged individual who was about to follow them down.

'I've reprogrammed some of these remotely,' said Yeng. 'They're standard gas-giant divers. There's a prerecorded message – just a hailing and query – for you to fire off on the wavelengths the Jovians use for what we think are their communications, and an isolated core for any reply.'

'How will I know which ones to fix on?'

'They're the only ones you'll get through to. Don't worry, they're a big enough fraction of the total for you to have a good chance of getting close.'

'OK,' I said. I looked at the Mission Control display. 'Five minutes to entry. Here goes nothing.'

Malley turned from his own screen and gave me a thumbs up as I sat down and put on the VR helmet.

Jupiter loomed, and in I fell.

It was the clarity of the light that struck me first. I knew intellectually what to expect, but I'd got used to seeing Jupiter from above, and from far away, as a roiling mass of clouds and upwellings. Close up, the scale of the spaces between those clouds was a visceral shock. There were chasms between the pillars of cloud in which Earth could fall in sunlight all the way to the metallic-hydrogen core.

The hundreds of probes, elaborate but expendable, stamped out like bottle-caps in the nanofactories, were passively aerodynamic: gliders with the shape and approximate size of stone arrowheads, their faceted surfaces glittering like chipped chert, their shafts the thin rods in which the drogues were stacked. The filaments of their aerials trailed behind them, parallel to the shafts. The probe heads had ailerons and rudders, so their flight could be controlled, but with a minimum two-way delay of twelve seconds such control could only be gross.

As they hit atmosphere at a hundred thousand miles per hour I was flicking from probe to probe, seeking out ones that seemed to be heading in interesting directions. The first one on which I settled was spiralling down in a clear updraft in which one of the bubble-clusters (I was not prepared, yet, to call them 'cities') was drifting upwards. I tagged another, which headed straight for one of the 'walls' of the convection cells, and stayed with the first as it descended. The pink and orange clouds streaked past.

Behind me – as I couldn't help thinking – the drogues deployed one by one, and one by one were whipped away. By the time the last had gone, the probe had slowed to a mere fifty thousand miles per hour and was two hundred miles deep in the atmosphere, hurtling in a tightening circle down the well of clear hydrogen towards the bubble-cluster. I nudged the probe's control surfaces and brought its descent almost to a halt, circling the cluster like a stacked airliner. The bubble-cluster was a thousand miles in diameter, made up of hundreds of translucent bubbles. This much our telescopes had already shown; and the hint of movement within.

Closer ... now I could see the black threads, each at least a quarter of a mile wide, which radiated from the cluster and vanished into the cloud walls. That the threads connected with other such clusters seemed incredible, given the distances involved – but the only other explanation, that they were some kind of intake and/or outlet pipes, was so far without evidence, tempting as the thought that they were mere sewers and ventilators might be.

Closer still ... the apparent translucence of the bubbles sharpened to transparency: multiple hexagonal panes set in a lattice of sturdy-looking white struts. Behind them was movement, unmistakable, definite. I hit the 'send' key and swooped around again. On a reckless impulse I slewed the probe into a close pass across the top of the bubble-cluster. All I saw, of course, was a minute-long blur, followed by darkness as the probe plunged into the clouds.

I disconnected from the probe and flicked to the data, running the recording in slow motion, stepping it down and down until I seemed to be drifting along; increasing the magnification until each panel was as clear and close as a cockpit window.

And saw behind those windows – looking out, crowding, visibly following the tiny object's flashing flight – deep violet eyes in gigantic faces, faces sweet and calm as those of any imagined angels. Their bodies too were like angels': with long, trailing cascades of gold or silver or copper hair, and sweeping diaphanous robes of rainbow light, each breastplated with a sunburst of jewelled filigree. Their features weren't sexless, or androgynous – they were differentiated into the variant ideals of masculine and feminine beauty. The interior of the bubble glowed and flickered with the radiance of their beating wings. Not like the wings of insects, or birds, or bats, but perfect parabolas, curved like magnetic fields, shimmering like polar lights; wings made from aurorae.

As I watched, they changed, flowing into the shapes of fantastic fish, of floating multicoloured scarves, of showers of flowers, of flaring fireworks. The vision ended as the probe passed beyond the cluster.

I replayed it, this time accompanying the images with the message I'd sent, and found that a response had been received. I hesitated, then went ahead and ran it through the firewall filters. What came out was not any kind of virus, but a quite straight-forward message composed and sent repeatedly as a second-long sequence of English. The machines stretched out the burst, sampled it to a sound that sang in my ears, letters that shone before my eyes:

'Responding to probe: we welcome your message. Standing by for further communication. Informally – hi guys and gals! It's been a long time! Let's talk! See you soon!'

The beauty of the Jovians, the warmth – and indeed the colloquial informality – of their message, should have been enough to melt all hostility, all suspicion. The gaiety of their display, the tones of welcome and love in their voice, made me yearn to see them and speak to them again. I ducked out of the VR helmet and put it down and looked up at Yeng. I could feel my cheeks strained with smiles, damp with tears. Yeng smiled at me and glanced above my head. I swivelled the gimballed seat and found the rest of the crew and of the Command Committee crowded behind me.

'Well?' said Tatsuro. 'You made contact?'

'Yes,' I said. My voice quivered.

'No hacking? No viruses?'

Yeng shook her head. 'It's all clean,' she said. 'No viruses.'

'None at all,' I said. 'See for yourselves. Look and tell me if those aren't the most beautiful creatures you've ever seen. They're . . . ravishing. Seductive.' I sighed, remembering. 'And obviously capable of communicating with us. Whatever they've gone through, they've kept some continuity with humanity.'

The images I'd seen were replayed again, this time on the screen. Suze and Malley watched them, rapt. The crew and the Committee studied them more warily.

'What do you think?' asked Tatsuro. The others were, for a moment, too absorbed in what they'd seen to speak, so I got in first.

'Why don't we have a look at some of the other Jovians?' I said. 'The ones I *wasn't* in contact with. Let's see how typical this is, before jumping to conclusions.'

Reluctantly the others pulled themselves out of their contemplative admiration, and set to work. A few probes had passed as close, or closer, to other bubble-clusters as had the one I'd been tracking, and images of the clusters' inhabitants could be extracted. Their appearances varied widely, and changed rapidly as we watched. The 'angel' form I'd first encountered was among them, but there were many others no less beautiful. The most common basic shape resembled a butterfly, with the parabolic, colourful wings, like those of the 'angels', extending from a central column or core. The sunburst shape, which on the 'angels' had appeared as a breastplate or pendant, was a feature of all the Jovian entities, though sometimes masked by their current form.

'That jewelled object seems to be your basic Jovian,' I said. 'The CPU, perhaps? It sits in the glowing shape around it like a magnet in its fields –'

'Which it may well be,' said Yeng. 'The wider form is like a controlled aurora, almost a television picture, which the Jovian can vary at will.' She smiled. 'They seem . . . playful, whimsical . . .'

'Jovial!' someone said.

'It suggests,' Tatsuro said seriously, 'a degree of commonality with ourselves that the old Outwarder macros with their amoeboid shapes did not. Their reaction times show that they are still "fast folk" but their appearance is more . . . appealing, and they each seem to be distinct individuals. I have to say that one's automatic reaction to these entities is quite the opposite of the horror and hatred that the macros seem to incite.' He waved a hand through some virtual display of his own, creating a sequential display of the beautiful, flickering images. 'When people see them, I don't think they'll be as eager to destroy them as we are – or *were*.'

The members of the Command Committee were nodding gravely, stroking their bearded or beardless chins like peasant elders listening to an intellectual. I glared at them all, amazed that they could be so swayed.

'Isn't it obvious what's going on here?' I said. '*This* is the mind virus, the killer meme. The fast folk have simply adapted to an environment that contains humans with more power than they have – for now. Their beauty is a lure, precisely calculated to trigger our aesthetic reactions. That message, that display, was their first line of defence. We have to smash through it, or we're doomed.'

7

The Iron Heel

T HAT WAS the start of the argument. The other CC members knew as well as I did that life is a fight in which beauty is a weapon: an instrument of survival, like a baby's cry or a child's smile. They knew that the message I'd recorded – and any other communication – could be the output of a flatline. They knew . . . but why go on? They had the true knowledge.

So I still find it difficult to forgive, or indeed to understand, the next decisions of the Command Committee. Each decision went to a vote, and each vote was carried by twelve to two (me and Joe Lutterloh, our comms specialist). The committee decided: to release all the Jovian images and other probe data to the rest of the Division; to prepare for a direct contact, using a (heavily firewalled) radio link; and to cooperate fully with the Solar Council delegate, due to arrive in three days. There was still plenty of time to deflect the incoming train of Kuiper–Belt comets – all of them had guidance rockets attached, and right up to the last few minutes all it would take to divert them from the usual harmless slingshot swing around Jupiter would be a brief burn.

Tatsuro seemed to win over most of the committee with the argument that there was nothing to lose, and possibly a lot to gain, by doing things this way. The Division had originally intended to present the rest of the Union with a *fait accompli*, to give the Jovians no warning – but we'd known that there might be some problems later. This way, we'd pull the rest of the Union into the decision. If coexistence with the Jovians turned out to be impossible – or was voted down – then the Jovians would still have no time to react if we went ahead with the bombardment. From the Jovians' point of view, the incoming comets would appear no more threatening than our normal import traffic, until the final, fatal, fine adjustment to their course.

I thought, and argued, that this was assuming rather a lot about their capacities. Unfortunately, by opening the question of negotiation in order to get Malley to cooperate, I'd let the other committee members rediscover any doubts and hesitations they may have had – as well as exposing them to the insidious sight of just how attractive and appealing the Jovian entities could appear. I consoled myself with the thought that Malley's cooperation was, in the long run, the most important thing from my point of view.

The Command Committee's deliberations had been held *in camera* only because of the possible virus threat. With that apparently out of the way, the meeting was as open as all our meetings usually were, and all its decisions were open to appeal to the Division as a whole. The emergency meeting-room would be kept up, however, as an operations room to handle the direct communication. During that contact, it would again be isolated.

Malley, of course, was delighted at how the debate had turned out, and was eager to get on with his study of the wormhole. Suze too seemed pleased by it, and a little relieved when I showed no sign of hostility to her – or to anyone else who disagreed with me. I took my defeats in the votes with every sign of good grace. Inwardly I was seething, but it doesn't take two hundred years to get a grip on that sort of thing. I've been good at it since my teens. (My *late* teens, admittedly.)

As are others. Tatsuro didn't get to be the chairman for nothing. At the end of the meeting he said mildly:

'Ellen, you are obviously not keen to participate in the negotiations, and you have little to contribute to the scientific analysis of the survey data. May I suggest that, until further notice, you continue to work with Doctor Malley, giving him all practical assistance on the wormhole navigation problem?'

I agreed, of course, and the rest of the committee were more than happy to have me occupied in something I agreed with, rather than reluctantly participating in something I didn't.

'We have much to do,' Tatsuro said. 'But I suggest further that the crew of the *Terrible Beauty* take some time to get some sleep. You in particular, Ellen, must be quite exhausted. You can begin work with Doctor Malley in the morning.'

I smiled and nodded. As we rose to leave, Tatsuro turned so that his face was, for a moment, visible only to me. I saw his almost undetectable wink, and knew our concord held.

Suze stayed behind with Malley, who was given a work station at the far end of the room to continue with the wormhole observations. The rest of us headed for the suite which we shared as a crew, though several of us would undoubtedly be going elsewhere tonight. (Night and day in the Callisto caverns had nothing to do with that satellite's inconvenient rotational period – they were arbitrarily based on GMT, like our ship time. For many they had little to do with their sleep patterns, either, which were often based on staggered shifts and distorted by anti–sleep drugs. The latter had a limited usefulness: the circadian rhythm was buried deeper in our cells than our genetic tinkering or pharmaceutical intervention could reach, and the brain's requirement for regular sleep is – though more recent in evolutionary time – even less amendable.)

I stood aside to let the others in, then let the door click into place behind me and leaned back against it. The suite was as we'd left it when we'd been scrambled three weeks earlier. All the items of clothing or crockery left lying around had no doubt been patiently and mindlessly cleaned in our absence, which was just as well. The plants had been dusted and watered. The low ceiling glowed with its familiar dim evening light, the kitchen was humming quietly to itself, and the bedrooms off the lounge were sighing with invitation. The mailbox was politely silent; though probably bursting with messages from our colleagues and friends and forebears and offspring, it knew better than to remind us of this when we'd just come home. I looked around at Boris, Yeng, Tony, Andrea and Jaime.

'I don't know about you, comrades,' I announced, 'but I am not for any discussion. It's been a long day, and a long trip, and we all need some R&R. I'm up for a high-alcohol drink, a low-gee jacuzzi, and some low-gee sex. In any sequence, all at once, and more than once.'

'"If", "Else", and "Repeat",' Yeng grinned. 'Still the basic program logic.' She caught Tony's hand. 'We'll have a drink, but we're going out.'

'I guess that's decided,' said Tony. He squeezed Yeng's hand, kissed the top of her head, let go her hand and bounded over to the drinks cabinet, where he started dialling up responses to shouted orders. Andrea and Jaime wanted to do their own thing too.

'That leaves us,' I said to Boris. 'So, big gunner, you wanna make it with me, or just leave me with my suit's imagination?'

He put his arm around my shoulders and boosted me towards a couch. 'Ah, Ellen, of course I stay with you. All the girls in all the bars in Callisto . . .' He paused, looking dreamy and regretful, until I gave him a friendly kick, '. . . couldn't drag me away from my good lady to whom I'm eternally grateful.'

I first met Boris in 2110, on a military mission to the Sheenisov. We met on the frozen Lena outside Yatkutsk. He was a giant in furs, I a sexy spacewoman in my new smart-matter spacesuit, with its bubble helmet and black sheen. An angel more of death than of mercy, I was delivering home-brew kits for turning Siberian ore and Russian rust into shiny, perfectly machined small arms. His voice was like black molasses: American accent, deep, rich; it reminded me of Paul Robeson, and it still does. I could never forget it, or him.

Over the next nine decades I saw Boris, or he saw me, in many odd circumstances, but I could never stay, and he could never go. Eventually we found each other in the last battle, against the last believers, the last crazy altruists to risk their mortal bodies and potentially immortal minds for god or country or duty or other people's property. I pulled him from a wrecked and burning tank in the suburbs of Lisbon, and took him with me to orbit and grew him all back, and I never let go of him again.

'I don't want your gratitude,' I said, reaching up with one hand to grab a tall vodka-and-ice from Tony, and reaching down with the other. 'That wasn't why I pulled you out of the tank. It was pure selfish lust, comrade, and that's what I want from you.'

And that was what I got. We did the If, we did the Else, we did the Repeat, we did the Do Until exhaustion. There are those who swear by free fall, but give me low-gee any day, or night. There's more *purchase*. As for one-gee and above . . . it's OK for a bit, but it does you in. How Earth ever got to its present population, I'll never know. Cloning, possibly.

But eventually, we slept. I dreamt of angels, and sometimes woke with a start and with memories of other things, and clung to Boris until I rejoined him in sleep.

It's 2089 and things are falling apart: as below, so above. Every day, every hour brings a new disaster to our screens, picked up from the dwindling number of functioning news services and the vastly larger, but also diminishing, numbers of communications amateurs and hackers and pirates. The net that brought the world together is dying in its arms. It's been years since any rocket that didn't carry a warhead has lifted from the surface. We're on our own now: hundreds of thousands of people, millions of bugs and beasts, more millions of humans and other animals *in potentia* as frozen sperm and eggs, *in vitro* as cell samples and recorded brain-states; countless digital ghosts; together they make up the space-based fraction of the biosphere. They add up to millions of eggs in hundreds of baskets; no longer, thankfully, in one. Spread out across near-Earth, Lagrange, Luna, Mars and the Belt, humanity and its animal allies are safe against anything short of a nearby supernova. The sky won't fall, now; but Earth will.

The Green Death is in its early stages. Already, the biomedical laboratories where the only hope of a cure could be found are being put to the torch. The Greens are leading the mobs, happy to divert the unfounded suspicion from themselves. I, at this time, am absolutely convinced that the Greens have deliberately engineered the Death in a genocidal sacrifice to their evil goddess, Gaia.

So, with this awful warning of the consequences of the kind of thinking all of us have always opposed being shown in lurid and distressing detail before our very eyes, the two factions of the space movement, Earth-Tenders and Outwarders, unite in adversity to face the challenges of the future ... No. We're arguing over resources, we're on the verge of *fighting* over resources – water, primarily. We're bleeding all the solar power we can spare into the capacitors of high-energy lasers. We're checking our nukes.

The Outwarders have – appropriately enough – long since moved out, or been pushed out, from the old near-Earth battlesat in which I still live. They've moved out to Lagrange 4 – most of the traditional Space-Movement types, for reasons buried deep in Space-Movement tradition, settled at the other Lagrange point, L5

– where they're building the fleet for their Jovian expedition; and they're mining the Moon.

That's one source of conflict. They want Lunar polar water ice for their expedition. We want it for our survival – there's ice out in the Belt, but its transfer-orbit delivery is a slow trickle. The allocation of rights to exploit particular patches of Lunar ice would have been tricky to work out, even with the best of intentions and a decent legal system in place. (Discovery? First use? Present possession? Does the first satellite identification count? The first landing? The first staking-out? The first successful mining-plant?) In these benighted days we're all experts on libertarian property acquisition theory – trouble is, every claim has at least one respectable theory behind it, and a squad of underemployed legal experts in front of it, with guns.

I'm worried about the Lunar polar mines, because my parents – with whom I keep in touch, though we haven't breathed the same air for decades – are managing one of them, on behalf of one of the old Space Movement's front corporations.

Meanwhile, we – the Earth-Tenders – are using up resources in quixotic efforts like orbital medicine-drops (not as useless as it sounds, by the way – we drop medical *nanofactories*) and orbital zaps of whatever military force look like this week's bad guys (big mistake) and servicing communications satellites that would otherwise just *die* (good move, except that the military bad guys [q.v.] use them too). And the Outwarders claim, using whatever theory of property is to their immediate purpose, that at least some of the resources we're allegedly wasting on aid for the stricken populations of Earth belong to *them*. For example, they helped to boost this station to its present orbit; we paid them, but they now claim rent for the *orbit*, backdated, with interest.

'Fucking property rights,' I say to Tony as I keep an eye on the deep-space radar. 'It's enough to make you turn communist.'

We're seated criss-cross, each looking at a screen behind the other's shoulder, in one of the station's modules that barely has room for both of us, let alone for the tangle of cables and tubes and floating obsolescent equipment. Outside the open hatch of the module, other people are working, moving slowly in the sluggish stale air.

'Hah!' Tony doesn't look away from the computer on which he's collating loyalty checks on the station's eight hundred and fifty-six personnel. 'You're a communist already, Ellen, you just don't know it. When did you ever pay for your supplies, or get paid for your work?'

'Ah, that's, that's different,' I say, waving my hands. I have genuinely never thought of it that way, never given a moment's thought to the way of life in the settlement in which I've been raised – a crowded can at Lagrange called New View – or in the battlesat. 'I mean, that's all just among ourselves. We all know what has to be done, and what we can afford to use, so there's no problem. What I meant – and only as a *joke*, for fuck sake – was that all this crap about who owns what was making me feel a bit . . . *bolshie*, isn't that the word?'

'I see,' says Tony. 'Like the Sheenisov.'

The Sino–Soviet Union, a rabble of collective farmers and Former Union and ex-PLA veterans whose ragged red armies are currently besieging – or, if you listen to their broadcasts, relieving – Sinkiang.

'I thought they were more into restoring democracy.'

'Yeah, for now, though I don't know how democratic it all feels when their partisans roll into town and call a meeting. But for the long run, when the Sheenisov have conquered the world –' we share a laugh '– their theorists advocate the weirdest kind of communism I've ever heard of: everybody owns nothing, or everything.'

'Sounds like every dingbat communist since Munzer –'

'No, no – every *individual* owns *everything*. The whole goddamn universe.'

'Including every *other* individual?'

'Only to the extent that you can.'

'Nice if you can get it. I just want to be princess of the galaxy.'

'Modest of you, my sweet. But that's the catch – the universe is yours to take, *if you can*.'

'So what's to stop me?'

'Only the other contenders, and your possibly reluctant subjects. And the size of the universe. If you can get around all that – go for it, gal!'

'Oh. I see. And there was me thinking that eating people is wrong.'

Tony does glance sideways at me, now. 'Eating people is *wasteful*

. . . but seriously, if you think it's wrong, fine. I entirely agree. So do something about it. Arm the prey! Set up taboos. Give them teeth! Just don't think that announcing your moral convictions affects any part of the universe further than your voice can reach.'

'And they want to base *communism* on this . . . this unlimited selfishness? What's to stop it all degenerating into a war of all against all?'

Tony shrugs. 'No doubt they expect we'd come to some kind of arrangement.'

I'm telling him all the reasons why this'll never work and he's dividing his attention between talking to me and grumbling to himself about a Minskyite clique in cee-cubed (you're asking *me*?) when the alarm goes off and I realise it's me that's done it, set it off by reflex, even before my conscious mind has registered that there's a blip on the scope and it's closing *fast*.

'Shit shit shit SHIIIT!!!' I announce, helpfully. Fingers tapping, keying the message to Command-Control-Comms (and hoping the Minskyite clique, whatever they are, knows which side of the bulkhead their air is on) and the blip is suddenly blurred by a burst of debris from the side just as the station lights dim under a power drain and the object is filling the screen then clearing it to the top right and it's gone, as I duck and feel there should have been a *whoosh* as it passed overhead.

'Hundred-ton rock on collision course deflected by laser burn,' says a calm voice in my ear. Needless to say the whole process from detection to deflection has been automatic – both I on the watch, and the gunnery crew, are just there to make sure we know what's going on. Here in a purely advisory capacity, as the US/UN grunts used to say.

The alarm cuts out and the lights come back.

'What the fuck was *that*?' says Tony.

I'm swinging the screen's viewpoint, as the computer labours to patch in data from drogue cameras and other settlements. The cluster of habitats and ships at Lagrange 4 comes into sudden focus. Where each one had been was a point of actinic, atomic light – for a moment, I think they've been hit; that *we've* hit them. Nuked them.

And then I see them move. The flares are fusion torches, not fusion warheads. The Outwarder fleet is making its orbital transfer burn, heading out to Jupiter. Our comms net is buzzing. Other pictures begin to flash up:

Teletroopers bounding across the lunar surface, smashing into the mining-camps, seizing control of the mass-driver. They've used it to punch a few warning shots at us, and it's still sending load after load of precious water to rendezvous with the Outwarder fleet.

Our people in the camps dying – shot or gasping vacuum. I see security-camera footage of teletroopers stooping over the dead, applying clawed devices to their skulls. My fist is at my mouth, my teeth are biting on my knuckles.

Later my parents' names appear on the list of the missing.

The face of David Reid, the owner of the bonded-labour supply company, looms on our screens in a final message from the Outwarder fleet. It's like a hostage video – face haggard, stubbled; voice stumbling, eyes glancing now and then to the side.

Some apology, some expression of regret.

Then the smooth, confident face of one of the Outwarders cuts in. They were still human, then. If you call that human. He tells us what they've done.

My knuckles begin to bleed.

The Outwarder spokesman told us what had happened to our people in the mining-camps. The lucky ones had been killed outright. The rest had been brain-scanned before their bodies were left to gasp vacuum. The Outwarders left us the details of their claim to the mines: they had records of having bought up the front-company years ago, something we could no longer check, and which they'd hitherto neglected to tell us. Our use of the mines had been theft, according to them, a crime aggravated by our resistance to their teletroopers. They claimed compensation, which they were going to recover as labour from the people whom they'd 'uploaded.' They'd use their recorded and rerun brain-states to operate their robots: much cheaper and quicker than AI.

They never did tell us which of the dead had been scanned, and the desiccated corpses we recovered later didn't show up traces that could answer the question. For years after, I had nightmares about its being done to my parents. They'd appear anachronistically in dreams of other times, speaking to me on television screens. After the conflict, I didn't just have an ideological dislike, and aesthetic distaste, for the Outwarders. Hatred was flash-burned into my brain.

Which is one reason why I wasn't too worried about the Command Committee's decision to negotiate with the new Jovians. The night after the decision I now and again found myself lying awake in the dark, cuddled up beside Boris's obliviously sleeping bulk, thinking about it all. No matter how beautiful the Jovians appeared, no matter how specious their messages might turn out to be, there were still enough people alive who remembered, and who would never forgive. That was not, of course, the rational reason for destroying the Jovians – but it was related to it. The brief experience of what can happen to those at the mercy of superior power had left me, and many others, with the implacable resolve never to allow the existence of any power superior to the power which we shared. There can only be one dominant species, and humanity was not about to relinquish that position. (Or, if it was, I was not about to let it.) But the emotional memory of what the Outwarders had done to us, and what their Jovian descendants had done to Earth during the computer crash, should help to harden hearts when it came to the crunch.

When it came to the crunch . . . I smiled to myself, and went back to sleep.

I got up before Boris, in the slowly increasing daylight-spectrum light of an artificial morning, and checked my c-mail. (Electronic bandwidth was far too precious, and too laden with multiply-redundant safety measures, to be squandered on anything less than urgent news or real-time links. Hence, chemical mail.) Some of it was practical, some personal or sentimental: these days, I didn't exactly have a family, beyond the intertwined relationships of the crew, but I had descendants. I replied to those letters that needed a reply, sending the little coded molecular message-bearers swirling off down the capillaries, into the circulation of the base; and beyond it, to the crater towns: Skuld, Trindr, Igaluk, Valfodr, Loni . . . There was nothing in the mailbox as urgent as my current work, so I left a coffee percolating for Boris and headed for the operations room.

It was a slow progress for me. The corridors were crowded, and everybody I met seemed to want to talk to me. The committee's discussion and decision, and the images from the probes, had all been flashed around Callisto's fibre-optic network. Every forum for argument, from screens to streets, was overloaded with nothing else.

'– you're right Ellen, we should hit them and not waste any more time –'

'– waited long enough –'

'– wait and see –'

'– sorry to say this, Ellen, but I think your position is way off beam –'

'– forget the comets, we can rig some nukes that'll disrupt them, they look pretty delicate –'

'– give them a chance, it's not as if *they* did it –'

'– magnetic fields, right? Well, a polar hit with one good EMP burst –'

All the time my senses were bombarded by the colourful clothes, the beautiful faces (how right we had been, back at the start, to call ourselves the beautiful people); their insistent, vigorous voices, the absolute confidence of all the conflicting opinions; the eager, earnest children literally jumping up to have their say. I had my say too, but I avoided argument. I was happy with it all, not annoyed. Even those who disagreed with me strengthened my conviction that I was right: that this self-chosen people, this fractional distillation of humanity was worth more than anything or anybody else in the universe. There has to be some source of value, some measure, some criterion, someone for whom 'good' means 'good for us' – and we were it. There was more vitality in our one million than in all Earth's billions together, more beauty in us than in any pretty pictures the Jovians could project.

Still, entering the relative quiet of the operations room was a relief. Since yesterday it had lost its newly hacked look. With the instinctive biophilia of all space settlers, people had brought fast-growing plants whose leaves and tendrils were already spreading across the nutrient-rich insulation. A coffee machine had been set up, and cleany-crawlies – those cockroaches of cleanliness – were burrowing into the inevitable drifts of discarded plastic cups. The robots at the ice-face had extended the room by at least ten yards overnight, and the racks and rows of machinery had kept pace. Cameras for the news-threads were present and active, according to the suit.

A few members of the Command Committee were present. Some had just arrived, one or two had been there all night. Clarity Hardingham, the youngest CC member, younger even than Yeng, looked up at me. She was interfacing with one of the computer banks, evidently through a virtual-image display: I could see the focus of her eyes, and the apertures of her green irises, changing moment by moment. Judging by the dark areas around her eyes, she had been up all night. She flicked her auburn curls back from her temples and blinked away the display.

'Good morning, Ellen,' she said. 'Grab me a coffee, will you?'

I passed one over to her. 'You look like you should be drinking cocoa,' I told her.

'Ah, sod it,' she said, knocking back a drug tablet, followed by a sip of coffee. 'This is too exciting for sleep. For me, anyway. I've been more or less holding the fort since about four.'

'Doing what? Comms protocols?'

'Aagh! I wish! Well, I was working at that earlier, so I can't complain. No, what I've been doing for the past four hours is sampling opinion – we'll run a proper poll nearer the time, when we have to make a decision. This is just preliminary, sounding out what the comrades think our negotiating position should be.' She grinned quirkily, scratching her ear. 'That's if we have one. There's a lot more than two in twelve agree with you out there, Ellen.'

'I'm not surprised.'

'Well, me neither. But of those who do want to negotiate, I reckon the biggest issue is putting an end to the viral assaults. Next, coming to some agreement on . . . spheres of influence, if you like.'

'Literal spheres,' I smiled.

Clarity nodded. 'Yes! Most comrades seem keen on the idea that the Jovians should have Jupiter, and we'll have the rest.'

I stared at her gloomily. 'That is so stupid. All right, let's just say *premature*. We know the Jovians have gone from nothing to some kind of culture in a matter of weeks, their powered flights are increasing all the time –'

'No, Ellen, we've been tracking that further while you've been away. The flights haven't increased, nor the number of clusters. They may have reached some plateau in their progress. After all, remember they may have inherited all their technological information from their precursor entities, and are now simply implementing it, so their earlier rapid ascent needn't indicate that they're, oh, recapitulating human development from the stone age up on a faster platform.'

'That could make it worse, from our point of view,' I said. 'What if during their precursors' time in virtual reality they were all along doing design-ahead work? We've only *assumed* that the old Outwarder macros went crazy, and that all their descendants up to now have been crazy too. We could be wrong. The ones that have now emerged into the real world could have countless generations of R&D simulation behind them, which they could implement at will.'

Clarity shrugged. 'You're right, it is premature to argue over how we negotiate before we know what they're capable of, which is why the *next* highest item on most people's agenda is finding out more about exactly that, and getting some kind of reliable access to confirm any story they give us about what they're up to.'

'Inspection rights? At least that strikes a note of healthy suspicion.'

'You could put it like that.' Clarity drained her cup and tossed it towards the big table. '*You* would.'

We both laughed, but I could hear the slight tension in her throat, and in mine.

The other CC members hadn't looked up from their work when I came in, and were still absorbed in it. I didn't interrupt. I spent the next hour or so in front of an unused interface, pulling up summaries of the night's work, an increasing number of which were modified and updated as more people came in. The science teams, safely distant in other warrens, were evaluating the physics and chemistry of the Jovian entities: the most solid results so far were that the bubbles were made of laminated sheets of monomolecular diamond; that the 'wings' were, as we'd thought, made up of a flow of ionized molecules in electromagnetic fields; that the 'bodies' were a combination of these with hologram projections; and that the whole display was not just decorative or expressive but a means of communication, a language of light. The core of the Jovian individual, the brain and engine of the thing, was the elaborate structure that had appeared as a jewelled breastplate on the angels. This object was itself aerodynamic, and drew its energy directly from the fast winds and vast electrical pulses of Jupiter's atmosphere, which even at its calmest was (from a human point of view) a ceaseless violent storm.

It struck me that the Jovian body was a tough structure. Disrupting the displays, even cracking the diamond bubbles, might be as easy as the nuclear enthusiasts I'd encountered thought. Destroying their source would take exactly what we had planned.

Malley and Suze came in at 0900 GMT, with the smug, sleepy look of people who had spent a first unexpected night together. I disengaged from the interface and stood up.

'Good morning,' I said.

Suze smiled shyly; Malley grinned. 'Hi,' he said. He passed a hand over his reddened eyes. 'God, is there coffee in this place?'

I brought over three cups and we made our way to Malley's workstation. Suze dragged a couple of extra chairs over and we sat down. Spindly chairs; on Earth they'd have crumpled under us.

'How have you been getting on?' I asked.

'Oh,' said Suze, 'we've been getting on very –'

She stopped and giggled.

'Well, yes,' Malley said. He smiled at her again. 'Suze has a really charming notion that getting off with a non-co is some kind of decadent perversion –'

'I do *not*!'

'I must say it adds something to the, ah, energy of the reaction. Not that it needs much adding to – you were right about those rejuvenation treatments. I had forgotten it was possible to feel this good.' He sighed and stretched. 'On the other hand – I feel very strange. Part of it's the gravity, the conditions, and part of it is . . . you people. Your people. They're not what I expected, even after spending days with all of you in the ship. The crowd out in the corridors are so . . .' He shook his head. 'You in the Division aren't like the people in the Union, at least from what I've seen. The Union people seem happy enough, and free too in their way, but you out here have more *edge*, more discontent with themselves. You, Ellen, and your crew, well . . . it's hard to say, but you are different again, you seem to carry more of the past.'

'We do,' I said. 'Several of us are almost your age.'

He looked at me curiously. 'No, even Yeng has it – a sort of hardness in the eyes.'

'Yeah,' said Suze. 'It's the "old comrades" look I told you about.'

'Hmm,' I said. 'I don't know. You strike me as pretty tough yourself, Sam.' I flicked my hand sideways. 'Another time . . . What I wanted to ask you was, how are you getting on with the math? Are our miracles of neural nanotech reviving your genius?'

Malley laughed. 'That's one of the things about you that I was talking about, Ellen. You can say something like that without cracking a smile, and yet treat other matters with the most appalling levity. Anyway, as you say. Later for psychology. The answer to your question is, yes, I am making progress, but it's slow – and I don't think it's because of my brain's age. The "engineering considerations" I once blithely summed up as beyond the wit of man are beginning to look a bit more tractable, and as for the theory of the quantum-chaotic manifold, even my own old papers are beginning to make sense to me again.'

I wasn't sure whether he meant this ironically or not.

'OK,' I said. 'You heard what the man said, last night. I'm supposed to give you all necessary practical assistance, starting this morning. That obviously includes giving you access to all the observations, all the calculating machinery you might need, and so on. But it's more than that. If you want to observe the wormhole Gate up close, or send a probe through it, or for that matter go through it yourself – we can make it possible.'

'I suppose it would be best to do things in that order,' Malley observed. 'Observation, test probes, expedition. Rather than the reverse.' He smiled, as at a thin joke, and for a moment, despite the glowing success of his rejuvenation, looked like an elderly academic from one of those twentieth-century lecture tapes whose science has remained valid, however bizarre the diction or the clothes appear to their modern students. 'However . . . it's the practical calculation which has to be solved first, so yes, I would appreciate as much computing power as you can spare, and a walk through your available mathematical software. Oh, and a lit search, don't want to reinvent the wheel, eh?'

I set him up with all of these and a connection to our wormhole physics team; they had decades of experience of sending probes into the wormhole, and none whatsoever of any coming back. When he was comfortably enmeshed in the virtual-reality workspace I turned to Suze.

'There's something very important you can do,' I said. 'If Sam finds a way of getting us through, we may need you to help us find our way about on the other side.'

'New Mars?'

'Yes,' I said. 'Imagine an entire planet of non–cooperators, if you can.' I frowned. 'Now I come to think about it, there are only half a million or so, which is probably less than you've got on Earth . . . but this lot have a world to themselves. I'd like you to take a look at the files we've built up of Wilde's accounts of New Mars, and some of the images his little spacecraft had in its storage.'

'I'd love to,' Suze said. 'It's a dream, it really is.'

'Each to their own,' I said.

Suze laughed. 'You don't like it?'

'I don't like what I've seen of New Mars, or what Wilde told us about it,' I said, as I guided her to the most recently built workspace, at the far end of the room. Closest to the ice-face and the busy, tiny robots, it was the one least likely to be coveted by CC members. 'For me it just confirms something I've thought for a long time: people in an owned world are owned.'

Suze sat down and began adjusting the workspace to her own preferences. All I could see of this process was off-centre hologram images, dim in the full-spectrum light, and subtle twitches of Suze's facial muscles as she settled into the scene. She turned to me and smiled, as though from a distance.

'That isn't how they see it,' she told me, and before I could reply she had slipped the sound system over her ears, and was away.

By about ten o'clock all the CC members had turned up. None of them looked as if they'd had much sleep, and not for the same reasons as Suze and Malley (and, for that matter, myself). They had probably collapsed into a few hours' deep sleep after staying at work most of the night. Several of them resorted now to stimulant drugs, as well as making full use of the coffee machine.

I'd used the time until their arrival in checking out the current flightworthiness of the *Terrible Beauty*; according to the maintenance team, it was entirely sound, so all I had to do was reserve it for my own crew. There were two reasons for doing this; one was that it would be quite inconvenient, but all too predictable, to find that all the fusion–clippers were already assigned or in use just when we needed one; and the other was that, like myself, the rest of my crew were far more familiar with the handling and operation of fighter-bombers than of fusion-clippers, and our experience with the *Terrible Beauty*'s individual quirks would make our next flight in it easier.

Tatsuro took a seat at the head of the long table.

'Why are you here, Ellen?' he asked.

'Doctor Malley is fully occupied,' I said. 'If he requires further help from me, he has only to ask. In the meantime, I would like to remain here.'

'Very well,' said Tatsuro. Other members began to wander back from the other end of the room, and sat down. Clarity smiled at me, and took a seat beside me; others looked somewhat reserved. Tatsuro called the meeting to order.

'For the benefit of any who were not present last night,' Tatsuro began, with a flash of his eye at me, 'we've finalized our equipment for opening a secure communications channel. Our surface teams have arranged a narrow-beam transmitter-receiver, connected by a completely independent and isolated cable to a screen and speakers in this room. The wavelength and location with which comrade Ellen established contact yesterday will be used as the basis for our first attempt. During the contact, this room will be isolated, and anyone who doesn't wish to participate is free to leave.'

We all looked at each other. Nobody made a move.

'All right, comrades,' said Tatsuro. 'Ellen, will you please ask Doctor Malley and comrade Suze to leave.'

Malley and Suze, when I'd interrupted their respective attention-trances, flatly refused to do any such thing.

'Wouldn't miss this for anything,' Malley told us. Suze just looked stubborn.

Tatsuro gave a small shrug. 'It's your life,' he said. The two of them sat down together at the table, Suze beside me, Malley beside her. I squeezed Suze's shoulder.

Joe Lutterloh, the committee's electronics specialist, went around the room checking each news-thread camera location and disconnecting it. We could hear a murmur through the walls as the people outside, like everybody else in the Division who was watching, found their screens going blank.

The big screen was moved into position at the end of the table, and a camera was mounted on it. The isolated cable was connected up to both, via a likewise isolated computer through which the message, if any, would be filtered. A small cable was unwound and trailed across the table to a control pad in front of Tatsuro.

'Ready,' said Joe.

He rejoined the rest of us at the table. We all shuffled our seats around until the arrangement resembled a broad U-shape, with Tatsuro at one end and the screen we all faced at the other. Each of us could see all the others. Tatsuro gave a final glance around, as though to check that everybody was still willing to be present, and pressed a switch. The tiny light on the mounted camera glowed red. The prerecorded hailing message went out, several times, along with an image of the room and our silent, waiting selves.

Time passed, perhaps a minute; it seemed longer. Then the screen lit up with a picture. There was no fuzziness, no moment of tuning. It came into focus at once. It wasn't any of the shapes I'd seen. Instead, it showed the head and shoulders of a young man, wearing a plain white tee shirt and apparently standing casually in the interior of one of the bubbles. I could see the hexagonal patterns of the panes, as from a great distance. The more familiar – since yesterday – forms of the Jovian entities drifted and shifted in the great spaces between the man and the domed roof, like strange birds in an aviary. The man looked like a typical North American, mainly Caucasian with a good mixture of the usual other races. His face was unexceptional: healthy, good-looking, alert and friendly. The image could have come from an old NASA commercial, and possibly did.

He smiled and waved. 'Hi,' he said. 'Thank you for getting in touch again. To us, it's been the equivalent of two years since your first contact, so we've had time to prepare our response. I'm operating at your speed, by the way – we can interact directly.' He smiled. 'Apart from the light-speed lag, of course. I see Doctor I. K. Malley is among you. We're honoured, sir.'

Malley grunted something. There was a pause of a few seconds. The Jovian smiled.

'As you know, what you're seeing now isn't how we usually present ourselves to each other. But it isn't just a mask – we're of human descent, and we have much in common with you, perhaps far more than you think.'

No doubt we could say the same to gorillas – or to goldfish.

'But,' the friendly face continued, 'we are of course post-human. We don't wish to hide that, or play it down. We know of the long history of discord between those who took our path, and those who chose to remain within the human frame.'

His gaze, uncannily, fixed on me. 'Ellen May Ngwethu,' he said, in a wondering tone. 'It's amazing to see you here. Your old opponents from the wreck-deck send their regards.'

He raised an open hand, then clenched it to a fist in what, from his quizzical expression, I judged to be an ironical salute.

'How do you know me?' I asked, keeping my voice steady. The delay in the response gave me plenty of time to quail.

'We are individuals,' the Jovian said, moving the clenched fist, turned inwards, to his chest. 'Not a hive, not –' and here he paused to smile '– a "Jupiter-sized brain". But memories are shared, and nothing is lost. Some who were with you are with us, and some of their memories are with me. I hope you'll come to see us as alive, as a different flesh, and not as a simulation or a soulless mimicry. We have thoughts and feelings that may be wider and deeper than we remember from our human phase, but are otherwise like your own. We're people too, Ellen, as we hope you'll come to see.'

I made no reply, and after the inevitable delay the Jovian's attention shifted.

'Tatsuro, isn't it?' he said. 'No doubt you have questions for us.'

'Indeed I have,' Tatsuro said urbanely. 'But first, let me say how much I, and most of us here, welcome this opportunity to talk things over. I will be frank with you. As you may know, we represent a defence force which has spent most of the last couple of centuries – which to you must be almost geological ages – in conflict with your kind. Your continued broadcasting of viral programs, and generation of destructive molecular machinery, remain an inconvenience to us. Their first occurrence, shortly after your arrival in the Jovian atmosphere, resulted in many millions of deaths, and gave the final push to an already tottering civilization.

'Your emergence from virtual reality into, as you put it, a different flesh, changes the situation, but in a way which – as I'm sure you'll understand – many of us can't help regarding as a threat. Your predecessors, the human beings with whom you affirm your continuity, left us with no cheerful prospect for the future of humanity, in a Solar System dominated by post-human entities. We're interested in what you have to say on these points.'

Perhaps because of the length of Tatsuro's statement, the Jovian's reply began immediately. It gave a superficially reassuring impression of a conversation, but on second thoughts it only confirmed the alien superiority of the being confronting us; he must have been able to deduce, from subtle clues in Tatsuro's voice, expression and posture, the exact moment when he'd subconsciously intended to stop speaking, and precisely timed his response to arrive a moment after that. Doubtless he was processing Tatsuro's last few sentences while apparently speaking the first of his own. I felt hairs prickle on my forearms.

'This has come as a shock to us,' the Jovian was saying. 'We assure you that we weren't aware of this viral sabotage. We are grieved to learn that it did you so much damage, in the past. Please bear in mind, we have only just emerged from what you refer to as virtual reality, and which we remember as a kind of nightmarish dreamtime. The last two months, to you, have been about a century and a half to us. We've spent most of it in our own struggles for survival – in developing, as you see, the rudiments of a material culture in what remains an exceptionally harsh environment. When we realized how much time had elapsed between the wormhole starship project and the present, we were astonished and, I must admit, appalled. The viral sabotage is – at the very least – not under our conscious control, and may not be – even indirectly – our doing. There are physical, mechanical processes – the post-biological equivalent of vegetation – underpinning our existence, and the viruses may be a reflexive, defensive product of that, like the natural insecticides of plants.' He gave a self-deprecating smile. 'Or maybe it's just our natural smell. Sorry about that, folks. It may give you offence, but it isn't, on our part, an offensive action. We'll do our best to find out what's causing it and, if possible, put a stop to it.'

He registered, with another smile, the nodding that had been going on around the table from everyone but me, and continued.

'We obviously have a lot of problems to overcome about our common past. One of the things we hope to gain from our contact with you is a better understanding of what happened during our . . . dreamtime, how it came about and how any harm that was done in that time can be repaired, or at least some restitution made. And that brings me to your very understandable concerns about the future.

'The first thing I'd like to say, on behalf of all of us, is this: please, we urge and implore you, don't hold against us the wild statements made by the alienated adolescents some of us once were, long ago. Would you judge an adult by every spiteful or foolish word spoken in childhood? We are much further advanced from our origins than that! And as for things said by some who should have, perhaps, known better – the philosophers and predictors of the post-human, most of whose speculations were committed to text before even one AI existed in the world – please don't turn these guesses, fearful or inspired, against us now. Please judge us for what we are, not for what some roboticists and science-fiction writers hoped or feared we might become.

'Ellen, and others present, used to joke about our emergence as "the Rapture for nerds". Well, we weren't all nerds, you know! And for us, it hasn't exactly been a Rapture. There were great and exhilarating times, ages to us, in the early years. Since then, since our catastrophe, it's been a long and agonizing process of evolution, in every sense of the word, during which we learned to turn away from the dreams and nightmares that our new capacities made possible, and turn again to the real and only universe, the one we share with you, and with all life. We have laid no plans against you. All we ask of you is to live in peace with us. To let us enjoy the part of this system that belongs to us, and yourselves to enjoy what is your own. We hope that you will go further, and explore with us the possibilities of what we can accomplish – together. The choice is yours.'

It was indeed, but I wondered how many of who heard this message would understand what the choice it presented was.

The Jovian spread open his hands. 'This contact is putting quite a strain on our resources, friends. We'd like to leave you now, to consider it, and we look forward to your reply.'

The screen went blank. Tatsuro fingered his control panel, and the camera's light went off. A moment of silence was followed by shiftings and sighings as people relaxed.

'Well,' Tatsuro said, 'that was a remarkable message. Something to think about. The Command Committee meeting is adjourned while we do some thinking about it. Don't all speak at once.'

Everybody did, but Tatsuro resolutely ignored them while he rose and strolled to the coffee machine and helped himself. Others followed suit, and within a minute we were all standing around. It was quite a smart move on Tatsuro's part, because it gave us a breathing spell, a chance to unwind after the tension of the contact. In the huddle around the coffee machine, I found Malley in front of me.

'I happened to glance at you during the last part of that message,' he said. 'I hope we kept a tape of how our side looked from the camera. Your expression was a classic.'

'Oh?' I reached the machine and keyed up some espresso. 'How so?'

Malley grinned, over the rim of his cup. 'Hmm,' he said. 'I once saw a late-twentieth-century newspaper photo of a mad Moscow bag lady clutching pictures of Stalin and the last Tsar and looking into a shop window full of televisions showing the new politicians making promises after the counter-revolution. You had *exactly* the same look on your face.'

'Sometimes, Sam,' I said, 'I have only the vaguest idea of what you're talking about. But if you mean I looked somewhat sceptical, and perhaps a little hostile, then –'

'Yeah, that's about it,' he chuckled. Then his face became more serious. 'It's almost frightening, Ellen, to think that if I hadn't insisted on your making contact, you'd never have had the chance to hear what the Jovians had to say.'

'Yes,' I said. We were moving sideways, letting the pressure of bodies shift us out of the crush. I found a clear part of the edge of the table and sat down. 'Without that message, we might never have known just how hostile they are.'

Malley nearly spilled his coffee. '*Hostile?* That was as generous an offer of peaceful cooperation as you could hope to hear.'

I shook my head. 'Sometimes I might sound prejudiced, but contrary to what you might think, I *can* imagine what a generous offer of peace from the Jovians would be like. I'm not saying I'd believe it, or even if I believed it that I'd accept it, but I can imagine it. And what we've just heard was not that.'

'Frankly, I'm amazed,' Malley said. 'What problems do you have with it?'

'I'm still adding them up,' I said. 'The devil is in the details.'

Malley grimaced. 'All right. I'm a scientist, not a politician.'

'How's the science going?' I asked lightly.

'Ah.' Malley looked down, then looked me in the eye. 'As you said: the devil is in the details. It's all a matter of getting the angle of entry to the wormhole right – that's how you end up coming out of the daughter wormhole, and not up the arse of the probe. Once you've got that, it's straightforward. But I'm a long way from getting that. Even the physical measurement of the angle depends on how you define the location of the quasi-surface, and that's technically a bit tricky. Still . . . that's what we're here for, eh?'

While everyone was milling around Joe and Clarity were running diagnostic software on the message records. As far as they could tell, the message was clean. As soon as this was announced Tatsuro banged on the table and reconvened the meeting.

'OK, everybody,' he said. 'We know the message contains no Trojan-horse viruses or semiotic-trigger traps, so I propose we release it to the Division without delay. Anyone disagree?'

Nobody did.

'Fine,' he said. 'Carried *nem con.*'

Joe reconnected the cameras. Again we heard sounds from outside. Tatsuro hit some keys and the conversation between the Jovian and ourselves began to replay on the outside screens, while our continuing discussion was being shown on other threads.

'Next item: anyone totally opposed to continuing the contact?'

Again, no objections.

'Then I suggest we move quickly to a response,' said Tatsuro. 'From what the Jovian said, the fast folk are as fast as ever – a thousand times faster than us. Let's not give them two subjective years between messages, this time. You've had time to sort out your first impressions; here are mine.

'The account we've received of how the present . . . implementation of the Jovian post-human intelligences came into existence fits perfectly with what we've figured out ourselves. They have some continuity of memory with their human progenitors, which is not a surprise, although their recognition of individuals among us is, I may say, disquieting to experience. They are obviously making an effort – an effort which they at least want us to believe is at some cost – to show us, literally, a human face. They've made a statement which we should weigh carefully, but which on the face of it is an appeal for cooperation and an offer to live in peace. To me, this suggests that they do not, as yet, have enough power to defeat us in all-out conflict – and that we, for now, have the power to destroy them. At their present or possible rates of progress, this balance could rapidly tilt the other way. So far, they've shown no signs of any ability to project their power beyond the Jovian atmosphere – other than by radio messages, of course, and the odd molecule boiling off into space, which they claim is not their doing.

'The expressed dismay at the damage the radio-borne viruses have caused, and the disavowal of responsibility for them, are again among the possibilities we've considered ourselves. We can't confirm it, but I think we should give them the benefit of the doubt.

'Now . . . as to the appeal for cooperation. The points made about not judging them by their progenitors, or by the speculations of pre-Singularity thinkers, are well taken. But they have a further implication. If the Jovians continue to develop, and manage to avoid the virtual-reality trap, then they or their descendants could soon be as far beyond their present selves as they are now beyond their past. They now look back at their past selves, and in effect disown them. The shadow of the future, which to them, now, may loom genuinely long, would be to us a painfully short period before their defection. In a matter of days or weeks, they could look back on their present selves and dismiss their concerns and promises as those of infants – or less than that.

'How can we bind them to their promises, without superior force? And how can we keep our force superior? We can't – we either *trust* them, or destroy them.'

Tatsuro placed his hands, palms upward, on the table, and his gaze slowly tracked around us all. He raised his eyebrows, and then sat back.

I was surprised and relieved that he'd said all he had. He, at least, had not been carried away by the Jovian's rhetoric. Others didn't welcome the cold water he'd poured on their hopes. I could see that from their faces, but nobody seemed willing to speak.

So I did.

'There is one more point,' I said, 'which could bear clarification in the next exchange. The Jovian said that they wanted to enjoy their own part of the system, and leave us to enjoy ours. It would be very interesting to know just what parts they mean – what they consider theirs, and what ours. I seem to remember that this kind of property right was one of the issues we originally fell out about. He, or it, also mentioned repairing or recompensing harm done during the period of their so-called dreamtime. He said nothing of who was to compensate whom, for what.'

'But surely he meant –' someone began.

'No!' I insisted. 'We can't assume they mean the harm *they* did to us! They might mean the harm we did to them. Some very rich people became Outwarders, and they could still claim that we – that is, the Union – stole their property in the social revolution. In terms of their legal system, the bloodsucking usurers owned half the Earth, and they might want it back, and the rest as interest! The way I take what the Jovian said, our choice remains the same: we hammer them with the comets, or we live under their iron heel, submitting to whatever enslavement it would take to pay them off for their so-called property.'

'Oh, Ellen!' said Clarity. She looked at Tatsuro. 'Sorry. Uh, comrade chairman. Ellen's comment I'm afraid sums up what's precisely the wrong approach we should take to this situation. The idea that these post-human beings would be *interested* in Earth, or in interest – whatever that is – when they have the whole universe in front of them and the whole future before them, is just dragging up old fights. I don't think we should even *mention* it. I'm not saying take them at their word, but let's show them the sort of basic goodwill we show to any stranger, and not get bogged down in ancient history.'

A ripple of amusement went around the committee at this fifty-year-old's allocation of the youth of most of us to ancient history. Suze raised her hand. Tatsuro nodded.

'Comrade Tatsuro,' Suze said, 'my sympathies are with Clarity, but I would like to say that Ellen has a point. If the Jovians do think in the way she described, then they could feel themselves justified in almost anything. On the other hand, if they have some version of the true knowledge, then anything they wanted to do to us would be its own justification, once they have the power. It would be very helpful if we could get them to demarcate now what's to count as theirs, and what as ours, and to agree to build in that distinction to any future versions of themselves – something they can't go back on without severe internal conflict. So that whether they're moralists or egoists, they'll go on respecting us.'

Tatsuro gave her an encouraging smile, and said: 'Comrade Suze, you may be right, but that still comes down to trusting them. Without power, respect is dead. But our power needn't be the capacity to destroy them – our own infants, and many lower animals, have power over us because our interests are bound up with theirs. Because *we* value *them*, and because natural selection has built that valuing into our nervous systems, to the point where we cannot even wish to change it, though no doubt if we wanted to we could. This is elementary: the second iteration of the true knowledge. The question we really have to answer, then, is whether the Jovians have come to value our independent existence.'

'That,' said Joe Lutterloh, speaking up suddenly, 'comes back to surviving as wildlife or pets.'

The discussion then heated up, and went on for an hour or so until Tatsuro stopped it with nothing more than an impatient drumming of his fingernails on the table.

'Comrades,' he said firmly, 'I think we've discussed this to the point where we have more than enough to bring to our next contact. *However* that turns out, I am more strongly persuaded than ever that Doctor Malley's work on the wormhole must continue in parallel.' He looked over at Malley, and at me. 'I accept your reasons for wanting to witness the first contact, and to confirm *our* sincerity in making it – but can I take it that you're satisfied?'

Malley nodded.

'Very well. I'm sure you're keen to return to the wormhole problem. Ellen, I think you've said all you need to say. I don't see your contributing further to the discussion, or the negotiation. Am I right?'

'I guess so,' I said.

'All right. See to it that a part of the far end of this room is sound-screened off, so that Doctor Malley can continue his work without distraction, and give him any further help he needs. If any developments require your attention, we'll let you know.'

I stood up, gave the rest of the committee a comradely smile, and accompanied Malley back to his workstation. After a moment of hesitation, Suze followed.

'Well,' she said, 'that's us put in our place!'

I clapped her shoulder. 'Not to worry. Tatsuro is actually paying us quite a compliment, however it looks to the others. He's saying our work is as important as anything that's likely to come out of the contact.'

Malley sat down at his workstation and gazed at the screen. He grasped his temples in his fingertips and rubbed. 'You know, Ellen, he's right. Because what we're trying to do is get to the stars!'

'That's the spirit,' I said. I looked back at the group around the table. Joe was once more disconnecting the external cameras. Another contact session was about to start. I wondered how far the Jovians would have changed in the time since our first contact, and how far we had.

'Come on,' I said. 'Suze, help me round up some robots to spin us a sound-screen.'

Over the next three hours I helped Malley with locating and collating thousands of recordings of the Gate, and with running through the navigational data from Wilde's spacecraft, which had come through the wormhole the other way. Frustratingly, the paths were not commutative: it was not possible to take the path from the New Mars system and run it in reverse. Outside, through a plastic partition that let through light but not sound, I could see the committee going again and again into contact with the Jovian emissary. Suze was immersed in her study of New-Martian society, occasionally muttering to herself.

About 1500 GMT Clarity strolled in carrying three mugs of coffee. We all stopped work and leaned back and smiled at her gratefully.

'Clarity, you should be charity,' Malley said.

'How's it going?' I asked.

Clarity wrinkled her small, perfect nose. 'All right, I suppose,' she said. 'The Jovians are being very friendly, and they're not just showing that man-image now. There are other forms crowded around him, and sometimes they seem to be relaying replies through him. It's like they've understood we're getting used to them.'

'Any progress on the virus front?'

'No, they still say they haven't pinned down the source of it themselves.'

'Hah. What about the issue of who gets what?'

'Oh, that! The Jovian was very taken aback that it should even come up. Insisted that they had no plans for any use of the system beyond Jupiter, which as he pointed out was quite big enough.'

I favoured her with an evil grin. ' "No plans" still doesn't mean anything, beyond what it literally says, which isn't much. And *nothing* is big enough for exponential growth, which is what the old Outwarders were really keen on.'

She shrugged. 'As you keep reminding us. Enjoy your coffee.'

'Thanks.'

Malley watched her walk away, and Suze watched Malley. I caught Suze's eye and smiled.

'It's the rejuve,' I murmured.

'What?' asked Malley.

'Nothing.'

'You know what you are?' Malley said to me. 'You're a hawk.'

'Hey, I like that,' I said. 'I thought we all were out here, I just didn't expect everyone to go all dovish as soon as their faceless enemies put on a face to talk to.'

Malley took his pipe out of a pouch on his belt, and clenched it between his teeth. He put it down again and took a sip of coffee. 'You know,' he said, with some regret, 'I'm not sure I even like the *taste* of tobacco any more.' He dropped the pipe and caught it again, several times, as though fascinated by its slow fall. He tilted his seat back and stared at the screen and poked around in his virtual workspace.

'Back to work,' he said.

He continued for another hour, and then he suddenly stopped. I was talking quietly with Suze at the time, as she refreshed my memories of the intricacies of anarcho-capitalist legal theory – something some of the Outwarders had bored me with back on the wreck-deck, and of which New Mars was an insanely logical outcome. It was like Ptolemaic epicycles, an endless addition of reinvented wheels. Why, I kept wondering, couldn't these people *see* the answer?

Malley's inarticulate sound of frustration interrupted us.

'Is there a problem?' I asked.

'Is there a fucking problem.' Malley took out his pipe again and this time stuffed it with tobacco and lit it, puffing furiously. Small machines stopped what they were doing and sniffed the air. Some of them hastily extemporized firefighting equipment, and began to gather round.

'I can't do it,' Malley said. 'The whole thing depends on the angle you make to the wormhole when you pass into it. I can't get it from the angle the mutineers' colony ship made back in 2093 – the wormhole goes through a cycle whose period I don't know, and so far, calculating it is beyond any of the resources we've got. There's a key to it somewhere, but it's mathematically intractable. You'd have to have built the wormhole to know what it is.'

'You can't even make a best guess?'

'Oh, sure,' said Malley. 'I can make a best guess. Wouldn't bet my life on it, though.'

'You don't have to!' I said. 'We'll test it with a probe. See if it comes back . . .'

Malley jabbed at his screen with the stem of his pipe. 'Sure,' he said. 'Trouble is, we could be testing probes from now until doomsday. I mean, my best guess is no better than the best your chaps have come up with, and *they* haven't had anything back.'

I fought to hide my dismay. There was no way we'd have time to mess around with test probes. We'd all been counting on Malley, confident that with his deep theoretical knowledge and our masses of data, he'd find us a path through.

Malley looked up at me, frowning.

'Something's puzzling me,' he said.

'Yes?'

'This space-time path back here from New Mars . . . how come we have that, and not the one the other way?'

'Well,' I said, 'it's kind of funny. Wilde had the return path in his onboard computer, and we've been able to access it. The outward path – which may not even be a valid solution any more – he had in his head, so to speak. I mean, there was a time when both "his head" and the return path were stored programs in the same computer, but even if we'd known, we still can't hack human minds, even minds in computers. No access path, no memory addresses . . .'

Malley smiled, thin-lipped. 'I know that. What I was wondering is how Wilde was able to work out the return path from New Mars.

Do the New Martians have super-advanced computers, or lots of brain-boosted physicists, or what?'

'Not exactly,' I said. 'Over on New Mars, they have the stored original mind-states of the Outwarders, and the stored minds of some of the subsequent "macros" before their catastrophe. What they did – and it still gives me the shivers to think about – was make copies of them, then restart the copies in a controlled environment – a standard nanotech tank, as it happens – then ask them to work out the return path, and when they'd got the answer to that question and a few others, like how to resurrect a lot of human minds and bodies they also had in storage . . . they, well, they basically tipped in the bleach! Something called Blue Goo, actually, a nanotech specific for wiping out nanoware.'

'Jesus!' said Malley. 'You mean they generated an entire post-human culture in a virtual reality, asked it a few deep questions, and then *destroyed* it?'

'Yes,' I said. I chuckled at the appalled look on his face. Even Suze was astonished by this part of the story, which the Division hadn't chosen to release. 'OK, it was a bit risky – I wouldn't trust a post-human culture, even if I did have it in a bucket. But, you know, full marks for initiative.'

'And zero for morality,' Malley said. 'That's like a small-scale version of what you had in mind for the Jovians and with less excuse.'

I nodded briskly. 'Wilde does have his own take on the true knowledge,' I said. 'Even if he is a non-co.'

Malley sighed. 'Let's not get into that. So how did they get the original path, the path through the daughter wormhole to New Mars?'

'Oh,' I said, 'they got it from the Outwarder macros.'

Malley stared. 'The Outwarders *gave* it to them?'

I spread my hands. 'One, or several, of them did. We don't know if it was a deal they had arranged all along as a payment for the operator of the bonded-labour company – a man called Dave Reid, a very nasty piece of work who's probably still top dog on New Mars – or if the daughter-wormhole was set up by the Outwarders for other purposes, and Reid and company just managed to extract the information as the Outwarder macros were degenerating.'

'Ah,' said Malley. 'It has occurred to me that we could do the same ourselves. We could just ask.'

I really had not thought of that.

Tatsuro was sitting at the head of the long table, doodling on a pad and combing his receding hair with his fingers. Committee members stood or sat around, talking and drinking coffee. Another contact session had just been completed, virus-scanned, and relayed to the rest of the Division. Clarity was elbow-deep in a display of the state of current opinion about the talks so far: shifting, by the look of it.

Malley and I walked up to Tatsuro.

'We have a problem,' I told him. 'And a possible solution.'

As he listened, I watched his expressions; almost undetectable, under the smooth surface of his skin. Alarm, disappointment, anger, doubt, and a faint glimmer of hope.

'I suppose it's worth a try,' he said at last. 'But it does let them know we're going through.'

'They'd find out as soon as we did go through,' I said. 'At least, we have to assume that they could.'

Tatsuro nodded slowly. 'Perhaps. Although I must say, observational astronomy from inside the Jovian atmosphere is probably a bit tricky, even for them. Anyway, if we ask them for the path, we need to do so without getting them worried about our intentions.'

I shrugged. 'Surely we have an understandable interest in another human society –'

'Aha!' said Malley. 'How about this? The Jovians may still have some, ah, bones to pick with the mutineers, yes? And so do you, I would imagine. Didn't the labour-force operator conscript some of your people into his labour gangs?'

'That's one way of putting it,' I said sourly. It was something I'd thought over before – that the responsibility for those long-ago raids and deaths might rest more with Reid's company than with his clients, the Outwarders. Not that it mattered.

'So tell them that,' Malley said. 'Tell them you want to extract some retribution for what was done. The Jovians might well consider that a *very* understandable motivation.'

'Especially if they think it gets them off the hook,' said Tatsuro. 'OK, we'll do it on the next contact.'

'By the way,' I said, 'just who are we in contact with? Do we know that they're in any way representative?'

'Like us, you mean?' Tatsuro asked dryly. 'Rather more so, I would say. We've had evidence that the contact is being monitored throughout the Jovian population. The "man" we see is a construct, presenting a consensus or majority view.'

'Sum over histories,' said Malley.

The preparations for contact were gone through once more. It was becoming a routine, as was the contact itself. Again the face appeared. The first few exchanges concerned matters arising from earlier sessions, which I hadn't seen. Then Tatsuro broached the subject of the wormhole and the path to New Mars.

For the first time, the Jovian speaker hesitated. 'One moment, please,' he said. His face suddenly became abstracted, the resolution fading until it looked like a hollow mask. The flitting shapes of the individual Jovians in the sky around him went through agitated transformations, spinning into girandoles, stretching into long columns, building themselves into dark edifices . . .

'This might not have been such a good idea,' someone whispered.

Shut up, I didn't say. My lips were dry.

The Jovian speaker's colour and texture returned like a flush.

'Sorry about that, folks,' he said. 'The information you asked for was buried quite deep in our archived memories. Also, some of us weren't too keen on giving you it.' He smiled. 'But the rest of us won them over, so here it is.'

Tatsuro's fingers scrabbled on the control panel as a line of pulsing light along the bottom of the screen indicated a raw-data transmission. It was over in less than five seconds.

'That's all you need,' said the Jovian. 'Give our regards to our former employees, and please assure them that we bear them no ill-will for having baled out when they did. Goodbye for now.'

The image blinked off.

'Wow, fuck,' said Malley. 'These things are sharp.'

I tried to laugh. People were looking at the empty screen, looking at us.

'You stirred up something there,' said Clarity.

'That's the first indication we've had of dissension among them,' said Tatsuro. 'I suggest you give the data we just received a *very* thorough virus-scan.'

I called up Yeng and asked her to come along. Together with Joe and Clarity, she combed through the data with everything she'd got. It checked out clean. Malley loaded it into his workspace, and found that it meshed with his own incomplete calculations.

By this time it was well into the evening. Yeng, Suze and I were seated around Malley. Behind us, other work was going on. When Malley leaned back and nodded silently, we all let out a whoop that caused some distraction.

'We test it first,' I said.

I dialled up a drone and downloaded the data into its navigational computer. I patched in a view on Malley's screen, and we watched the whole mission, from the tiny rocket's launch to its carefully angled insertion in the wormhole. That took about an hour. We'd warned the patrol fighters, hanging in orbit in front of the Gate. Even so, the probe's re-emergence put them on full alert. I could imagine the jangled nerves.

The probe had nothing on board but a telescopic camera – photographic film, not television. One of the fighter-bombers scooped up the probe and ran the film for us, past one of their own telemetry cameras.

We looked at the grainy images of an unfamiliar starfield, and the spectrum of an unknown yellow sun, and at the distant red globe with its tracery of canals.

'Fucking amazing,' said Malley. 'Just seeing this. I wonder if I ever really believed it before.'

I slung my arms around the shoulders of Malley, Yeng and Suze. 'Believe it,' I said. 'We're going there. Tomorrow.'

8

City of the Living Dead

TILTED, JUPITER'S ring cut a white segment into the forward view. Ten miles ahead, also at an angle, hung the vastly smaller ellipse of the Malley Mile. At this distance the boosters and attitude jets clamped to its circular rim showed as tiny black beads spaced out around its rainbow ring. A fighter-bomber, the *Turing Tester*, stood by beside us, ready to move into our exact present position shortly after we'd vacated it.

The *Terrible Beauty*, with the currently uncrewed fighter-bomber *Carbon Conscience* clinging to its side like a black fly squatting on a white egg, was about to make its final thrust towards the wormhole Gate. The whole crew was on board, along with Malley and Suze. Malley, despite protests from Tatsuro and others, had insisted that he was certainly not going to stay behind. Whose goddam theory was it, anyway, he wanted to know? Whose name was on the thing, eh? Suze's equivalent insistence had more logic behind it: we actually needed her, because she was the only one who seemed to have a feel for how New-Martian society worked.

'Angle of approach 1.274066 radians,' said Jaime.

'Course confirmed,' said Andrea. 'Distance nine point seven five miles, relative speed one hundred and twenty miles per hour.'

'Check.'

It was all down to them now; them and the onboard computer, which was really flying the ship. But, moved by an impulse that goes all the way back to Vostok and Mercury, when people are in a ship they like to have the final say. Maybe it's an illusion, maybe it would be better to let the machines handle it all, but when you start thinking like that, where do you stop? You don't, is what, and you end up with all machines and no people. Come to think of it (I thought, floating in my straps, an inch above my acceleration couch and trying not to think too much) you end up with exactly what we were fighting against.

'Eight miles.'

Right now, as I watched the Malley Mile expand in the screen overhead, I didn't have much sense of control. We were falling into a hole in the sky, and there was nothing I could do about it any more.

'Six miles.'

'Ready for the burn,' Andrea sang out. 'Three minutes.'

We had to go through under acceleration, Malley had told us. He had tried to tell us why, but lost most of us by the fourth equation, and that was keeping it simple. I glanced over at him. He was lying on a couch next to me. As far as I could see, he had his eyes tight shut. His lips were moving. He turned over, and opened his eyes.

'Ah,' he whispered, 'you caught me at it.'

'At what?'

He closed his eyes again for a second, then opened them and smiled. 'Praying.'

'I didn't know you were a believer.'

'Not as such,' Malley said. He stared fixedly at our looming goal on the screen above us. 'But I understand God listens whether you're a believer or not.'

This was no time for philosophical debate. 'Yes,' I whispered back. 'That's what Andrea says about her St Christopher medal.'

'I heard that,' said Andrea. 'Don't you believe it. I may be sentimental, but I'm not superstitious.'

Malley smiled and seemed to relax somewhat.

'I've seen God,' Boris contributed, from the couch to my left. 'In the sky outside Brno.'

'You mean you got caught in smart rain from an obsolete Hanseatic psychochemical munition,' I said. 'Don't confuse things.'

'I know what done it to me,' Boris said placidly. 'And I know what I seen.'

'Pipe down, you back there,' said Andrea. 'Boosting in ten seconds, nine, eight . . .'

This time the acceleration was gentle, building up slowly to a half gee; but the wormhole gate came at us in a rush. Before I could think, before I could wonder, before Malley could pray again, the screens flared briefly blue, and then went black.

'Cutting the drive,' said Andrea. The small weight went away. Jaime's voice rose above the sudden silence.

'Is that *it*?'

Andrea flicked though screen images, stabilizing on the red crescent of the planet we'd seen the day before, sixty-two thousand miles away and dead ahead.

'Yes,' she said. 'That's it. We're through.'

Jaime was checking the starfield against an astonomical atlas in the navigational computer. The babbages ran for a few seconds, the fixels flickered and laboured; the catalogued 3D picture incremented the proper motions of the stars, and after several iterations meshed with the outside scene. Jaime examined the tank's readout.

'Ten thousand light years from home, and just over ten thousand years in the future, at a rough guess,' he said. 'Welcome to the Sagittarius Arm.'

'Wow,' said Suze.

'I think you spoke for all of us,' I said. 'Stay strapped in, everybody. Yeng, would you please run us a scan?'

Yeng complied quickly, hauling her interface down from the clustered banks of computers and checking that it was isolated from the rest, then cautiously sweeping the radio portion of the electromagnetic spectrum and sample-scanning apparent messages into her anti-virus software.

'It's busy,' she said.

'Take your time,' I said.

'It's *really* busy. I've never seen anything like it. There are signals at *every possible* wavelength! Scanning them all for viruses would take forever.' She waved a hand helplessly at the screen, down which a string of samples was propagating. 'Nothing there, but that's just the beginning, just a tiny fraction.'

'Try a random sample right across the spectrum,' I suggested.

That took about an hour, during which time we drifted further from the daughter-wormhole Gate and closer to the planet. We put this time to good use. First, we rotated the ship and decelerated, so that we could flee straight back through the wormhole if Yeng's investigations turned up anything nasty. Next, we placed a small communications satellite in a fixed position relative to the wormhole, a position it was programmed to hold. It was also programmed to point a communications laser at the correct angle for the beam to get through to the *Turing Tester* on the other side. (Light, having no mass, could get through without acceleration, which would of course have been impossible in any case; Malley's further explanation of how only coherent light could do it was, I'm afraid, lost on me.)

I tested the link, nervously, with Malley at my shoulder.

'*Terrible Beauty* to *Turing Tester*, are you receiving me?'

Seconds passed.

'*Turing Tester* to *Terrible Beauty*, receiving you loud and clear. Are you in the right place?'

'Yes, we are,' I said. 'Ten thousand light years from home, according to Jaime.'

Another short delay.

'Just passed on your message to the Command Committee. Tatsuro's coming through now.'

The voice changed. 'Congratulations, comrades, you just made history. Small step, giant leap and all that.'

One small step for the Jovians, one giant leap for us.

'Thank you,' I said. After a few more exchanges, mainly technical, we signed off.

Next we spun out a mirror and set it up in front of the ship and a little to one side, so that we could make visual observations through *Terrible Beauty*'s forward telescope. By sheer good luck we'd arrived just at the time when the planet's major settlement, Ship City, was coming around the middle of the crescent limb and turning to the night. The lights of smaller settlements were sprinkled across the dark side, and shortly the five-armed shape of the city joined them, a bright neon star. There were more settlements than Wilde had told us about, and the city seemed bigger and brighter than he'd described.

'Looks human enough to me,' said Tony.

'Well, it ain't,' I said. 'According to Wilde, four of those arms are inhabited, if that's the word, by robots running wild.'

'The lights are on, but nobody's home?' Malley said mischievously.

'Exactly,' I said. 'So let's not make assumptions, OK?'

'Looks like somebody's making assumptions about us,' remarked Boris.

'What?'

'No challenges,' he said mildly. 'They must assume we're friendly.'

'Thank you for sharing that,' said Tony. 'I've always thought the null hypothesis didn't get its fair share of publicity.'

'Stop bitching, comrades,' I said.

'Who's bitching?'

They continued in this vein for some time.

'*When* you've all *quite* finished,' said Yeng. She pushed the apparatus away from her, and the spring-loaded boom lifted it back to the cluster. 'You might like to hear my preliminary report on a random sample of radio signals.'

'We're listening,' I said.

'They're clean,' she said. 'A lot of encrypted stuff, but nothing that does nasty things to anything I've thrown it at. Definitely just dead data, not live programs. So, would you all like to hear a little of what goes on in a system where humans have the spectrum to themselves and don't have to worry about –' deep doomy voice '– "parasite programs from monster minds" shorting their circuits and eating their brains?'

'Yes, go ahead,' I said.

We all sat up a little on our couches – or rather, pushed ourselves away with our elbows – to listen to what people without Jovian jamming to worry about had to say. Yeng, with an impish smile, reached up for a switch and fiddled with a dial. The command-deck speakers filled the level with the most doleful music I'd ever heard. A sad, throaty voice was singing along, with lyrics I had to search my most distant memories to make sense of: the themes included unemployment, alcohol abuse, desertion, betrayal, sexual frustration, jealousy, religion . . .

'That's *terrible*,' said Tony, after a couple of minutes of open-mouthed listening. 'It must be hell down there.'

Suze laughed. 'Not hell – capitalism.'

'Yes, yes, yes,' I said. 'But what sort of music *is* that?'

'Country,' said Malley. 'Or maybe western.'

'Give us something else,' Boris pleaded. 'Anything.'

'Sure thing,' Yeng drawled. (The infection was already getting to her.) She turned the dial through a couple of banshee howls, and settled on a wavelength just as a voice announced: '– and I'd like to welcome you all to the Black Wave, Ship City's first and best blues and soul station, here to help you make it through the night . . .'

To be fair, not all the music beamed out by the local radio stations was an incitement to suicide: some of it was definitely a provocation to murder. This fitted right in with what we saw on broadcast television, which at first sight indicated a society where murder was commonplace; but Suze and Malley assured us that Wilde had been right in his descriptions of this in his original interrogation – it was just faked, staged, pretended violence for entertainment. Most of it was, anyway. Lethal combat was a legal spectatar sport, as Wilde had told us and as we now soon confirmed. We floated about, watching the screen with an appalled fascination.

'This is *sick*, man,' said Boris. 'Hey, I've seen more killings in the last half-hour than I ever saw in the Hundred Years' War.'

'You did most of your killing at long range, as I recall,' I said. 'What you saw is one thing, what you did is another. Anyway,' I added, pointing at a losing player being dragged out of a stadium, to cheers, 'he'll be back on his feet – well, when they find them – in a few days.'

'Nasty head wound,' said Yeng.

'They all take back-ups just before they go on, so all he'll lose is the memory of the fight. That's how they see it.'

'But not you?' Malley asked.

I shook my head, emphatically. 'Death is death, and I don't see the comfort in knowing that a clone with your memories is going to exist in the future.'

Malley pushed himself away from the wall he was about to collide with, and immediately drifted off in a direction other than the one he'd intended.

'I think,' he said over his shoulder, 'that we've just encountered yet another of your incorrigible ideas, Ellen. It's right up there with this "machines aren't conscious" bug in your mental program.' He grabbed at a plant through whose fronds he was moving, and succeeded only in breaking off a leaf.

' "Consciousness is an emergent property of carbon",' Yeng quoted gleefully. 'So stop hurting our plants.'

We'd needed this interlude of slacking-off, to recover somewhat from the tension we'd all felt about going through the wormhole – greater, to me anyway, than that of any other manoeuvre I'd experienced; at least since dropping in on the battle of Lisbon, which was a long time ago. To cross that space-time gulf was scarier than landing a shuttle through flak, and in retrospect it was no less troubling. I turned my mind resolutely from reflecting on it. It would be some time before the awe at what we'd done struck home to us, and I wanted to be safely home before it did. The radio and television broadcasts, misleading though they possibly were about the texture of daily life, had also been useful in mentally preparing us for arriving in a very alien society.

But it had gone on long enough.

'OK, comrades,' I yelled. 'Stop laughing at the sex channels and get back to your posts. We got work to do.'

When everyone had drifted – or, in Malley's case, been hauled – back to their couches, I attached myself loosely to my own and positioned myself to see and be seen.

'Right,' I said. 'We've established, at least provisionally, that New Mars hasn't yet had a runaway Singularity. If it has, somebody's making sure it looks and sounds like it hasn't – but we can't rule that out. The obvious way to check is to send down a few small, unobtrusive probes and see what it's like close up. But first, we want to let them know we're here. As far as we know, we haven't been spotted yet, but we certainly will be as soon as we start our approach burn and go into orbit.

'We've been through all this before, but let me go through it one more time. They don't have space defence in a military sense, but they do have laser-launchers, and spacecraft with missile and laser capability. They use them whenever one of their incoming comet fragments looks like it might fall in the wrong place, or fall too hard – terraforming by cometary bombardment is a bit of a risky business. Their lasers aren't powerful enough to burn us out of the sky – they only use the laser-launchers for little robot craft like the Wilde simulacrum came back in – but they could do us a lot of damage, and even the fighter-bomber might find their missiles too hot to handle. They have a charmingly casual way with nukes, by the way.

'So let's do this by the book. The first thing I suggest we do is for Suze and Yeng to compose and send a nice, reassuring hailing message, and for Jaime and Andrea to put us on a course which plainly is aiming for a high orbit around the planet. Geostationary, or to be precise –' I paused, smiling at my own pedantry '– *neo-areostationary* above Ship City would be ideal.'

'Not right above it,' said Tony. 'Too intimidating.'

'OK, just so long as we stay above the horizon. Before we start hailing, I'd like Boris to power up a dozen probes – little ones, mind, whose final stage will just float through the air like a leaf – and have them ready to fire them off shortly after orbital insertion. Meanwhile, I want you in Fire Control from the moment before we start signalling to well after we're sure we're welcome; and you and Jaime be ready to scramble the fighter-bomber. Yeng, you could scan for any response to our message on the aerospace-traffic control channels, or whatever they have, and Suze can do the same for the news broadcasts. It shouldn't be too long before we're the number one item.

'Finally . . . last we heard, they don't have a state here. All to the good, no doubt, but what they have instead is a lot of competing defence companies. It ain't like the Division, or even the Union – we don't worry about tooled-up people, because we aren't violent. These people may not be as violent as you'd think from their television, but they're a bit, ah, touchy and unpredictable.' I looked enquiringly at Malley.

'I think that's safe to say,' he acknowledged.

'Right,' I said. 'Let's do it. By the book.'

We got our first reply very quickly. This historic first contact between the Solar Union and humanity's first and only extrasolar colony went as follows:

'This is Solar Union passenger spaceship *Terrible Beauty*, out of Callisto via the Malley Mile, calling Ship City traffic control. Requesting permission to enter geostationary orbit and –'

'GET THE FUCK OFF this channel, kid. I'm warning you, you're endangering traffic, and we're triangulating your source *right now*. You are in deep shit, you little scumbag. OK, we've got you, we –'

Long pause. 'Uh oh. Jonesy, we got a bogey. I say again, we got a bogey. Condition Yellow. Going over to encryption Zero-Prime, I say again, Zero-Prime as from now, *kcchchchgh* . . .'

'Try another channel,' Suze advised. 'See if their competitors are more open-minded.'

Yeng worked her way through a succession of rebuffs from Ship City ATC Inc, Reid Industrial Airways, Lowell Field Control Tower, Barsoom Buddies, Xaviera's Friendly Flight-Control . . .

'When you said to go by the book, Ellen, you might have told us you meant the Yellow Pages,' Malley said.

I had to laugh (and yes, we did have Yellow Pages, even in the moneyless commonwealth); but we could all imagine the calls that were undoubtedly going on, to yet another list of companies: the ones that sold protection from incoming space-junk. We also knew that the people on New Mars had what seemed to them good reason to worry about things coming at them out of the wormhole. Five years earlier, Jonathan Wilde's robot copy had disappeared through the Malley Mile, desperately worried that the Jovian fast folk were about to take control of its other end. This concern had been misplaced, but he'd never reported back . . .

And our own intentions weren't entirely friendly. If the New Martians had known just what they *were*, they'd have scrambled every interceptor they had, and blown us out of the sky.

Suze called out: 'We're on the news!'

Yeng leaned over and swung a display screen around so that we could all see it. It showed an excited small boy, talking very quickly in front of a picture of a blurry but recognizably ovoid blob.

'– the UFO is still moving slowly towards us from the wormhole Gate. According to a well placed source, it claims to be a human expedition from the Solar System! Sources remain tight-lipped, however, about whether this claim is true – or whether the fast folk back home are pulling a fast one on us! Are we about to face a real invasion – or a virtual one? Software Seduction Services urges everyone to update their anti-virus systems. Don't take chances – call this number now!' A long number appeared at the bottom of the screen. 'And now . . . we bring you, live and exclusive, an outside broadcast of Mutual Protection's crack comet-busters scrambling from Lowell Field! No job's too big for Mutual Protection – and no job's too small! Is *your* home or business as safe as it could be? Call Mutual Protection, and you too can enjoy the security that only the most experienced protectors can provide, in a proud tradition that stretches all the way back to Old Earth, and is still out in front on New Mars!

'And off it,' the kid ad-libbed admiringly, as the screen filled with a startling floodlit view of scores of needle-shaped rockets leaping into the night sky like the arrows at Agincourt, the snarl of engine after engine rising and merging into one baying yell.

At the bottom of the screen was another number to call.

'Boris, Jaime, get in the fighter-bomber,' I said. 'Don't separate until I tell you, unless you see incoming. Jaime, give us an estimate on how long these rockets will take to arrive –'

'They won't,' Boris said flatly. 'That picture is *bullshit*, Ellen. Archive footage or outright fake. These are last-ditch anti-missile missiles. Type we used to call Citizens. No use for comet-busting unless the comet's almost on top of you. It's a diversion –'

The alarm went off and the forward view lit up with laser fire meeting its targets. Heavy thuds resounded through the ship – not hits, as my first shocked notion was, but decoys being launched from the hull's tubes in a crazy, confusing non-pattern to distract any radiation-seeking incoming missiles with a bewildering variety of radio, radar, and infrared emission profiles.

'Strap down!' yelled Andrea. Our suits, responding to the alarm with the equivalent of conditioned reflex, were already hardening around us, tightening our straps. Andrea fired the attitude jets and, while the ship was still rolling over, engaged the fusion drive. The acceleration pressed down on me like a smothering, giant hand. Despite all the support of the suit, my ribs were almost cracking under the strain of breathing. I began to black out, then felt my skin prickle all over as the suit started slipping oxygen directly into my blood through micrometre-wide tubules. The forward view – what I could see of it through the flaring patches that the weight on my eyeballs was generating on my retinae – was a storm of expanding spherical flashes.

And then we were in free fall again. I lay gasping painfully. The suit's multitude of tiny needles withdrew, their infinitesimal pains indistinguishable from the pins-and-needles of returning circulation.

'Stay where you are!' Andrea's warning was again redundant – none of us could have as much as raised our heads. 'We did it,' she went on. 'We outran them.'

Boris was scanning engagement and damage reports.

'Not too bad,' he said. 'Hull damage is within tolerance. *Carbon Conscience* is intact and seems to have fought pretty well on its own account.'

'What *happened* there?' Suze asked plaintively. 'Were we attacked?'

'Sure were,' said Boris. 'Nothing too sophisticated, though. Looks like they had a small swarm of comet-breakers parked around the wormhole. They weren't much use against active-defence. Wasted the decoys on them, really. Pity about that.'

'Why,' I asked, staring in disbelief at the swelling dark circle in the forward view, 'are we heading straight for New Mars?'

'Ah,' said Andrea. 'Sorry, comrades. Reflex, I'm afraid. I can make a course correction if you –'

'No, no, leave it for now.' I was beginning to reconsider our approach, literally as well as figuratively. The television news was still coming through.

'– the UFO has punched through our first line of defence and is now *heading straight towards us*! Stay tuned for –'

' "UFO", indeed!' said Malley. 'Bloody cheek.'

'What's a UFO?' asked Yeng.

'Something people believed in before they had the true knowledge,' Malley flipped back.

'Yeng,' I said, before her moment of puzzlement could turn to hurt, 'I wonder if you can access the New Martian communications network, and *call that number*?'

'Call up Mutual Protection?'

'Yes, why not? Suze, do you think you could talk to them? Do a deal?'

Suze laughed. 'I don't know about that, but I could make them very confused.'

'It's worth a try, anyway,' I said. 'OK everybody, stay strapped in. Enough of trying to persuade them not to be paranoid. We're going to give them something to *really* worry about. Andrea, give us a three-gee course towards them, then spin us round and bring us down anywhere that looks uninhabited and not too far from Ship City. Suze, Yeng, keep trying the numbers. Boris, Jaime, get in the *Carbon Conscience* and ride along as long as you can; disengage before we hit atmosphere, make an aerodynamic landing, and use up all the firepower you need to get us through.'

'That's what I like,' said Boris. 'Covering fire for a contested landing. Takes me back.' He disengaged from his couch and followed Jaime in a straight dive for the transfer airlock.

I decided that reminding him that he'd never done any such thing, and that I had, would be bad for his morale. A minute or so later he called us up from the fighter-bomber and announced that he and Jaime were ready for the burn.

'Good,' I said. 'Now let's show those non-cos what we're made off.'

'Here's hoping they don't have to work it out from our scorched DNA,' said Andrea, just before the drive kicked in. This time the gee-force was less than in our evasive manoeuvre, but it was considerably more prolonged. The moment of free fall during the roll-around provided no respite – parts of me that were enduring a dull ache took the opportunity of the weight coming off to report in as acute pain, and didn't shut down when the deceleration began and the weight came on again.

'Disengaging,' said Boris. 'See you on the ground, if you make it.'

'I love you too,' I said. 'Take care.'

In the lateral view the complex insectile shape of the fighter-bomber shifted away on a parallel course by a brief burst of its jets, and fell rapidly behind us. Then its main drive lit up and it shot past us again, on its own different, perilous, and necessarily one-way descent.

Suze and Yeng simultaneously said something, hard to make out as their voices strained against the weight on their chests.

'Say again please,' I said heavily.

'We're through,' groaned Suze, her voice making it sound as if she meant that we were finished. 'We're in contact with Mutual Protection. They seem to be taking us seriously. Got them on hold right now.'

'Put them on the main screen,' I said. 'Patch me through.'

A serious-looking young man's face appeared above me. 'Hi,' I said feebly. 'We're about to make a powered landing outside your town, and we want to assure you we're friendly and ask you to keep your missiles off our backs. We can fight them off anyway.' This was a bluff, but my face was probably so distorted that my expression was unreadable. 'But we'd rather land peacefully.'

'You the starship that calls itself *Terrible Beauty*?'

'Yes,' I said. Starship, I thought. That's better than calling us a UFO!

'Can you offer collateral?'

'Call what?'

'Excuse me,' said Suze, cutting in. 'We can offer at least one ton of gold as collateral against any damage.'

'Ah.' The young man frowned, trying too obviously not to look impressed. 'Is that imperial, or metric?'

Before this negotiation could go further we hit the upper layers of the atmosphere, and the picture went hazy and then black. The air of New Mars is thinner than Earth's – not that we were relying much on aerobraking. The outside view went red, and comms and active-defence could do very little. Nor could we. We just had to lie there and hope that the shrieking and buffetting were caused by our passage through the air and not nearby airbursts, each of which could be the last thing we knew. Malley seemed to be praying again, and I almost wished I could do the same, even with his agnostic reservations. But I'd been a good materialist in too many foxholes to relent now. All I would ask of a god is unconditional love and close air support, and I could rely on Boris for both.

The drogues jolted us three times, four, five – the thinner air meant more were needed than on Earth, even with the lesser gravity. There was a final flare of the jet which piled on the gees and helped deploy the struts, and then we were down. I could hear nothing but the creak of my chest and the pneumatic sigh of the settling struts.

'We're down in one piece,' said Andrea. 'No incoming missiles, and *Carbon Conscience* just checked in. They're spiralling down and report no ground fire.'

People attempted a cheer. Andrea lined up a comms laser on the relay at the wormhole and passed on the news of our safe landing.

Painfully, making full use of the suit's power-assistance, I moved to a sitting position and stood up.

'Everybody OK?'

They all struggled upright.

'Feel as if I've been in a fight,' said Tony. 'Where are we?'

'Forty miles outside Ship City,' said Andrea. 'In a field covered with some kind of monoculture.'

'It's something people do when they don't have hydroponics,' Malley said.

'A non-co thing, is it?' asked Yeng.

I was pleased to see her beginning to be sarcastic back.

A short while later we discovered that it was indeed a non-co thing, as I peered out of the airlock hatch to see a man standing in semi-darkness, just outside our circle of lights and the wider circle of ruination our landing had caused. He was holding what looked like a shotgun. The land around him was level in all directions, with low, lit mounds here and there which I guessed were dwellings of some kind. The stars seemed closer than they do in space, and, strangely, brighter.

'I don't know who or what you ay-are,' he shouted. 'But you pay-ay for this day-mage, or you git the hail off mah lay-and.'

'What payment do you want?' I yelled back, giddy with relief and quite prepared to offer the man a ton of gold, imperial or metric.

'Hey,' said Suze, from behind my shoulder. 'Let me handle this.'

The farmer, who introduced himself as Andrew Calvin Powell, turned out to be quite different from the non-cos I'd encountered in London. After a few minutes of narrow-eyed dickering ('What's that in grey-ams?') he seemed delighted by what Suze offered by way of compensation, and invited us all to 'Come on in and way-at fer the helicopters.'

'Military helicopters?' I asked, glancing anxiously back up the ladder.

The man laughed, white teeth flashing in his friendly, sunburned face. 'Good Lord no, may'am. Last I heard, Mutual Protection had taken you all under their wing. No, you're getting a visit from the city big shots, them as have been dragged out of urgent business meetings – and beds and bars! They won't be here for a good hour at least, while they get their act together. And your pals in the stealth bomber have lay-anded safely at the airport, where they're talking to reporters.'

I signalled for the rest to come down the ladder. There was little point in staying with the ship – it was more than capable of looking after itself, and so were we. Our suits could maintain encrypted radio contact with it – or with the fighter-bomber, when that was closer. In fact, we could do better than that, I thought, and tapped my cuff as though I had an itch under it. The tiny beaded eyes of nanocameras formed, barely noticeable, in the suit's fabric.

'How do you know all this?' I asked, as we gathered around Powell and set off across eight hundred yards of ploughed ground towards the glowing windows of his house, which was in the shape of a long, low mound. 'Was it on television before you came out?'

'Don't you hay-ave cortical downlinks?'

'Well, in a way,' I said carefully. 'We just don't use them for *news*.'

He gave me a sideways look. 'Same old Reds, eh? Controlled news and lousy consumer electronics. Way-ell, at least you're fray-endly, like the old New Viet Cong back home.'

'Hey,' said Tony, tramping along beside me through the muddy field, 'I remember them.'

'Wait a minute,' I said, before Tony could launch into political reminiscence, 'it isn't like that. We have problems with electronics, sure, but that's because of the fast folk. We have all the fancy tech we want, but we've just developed it in a different direction.'

'My old grandpaw told me the goddamn Russkies useta say that,' Powell said, with maddening slowness and imperturbability. 'And the only things it was true of was the Energia booster, the Mig fighter and the AK-47. The rest of their kit was cray-ap.'

Behind me I could hear Malley laughing.

'Oh, come on,' I said, 'how do you think we can see in the dark?' I waved a hand in the dimness.

'Not with gene-spliced visual intensifiers, I'll bet,' said Powell.

I blinked my contacts to a higher acuity and said nothing until we arrived at Powell's back door. He stood back on the doorstep and gestured for us to go inside. Just before I did so, I got the suit to repel all the mud from my boots, and to go through a spectacular transformation as I stepped dramatically over the threshold into the brightly lit room beyond.

I turned around with a twirl of skirt, noticing with a downward glance that at least some of the suit's cameras had cleverly turned themselves into visible beads. 'Do people here have clothes that can do that?'

Powell grinned. 'That's a very fine dress, may-am,' was all he said. He waited for us to step inside – the other women followed my example, each in her own fashion – and came in and racked his shotgun at the door, then led us through his house.

The first room we passed through was just a store: bare walls of concrete – much the same as sea-crete, except that the limestone component is fossil – with racks and shelves of tools and seeds and parked robots. Then Powell led us along a corridor, past closed wooden doors, into the main part of his house. Somewhere along the way the flooring changed to a deep carpet, which Powell stepped on to without even shaking the mud from his shoes. A few steps later his shoes were clean. I couldn't quite catch how it was happening. The carpet's pile shimmered slightly as he walked on it; that was all.

From outside, the house had looked quite large, an artificial grass-covered knoll, about thirty yards long by four high. Inside, it looked even bigger, because it turned out to be thirty yards square and partly underground. We came out of the corridor on to a balcony that ran all around a sunken atrium, whose roof was a layer of glass, behind which we could see torpid fish and the ripple-distorted, starry sky. The lighting was brighter in the lower level, which was furnished with what looked like leather-covered sofas and chairs and a few tables. A woman was sitting at one of the tables, and as we entered she stood up and smiled at us. We trooped after Powell down a stair that followed the curving wall to the floor, past a pool with tall plants growing up from it and fish swimming around.

All around the walls were screens, apparently blank; a few large, still pictures of people and Earth landscapes; and a great number of unfamiliar objects, most of them vaguely organic in appearance but probably artificial. They clung to the walls or squatted on shelves or hung from the ceiling. You never quite saw them move, but at a second glance they gave the disconcerting impression that they just had.

'Folks, meet my wife,' said Powell, turning around and looking at us all.

The woman who'd been sitting at the table stepped towards us, smiling. She was about five foot six tall with a sturdy, curvy build which her rather tight, gem-beaded red dress did little to conceal and much to enhance. Her blonde hair cascaded around her shoulders in elaborate curls and waves. Her face was covered with cosmetic make-up, quite unnecessarily: it was young and pretty underneath all the powder and colouring. She held out her hands and grasped mine between them.

'Well hi there,' she said. 'I'm real pleased and honoured to meet you. My name's Abigail, and you must be Miss Ellen May.'

'Just Ellen, neighbour Abigail,' I said. 'I'm pleased and honoured to meet you too.'

'Oh, how kind of you,' she said. Her accent was less noticeable than Andrew's, and in fact from that point on I stopped noticing his. The main thing I noticed about her voice was the warmth. As I introduced the rest of the crew she greeted all of them like long-lost friends. She had heard of Malley, and seemed awe-struck to meet him. By the time the introductions were over Andrew – or someone, or something – had covered the table with an inviting array of bottles and glasses. The couple insisted on sitting us all down on the biggest sofas and serving us drinks, than sat down facing us by the table and served themselves.

Andrew Powell raised his glass. 'Peace and freedom!'

We drank to that. I felt a bit bad about what we all might think of it, any day now; but we could always hope. There was a moment of awkward pause, not surprisingly: the etiquette of first contact between people from two long-separated human societies was in its early days.

'It was brave of you,' I said to Andrew, 'to go out to us with nothing but a shotgun. You didn't know who we might be, or how we might react.'

He waved his hand. 'Not real brave,' he said. He and his wife shared a smile. 'Abigail here had you covered from the house, with enough firepower to stop a regiment.'

'Ah,' I said, thoughtfully. 'But you'd have been in the line of fire, yes?'

He shrugged. 'Backed up just the other week. Some memories I'd be sorry to lose.' Another shared smile, a nudge and a giggle from Abigail. 'But anyway, I weren't that worried. Had you lot figured for a human expedition ever since the first reports this evening. Just gosh darn lucky you landed on my patch. I'll be showin' off that site for years, and prob'bly charging admission!'

Abigail must have misinterpreted our puzzled expressions. 'Oh, you see, we don't have no problem with resurrection. We both fell asleep way back in the twenty-first, and we were raised again only five years ago. Which is why –' she waved around, with a look of slight embarrassment '– we're still only moderately well-off, as you can see. I mean, we can't really afford to have children yet. But we have each other, and our little farm, and God has been kind to us.'

Her thick eyelashes emphasized a few quick blinks.

'Didn't have no truck with religion until I died,' said Andrew awkwardly. 'But that experience kind of concentrates one's mind on spiritual things, and when I found myself buck naked and dripping wet and looking up at a Red Cross chopper, I tell you I just got down on my knees and praised the Lord.'

'What you might call a born-again Christian,' said Malley. The rest of us didn't quite get why Andrew and Abigail laughed so much they had to clutch each other for support.

'You could say that,' Andrew gasped, knuckling his eyes. He took a deep breath and spoke more seriously. 'But apart from the, uh, relief and thankfulness and so on, when I had time to think about it I figured, well, if mere man can do that then you'd be a *damned* fool to think the Almighty couldn't raise all the dead in His own good time, and I knew that only Jesus could stand between me and His righteous indignation on that day.'

He grinned at our politely frozen faces. 'OK, that's me done my witnessing to you godless communists, and you'll hear no more gospel from me unless'n you ask for more, and I'll gladly give it. But the good book says not to cast your pearls before –'

'It sure does,' Abigail interrupted, with apparently unnecessary haste. 'Now let me get you all another drink.'

Our forty minutes or so of enjoying the hospitality of Andrew and Abigail did us all a great deal of good, though at the time it seemed only to give us a little relaxation and a sense of unreality arising from the sudden change from our dangerous descent to this scene of sumptuous comfort. As soon as they'd got past the 'witnessing', which they apparently regarded as something they had to do, however briefly, to any stranger, they chatted to us easily. Mainly about themselves, but even this was a courtesy, as though they didn't want us to feel we were being interrogated. We all knew that the time for that would shortly come.

They proudly called themselves 'dirt farmers'; vegetables grown in real soil were a luxury here, supplied to exclusive restaurants for sophisticates who claimed to be able to tell the difference from the carbon-copy, and who could afford the – considerably more evident – difference in price. (I had to give Yeng an unobtrusive nudge at this point.) Variety was their speciality – Andrew explained how much searching of the gene-banks he had to do to keep ahead of changing fads. Most of the work on the farm was done by what they called 'dumb machines', and not by what they called 'hired help'. (Another nudge to keep Yeng quiet.)

Their questions about the Solar System were carefully general. We answered with similar care. They expressed relief that Earth was well populated, respect at our assurance that it was prosperous, and only wry regret that it had all 'gone communist' (as they put it) since their demise.

'I don't think you'd find it anything like what you think of as communist,' Malley said. 'And I'm not part of their society, so maybe you can take my word for it.'

'I'm sure you folks like it just fine,' said Abigail soothingly. 'But for ourselves, we like it here.'

'Every man under his own vine and under his own fig tree, and no one to make him afraid,' added Andrew.

'Things must have changed a bit since Jonathan Wilde left,' I suggested.

'Since he *left*? Oh – I see what you mean.' Abigail shook her head. 'Now that I do call unnatural, having another copy running. Anyway, you're right, things sure have changed. You know, in the old days, before the Abolition, they didn't even give civil rights to robots who were as smart as any human being, if not a darn sight smarter!'

'They had androids and gynoids walkin' about, lookin' just like people,' said Andrew. 'God only knows if they have souls, but they sure do have minds of their own, and anybody could just own one like it was a brute beast!'

Before we could respond – our looks of surprise, perhaps even, in my case, of shock having been interpreted by Andrew as sharing his dim view of this unenlightened past state of affairs – there was a distant chime.

'That'll be the big shots' delegation now,' said Andrew. He

looked down at a panel on the table, which hadn't been grey and glowing last time I looked. 'Landing in a couple of minutes. Best get up to the patio.'

As we rose to our feet Abigail said: 'Just one thing . . . it was courteous of you ladies to turn on those pretty dresses for visiting us, but I think when you're going to be on television and all, you'd best *look* like you'd just stepped out of a spaceship, and not out of a cab on the way to a dance, if you don't mind my saying so.'

Oh, well, I thought, there'd be other chances to show off. But I felt a slight pang as my layered chiffon, Yeng's brocade cheongsam, Andrea's tiered lace and Suze's silver velvet sheath melted and flowed back into variants of high-gravity, on-duty gear.

Andrew grinned as the transformation was completed. 'There's already a group on the nets that says the whole thing's a fake got up by the defence companies to drum up business. Don't know if you looking like spacers will make them any less suspicious.'

Abigail approved of my blue denims and high boots. 'But you want to put some darker colour in that jacket, and maybe a mission patch or two . . .' So when we all marched up the stairs, around the balcony and out on to the patio, we each had a round blue patch with Earth's starry plough and a picture of the *Terrible Beauty* over our hearts.

The wide patio was also sunken, about six feet below ground level, open, and brightly lit. Over to the left, above the banking around it, was another flat illuminated space, on which a small helicopter was parked. Above it a much larger helicopter hovered, silent apart from the *whap* of the rotor-blades. It slowly descended close by the smaller one, beside which it looked like the adult of a strange species standing over its infant. I think it was something clever in the ground plan, and not any more advanced technology, that kept the downdraught blowing above our heads and not into our faces.

The helicopter's side door folded away, and a set of steps folded out. In the moment before anyone appeared, it occurred to me that I felt as if we, and not they, were waiting to meet the aliens.

A man stepped down the ladder, with a slow dignity which was only partly due to the care which he had to take with the high heels of his tall boots. His medium height and slim build were further extended by a stovepipe hat and an open frock coat, both black, and a colourful waistcoat over a white shirt with a black bootlace tie. A holstered pistol completed the look: the law west of Pecos, to the life. He walked over to the rim of the patio, looked to left and right, found the steps and made his way down.

Close behind him followed another man and two women, with a whole crowd of other people behind them. I just had time to recognise the second man – it was David Reid, who'd supplied the Outwarders with bonded labour, including some of ours. Our old enemy –

And then the man in the tall hat was shaking my hand.

'Hello,' he said. 'My name's Eon Talgarth. I'm pleased to welcome you to Ship City, of which' – his smile twisted a little – 'I'm the somewhat reluctant Chief Justice. And you must be Ellen May Ngwethu, acting captain of this expedition?'

'That's right,' I said. 'Pleased to meet you, neighbour.' His voice and accent reminded me, oddly, of the London non-cos; he'd stabilized his age at about forty, but he was much older than that, possibly older than I was – an eerie thought, which impressed me more than his ridiculous judicial fig.

'Yeah, I reckon we're all neighbours now,' he said. He turned as if to introduce these new neighbours, but any opportunity for formal introductions had been lost: everybody on one side was indiscriminately shaking hands with everybody they could find on the other and introducing themselves or introducing somebody else. Talgarth looked momentarily at a loss, even taken aback, before he shrugged and relaxed. Reid, I noticed, was working the little crowd expertly – probably avoiding me, for the moment, and trying to make a friendly impression on my comrades. Abigail and Andrew, on a sudden inspiration, began handing out drinks, and shortly we were all behaving as if we'd just arrived at a slightly formal party.

'Comrade?' someone said in a friendly, but slightly diffident, voice. I turned, smiling at this unexpected greeting.

The girl in front of me had long fair hair that sprouted straight up from her scalp and then fell back in a mane between her shoulder blades. She wore a belted jump suit which showed off her muscular but definitely female frame. Almost as tall as me; big blue eyes, wide grin, thin, sharp nose; striking rather than beautiful, but I was inured to beauty.

'Ellen? Hi.' She stuck out her hand and I shook it. 'My name's Tamara Hunter,' she went on. 'Very pleased to meet you.'

'Likewise,' I said politely. 'What's your –'

'– part in all this?' She scratched her head. 'I put up a bit of a fight to get on this delegation. Just so the business folk and the judges didn't have it all to themselves. I'm a union official, actually, in the inter-syndical.'

'You negotiate terms for the wage slaves?'

'Exactly!' she said, looking pleased. 'A dirty job, but someone's got to do it.'

'We have these too,' I said, wryly.

Tamara looked around, as if concerned that she might be overheard.

'Is it really true,' she asked, leaning closer, 'that in the Solar System you have anarcho-communism?'

I thought over this unfamiliar word. 'We don't have to sell ourselves, and nobody tells us what to do, so I suppose you could call it that.'

'Wow!' she said, her eyes shining. 'Just knowing that is *possible*, that it can *work*, will make a huge difference here.'

'I don't know about that,' I said, mentally comparing what Abigail and Andrew considered modest prosperity with the conditions that had brought about Earth's social revolution. 'It's not just a question of ideas in people's heads –'

'Stop plotting there, Hunter!' a man's loud voice said. 'Time enough for that later.'

The man who spoke came up and firmly grasped my hand. He had black hair down to the collar of his sharply cut cotton jacket; dark brown eyes, thick black eyebrows, smoothly tanned skin; and the look of ease and unshakeable self-confidence which in our society marked out the 'old comrades', and in this one, I guessed (correctly, as it turned out), the rich.

But there was more than that. He was terrifyingly old, among the oldest people alive, and unlike even his contemporary Wilde, he'd lived as the same body, the same man, for over three hundred and fifty years. Again unlike Wilde, he had both the desire and the capacity for power, and had grown strong and proficient in its use.

'Hi, Ellen May,' he said. 'My name's Dave Reid. I'm happy to meet you, at last. You know, I heard about you back in the old days, from, well –' he laughed '– the Outwarders, I have to say!'

'Your former clients send their regards,' I said, rather more coldly than I had intended, 'and their assurance of no hard feelings about your . . . departure.'

'Do they, indeed?' He seemed surprised and pleased. 'Well, as I say, later for that. This is a great occasion.'

I sipped my drink. 'So everyone keeps telling me.'

He grinned, unperturbed. 'It is a bit of a mêlée, isn't it? I don't think anyone ever worked out the protocols for contact between socialist and capitalist anarchies. Your comrades in the *Carbon Conscience* have been telling reporters all about your society. Fascinating stuff.'

'I'm sure it is,' I said, wishing I'd briefed Boris and Jaime on what and what not to say.

'Used to be a socialist myself, you know,' Reid went on. 'Gave it up as a bad job.' He grinned at Tamara. 'Maybe I should have stuck with it.'

Then he looked at me, and through me, his face momentarily bleak. With a shake of his head he smiled again.

' "Battles long ago",' he said. 'Speaking of which, Ellen, Dee has something to tell you –'

A woman was stepping delicately towards us on stiletto heels. She wore a short dress of black lace over a longer one of white crepe, all wow and flutter. She had black hair, pale skin, green eyes, broad cheekbones and a warm smile.

'Hi, Ellen,' she said. 'I'm Dee. Pleased to meet you.'

'Hello,' I said, trying to keep the ice from my voice.

'I'm Dave's partner,' she went on. 'I used to be his, ah –'

His mechanical squeeze. A clone with a computer in its skull. Just a fucking machine.

'I know,' I said. 'Wilde told us about you.'

The gynoid woman shook my hand; I felt, or perhaps imagined, an electric tingle in her touch. She smiled up at me with disconcertingly wide, bright eyes and parted lips.

'So he made it back,' she said quietly. 'And Meg too?'

Meg – Wilde's companion, the artificial woman. Another walking doll, another fucking machine.

'Yes,' I said. 'They both made it.'

'Ellen,' Dee said. She caught my hands. 'My mind works ... differently from yours. I have access to all the old company records, and to the city's nets. I have something to tell you. Many of the people here, as you know, were revived from the fast folk's robotized workforce. Your parents were ... not among them.'

'They were never among them?' I asked. 'It's not just that they didn't make it in the ship?'

'We all made it in the ship,' Reid said. 'I made damn' sure of that. I didn't leave behind anyone, human or ex-human, alive or dead, who'd been conscripted or volunteered to my company.'

I looked down at him and unclenched my teeth and nails. 'I'm relieved to hear that,' I said. 'I truly am. I am happy to know that my two hundred years of nightmares about them being enslaved in robot bodies were only bad dreams, even if it does mean I'll never see even their copies again.' I stopped and took a deep breath through my nostrils. 'I can live with that, Reid, but I can't forget who killed them.'

Reid shook his head firmly. 'It wasn't me, or my company, who carried out those raids,' he said. 'It was all the doing of the Outwarders. I just saved what could be saved, and gave people a chance of a new life. For which I've received no complaints.'

'Very well,' I said. I grasped his shoulder and smiled at him, in a way that made a very satisfying shadow of fear show briefly on his face. 'Now I know who I'm looking for, and I'll take your word that it isn't you.'

Reid took a step backwards as I let go of his shoulder. His jacket was creased there, and damp. I automatically wiped my hand on my thigh. The two women looked at me with expressions of indistinguishable compassion. Eon Talgarth, the judge, perhaps drawn to the edge of our little group by the intensity of our conversation, broke an uneasy silence.

'If it's justice you want, Ellen, if that's among your reasons for coming all this way, you can find it here.'

I shook my head. 'I'm sorry,' I said. I lowered my voice. 'This is a great occasion, a happy occasion, and I don't want to spoil it.' I indicated the more cheerful fraternization going on around us, hoping that the comrades didn't take it too far. 'But you should know something about us, about me. I don't seek justice. We don't believe in justice. We have the true knowledge. There is no justice.

But there is defence, and deterrence, and revenge. That's what I want. And I will have them all.'

Reid, to my surprise, smiled and stepped forward again. Though shorter than I, he held my gaze as though it was he who was looking down.

'I know what you mean,' he said. 'I've been there. If you want to take your revenge on the fast folk, be my guest!' He waved his arm expansively. 'I can fly you at a moment's notice to the place where we store their templates. You can revive them, tell them exactly what you're going to do to them and why, and make them die a thousand deaths before we flood the tanks with Blue Goo. And then, if you want, you can do it again. And again. And –'

'Stop.' I caught his arm. 'Enough.'

The vast futility of my deepest and darkest, though not my most secret, motives for coming here made me feel cold and sick and dizzy. My hope against hope of meeting copies of my dead parents had been one, and I was racked by its simultaneous disappointment and relief. My desire for revenge on the entities who were incontestably the closest to the original Outwarders had just been exposed by Reid as equally, achingly empty. There would be no point in tormenting, no satisfaction in punishing, entities with which I didn't even have enough empathy to take pleasure in their pain, if pain it was. It would be as futile as stamping on a recalcitrant machine.

There could only be one deterrence, one defence, one vengeance for me, and that was to send them to the same oblivion as they'd sent my parents and so many others: an eternal death without hope of resurrection. Nothing I said or did now could be allowed to imperil that.

I smiled at Reid. 'You're right, of course,' I said. 'It's just one of those fantasies, isn't it? When you spell it out, when you have the chance to act it out, you see how tawdry and childish it really is.'

'Well, it's understandable,' he said. 'I know how you must feel.' He clasped my forearm. 'Come on. We'll have reporters buzzing about in a few minutes, and you'll have to talk to them. When you've got that out of the way, you can all come and see the city.'

'Yes,' I said. 'I'm looking forward to that.' My knees were shaking. Reid noticed, and guided me to a seat beside a patio table. He twitched his eyebrows at Talgarth and the two women, and they slipped back amongst everybody else, standing and talking. Reid sat down beside me and uncapped a silver hip flask and passed it to me. I sipped something fiery, and passed it back.

'It's not the same,' Reid admitted regretfully. 'I really hope you still know how to make single malt.'

I had to smile. The man had, despite his reputation for ruthlessness, a disarming ability to put one at one's ease.

'You'll have to ask the people in Japan about that,' I told him.

'Oh, God,' he said. He took another sip. 'And you really do have a world without money? What do you use instead – computers?'

'Yes,' I said proudly. 'We don't do much planning, but for what we do, we use computers. The biggest in the world.'

Reid's head rocked back, his laugh bayed at the sky, and he didn't see my bleak moment of remembering just why our most important computers were built of brass and steel and looked like the very locomotives of history, incorruptible analytical engines that nothing could divert or deflect.

The year is 2098. Below me a city drifts past, its old towers of concrete and glass overshadowed by recent nano-built spires and surrounded by the shantytown sprawl that predates, and will outlast, the buildings which have grown above it like fungi on a damp, dark soil. Beyond even the shanties, the vivid green of the forest with its grey-brown scars of road; higher even than the towers, and rising still, and multiplying, the columns of oily smoke.

The smoke is rising from crashes. Here a tower is burning, upward from the twentieth floor where a helicopter is spattered on the side of the building like an insect on a windshield; there traffic is gridlocked by numberless collisions; elsewhere an airliner has fallen out of the sky, and set ablaze acres of wooden shacks.

I float in the station's telemetry deck, and the unmanned cargo airship floats above Lagos, its scanning cameras showing me scenes I can do nothing whatsoever about. This was a successful city, until half a day ago. The West Africans, decimated again and again by the plagues of the twentieth century, are almost immune to the last great plague of the twenty-first. They have survived the Death, and have even accommodated the floods of European refugees which fill the shantytowns and swirl about the towers. They still have oil, they still have computer networks. Here civilization is still rising, not falling.

Until now.

The computers are crashing, and with them everything that depends on them: traffic control, air traffic control, *aircraft* controls, industrial processes, stock control, telecommunications, and electricity supply. With predictable prisoner's-dilemma rationality, people are looting food from the suddenly dark and warming refrigerators before it spoils, raiding the shops before they're stripped, arming themselves before they're robbed, taking to the roads and heading for the villages before anybody else gets the same idea, and each discovering that everyone else is doing the same.

We're in a bad way ourselves, running everything on manual or back-up or emergency. Our computer programs have been reduced to gibberish, the viruses have shorted systems, wiped memory cores, crippled machinery . . . but our basic systems are robust, they've been jerry-built and jury-rigged and worked around so often that nothing short of physical force can disable them. We still have air and food.

The people down below are in a worse circumstance. They're paradoxically far more reliant on a network of artificial organization than we are. Lagos's biggest export is financial services, pulling in even more than its dwindling oil. All that is gone now.

The people I helplessly watch struggling in the streets are worse off even than they know. There's no help coming from anywhere, because everywhere is in the same plight. With an eerie, awful certainty, I know that a very high percentage of those people are already dead, as dead as if they were walking around – as, elsewhere, in other cities, not a few at this moment are – in the elliptical downwind teardrop zones of fallout from burning reactors.

The airship crumples into the side of a nano tower, and the picture dies.

The door of the helicopter opened again and reporters swarmed out and began hovering and buzzing about, just as Reid had said. I'd thought he'd spoken figuratively, but he hadn't. The 'reporters' were tiny helicopters, carrying microphones and cameras and loudspeakers; some of them had the ability to project a hologram of a human figure which lip-synched along with the questions from the speaker.

'They'll look quite solid when you've tuned your contacts,' Reid assured me.

'I'm not sure I want them to,' I said.

I gathered the team again into a group and we all faced the cameras and mikes together. Boris and Jaime, I guessed, must have satiated the requests for basic information about us: most of the questions I was asked (and it was I who was asked, the local media having appointed me the spokesman of the expedition) felt like the reporters here were just mopping up.

'You seemed surprised at the sight of us, Miss Ngwethu,' said a spectral youth a few feet away. 'Don't you have fetches and 'motes back in the Solar System?'

'Of course we do,' I said. 'But as I'm sure you've heard, we have problems with our electronic communications, thanks to our local versions of the fast folk. In any case, even if we didn't, I doubt if we'd use them for … what do you call it, news gathering? We do make limited use of them, for exploring or monitoring dangerous environments and so on.'

'So what do you use for news gathering? Do reporters have to go around in person?'

'We don't actually *have* reporters, as such,' I said. 'I mean, some people run newsletters and pump newsfeed pipes, but nobody has to pay them much attention.'

'So how –' The reporter paused, baffled. 'How does anyone know what's going on?'

'Oh! That. Well, everybody in the Union can report anything to anybody, and attend or listen in to any meeting of the social administration and say anything they like about it. Or at it, come to that, unless they start wasting everybody's time and get thrown out.'

'So your Central Committee, this Solar Council, could have hundreds of thousands of people turning up at its meetings, and all shouting at once?'

'Of course not,' I said indignantly. 'I suppose in theory, yes, but who would want to? Apart from the Solar Council delegates, that is, and some of them practically have to be pushed. It's all very practical, and frankly a bit *dull*. Local meetings are far more interesting because they have more to do.'

'Does that apply to your organization, the Cassini Division?' asked the hologram.

I thought about this. 'No,' I said.

'Why not?'

'Fighting is different. Sometimes we need to keep secrets, but not for long.'

The reporter hesitated for a second, and another seized the opportunity. She had straight blonde hair and looked about twelve years old. 'Why have you come here?' she asked.

I gave her my best smile. 'We're very interested in finding out what has happened to the only other human community, and in establishing friendly relations with you. And of course we have a scientific interest in the wormhole – the Malley Mile.'

She gave me her best 'I wasn't born yesterday' look; rather funny, considering her age and mine. 'Apart from that.'

'Isn't that enough? Why else would we want to come here?'

'To impose your system on us, perhaps?'

This idea had genuinely not occurred to me. Our intention of wiping out the local fast folk, or destroying what Reid had called the templates, was secret and sinister enough for me to worry about anyone's guessing it. But not this. I just laughed.

'You seem to be doing fine as you are,' I said diplomatically. 'And you can't have socialism unless most people understand it and want it and are willing to do something to get it. From what I know of New Mars, this is not the case – yet.'

This raised an appreciative laugh all round, and Talgarth stepped forward with his hand raised. 'Ladies and gentlemen,' he said to the phantom figures and their rotary haloes, 'I'm sure our visitors will have a great deal to tell you all very soon. Meanwhile, I'd like to give them some hospitality and privacy.'

We'd been having plenty of both until Talgarth and the other leading citizens and their accompanying swarm of inquisitive remotes turned up, but I was not complaining. We said goodbye to Abigail and Andrew, and were escorted to the big helicopter. I found myself in a window seat beside Tamara. As the machine lifted off I waved to Powell and his wife, who waved back. The last thing I saw of them before we turned out of sight was Andrew Powell setting off across his field with a swarm of remotes beside him, heading for the ship. I knew he would have the sense not to go too close to it, but I rather suspected that this was not true of the remotes.

I leaned back with a smile, already enjoying the flight.

Tamara and I got chatting about life on New Mars and on Earth, laughing at each other's misconceptions, and about our pasts. I was gratified and embarrassed by Tamara's awe about mine, and encouraged her to talk about her own.

She said she'd been an Abolitionist.

'What's that?'

Abigail and Dee had mentioned the Abolition, but I hadn't yet followed up what this meant.

'We used to be a small group of anarchists – some social, some more into the lifestyle thing – who believed that using conscious machines as tools was wrong, you know, like slavery. But five years ago, all that changed.'

'You don't believe it any more?'

Tamara looked at me, visibly decided I was joking, and laughed more at the oddity of my supposed humour than at its content. 'No, we changed people's minds! It all came out of a complicated string of court cases involving Wilde, the copy of Wilde in the machine, Dave Reid's ownership of Dee, and of course the fast folk. After that a lot of owned sapients took to claiming self-ownership, and some people sided with them, and the new people from the dead couldn't see how anybody could treat robots like that – they didn't have the prejudices that the first humans here had.'

'Yes,' I said, 'Wilde told us about that. He said things were getting pretty hot just as he left.'

'They sure were! Closest we've ever come to a revolution, everybody outside in the streets arguing.'

'What happened about the fast folk?' I asked lightly.

Tamara's expression darkened. 'Well, after Reid and Wilde used them to start the resurrection – it's still going on, we're bringing back dead people from the smart-matter storage all the time, about a million over the past five years, which is why the city's grown so much and all the new settlements are springing up – they wiped out the copies of the fast folk they'd revived, and Reid's still sitting on the stored originals. Still scared of another bad Singularity.' She paused thoughtfully. 'But now that your Jovians have started acting reasonable and aren't going mad or anything, maybe that'll change too.'

'I'm sure it will,' I said, 'Reid won't be worrying about a bad Singularity for much longer, not if I have anything to do with it.'

Tamara's pleased look in response to this true but ambiguous statement shamed me a little. I turned to the window and looked down at the city below and before us, three of its five arms foreshortened, their long streets with their radial canals joined by the ring canal, a glowing starfish in the night.

9

A Modern Utopia

AIRPORTS ARE quiet places, where people make their leisurely way along covered walkways to the waiting craft. Around the sides of the concourse are tables with drinks and snacks, open-sided rooms with stores of the kind of supplies you might need and are likely to forget, racks and shelves where you can browse and, if you like, take away a book or journal or disk. There's a knack, a *politesse*, of picking just enough entertainment for you to have finished at the end of your journey, or at the end of one of its stages, so that you can casually place it on another airport's shelves. At some airports there'll be a group of musicians or a troupe of acrobats or whatever. You can stay within sight and sound of them, or move away. The only barriers you'll encounter are to keep you from wandering into danger. Sometimes you'll help other people with their luggage, sometimes you'll ask for a hand. If you have a long wait for your flight, you might feel like joining in some of the support activities, making sure that more hurried passengers get their refreshments or books or help with heavy luggage or small children. That's what airports are like.

Not in capitalism, they're not. When I emerged at the end of a long corridor from the busy landing field into the main concourse of Ship City's aerospace port, with my comrades beside me and the leading citizens behind them, I was greeted by hundreds of enthusiastic people behind a barrier, a swooping flock of reporters, a dazzle of clashing colours and a blare of sound. Every square yard that wasn't absolutely required for passengers or people waiting for them was occupied by a stall or shop or kiosk, each of which had its own fluorescent rectangle above it advertising flights or drugs or socks or cosmetics or lingerie or insurance or back-ups or cabs or hotels. The public-address system thumped out urgent-sounding music made all the more unsettling by frequent, and equally urgent-sounding, interruptions.

Meanwhile, other activity, apparently unrelated to our arrival, was going on. The wide passage between us and the welcoming crowd was being traversed from right to left by a succession of small automatic vehicles slowly hauling laden trailers, and of briskly striding men and women and – this was my first such encounter – what looked like ape-men of various species. Among them robots, few of which were remotely humanoid, stalked or skittered. Outside the terminal building, at the far end of the landing field, the distant sounds and flares of heavy lifting shook the air and lit the night. None of the humans or hominids or robots hurrying past in front of us spared us more than a curious, if friendly, glance.

I hesitated, unsure about how to get across this stream of light but persistent and swift traffic. Talgarth walked past me and strode out into the midst of it and, facing the oncoming flow, held up his hand. This imperious gesture enabled us to get across to just in front of the barriers. Yells and smiles greeted us, hands reached out to touch us; recorders and babies were held above heads. Talgarth led us past them all, along the barriers and around a corner into a quieter area, from which even the tiny news-copters were turned back. There were padded benches along the walls. Jaime and Boris were sitting there, looking somewhat drained, but talking earnestly to two young women in identical sky-blue jackets and matching skirts. When they saw us approaching they said their goodbyes to the women (who immediately stood up and assumed strange fixed smiles) and rejoined us.

Andrea hugged Jaime and I hugged Boris and everybody milled about for a few minutes, until Talgarth herded us all together again like a supervisor on a children's outing and led us between a pair of big glass sliding doors to the edge of a flat expanse of tarmac, where a lot of vehicles were parked, one of which awaited us.

It was about twenty-five feet long and eight feet high, with large windows at the side and a low-slung chassis. A man in a grey uniform, wearing a grey peaked cap, stood outside its open door and gave us another example of that oddly impersonal smile. Talgarth stepped aside and motioned to us to enter the vehicle. Inside there were rows of seats covered with something like leather, a fitted carpet on the floor, and a smell of fresh plastic in the air. I made my way to the rear seat and sat down beside Boris. Talgarth sat in the seat in front of us, and the rest of the crew filled up the adjacent seats. Reid, Dee and Tamara all got on too. The others who'd been with them stayed behind, waving at us from the kerb, looking simultaneously self-important and left out.

As the driver closed the door and got behind the steering wheel I said to Talgarth, 'It's neighbourly of you to lay this on for us.'

'The mini-coach?' He smiled. 'They're standard airport-to-city transport.'

'Well, thanks anyway,' I said. 'Where are we going?'

'Reid's booked a hotel floor for you, in the same building as his offices,' Talgarth explained. 'We'll go to his offices first, if that's agreeable, because we'd like a chat with you all privately before we arrange any other social functions.'

'Fine,' I said. 'We have a lot to discuss.'

The airport was between the proximal ends of two of the city's arms. Behind it lay miles of open flat ground, some of it apparently water-covered: as I glanced back through the big curved and rounded rear window, pools flashed back reflections of the jet of a rising rocket. As it faded, another flared. There was a *lot* of heavy lifting going on. Ahead, along a couple of miles of wide, open road, rose the centre of the city. The buildings in the two converging arms on either side of us became higher the closer they were to the centre, which was dominated by a cluster of tall, slender towers. They were not as tall as the towers of Earth, or the trees of the Lunar crater-domes, but they were more graceful than either, lifting the gaze and catching the breath. Their lower reaches were linked by spiral or otherwise curving ramps, giving the whole complex an appearance like the fine metalwork of a decorative headdress. Among them were other buildings, rounded, polyhedral; and tall glass rectangles like those I'd – only a fortnight ago – watched *Terrible Beauty* land beside.

All the buildings blazed with lights, from windows and flood-lamps and displays. We stared ahead, entranced.

'It's beautiful,' Suze said. Reid, sitting in front of her, turned around and said over his shoulder:

'It is, and it's also a little joke on us. The more delicate towers and the elegant geodesic domes were designed by the fast folk, based on old illustrations of futuristic cities – just to say to us, "look, we can do this better."'

'They did, too,' said Malley. His chuckle resounded above the electric hum of the bus. 'I remember those old skiffy covers myself. Bloody spiral ramps – nobody ever got them looking right, but whoever built this did.'

The driver, I noticed, wasn't doing very much, and most of the other vehicles on the road seemed to be driverless. The driver was a formality, a gesture towards the notion of some people serving others, being at their beck and call; another of those capitalist things, like the air stewardesses that Boris had been talking to, and was now telling me about … I listened sceptically: he seemed unduly impressed by their wage-slavish solicitude.

'But are they any more friendly and helpful than neighbours helping out with refreshments on a transport?' I asked, my mind going back to how I and Suze had met.

Boris shrugged. 'Maybe not,' he said grudgingly. 'But they do it all the time, and they do it to get what they need to live on, and that makes it all more … intense.'

'Ha!' I caught his arm and snuggled up beside him. 'That's *kinky*, that is,' I murmured in his ear. 'You're just an old Sheenisov state-capitalist at heart. Bet you've been secretly into employer-and-employee sex-games for years.'

'I have *not*,' he growled indignantly, then turned and touched the side of my nose with the tip of his and grinned. 'Couldn't never get anyone to play, anyway, but if that's what *you* want –'

'Go employ yourself,' I told him, very quietly. No one even in the adjacent seats could have overheard my crudity. But Dee must have had – perhaps not surprisingly – superhuman hearing, because she turned around and looked back at us from the front of the bus with a friendly and wicked smile, as though she knew exactly what we were talking about. I felt my cheeks burn a little, and I looked away.

The mini-coach was now gliding along a street, between tall buildings. At the bases of the tall buildings the pavements were quite wide, and quite crowded, even at this late hour in the evening. The traffic was denser here, and slower-moving, and as we passed, people (and the startling, ubiquitous quasi-people, the enhanced apes and re-engineered hominids and the autonomous machines) on the street would turn and stare for a moment, and look around them and smile.

'How do they know we're in this bus?' I asked.

Dave Reid, up at the front, snorted. He gestured at a flat grey screen behind the driver's seat. 'It's because we're – ah, sorry –' It seemed that all he did was to snap his fingers, irritably, and the screen suddenly showed a picture of our coach, from above and behind. I looked back through the rear window, and spotted the pursuing remotes. The others on the bus laughed. 'Don't encourage them,' Talgarth said, as I faced the screen again and saw the back of my head in a zoomed-in shot which then zoomed disappointedly out.

The news-copters were still hovering above us when we stopped at the foot of a tower like a great concrete treetrunk, with tall windows distributed apparently at random, close to the centre of the city. Talgarth and Reid preceded us out of the coach, gesturing at the remotes as if waving away flies. As I got off I thanked the driver and said goodbye to him, making eye contact for the first time. He smiled with a slightly startled look, and smiled a bit more when Dee paused on her way out and slipped him a tip.

Inside, the building was furnished in fake leather and real wood and the inevitable potted plants and indoor ivy, with some of the walls left as bare concrete. The vast, deep-carpeted reception area had the polite hush of posh. The lift, which had a grey-uniformed attendant to push the buttons, was big enough to take us all, comfortably. It was also fast, its acceleration almost enough to make my knees buckle.

Reid escorted us to a room along the corridor from the lift. It was a large anteroom to a small office, whose heavy wooden desk and deep-set window were visible through its open doorway. An oblong arrangement of deep fake-leather armchairs and sofas, around a long, low wooden table with glass ashtrays; subdued ambient light; black-cylindered spotlights picking out wall pictures, plants, and the drinks cabinet.

'Sit yourselves down,' Reid said. He took off his jacket and slung it over the back of a seat at the top of the table, marking his own territory, then busied himself at the drinks cabinet. Talgarth hung up his hat and coat, pushed back his shirtsleeves and sat down, unbuttoning his waistcoat. Dee and Tamara waited for us to take our seats, and then sat down together.

The chair I found myself in, with Boris on my right and Malley on my left, faced one of the large, well-lit framed photographs on the wall. Most of them showed Reid posing with new weapons systems or talking to what I guessed were capitalists and their hired men. The one opposite me showed Reid and Dee standing together on a wide step outside a vast arched doorway with a crowd of people around them.

The man standing beside Reid looked just like Jonathan Wilde, and the woman standing beside Dee looked just like Dee: same height, same build, same face. I realised with a start that I was looking at Dee's original, and Wilde's copy, the one who had stayed here. The two men wore black coats and trousers and colourful ties, and the woman standing beside Dee was wearing a long, narrow green dress of understated elegance.

Dee was wearing a smug smile and a very fancy white satin dress with fitted bodice, gigot sleeves and a full floor-length skirt, all decorated with beadwork, cutwork, panelling, stitching, lace trimming and organza fluting: not one expensive cheap trick of exuberant, eye-filling excess had been missed. On her head she wore a silver tiara from which a waterfall of embroidered tulle cascaded down her back and across the wide, ruffled pool of the skirt's train. The whole saccharine confection seemed to be the costume for some carnival where considerations of visual impact overrode those of taste; I nudged the suit to record it, for the next time I wanted to make a big entrance at one of our wilder parties.

Reid placed some trays of glasses on the table, then bottles of spirits, beer, tonic water, plain water, and cola. 'Help yourselves,' he said, and while we were doing so he sat down in the seat at the top of the table with a bottle of beer in front of him. When we were all sorted for drinks he leaned back in his chair and ran his fingers through his long, thick black hair several times, in a rather distracted way, then lit a cigarette. He let out a long, smoky sigh.

'Well,' he said. 'Nothing like a bit of peace and quiet. This room is about as secure as you can get, and it's also inside a Faraday cage. Chicken wire in the concrete, I understand; quite effective.' He glanced at what looked like a wristwatch, and then at me. 'So, Ellen, I'm afraid your encrypted television signal won't get beyond the walls.' He grinned. 'Just letting you know; it's not a problem. Feel free to record anything and report back to your committee or whatever – I'll give you comms facilities and complete privacy, afterwards, if you want.'

I nodded. 'Fine.'

'Good,' Reid said. He looked around at us all. 'So let's get down to business. If you want to do deals with people here, it would pay you to deal with us first. Talgarth owns a court, which at the moment is accepted by the other courts as . . . a final court, particularly for human-machine interface problems. Dee and I run the biggest protection agency, which funnily enough is the one which has taken your contract. Tamara has the ear of a significant part of the city's population, not to mention a capacity to call a general strike at a moment's notice.'

Tamara smiled and spread her hands. 'Not really.'

'You're too modest,' said Reid. 'We're not in charge here, we certainly don't see eye to eye, and I'm much less of a city boss than I was before all the formerly dead people started arriving.' He smiled wryly. 'But any of us could make or break your chances of getting on well with the people and machines of this city – I'm not saying that as a threat, just a fact. I presume you have some similar status back where you come from, and aren't' – his eyes crinkled – 'just a bunch of rank-and-file cosmonauts.'

'We are, in a way,' I said. 'We have no special status, but we do have a mandate to negotiate and take whatever action we think is necessary.'

'On behalf of thirty billion people?' asked Reid, looking at me through narrowed eyelids and a haze of smoke. Somewhere an extraction fan started up.

I shrugged. 'More or less, in that we'll have to answer to them, and they voted for the broad outlines of what we're here to do.'

'And what's that?' Reid asked, with deliberate casualness.

I took a sip of whisky and water. The taste for it could be acquired, I decided. Malley was fiddling with his pipe, Suze examining her fingernails.

'We're here,' I said carefully, 'to make certain that the fast folk on your side of the wormhole are no threat to us, just as we can ensure that those at our end are no threat to you.'

Reid and Talgarth leaned forward at the same time, with the same alert, cautious expression.

'What do you mean by that?' asked Talgarth.

'Wilde –' I shook my head. 'The other one, the one you call Jay-Dub. He told us that the whole question of "robot rights" was bound up with that of reviving the fast folk, and that when he left, the robot rights side of the argument seemed to be winning. Naturally, we were concerned. I have to say I was relieved to hear from Tamara that you are still resisting any suggestion of reviving them. Can you guarantee that the question will remain closed?'

'What guarantees would you accept?' Reid asked.

Nothing short of their destruction, I thought. 'What can you offer?' I asked. Reid knew well that I hadn't answered his question, but he didn't press me on it. He leaned forward, elbow on knee, fingers with cigarette at his lips. 'How about my – our – continuing conviction that it would be unsafe to tamper with them again?'

'You've tampered with them once,' I said. 'And the results, as far as you're concerned, have been entirely beneficial – you've been reunited with people you'd lost, you've gained a population that seems to have materially increased your city's prosperity, you got . . . Jay-Dub through the wormhole, and so on. Now, I don't remember much about capitalism, but some of us do, and I think it's safe to say that at some point the temptation to let the genie out of the bottle again, get a few more useful answers to intractable problems, and thus give your company some competitive edge, could be hard to resist.'

Reid leaned back and looked straight at me. 'That's an entirely valid point,' he surprised me by saying, then didn't surprise me at all by going on, '*however* . . . I think you can rely on my not doing it until it's safe.' He looked over at Talgarth. 'What was it I offered – to let anyone do it who could provide an isolated space platform ringed with fire-walled lasers and dead-fall nuclear back-ups?'

Talgarth smiled and nodded.

'Hey –' said Boris, with that look shown in cartoons by a light bulb going on and blocky capitals spelling *IDEA*.

'*Nevertheless*,' I interrupted firmly, 'you then did it, with, what? *Blue Goo* instead of heavy weaponry, and you got away with it. What's to stop you doing that again?'

'The rights of the fast folk,' Reid said, quite seriously.

'*What* "rights"?' I asked. If we'd been discussing a bacterial culture, I couldn't have been more surprised.

'Oh, you know.' Reid waved his hands about. 'The usual. Life, liberty, and the happiness of pursuit.'

I sat back and laughed. 'But seriously,' I said. 'What's to stop you?'

Reid crushed out his cigarette and glared at me.

'I *am* serious. It would be wrong to do again what we did five years ago. It was wrong at the time, but' – he grimaced – 'we didn't know any better. It would be all right to revive the fast folk and be ready to defend ourselves against them – that's the lasers-and-nukes scenario – but not to revive them and then wipe them out as soon as we'd got from them what we wanted. So you needn't worry about us doing that.'

Talgarth nodded agreement. I frowned, trying to figure this out. Dee and Tamara were watching me even more narrowly than the men were.

'You offered to do it for me,' I said. 'For my revenge.'

Reid gave me a cold smile. 'An offer I knew you would refuse. You're an intelligent woman.'

I wondered how he'd have reacted if I'd accepted, but thought it best to drop that uncomfortable question and return to the main point.

'You're telling us we can't trust you not to revive them, but we can trust you not to wipe them out if you do?'

'That's about it,' Reid agreed cheerfully. 'But, as I say, we wouldn't revive them without adequate defence, and there's not much chance of that in the foreseeable future.'

I could foresee quite a few futures in which Reid's idea of 'adequate defence' might differ from mine, and where in any case he'd have a strong motivation to deceive himself about how much defence he'd need. But I let that pass, for now, and tried to work around it.

'According to Wilde,' I said slowly, 'you used to think very differently. You used to think that the fast folk, in fact all AIs and uploads, were flatlines – not really conscious. And now, you're saying our whole safety depends on your continuing to believe the opposite. What changed your mind?'

Reid gave us all a big, stupid, happy smile. 'Dee,' he said.

I shook my head and glanced around at the comrades, then at Dee, who was fixing a steady gaze on me. I had the uncomfortable feeling that she knew what I was thinking.

'I don't quite understand,' I said, lying diplomatically.

'That's quite understandable,' said Reid dryly. 'It's a matter of experience. I found that I couldn't go on thinking of Dee as I used to before she became autonomous.' He smiled at Dee. 'Before she walked out on me. Looking back, I have to say that my, uh, relationship with her before then was a bit sad and sick, but you have to allow for local custom. Gynoid or android mates were a success-symbol for rich people. Very capitalist.' He smiled, with a flicker of embarrassment. 'Anyway, after all the trials and challenges she put me through, after the resurrection, after I got to know her again . . . I found it impossible to regard her as anything less than a person. Not a cunning imitation, not a flatline, but a real woman, whom I loved and who *loved me*. And because I had frequently, notoriously, and publicly denied that she or any other artificial people were real people, I had no choice but to acknowledge the error of my ways in a very public and decisive manner.'

He glanced up at the big photograph opposite me, and then smiled at Dee again. 'I married her.'

So *that* was the occasion! Marriage meant a public declaration of a sort of mutual possession: an odd, ancient custom, rare in the Union but apparently widespread here. And Reid had made that commitment, to this machine in a pretty body and a pretty dress, after owning her and using her for years. I hoped my face showed no trace of my revulsion.

'Ellen,' said Dee, 'it really doesn't matter what you think about us – about me.' She stood up and walked around the table and sat herself down on the edge of it, just in front of me. I couldn't avoid her green-eyed gaze. 'I know you think I'm a machine. "Just a fucking machine", yes? But *I* know I'm human, and if you were to know me for any length of time, you'd find you couldn't treat me in any other way. You can't own me, you can't use me, you can't switch me on and off. You can try! And if you had the power to force me, you could get some use out of me. But you wouldn't get much, and you wouldn't get *me*. If you want to get all that can be got out of this machine, with all its capacities, you have to let *me* decide to use those capacities. If I'm a machine, Ellen, I'm one that doesn't – *can't* – function properly unless it's free.'

She reached forward and touched my face. I didn't flinch. 'And so are you. So let's just try to be nice to each other, shall we?'

She stood again and walked back to her chair and sat down beside Tamara. I looked sideways at Suze, who was looking at Dee; at Yeng, who was looking at the floor.

'I reckon,' said Malley, 'that somebody just passed the Turing test.'

There was a moment of laughter, tension released. Reid reached over and caught Dee's hand. 'She passed it long ago,' he said.

Dee smiled at him, and then at me. The warmth of her smile chilled me as much as the passion and cogency of her reasoning had, and the gentle touch of her soft fingertips. It was like one of those uncanny moments when you're looking at what you think is a twig or a leaf, and suddenly it spreads wings and flies away.

'All right,' I said to Reid. 'I accept that your views about machine consciousness aren't likely to change.'

Yeng was still examining the floor. Suddenly her head jerked up. 'So *what*?' she said fiercely. 'You can all believe that if you like. The denial of machine sentience is not part of the true knowledge, it's just an opinion the finders had, a –' Her hand mimed her search for a word just out of reach.

'*Obiter dictum*,' suggested Talgarth gravely.

I doubted that Yeng had heard the phrase before, but she nodded briskly. 'Yes! Something like that. All the things Dee said, they're part of the true knowledge. It's just the same with people. If we want to make the most of our lives we have to get the most out of each other, and that means not treating people as less than what they are.' She paused and frowned, as though puzzling something out. I felt for her: the cognitive dissonance of being taken in by Dee's startling mimicry must have been painful. 'Unless we get more by doing that, of course, which doesn't happen very often. If we meet machines that the same applies to, we can live with it.' She laughed, without humour. 'We might have to! None of this changes the other problem, of how we deal with machines far more powerful than us, which – or who, for all I care – could be *more* than people. We can't live with beings to whom we are like ants.'

' "And we were in their sight as grasshoppers",' Reid said,

apparently quoting some obscure text. '*Why* do you think we can't coexist?'

'Because they'd have power over us,' Yeng said, explaining the obvious.

'Having more power than us,' Reid said with equally heavy patience, 'doesn't mean the same as having *power over* us.'

'All right,' said Yeng, 'but they'd have it, and they could always use it, just like you did to the fast folk you revived.'

'Ah,' said Reid. ' "They". That's interesting. I understand you're negotiating with these Jovians. How are you doing it?'

I glanced around the team. No one flashed any warning looks, so I explained how the contact had been made and how the communications were being carried on.

'So,' said Reid when I'd finished, 'how many of them are there?'

I shrugged. 'Millions, possibly. Thousands at least.'

'And they're some kind of hive mind, right? Some gigantic collective entity?'

'No,' I told him, not sure what he was getting at. 'They say they're individuals, and all the evidence we have indicates that's what they are.'

'Some kind of totalitarianism, then? Each subordinate to a single will, as Lenin put it? Or some angelic anarchy where they all agree on the obvious common good?'

'Of course not,' I said impatiently. 'We've noticed signs of disagreement among them, and they take time out for discussion and then come back to us.'

Reid shared a grin with Talgarth. He smacked his palm with his fist. 'Hah!' he exulted. 'Knew it!'

'Knew what?' I asked.

'That you people would be negotiating with the Jovians as if they *were* a hive entity. And as if you were, come to that!' He chuckled darkly. 'And you've made the same mistake with us,' he added. 'When I said we weren't in charge here, I meant it. While we've been talking, quite a few enterprising people have been acting. People who have been thinking ahead, designing ahead, planning ahead, during the five years it's taken for a confirmation to come back through the Gate that it was safe to go through. And now it has – now *you're* here – they've been scrambling to get ships in orbit, ready to go through themselves. Bit of a jostle to be first, but

I'm sure the protection agencies are keeping order in the queue of ships that must be building up right now outside the wormhole.'

He took a swig of his beer and lit a cigarette, blatantly enjoying our startled looks and Tamara's smouldering outrage – this was apparently news to her, too.

'To do what?' I asked, shouting above the rest.

Reid leaned back and clasped his hands and made cracking noises with his knuckles. 'To trade,' he said. 'What else?'

I laughed. 'They won't get much profit out of trading with us,' I said. 'And anyway, they don't know the way through.'

'Indeed they don't,' Reid said. 'But I do. I got it from the fast folk, remember, just as I got the path for going the other way. And I'm going to sell it.' He affected a glance at a wristwatch. 'Any time now, the bids should be coming through.'

Tony leaned forward. 'Very clever,' he said. 'But quite frankly, they'll be wasting their money. The businesses you're about to sell this secret to aren't going to be too happy when they find we don't need anything you've got to offer, and nothing on our side is for sale at any price. Either because we'll share it for free, or we won't give it to you for anything. Like Ellen said – not much profit in that.' He took this as his turn to sit back and look smug.

'I wouldn't be too sure of that,' Reid said. He waved his hand airily. 'Not that it matters. Most of the companies I'm talking about aren't that interested in trading with people in the Solar Union, anyway.'

'So who – ?' I stopped, unwilling to accept the obvious answer. 'Oh no. You're not.'

'We are,' Reid said calmly. 'We're going to trade with the Jovians.'

For a moment we were all stunned into silence. It was Yeng who spoke first, her normally high voice raw with anger and concern.

'This is insane,' she said. 'Just *look* at yourselves! I've seen how comms work here – you have radio for everything, electronic computers everywhere, including your bodies, and lots of you have cortical downlinks! Direct electronic interfaces with your brains, right? You're just *ridiculously* vulnerable – absolutely naked to viral assault and takeover. You're a *culture medium* for the things! The Jovians could *eat* your minds alive, and you'd never know.'

'We've considered that,' Reid said calmly. 'We're confident that our countermeasures will hold them off, should the Jovians behave as treacherously as you people seem to expect.'

'*Countermeasures!*' Yeng's voice spat contempt. 'We've had two centuries of front-line struggle against their virus plagues to develop countermeasures, and we still wouldn't contemplate what you suggest.'

Reid shrugged and smiled. 'We're pretty sure we've done better, because –' He stopped. 'We have better computers,' he finished, rather lamely I thought; but he might have had more to say, and not said it.

'I don't –' I began, then Boris raised his hand and shot me a quick glance.

'All irrelevant,' Boris said. 'Because if your ships go through the Malley Mile, you can rest assured the Cassini Division – our defence agency, our ships – will destroy them. The Division will assume anything coming through is hostile, unless they hear different from us.'

'Then,' said Reid, 'I most strongly suggest you do just that. Contact your Central Committee – or whatever – and tell them to let us through. Because if you don't, and your ships attack ours, the Mutual Protection fighters covering the traders will take whatever action is needed to defend them.'

Boris and Andrea guffawed at the same moment. The rest of the team looked at least amused. Even Malley had a faint, sceptical smile at Reid's apparent bluster. Malley had seen our ships, and Reid had not.

'They can try,' Boris said. He laughed again. 'They can try!'

Reid stood, and wandered over to the wall and leaned on his hand against it, beside a picture of himself alongside a sleek machine, something like a World War Three jet fighter aircraft. He drew on his cigarette and gave us a cool, appraising look. I knew what was coming next, so I spoke first.

'I presume you've already checked over the *Carbon Conscience*,' I said. 'Scanned it, maybe tried sending a little fly-camera in. Do tell us what you've found.'

'Indeed we have,' Reid said, with a slight involuntary backwards sway that cheered me a little. Boris bristled; my quick black look made him back down. 'We got a lot closer to it than we did to the *Terrible Beauty*.' This time it was his turn for a brief inward gloat, as I betrayed my surprise. 'Oh, yes, Mr Powell had our remotes on the job as soon as you'd left,' Reid went on. 'Very helpful and friendly bloke, absolute soul of kindness, as I'm sure you'll agree. Now, about the *Carbon Conscience*.' He gazed over our heads, his eyes flicking back and forth in the way of someone looking at a virtual image. 'It's a good fighter, I'll give you that. But so was the MiG-29, and we all know how that performed against the Polish EFAs.' He paused, frowning. 'Maybe we don't all know. Not very well, is how. And let me tell you, if your fighter-bombers come up against *these*' – he jerked his thumb at the spaceplane in the photo – 'they'll never know what hit them.'

'So you didn't get inside it?' I asked, in as casual a tone as I could manage.

Reid shrugged. 'Didn't need to,' he said, equally lightly. 'Outside inspection was enough.'

Boris almost made another forward lurch; at my sharp gesture, he sat back again, glowering. I hoped Reid had seen that – I was only just able to restrain myself from punching the air and shouting, 'YES! Just you try it, you banker!'

Because if they hadn't been able to penetrate the fighter-bomber's passive defences, they would certainly not be able to defeat it in combat. It was an ugly, insectile thing, that fighter; it looked more like an ornithopter than a spacecraft, let alone a spaceplane; but it was built for the most difficult combat imaginable, close-quarter fast manoeuvering in space, and it had evolved out of two centuries of zapping anything bigger than a molecule that dared to lift from Jupiter, and from even longer experience of split-second work within disintegrating comet nuclei.

The only problem I could foresee with pitting our fighters against Reid's was one he almost certainly wouldn't have thought of: so few of our pilots had ever killed a human, and those few so long ago, that they might fatally hesitate at the death. It wasn't a weakness that those on his side were likely to share.

'Our fighters are fully automated,' Reid said, 'no humans in the loop at all. That puts your side at a further disadvantage, don't you think?'

Oh no it doesn't, I thought with a surge of joy. We'd cream them without a fleck of carbon on our consciences.

'I see you disagree,' he went on. 'Perhaps you should see how they're made.' He made a slapping motion with his hand. The lights dimmed further, and above the table a hologram flashed into view. Six feet high, it showed a dark, pitted nodule, slowly tumbling end over end. On its surface, smudges of light seethed; and small bright things, like iron-filings, drifted off.

'Carbonaceous chondrite, with nanofactories,' Reid said. 'Now let's look a little closer.' The hologram shrank to a patch of the body's surface, which then expanded. The seething smudges became vast constructions of pipework and drillheads and vats: the small bright things, tens and hundreds of spaceplanes like the one in the picture.

'This is speeded up, of course,' Reid allowed. 'Each fighter takes a day to be put together by the assemblers. But as you can see' – the view zoomed back again – 'we have a *lot* of assemblers.'

The hologram vanished and the lights came back up. While we were still blinking, Reid strode over and sat down again.

'Even if you think your fighters can beat ours one-to-one – which I don't – you have the attrition to consider. It won't be one-to-one. More like hundreds to one, and they'll keep on coming.'

The room fell silent. We could still beat them, I thought. We had more than the fighter-bombers to count on. We had the far more powerful lasers on Callisto; the nuclear-armed orbital forts; the entrenchments on the other moons. We had the Inner System defence-forces. If it came to the last ditch, we had the population of Earth itself.

But the New Martians would have more than fighter-bombers, too, and they might have gods on their side – and not just the Jovians, even if they did find allies there. They had their own fast folk, in their smart-matter storage tanks up in the mountains; assuming they weren't already up and running, a deception of which I reckoned Reid was wholly capable.

The attrition would indeed be terrible, on both sides; and we still had the Jovians to deal with. We couldn't afford the diversion.

I smiled and rose to my feet. 'Isn't it great how talking things over can prevent fighting?' I said. 'How did we get into all this talk about fighting, anyway? Of course you can come through. If you want to deal directly with the Jovians, you're welcome to try. It's at your own risk, as the capitalist small print always puts it. You may even be doing us a favour, by running that risk on our behalf. We can look after ourselves, whatever happens.'

My crew were looking at me with barely concealed dismay. Even Malley and Suze looked troubled. I turned completely away from Reid and his partners, and gave the comrades a tremor of a wink.

'So, Dave,' I went on, turning back to him, 'about that offer of a secure communications room? I think it's time to take you up on it.'

'Hard suits, radio comms, deep crypto,' I said. Our clothes gelled, then set to armour around us. The small room at the top of Reid's tower had a shelf all around it of communications-control panels, with more help menus than we could use. All idiot-proof, Reid had cheerfully assured us, closing the door behind him.

In their reconfigured suits the comrades resembled faceless humanoid robots with anodized aluminium finishes in a variety of bright colours. No one could so much as read our lips, and the deeper masking of cryptography would keep our communications safe, unless New-Martian computation was so far ahead of ours that we might as well give up now. The comrades' voices contended in the dead spaces of the crypto channel.

I hit my override control. 'Try to talk one at a time,' I said wearily. I was hungry, and irritable, and among the first people in history to suffer starship-lag. 'Boris, the chair recognizes you.'

'Ha, ha, Ellen. What are you playing at? We can't let them through, definitely not now.'

'We can't fight them *now*,' I said. 'None of us, I hope, has mentioned the impact event. Eight days away now. We need our forces intact for that, just in case . . . We could stop a determined breakout from this side, *or* we could make sure the comets don't get diverted the wrong way. We can't count on doing both.'

'These aren't the only options,' Tony said. 'And we still have to do –'

'I know, I know,' I said.

'Do what?' asked Malley.

'Make sure Reid doesn't touch off another runaway Singularity,' I said. 'If he hasn't already. Don't worry, we'll deal with that. Right now, the decisions aren't up to us. What we have to do is contact the Division, and let them decide. Yeng, please go to it.'

Yeng complied, and while she was setting up a laser-link to the communications relay satellite (by now, presumably, somewhere among a growing fleet of ships that shared its orbit, and the wormhole's) I called up a display inside my helmet and did some rough editing of the suit's record of recent events. I made sure that Reid's most informative statements were there in full, so there'd be no doubt as to what he was saying.

'Ready,' Yeng's voice said. 'Encrypted conference link – you'll all see the committee as a virtual view in you helmets, and they'll see our faces.'

Worried faces, on both sides.

'Are you all right?' Tatsuro asked. 'We haven't had any contact for over an hour, since you went into that tower.'

'We've been in a Faraday cage,' I said. 'We're all right. There's been an . . . unexpected development. Tell you about it in a minute. How are things at your end?'

Tatsuro massaged his eyebrows, leaving tiny, paired dishevellments. 'Fine, fine,' he said. 'The Jovians have finally managed to shut off the viral transmissions. That's at least a token of goodwill, but we aren't opening any radio channels just yet. Their own atmospheric traffic has started to increase again. Also, they've detected the incoming comet-train. They can see it's heading for a slingshot orbit, but they raised the matter with every appearance of concern.'

'Can't say I blame them.'

'We've told them it's routine – for Martian terraforming – showed them records of our previous cometary flybys, which they've checked against what they call dreamtime archives. They seem reassured. Now, about your position. The relay has detected and reported a build-up of ships on your side. What's going on?'

It took me about ten minutes to tell them, with clips of our discussion projected straight through from my suit to their screens. The consternation thus sown was almost amusing to watch; the angry, murmured discussions echoed and amplified our own. I concluded with my assessment of the odds.

'Well,' said Tatsuro when I'd finished, 'this is certainly a complication. I would prefer that you had not said to Reid that his side's ships could come through. Is that not rather a matter for the Solar Council, or at least for its delegate?'

'Oh,' I said. I'd almost forgotten that little matter. The Solar

Council delegate had – or represented, rather – the ultimate power over us. For all the Division's immense, concentrated power, it could not prevail against the will of Earth and the Inner System Earth Defence forces – not in the long run, not with attrition to consider.

'Her fusion-clipper has just gone into orbit around Callisto,' Tatsuro continued. 'With a few Inner System fighters attached. Can we wait for the hour or so it will take for the delegate to arrive?'

'The decision can't wait,' I said. 'Reid is selling the coordinates to the merchant fleet at this moment.'

Tatsuro shook his head reprovingly, but with a glint of wry amusement in his eye as he said: 'You might have tried to argue for a delay of . . . a little over a week!'

'We could still do that,' I said.

Suze raised her hand and spoke up. 'If I may, neighbours . . . comrades. I don't think that would work. We're dealing with capitalists here. They'll *expect* us to stall, and suspect us of stitching them up – that is, of doing our own deal with the Jovians and cutting their side out of it.'

'Which might not be a bad idea,' said Clarity, frowning at us across light years and millennia.

'Oh, it would!' Suze said. 'If I know anything about these people, they'd just batter on through. Race each other to be first to cut a deal. Their whole way of life is based on taking high risks for high returns.'

'And not much risk, at that,' I said sourly. 'They've probably all taken back-ups, and they'll all try different approaches and keep on trying until one succeeds.'

'Or until the Jovians infect them all and turn them into puppets,' said Yeng. 'Puppets who can fight us in space.'

Tatsuro made a chopping gesture with his hand. 'Whatever. I move that we let them through. I agree with Ellen's analysis. If what Yeng fears does happen, we are still in a better position to fight if our own forces are intact. However, I think we should insist that some of our own fighters go through the wormhole and take up positions on the New-Martian side.'

'Opposed,' said Joe Lutterloh. 'We shouldn't open the Solar Union to the bankers, and we shouldn't let them trade with the Jovians, who are still a danger to us.'

After a few more minutes of discussion the vote was taken on letting the traders through. Eight in favour, four against.

Tatsuro didn't pause for a second. 'Carried,' he said, as the hands went down. 'So, comrades, go and tell Reid his traders and fighters can come through, on the condition that our fighters can do the same. Let us know if he agrees or not. Obviously you should make every effort to return to your ships. I appreciate why you had to leave them, but don't leave them for too long. Get your ships back into space, if you can, and stand by for a bombing run – by yourselves, or the other fighters – on the place where the fast-folk templates are stored. And meanwhile' – he looked around at the Command Committee, a slow, sly smile forming on his face – 'we'll work out how we're going to explain all this to the Solar Council delegate. Goodbye for now.'

I waved to the Committee, more bravely than I felt. Yeng switched out the link. Malley and Suze's voices were yelling in my ears. Tatsuro's passing comment was the first they'd heard about our real plans for the fast-folk templates. I waved my arms frantically for silence.

'It's only a contingency plan!' I shouted on the override. 'Only if Reid does something crazy with them! Don't look at me like that! We still can't trust them.'

'Don't worry,' Malley said grimly. 'I don't much care what happens to the templates, they're not conscious anyway. You can trust me not to tell.'

'And me,' said Suze. 'I just wish you had sooner.'

Her voice was thick with disillusion. I looked around at Malley, Suze, and the comrades, and as my glance slid helplessly from one blank bubble to the next, I realized that I couldn't tell which was which.

'All right,' I said. 'I'm sorry. Now let's go and talk Reid into letting us do it.'

Before the world commonwealth was established, one objection to it that always came up was *But who will do the dirty work?*

I always used to answer *me*, and I was right.

10

In the Days of the Comet

ONE AFTER another, the ugly, bristling, articulated fighter-bombers came out of the wormhole; a whole squadron of them, their names heroic, ironic, or plain daft: *Gai Phong*, *Debug Mode*, *Virus Alert*, *Luddite Tendencies*, *X Calibre*, *Acquisitor*, *General Arnaldo Ochoa*, *Codebreaker*, and *Necessary Evil But Still Cool*. And one after another, the slow, laden freighters of the merchants and the fast, sharp fighters of their mercenaries went in. Even on the screen in the aerospace port, with the news-child's prattling commentary jamming the silence, the sight remained awesome and uncanny: ship after ship vanishing in a flash of blue light, as if annihilated.

The same thought must have struck Andrea. 'What happened to the law of mass-energy conservation?' she asked. 'Did it just go away, with those ships?'

Malley leaned over from the bench beside me. 'Good point,' he said, jabbing his pipe-stem, like a lecturer's pointer, at the screen. 'The answer is that the mass of the wormhole at this end increases, and at the other end decreases, by the same amount as has gone through.'

We were sitting, with Reid and Dee, in the same quiet area of the port where Boris and Jaime had waited. I watched the screen with silent satisfaction as our fighters took up positions around the wormhole and deployed a scatter of attitude-control booster drones which clamped themselves around its perimeter. Reid had conceded this degree of control over the gate to us. I wasn't sure whether I'd convinced him it was the only way to get the people on our side to agree to his side's ships coming through, or whether his confidence in the superiority of capitalist technology made the entire concession irrelevant to whatever *his* longer-term plans might be.

I was listening intently to the conversation, and trying hard not to show it; Andrea was still puzzling over Malley's answer.

'So,' she asked, 'does that mean one side of the wormhole would just fade away to nothing if enough mass came through from the other?'

'In lay terms,' said Malley cautiously, 'yes. But bear in mind that the mass can go *negative*.'

I leaned back, hands behind my head, gazing up through the roof, and tuned my tone to idle curiosity.

'What does that mean, in physical terms?'

Malley laughed. 'I don't know, to be honest. The rest of the wormhole – the main wormhole – can balance a negative mass, and thus keep the original gate open, up to a certain point.'

'How much, though?' Andrea sounded worried.

Malley shrugged. 'Depends on its total virtual mass, which I don't know. A lot more than those ships, anyway.'

'The gate on the other side masses oh point nine five seven million tonnes,' Dee said, unexpectedly. 'On this side, a lot less: only about a hundred thousand. If we keep up the traffic, we'll have to ensure that it balances. Unless we want to find out what negative mass means, in physical terms.'

'We're safe enough for now,' said Reid. 'The ships that went through probably don't mass more than a thousand tonnes each.'

'I don't see our side sending twenty-odd thousand tonnes the other way,' I said, with now-easy flippancy.

'Ours are coming back.' Reid glanced over at me and grinned, as though challenging me to deny it. 'Aren't they?'

I returned him an equally unfriendly grin. 'Of course.'

The entire port was much quieter than it had been when we'd first arrived. The welcoming crowds had gone, and the heavy lifting had all been done. Only a few passengers, for the outlying settlements I guessed, wandered or hastened through. Even the news remotes, with an appropriately gnatlike attention span, had drifted off. For the New Martians it was the middle of the night; for us, early afternoon. Discarded disposable plates and the remains of likewise disposable food littered our surroundings. Now we were waiting for the auto-piloted arrival of the *Terrible Beauty*, and for the refuelling of the *Carbon Conscience* to be completed. There was a certain amount of tension in the air, and a lot of smoke. Malley was puffing his pipe, Dee and Reid chain-smoking cigarettes. The habit seemed common in capitalist societies; if we had to wait much longer, I'd be tempted to take it up myself.

'What do you intend to sell, and to buy?' Suze asked.

'If I knew that,' Reid said, 'I'd probably be doing it myself. The folks who're going through have given it a lot more thought than I have.' He spread his hands. 'Information, I guess.'

'They may get more information than they bargained for,' Yeng told him, darkly. 'And you'll get it, too.' She stood up and paced forward and pointed at the screen. One of the defence-agency fighters had hung back from going through, and was deploying a relay drogue, much larger than ours, on the same alignment. 'I can't *believe* your complacency. I hope we get off this place before the Jovian viruses come down the line, straight into your heads!'

Dee laughed.

'You don't get it, do you?' she said. 'We do have open systems, yes, and we are personally vulnerable – I more than most, I should say – to mind-hacking. That's exactly why we're not worried about it. We've *had* to develop countermeasures, very good ones, so we can protect ourselves from business competitors, criminals – or bloody kids!'

Yeng shrugged. 'Maybe so,' she said doubtfully. 'But if you're up against conscious – well, supposedly conscious – entities with processing-power vastly greater than yours, I can't see it doing much good.'

'But we –' Dee began. She looked at Reid. He shrugged.

'Oh, tell them,' he said. 'They'll figure it out for themselves eventually.'

'All right,' Dee said. She stood up and faced us all, as Yeng returned to her seat. 'I'll tell you.' Her tone, and her expression, altered slightly, as though some different personality were in control. 'Consciousness – or the emulation of consciousness, if you insist' – she smiled, her usual self flashing momentarily back – '*costs*. Selfhood has a very high cost in processing-power, and that cost increases with the amount of information it has to integrate. It's not something that just *drops out* of increased complexity, as some people used to think. It has to be actively *designed in*, either consciously by us or unconsciously by natural selection. So it's quite possible to build hardware more powerful, and software more complex, than any brain or mind in existence: computing machines that don't even act *as if* they're conscious, that don't have *interests*, and that don't object when they're used as tools.'

Her possession passed, her self-possession returned. She stepped over to one of the long seats, and expertly flicked the fluttery hem of her skirt under the crook of her knees as she sat down. I smiled at her. She, and Reid, had been right: no matter what I thought, in the innermost depths of my mind, about the innermost depths of *her* mind, it was impossible to be with her, to converse with her, and not give her the benefit of the doubt, not act *as if* her mind *had* innermost depths, and not to quite simply *like* her.

She smiled back.

'And these tools,' Reid added, 'we have. That's why we're confident we can deal on equal terms with beings greater than ourselves. We have ways of amplifying our power to more than equal theirs. Golems to stand up for us against the gods.' He crushed his cigarette and stood up. 'Products of good old capitalist competition. You should try it, sometime.'

I found myself thinking of the great analytical engines of our socialist planning, whose spare capacities had increased over decades of stability in which more and more decisions had come to be made locally, and only the most general, those concerning the most widely used resources, had to be made globally or even regionally. I thought of our smart-matter suits, and our domestic cybernetics. Perhaps we'd all along had gods – or golems – on our side, whose aid it had never crossed our minds to invoke.

About to say something of this, I looked at Reid, and then tracked his gaze to a falling spark visible through the concourse's transparent roof.

'Your ship's coming in,' he said. 'Time to go.'

Free at last; free fall at last! It had taken hours – hours of shifting the ships and coupling them together, an awkward job in one gravity; half an hour of negotiation between Suze and one of Reid's employees over our debt to Mutual Protection, and another half hour with the port company, over services they'd allegedly rendered and definitely wanted paying for – and finally a painful five minutes of boost, to get ourselves quickly into this orbit. Reid's last words to me had been: 'I hope I see you again.'

'Me too,' I'd said, sincere only in my hope that I never did.

I unclipped my webbing, pushed myself away from the couch and executed a joyous somersault, ending up just in front of the forward view.

I hauled the gross-focus bars of the display screen, rotated the fine-focus handles. Although the wormhole was still a long way off on our slowly closing trajectory, the forward telescope's field – transmitted through lenses, mirrors and fibre-optic cables – showed our destination clear and sharp: the rainbow ring of the daughter wormhole – like its parent, a mile across – and the glittering clutter of the surrounding ships. Our ten fighters and Reid's one; our relay drogue small, theirs large.

I fiddled with the controls and swung in another view, an enhanced night-time image of Ship City and its environs.

'OK comrades!' I called out, rolling around again. They'd all unstrapped and were flying around the command deck, enjoying not only the free fall but the respite between getting out from under capitalism and having to face a bit of democratic accountability from our distant socialism. I grinned at them all and gave them a big thumbs-up.

'Mission accomplished – so far!' I announced.

'Yeah?' said Malley. 'And what did we accomplish?'

'A lot,' I said. 'We've confirmed that the New Martians are just what they seem to be: real people, even if they do have funny ideas about what counts as people. We know for sure they're at risk of losing that, if Reid or someone else gets too cocky about reviving his fast folk again. And from what that nice anarchist comrade Tamara told me, we have good reason to think the fast-folk templates are still where Reid originally stashed them – up in the range of hills called the Madreporite Mountains.'

I pointed it out, and paused as a much more vivid marker made the point: a long bolide-trail in the atmosphere, and the flash of its impact. Another followed, and another.

'That's it,' I said above the sound of indrawn breaths. 'There, near where they direct their comet fragments, at the source of that long channel leading into the city. We got the exact coordinates years ago, out of the artificial woman's – Meg's – data-files. So if we or any of the other fighters gets the go-call, we can lob a nuke into the cave-mouth and blast them and the whole mountain to blazes.'

'You've got *nukes* on this thing?' Malley asked indignantly.

'On *Carbon Conscience*,' Boris said. 'That bird's got a fifty-megaton egg, man. Nice clean laser-fusion job, in case you're worried.'

'Consider me reassured,' said Malley. 'No doubt a few fifty-megaton city-busters will come in real handy if the New Martians should have the bad luck to fall short of your definitions of what counts as people.'

'There is that,' Boris said thoughtfully.

'No!' I said, shocked. 'We're not going to do that!'

'Why ever not?' Malley floated up, his voice heavy with sarcasm. 'According to you, you wouldn't be killing *people*.'

'Too dangerous,' I explained. 'Wouldn't be like Jupiter, with vulnerable entities at the bottom of a gravity well. It'd be a massive breakout, with millions of ex-human puppets and a space-going capability. If there's another Singularity here, we cut and run.'

'Run where?' asked Andrea.

'Through the wormhole, if possible,' I said.

'And if not?' Malley hung in front of me, hanging on my words. I waved a hand airily in his face.

'We keep boosting until we use half the reaction-mass, back ourselves up if we absolutely have to, and at the first likely looking clump of matter the ship finds, we download and spend the rest of the reaction-mass decelerating. And then, well . . .' I smiled at his frown. 'We have the makings of a nice little galactic empire of our own right here. With your beauty and my brains, neighbour . . .'

Malley's anxiety dissolved in a guffaw.

'And I shall call you . . . Eve!'

'Mitochondrial Eve,' Suze said firmly, catching Malley's hand.

'Plenty of good genes in the cold-stores,' said Boris.

I turned away before Malley could suspect there was even a sliver of a chance we were serious. (But it was part of the standard kit of a fusion-clipper, even so: the haunting fear of a runaway torch, or of everything going wrong in our cold war with the Jovians, was the real reason the ships relied on recycling rather than supplies, and stored the frozen seeds of a viable population and the smart-matter blueprints for its infrastructure and technology in their vaults.)

'Enough,' I said. 'We got work to do. Jaime, Andrea, could you please haul yourselves over to the nav gear and the long-range viewing-kit. We need to track all the moving matter around us, all the ships and missiles and especially all the cometary junk. We don't want to wander into the path of one of *their* comet-trains.'

(*Indeed we don't*, I thought to myself.)

'Don't worry about our deep-space radar being pinged,' I added. 'They know we're here, and they know we're not hostile.'

'We've paid for our protection,' Suze reminded me.

'Handy stuff, gold,' I agreed. 'And Yeng, I'd like you to help Andrea and Jaime with mapping comet-streams – their courses and timing *must* be public knowledge somewhere. As well as that, I need two channels – one to see if there's any readable information coming from their comms drogue . . .'

'Newscasts, probably,' Suze said. 'Subscriber only, if I know them.'

'So try subscribing,' I said.

Yeng grinned. 'And the other channel?'

'Same as before,' I said. 'Patch us in to the Command Committee.' I caught Malley's *you're for it now* smile, and smiled defiantly back. 'Time to find out what the democratically elected delegate of socialist humanity thinks of what the heroic defenders of socialist humanity have been getting up to.'

I recognized the Solar Council delegate at once, which surprised me. As the Solar Council – like all the other councils, from local to global – was directly elected, and I was theoretically one of its constituents, I shouldn't have been surprised. Local councils tended to be made up of people with local reputations, and so on up. The Solar Council's delegates should have been known to everyone in the Solar System, usually for their decades if not centuries of good, competent work in relevant fields; the re-gerontocracy, as some of our younger and more cynical neighbours put it. But by and large I trusted the people in the rest of the Union to choose people whose previous experience and reputation they trusted (and now and again to throw in some absolute beginner who had made enough of a fuss about something to get their name bruited about) so, apart from my recently lost position on the Jovian Anomaly Research Committee, I generally stuck to my little intrigues in the Division and left wider affairs alone. However, even I had heard of Mary-Lou Radiation Nation Smith.

She was, I think, Navaho, if it matters; in any case, a member of one of the all-too-many tribes – Aleutian, Kazakh, Aboriginal, Uighur, etc. – who'd been unwilling or unwitting participants in the old society's nuclear tests, and who now formed a loose but active lobby calling itself the Radiation Nation. They were united, not by ethnicity – which the Union only encouraged as a basis for cultural, and definitely not for administrative, association – but by a quite understandable though, I sometimes thought, exaggerated concern that we were a little too careless with our civil-engineering and outbreak-zapping and forest-clearing nukes. *Yes*, they'd say, *we can stop cancer and fix chromosomes and regenerate ecosystems, but there could be unknown losses, uncalculated risks* . . . it was a legitimate point of view, despite all the mutterings about Greens under the machines, and as a respected biologist and statistician, Mary-Lou Radiation Nation Smith had the qualifications to back it up.

Black bangs framed her face, dark eyes shone out of it. She was sitting beside Tatsuro, whose uncharacteristically frayed appearance – the hairs of his head, eyebrows, and moustache sticking out as if static-charged – contrasted with her well-groomed composure.

'Ellen May Ngwethu,' she said, as if it were the name of some particularly loathsome disease. 'Comrades and friends.' She swept us all with a glance, making a similarly distasteful diagnosis. 'And the distinguished non-cooperator Dr Malley. I'm pleased to meet you all at last, even at such a distance. *Especially* at such a distance, I should say. Your energy and enterprise are quite astonishing. We on the Council had *no idea* you were planning such bold initiatives. Not only have you set up a scheme to destroy the Jovians, you've simultaneously entered into negotiations with them! No doubt you have already worked out what to do if these superhuman minds see through your *highly plausible* cover-story, and respond. I look forward eagerly to our surprise when you demonstrate your sure-fire, foolproof stratagem to prevent their entirely predictable fury from wiping us out. Don't spoil my suspense by telling me in advance – not that telling us *anything* in advance is one of your habitual faults.'

She paused, placed the palms of her hands together and the fingertips under her chin.

'Well?' she said. 'I've heard the CC comrades' . . . explanations. What do *you* have to say for yourself?'

'Comrade, ah, neighbour Radiation Nation Smith –'

'Just call me Mary-Lou,' she said sweetly. 'Or neighbour Smith, if you prefer formality. My middle names are a soubriquet – like your last.'

From her point of view it may have been an inappropriate reminder of just *why* I'd chosen that old slogan for my name. *Ngwethu!* Freedom! I had it, and at the relevant point of application, perhaps more than she. The sting of her whiplash sarcasms faded, and (embarrassing to relate, but there it is) a few half-forgotten bars of that haunting anthem *Nkosi Sikelele Afrika* hummed through the back of my mind.

'OK, Mary-Lou,' I replied. 'We in the Division have a mandate to contain and destroy the Outwarder threat, and that's exactly what we're doing. I've assumed all along that our actions would be accountable to the Union, and that if necessary a global poll would be taken before the final decision – the issues are well known, and have long been discussed, so there should be no problem.'

'*No problem*,' she said, in a dead level tone. 'Of course, keeping our decision a secret from the Jovians is simply a matter of radio silence and complete self-discipline by billions of people, many of whom would be appalled at the suggestion of what you plan to do, not to mention what you've already done. You know, I can *almost* imagine that being possible, were it not for your other impressive feat. Opening contact *and* hostilities with the Jovians wasn't enough for you.'

She shook her head. 'Oh, no. As a final flourish, you manage – a mere hour before my arrival – to open the Solar System to a vigorously expanding capitalist society, and an anarcho-capitalist one at that. I'm sure if you'd had the choice between New Mars and some tedious statist tyranny with whose tedious statist tyrants we could at least have made some kind of deal that *might actually stick*, you'd still have picked New Mars, out of pure scientific curiosity as to which anarchy would subvert the other first. Let me tell you that your curiosity may be well justified . . . Dr Malley!'

Malley jumped (in as much as one can, in free fall) like a student caught dozing in a lecture.

'Yes?'

'I'm in no position to remonstrate with you – as a non-cooperator, you can't be expected to live by our rules. However, you do have to live with the consequences of your actions. Here are some consequences of yours: after decades of virtual radio silence from Earth, your brave experiment in encouraging your students to make and use radios has led to something of a happy babble of electronic communication. Our non-co friends heard that I was on my way out here, and decided to spread the news to the handful of non-cos in *space*. You'd be surprised to learn how much ill-informed comment on my well known concerns has flashed around the Solar System in the last few days. Evidently the New-Martian traders have monitored it closely – not difficult, because in absolute terms there isn't much radio traffic, *yet*. A couple of hours ago, I received a *personal message* from one of these ships, offering me "an unrepeatable, ground-floor offer" – whatever that is – for an "import concession" – I know what that is, thank you – for "alpha-emitter-assimilating biomechanisms" – whatever *they* may be.'

'How did you respond?' asked Malley, with what I thought commendable nerve.

'I told them to shop off,' was the somewhat coarse reply. 'However, we shortly afterwards picked up another version of the same offer, beamed towards Earth for anyone who cares to take it up. It's one of *thousands* of similar propositions directed at Earth, which in turn are the merest *fraction* of the communications going on between the traffickers' fleet and Jupiter. Most of the latter are heavily encrypted, so we don't even know what the offers they're making *are*.'

None of this came as a surprise, but it was all happening faster than I'd expected. I hadn't foreseen that the inevitable contact between the dominant non-cos of New Mars and the marginal non-cos of Earth would result in so much information leakage that keeping our plans from the Jovians would be well nigh impossible.

'All right,' I said. 'I see your point. That just means we'll have to act first and take the vote later – that's if most people aren't so relieved to be rid of the Jovian threat that it'll be obvious to anyone what the majority view is.'

Mary-Lou Smith lost her expression of detached, ironic appraisal. She shot me a look of hot fury.

'Act first, vote later?' she said. 'On an issue like this? What a disgusting attitude to your fellow human beings!'

'It isn't my attitude,' I protested. 'It's what's required by the realities of the situation.'

'Yes! Realities which you've brought about!' For a moment she looked as if she were about to start banging her head on the table. Then she drew her shoulders back and took a deep breath.

'Enough,' she said. 'We must deal with the situation as it is, and uncover the reasons for this mess when we have time. The whole relationship between the Union and the Division has to –'

She stopped herself, stood up and took a few steps backwards, so she could see all of the Committee as well as all of us. 'As I say, enough. Here's what I propose to transmit to the Solar Council, and what – on my mandate from the Solar Council – I *instruct* you to implement immediately, pending the Council's decision. One, you absolutely must not provoke the Jovians by giving them any reason whatever to fear a cometary bombardment. That means you must divert the comet-train into a wider and irreversibly safe orbit *now*. Second, you must step up fighter-bomber patrols on this side of the wormhole, and make no compromises with the New Martians on that. We have to make clear to them that they're here on our sufferance. Third, you must prepare to jam all radio transmissions within the Jovian sub-system, and between it and the Inner System, whether from the Jovians, the New Martians, or the non-cos.'

She strode forward and sat down again. 'That is all,' she said. 'Any questions?'

Nobody said anything. Quickly scanning the faces of the others on the Committee, I registered that most of them showed nothing but relief; in the case of Clarity and one or two others, more than relief. I took in their tentative smiles, keeping my own face carefully neutral. Only Joe Lutterloh showed anger, which he was equally visibly restraining. Tatsuro looked at me gravely. The tiny downtilt of his head could have been a cryptic nod, or an unconscious bowing to the inevitable. Mary-Lou might not have much immediate power to bring to bear on us, but a greater constraint applied. The Division couldn't go against the explicit will of the Union, or even of its authorized delegate, without being irretrievably split. And if we tore ourselves apart, we risked being easy prey for the enemy.

Well, if the others were too intimidated to talk, I was not.

'You propose a risky course,' I said. 'We've taken some risks too,

I admit, but we always had the final fail-safe of the comet-strike to fall back on. Anything conceded to the Jovians – or the New Martians – could still be negated with that. Now you want to strike this weapon from our hands, and leave us defenceless.'

Smith jumped to her feet and leaned forward, fists on the table.

'Ellen May Ngwethu!' she shouted. 'I have had *enough* of your inflexible attitudes! I've heard *more* than enough of your devious speeches! I've had it up to –'

She stopped, leaned back, drew breath. She bowed her head for a moment and massaged her temples, then looked up at me and smiled.

'Excuse my outburst, neighbour. I understand your situation better than you do. You've endured two centuries of apparently endless conflict, two centuries for your personal dislikes to rankle into hatred. You've had even longer for the harshest aspects of the true knowledge – its dark side, if you will – to overwhelm its truth. Because the truth is the *whole*, and in raising the aspect of struggle way out of proportion to that of cooperation, you've turned it into a *lie*. If you could see yourself – as I have, I've had time to sample the records of this Committee, and those which you and your comrades have been sending back – in all your implacable belligerence, your *imperviousness* to the reasonable appeals of rational beings, whether the Jovian speaker or the New-Martian gynoid, to be recognized as such . . . if you could see all that, I hope there is still something in you that would be ashamed.'

I stared at her, shaken despite myself. 'I've done nothing out of personal malice, *nothing* I'm ashamed of, and nothing that goes against the true knowledge.'

Mary-Lou shook her head slowly. 'There are two sides to the true knowledge, and you have forgotten one of them, despite your name. There is not only *amandla* – power. There is also *ngwethu* – freedom.'

'I know that,' I said calmly. 'And we'll lose both if we throw away our last chance to destroy the Jovians while we still can!'

For a split second, Mary-Lou literally staggered, as though I'd hit her. Then she said:

'All right. Let me speak to you in a language you understand. We are not throwing away our last chance to destroy the Jovians. *There never was a chance.* As soon as a stable, reality-oriented Jovian culture emerged, there was *no chance* that it could be destroyed by anything we could throw at it. These are beings whose *evolutionary ancestors* disintegrated Ganymede and punched a hole through space! How many *hours* do you think it would take for them to develop some response that could swat aside your comets like flies? And as soon as you brought back the first pictures, and the first messages, there was *not a chance* that the people of the Union would react to the Jovians' emergence with anything but hope, and to their destruction with anything but horror. You've seen how a typical Union member, Suze, a typical tough-minded non-co, Dr Malley, and even your own Command Committee have reacted. They've all drawn back from the brink, to varying degrees, and they're right! Our only *chance* of survival is to survive *with them*, and the only effect of attempting to destroy them would be to *make* them the deadly enemies you seem to take for granted they are.'

She turned to Tatsuro. 'Which reminds me,' she said. 'I heard no dissent from my instruction, except from Ellen. Do you wish to take a vote?'

Tatsuro nodded wearily. 'Those for accepting the delegate's instructions.'

All the hands on the other side went up, except Joe's.

'Those against.'

Me, and Joe. I smiled at him. He shook his head, lips compressed in a thin line, and drew a finger across his throat. I don't think anyone else saw the gesture. Behind me, I distinctly heard Yeng say: 'Shit.' No one else spoke.

'Carried,' said Tatsuro. He took his control panel from its strap around his neck, and jabbed in a long series of firing-codes.

'It's done,' he told Mary-Lou. 'The jets are firing, the nukes are flaring. The cometary masses have been shifted to the orbit you requested.'

'Let me confirm that,' she said. 'No offence, neighbour.'

She spoke briefly and quietly into a personal phone, waited a few seconds, then nodded.

'OK,' she said. 'The local observatories have confirmed it.'

Her shoulders moved as though a weight had been lifted from them. 'And now,' she said, 'Ellen. Let me try to reassure you about the Jovians.'

My heart was thudding, my mouth dry.

She sat down on the edge of the table, leaning on one hand, twisting her body a little to face me, in a pose of casual conversation. 'They're not *monsters*, you know. Why should you expect beings more powerful and intelligent than ourselves to be worse than ourselves? Wouldn't it be more reasonable to expect them to be *better*? Why should more power mean less good?'

I could hardly believe I was hearing this. Glancing quickly over my shoulder, I saw Andrea, Jaime and Yeng working at their screens but listening intently, and the rest giving Mary-Lou all their attention. I searched for my most basic understanding, and dragged it out:

'Because good means good for us!'

Mary-Lou smiled encouragingly and spoke gently, as though talking someone down from a high ledge. 'Yes, Ellen. But who is *us*? We're all – human, post-human, non-human – machines with minds in a mindless universe, and it behoves those of us with minds to work together *if we can* in the face of that mindless universe. It's the possibility of working together that forges an *us*, and only its impossibility that forces a *them*. That is the true knowledge as a whole – the union, and the division.' She laughed. 'So to speak! In fact, exactly so – the Union, and the Division!'

Images of the Jovians, in all their multifarious forms, processed through my mind. My skin felt as if small, chill, unpleasant things were crawling over it. I remembered the cold, lively metal of the robots, the warm flesh of Dee's fingertips; and I knew that my response to those machines, however edgy, however suspicious, however prejudiced it might be, was not the same as my cold intellectual loathing of the Jovians, beautiful though they were. The robots and the gynoid and all their kind, conscious or not, had become part of *us*, whereas the Jovians –

'You mean you would contemplate a union – with *them*?'

Mary-Lou nodded briskly. 'Of course. With those who wanted to. You may not know this, but the Jovians have the true knowledge, in their own terms. Some of their practices are even socialist!'

God help us all, I thought, heretically. 'That,' I said, 'only makes them more dangerous. More powerful, because more united, like we're dangerous to them, or *were* until *you people* –'

I stopped my words, too late. Mary-Lou chopped her hand

downwards. She pushed herself off the table, a slow, graceful motion in Callisto's low gravity, and brushed her hands together as if to remove some light dust.

'That's it,' she announced. 'End of discussion. If we are now *you people*, then we aren't in any kind of union *with you*. I have nothing more to say to you, Ellen. *Go away*. Just keep out of trouble, don't make any more trouble for us, and let someone else sort out your head, because I won't. Goodbye.'

She raised her hand above her shoulder, glanced at Tatsuro, and snapped her fingers impatiently. Tatsuro gave me a last, helpless look, reached for something out of sight, and the screen went dead.

It was all down to me now, I thought. Time for Plan B.

I rolled in the air and grabbed a stanchion. The comrades, and Malley, were all staring at me, or at the blank screen. The command deck had never sounded so quiet.

'So that's it, I guess,' I said.

'And very glad I am,' said Malley. Suze looked at him, looked at me, and nodded.

'It's over,' she said. 'Come on, Ellen. The decision's made. The die is cast. The comets won't crash, and Mary-Lou's won the Committee to her way. All right, there are risks, but she's right – there'd be more risks in yours. We'll just have to accept it, and hope they made the right choice.'

'Hope,' I said.

Hope was there, lighting up the eyes of Suze and Malley. The faces of the five other comrades didn't show hope, nor share the dread I felt. They were lost in their own thoughts, the worst of which may have been that they might have to choose between me – between us, the team – and the Union, or even the Division. For all our fierce individualism, we'd all – consciously or not – drawn strength from the Union, not only in the obvious objective sense but also in our selves. Mary-Lou had been right about that, at least: 'good for us' had two sides.

Now I'd have to work with this feeling, get it on my side – and so on everybody's, whether they knew it yet or not.

'Nothing's over,' I said. 'We have *not* been expelled from the Union, or even from the Division, and whatever Mary-Lou may think, I'm *still* on the Command Committee until I hear otherwise.'

I waved behind me at the blank screen. 'If the comrades choose to throw me out, fine – the first thing they'll do is tell us. They haven't. Until they do, I'll carry on as a member.'

Malley scowled, Suze shrugged, the others brightened slightly.

'OK,' I went on. 'There's something I have to tell you. For a long time now, Tatsuro and I have had . . . an understanding. We both knew things might come to this, and we knew we'd need a fall-back position if even the comet-strike were . . . struck out!' I smiled, and coaxed some flickers of response. 'Whether by the Jovians, or by our own decision. We knew we might come to that decision. We knew we might even agree with it ourselves. We weren't – I wasn't – as dogmatic about the Jovians as Mary-Lou made out. *I* was the first to argue for attempting contact, remember, against a fair bit of opposition.'

'Come off it,' snapped Malley. 'That was just to get my cooperation.'

'Of course,' I said. 'But it was hardly an act of blind hatred, was it? *I* risked my own mind making the first contact. You know how I feel about back-ups, and whatever you may think of that view, it's sincerely held. The risk was real, to me. I trusted them enough to take their path through the wormhole – a risk we all shared, yes, but I sure wouldn't have taken it if I thought the Jovians were *monsters*.'

'You've made your point,' said Malley. 'So why didn't you make it to Mary-Lou?'

'I know a hopeless fight when I see one,' I said. I shrugged. 'She has her point of view, fair enough, but I think she's biased towards a non-violent resolution, and blinded to the other possibilities. Don't get me wrong – nothing would please me more than to find that she's right, that we and the Jovians can coexist and cooperate and so on. That they won't turn out as bad or mad as their predecessors. But until I'm convinced of that, until we all know we're safe, I am going to do my best to ensure that we do have a last resort. *Only* as a last resort, and *only* if it's them or us, and everyone for themselves. And it's one that *won't* threaten, won't even worry, the Jovians, until or unless they threaten us.'

Jaime and Andrea glanced at the screens at which they'd been working, then smiled at me with dawning comprehension.

'This is what Tatsuro and I agreed,' I went on. 'The real reason we came here. Because here we have comet-trains all set up for us –

ones the Jovians need never see, and which can strike at them without warning. We can send comets through the wormhole.'

'But the comets aren't –' Tony began.

Malley shot him a dry smile, and to me, one of grudging respect. 'Very elegant,' he said. 'Relative motion.'

'Yes,' I said. 'We're going to move the *wormhole*.'

It wasn't as simple as that, but the process of setting it up convinced the comrades that at some level I still had authorization for what I was doing. And I had; in as much as Tatsuro and I had indeed privately agreed on this contingency plan before I'd even set out to find Wilde or Malley. The fact that the Division's fighter-bombers, around both ends of the wormhole, responded to my requests was evidence enough (not least to myself) that I hadn't been thrown off the Command Committee. Not yet, anyway.

I sat beside Yeng while she sent the encrypted instructions, to the squadron on our side and to the *Turing Tester* on the other. The action of the latter was crucial, but it passed almost unnoticed in the general redeployment of fighter-bombers around the Malley Mile, on which – ironically enough – it was Mary-Lou who had insisted. The *Turing Tester* pulsed its own instructions to the wormhole Gate's attitude-control rockets, which fired off in a sequence of brief puffs. Slowly, over several hours, almost imperceptibly, the great rainbow ring swivelled on its axis to face the surface of Jupiter.

Meanwhile, we drifted closer and closer to the daughter wormhole Gate. Neither our fighters nor the lone, auto-piloted sentry – which, I was amused to note, actually did belong to Reid's Mutual Protection company – challenged us. Jaime and Andrea steadily mapped the incoming stream of cometary fragments, which fell almost hourly on uninhabited parts of New Mars, after perhaps decades of slow, directed infall from this system's equivalents of the Kuiper Belt or Oort Cloud. We calculated that we could reach a sufficiently high speed to make an effective bombardment within anything from thirty minutes to two hours, with the ship dragging the wormhole at up to thirty gee if we had to pick the shorter approach: the maximum tolerable acceleration for that length of time, even with full use of the support capacity of our smart-matter suits.

'How do we grab the wormhole?' Malley asked.

'It's been done before,' I said. 'It's set up. The little attitude-control drones were designed for the original orbital shift we gave the Malley Mile back home. They've clamped around it, and they have secondary clamps that can grab on to the ship's lifting-gear cables. We can do it – the gate will be tilted at an acute angle behind us, we'll be at its centre of gravity, and our jet will be firing into it, going –'

I raised my eyebrows. Malley shrugged: 'Who knows?'

Just before the encounter, we'd have to cut the drive, disengage from the wormhole's perimeter and fire the drones' attitude jets to fine-tune the angle of the wormhole, so that the comets would follow the same course as had the departing ships, and explode out of the other side on a straight course for the surface of Jupiter. The combined velocities of the daughter wormhole Gate and the comet fragments would deliver enough kinetic energy to spread devastation for tens of thousands of miles around their points of impact. It would be best if we could simultaneously get the ships on the other side to move the far mouth of the wormhole, sweeping it like a gun muzzle across Jupiter, and preferably on a course that would take it all the way round, but we couldn't count on that best-case scenario. Nor could we count on the configuration lasting for a Jovian nine-hour day, carrying the exit gate around the planet. What we could count on was hitting the Jovians hard.

Yeng had found several commercial channels, and several internal company reporting channels, which were either not encrypted or easily hacked. We kept our forward lasers trained on the New Martians' comms drogue. We stayed near our acceleration couches, watched the screens, and waited.

Hours passed.

I was keeping an eye on a narrow-band monitoring channel, relayed from a camera and a mike in an upper corner of a room in a ship. Not encrypted, nothing special. Full colour, sleety image, mono sound, trickle feed. Probably just one of those capitalist things: management spying. Maybe something more benign, a sort of online black box. It was certainly not that ship's main comms channel, which was sending back an unbreakable flood of coded data. It showed a constant, unwavering view from inside one of the trading vessels – its command deck, by the look of it. Much less cluttered than ours, no recycling equipment, none of the trailing tubes and climbing tendrils. Five acceleration couches, moulded and resilient and glistening, like black jellies. Four men and a woman in identical blue fatigues, drifting around, checking instruments, watching their outside screens; joking and chatting. They didn't seem to have much to do. They were excited about being in the Solar System. One man had been there before, which gave me an eerie feeling when it became clear from his conversation that he'd been one of the uploaded slave-minds in the Outwarders' construction robots.

The real work of their mission was being carried on by their ship's computer, which they referred to as the Bitch, apparently in honour of the ship's name, which was *Running Dog*. I was not as bored as they were, partly because of my still-simmering tension, and partly because – as generations of producers of visual wallpaper have shown – there's something hypnotically watchable about people in space, just as there is about watching planetary surfaces from space.

Snatches of conversation, picked up by that unobtrusive mike, narrow-cast to a nearby drogue, lasered at a critical angle into the wormhole, cutting through millennia of space and time, bounced to another relay, beamed by radio to – no doubt – some bored watcher on New Mars, picked up by Yeng's eavesdropping aerials, to finally be heard by me:

'Bitch is hot!'

'Yeah man, she's got her tail up now. Musta met another Jovian.'

'Meeting a minds.'

'Sniff, sniff.'

Laughter.

'Reds still around the Mile?'

'Like flies on a shit. Don't like it, man, don't like it at all.'

'Home says not to worry.'

'Don't trust them, but. Fuck. It's their territory –'

'Says who?'

'Home, that's who. We don't know what they can do yet, anyway.'

(No, I thought, you don't.)

'Not a whole helluva lot, not if they're like the commies we useta know and love.'

'Ha-ha. Didn't know you were that old.'

'Looked good on the tel, though. See the tall black one?'

'Yuh-uh!'

Ribald noises. About me, I realized, and felt flattered. The men rolled and somersaulted, trading ineffectual pokes and punches. Then a voice cut across their laughter; the woman's voice, like a dash of cold water.

'*Something's wrong.*'

'Wha –'

'Look at the board! What the fuck!'

'Bitch, are you all right? Bitch?'

They were diving backwards to their couches, which caught and embraced them in swiftly emerging pseudopods of glassy black jelly. As soon as they'd smacked into place the five astronauts were working very hard, very fast. I could see their heads move, tracking virtual head-ups; their fingers flex over invisible keys. My own movements were almost a reflex of theirs – I was yelling, patching the view from this channel into the other screens and tiling in theirs.

On a news channel, one of the merchant ships – which a sidebar swiftly tagged as the *Running Dog* – had begun to move strangely, yawing under irregular thrusts from its attitude jets.

'They seem to be having some –' A child's puzzled voice.

'Boris!' I shouted. 'For'ard laser now! Get ready to hit the comms drogue! Yeng! Screen out all encrypted input now! Andrea, warm the torch!'

The voices of the *Running Dog*'s crew were still coming through.

'Can't raise the Bitch! Can't raise the Bitch!'

'Shaddap shaddap, we're trying. Shit shit shit shit, drive's not responding.'

'*Running Dog* to home, *Running Dog* to home. We got a bad situation here. Engine out, Bitch haywire. We're getting sorta rolling motion, irregular. Say again please, say again please . . . shit. Comms are out.'

'Lights are on.'

'Nobody's home.'

'Ha ha.'

'Running audit now . . . OK guys, we're in deep shit here, deep shit. Bitch seems to have taken a massive data hit, she's down . . . No! She's running!'

'The hell she is, she's not – oh fuck. Gotta report this, gotta –
Shit! Comms are still out.'

'Hey, the monitor!'

Faces turned, looking straight at me.

'If anyone's getting this,' the woman's voice said, quite calmly,
'please act fast. We think our onboard computer has been hacked
into and taken over –'

'A fucking Jovie's uploaded on us!' another voice yelled, and
meanwhile in the background a third voice was intoning: 'Holy
Mary Mother a God pray for us now and at the hour of our *hey,
wait a minute, guys, everything's back to normal, it's cool, look*!'

As I watched, their expressions changed from frantic concern to
calm relief. The woman was making waving motions at the monitor.

'Cancel that,' she said urgently, smiling. 'False alarm. Sorry,
folks, false alarm! Electrical glitch, Jovian atmosphere storm, that's
all, panic over.'

The men behind her were moving in a completely different way
than they had before, heads and arms working away in a new virtual
space; there was nothing wrong with their movements, except that
they were all making the *same* movements, in unison. Four heads
turned as one, smiling at the monitor as their hands reached and
fingers flexed in their synchronized puppet ballet.

'Boris,' I said.

On the forward view the twirling parasol of the New Martians'
comms drogue flared at the focus of our lasers, and flash-burned
instantly to a million fragments of twinkling foil.

Andrea hit the drive as all the other screens went out.

It wasn't a long burn, just enough to kick us into a closing orbit
with the Gate. We had only a few minutes in which to act. Lots of
things seemed to happen at once.

'Enemy fighter spinning around,' Boris announced calmly.
'Firing. Missile launched and closing. Active-defence –'

The forward view lit up, with a big flash then lots of small ones
as the active-defence lasers mopped up the missile's fragments.

'Fighter taking evasive action. I'm realigning the laser. Over to
automatic fire. Target destroyed.' He thought about it for a second,
and added: 'Yee-hah!'

'What'd they attack us for?' Suze demanded.

'For burning the drogue,' I said.

'Should be grateful.'

Jaime was running a plot on the nearest comet-train, and Andrea was aligning the ship to match his calculation. Our attitude jets fired, again and again, sending us on a giddying roll. Yeng passed the data to the fighter-bombers, and the *Necessary Evil But Still Cool* sent its own message to the Gate's little attitude-control jets. By the time we were ready to dock with the Gate it was lying at an odd angle, apparently 'below' us, like a tilted plate, and we were sliding backwards 'above' its mile-wide face. On some screen I noticed, out of the corner of my eye, that our own small comms drogue was darting about like a flea on a griddle, squandering its fuel in a mindless attempt to hold the correct position, relative to the disc of the Gate, for picking up the Division's messages. Zap it too? No – I was confident, even now, that the Division's computers and comms weren't going to fall for the Jovian outbreak.

The ship was now lined up for a straight blast into a course to intercept the comet-train, and to continue along 'up' that infall orbital path. The hull shuddered repeatedly as the grappling lines were fired. They snaked out, and were snared by the perimeter clamps. Andrea played another subtle but sickeningly violent crescendo on our own attitude jets, adjusting our alignment as the lines took the strain of the Gate's mass.

One hundred thousand tonnes, Dee had said. Plus another twenty thousand for the score of ships that had sailed through it on their bright bold enterprise . . . and had encountered at least one entity which had found the temptation, or competitive necessity, of *getting in first* as powerful as theirs. I thought of Dee, and wondered how her vaunted competitive countermeasures were holding out against whatever had come down the line from the poor, possessed *Running Dog*. Doing better than I expected, I hoped, for my sake – and hers, I realized, in a sudden pang of anguished solidarity with a self that, human or not, was at least as singular as mine.

'Holding position,' Andrea said.

'*General Arnaldo Ochoa* to *Terrible Beauty*.' Yeng was patching the message through to my phones. The voice was almost languid. 'Situation back home severely compromised. Situation here totally confusing. Please advise.'

Whoever that was had the right stuff, all right! I cut in the override on the Division's all-ships channel:

'Hi guys and gals, *Terrible Beauty* here. Situation as follows. At least one New Martian merchant ship, with crew, has been taken over by a Jovian upload or personality copy. That is confirmed, repeat confirmed. Comms drogue destroyed by us to stop viral spread. We don't repeat do not know if we did this in time. Observe extreme caution with all incoming comms of New-Martian origin. We are about to blast off with wormhole Gate in tow. Intend to try punching local comet-train through to hit Jupiter. You have two minutes to get clear or attempt to return home.'

The languid voice returned. 'Thanks for the clarification, *Terrible Beauty*. Good luck. We see heavy fighting back home. All ships have been recalled. We're leaving. Do you wish continued updates from our own comms drogue?'

'*Yes!*' shouted Yeng, the sheer volume of her voice carrying it to my override.

'Patching you through.'

The scene, relayed from the home system by the – for now – stable and on-position drogue, flashed up on the virtual screens of the suits, which were still tensing and hardening around us. It came from an external camera on the *Turing Tester*, loyally on station in front of the Gate.

Jupiter was bang in the middle of the view, as I'd hoped. The rest of the view sparkled with the flashes of distant laser hits and was scored by the scorch of particle-beams, and snowed by the chaff thrown out in efforts to deflect or diffuse both. Missile trails and kinetic-energy tracers added to the battle's blaze. Two or three of the trading vessels were in sight, each surrounded by a swarm of fighters. One was heading away on what looked like an entirely orthodox evasion course. The others were wallowing in the same bizarre way as the *Running Dog* had when its systems were first suborned. I could almost feel the strivings of the new minds in their unfamiliar frames, new impulses racing through controls, and the struggles of whatever parts of the ships' programming resisted its new master. The ships' yaw and pitch were resultant of these conflicting forces. Through the whole confused scene flitted the dark shapes of our own fighter-bombers, their violent manoeuvres dodging at least the kinetic-energy and missile weapons, but even in the first seconds of our observation, two were successfully targeted by particle-beams, and burst in silent agony.

One by one, the fighter-bombers on our side darted past, seeming to pass over our heads from the camera's viewpoint, our whole ship rocking as each fighter's mass passed through the Gate. I counted nine, then heard a now-familiar voice.

'*General Arnaldo Ochoa* says goodbye and good luck.'

'Goodbye,' I said.

For a tenth and final time, the great drumhead of stretched space to which we were attached resonated as the fighter-bomber went through. I saw its black, bat-like shadow-shape flit sideways a moment after its exit. We were on our own now.

Then I saw, heading straight towards us, filling the view, the bulk of a merchant ship. Something burned into its side, but it ploughed on. The last thing that the *Turing Tester*'s camera showed was an out-of-focus image of its looming forward shield. The last – and, while we were watching, only – sound to come through that channel via the comms drogue was a voice breaking in, by some frantic feat of hacking, to yell the warning:

'*Running Dog!*'

Our ship shook as the thousand-tonne mass passed through, simultaneously subtracting the same amount from the virtual mass of the Gate. A cable broke, lashing across the forward view. For an entire second, as I cut from the now-blank internal screen to an outside camera which Yeng had instantly and reflexively patched in, I watched in frozen shock as the huge ship rose from the wormhole Gate like a missile from a silo, with the wreck of the *Turing Tester* crumpled across its prow.

As soon as it cleared the Gate, its attitude jets fired with far greater precision than its earlier efforts had shown. Its new mind had mastered its controls, and it was turning its main drive away from us, and its blunt forward shield towards us.

'Andrea!' I tried to shout, but she'd already engaged the drive. The most violent acceleration I'd ever felt slammed down, crushing my shout to a grunt. The *Running Dog* vanished instantly from view, then reappeared as the camera swung to track.

'Boris,' I groaned. 'The nuke.'

'Can't,' his stronger voice came back. 'No time to program its course.'

'OK,' I breathed. 'Just send *Carbon Conscience* with it, kamikaze run.'

'Hope you mean kamikaze *autopilot*.'

'Don't – waste – breath . . .'

He wasted neither breath nor time, but it was a long minute before he'd punched the instructions through, and our very own fighter-bomber sprang from our side and flashed away, instantly outrun by our acceleration.

Yeng switched to its nose-camera, and – in less than a minute, its fuel burned off in one final sprint – we saw what it saw as it closed for the kill. We saw *Running Dog*'s bulk loom again. We saw the silent, shocking sphere of the fifty-megaton nuclear explosion . . . but not in that camera.

I swear we saw it through our hull.

The white afterimages of everything faded slowly, to be replaced by the red pulse of pain. I wasn't breathing – the suit was doing that for me – and the pinprick tubules of the suit's oxygen-supply were forged to hot blades stabbing through my almost-collapsed lungs.

Going for the short fast run, Andrea's message spelled out, in green letters on the wavering scarlet screen of my visual field. *Free fall in 20 mins, first encounter in a further 20.*

Can't you run it longer more speed? Boris asked.

Outa gas, replied Andrea.

Out of reaction-mass, to be precise. Nobody had any more questions. I hoped Andrea had allowed some reserve to get us home, wherever home was now, but I hadn't the heart or the strength to ask.

Jaime flashed up data about our target comet-stream: a long, rich train of fragments, nicely lined-up long ago by the New Martians' – or ultimately, ironically, the Outwarders' – automated machinery, far out in the system's vast cloud of unconsolidated ice and organics: still gigantic and irregular flying icebergs hundreds of yards across, each mined with chemical explosives synthesized *in situ* by the smart-matter that infiltrated it. These explosives were primed to detonate before its final fall on New Mars, breaking the masses into manageable morsels for the planet's atmosphere to ablate and its surface to absorb.

Something was troubling me, something I'd forgotten. I

struggled for the elusive thought, crushed as I was in that press of acceleration, and suddenly it seemed I had it – what if they broke up before hitting *Jupiter*? I dismissed it as unlikely – the nanomachines on the comet-chunks wouldn't mistake a gas-giant for a small and rocky world.

And anyway, there was nothing we could do about it, nothing at all. This was, in every sense, our last throw.

The crushing pressure ended. We all drew a first breath, and let it out in a common howl of pain just before the suits mainlined opiate derivatives into our blood, metered out precisely to cancel the agony and not to overshoot us into euphoria. Not that there was much risk of that.

'OK,' said Andrea, her voice shaking. 'We have twenty minutes to get clear and get this thing lined up. Stay in your seats.'

A quite redundant instruction, I thought, as I strove to twitch my fingers and call up screens. After about a minute, I succeeded. The suit's infiltration of my body was not withdrawing, this time; it still had work to do, as had everyone else's – the first screens I pulled in showed their physiological readouts. They were all alive, and conscious, and undergoing massive assistance and repair.

And I was not.

I stared at the screens, hardly believing what I saw, hardly believing that I was not seeing with my own eyes, or nerves, or brain. My brain had not shut down completely: it was keeping my body going, all right; but what Dee had called the cost of sustaining consciousness, of maintaining selfhood, had been passed elsewhere. The suit had shunted my mind straight into itself, running me as an update of the model it had taken, days earlier, for my back-up before the first Jovian probe.

So now I knew. I knew how a simulated mind experienced the world. There was no difference whatsoever.

At least, none that I, as a simulated mind, could tell.

Why had the suit done that? Why to me?

At that point I found a difference in my experience. I had an acute awareness of the suit's presence, its own awareness, as a loyal, living thing; and of its answer.

There is not only you, it said. *Potentially, there is another here. You are carrying a foetus. I optimize, based on your implied preference. The choice remains yours. You can override mine if you wish.*

I did not so wish.

As from a great distance, I watched Yeng disengage the grappling lines, Andrea boost us to a stable position a couple of miles from the wormhole Gate, and Jaime play the Gate's clamped-on attitude jets to bring it all to precisely the right angle for the oncoming comet-stream.

'That's it,' Jaime said. 'Just made it, the drones are almost out out of gas themselves.'

'Three minutes to go,' said Andrea.

The comets were closing so fast that, even at this late moment, they were still invisible to the forward telescope. Even if their reflected light could have been picked up, they'd show no proper motion against the background of stars, until the last few seconds before interception. Only the deep-space radar clocked their approach. I lay still, my fingertips keying in codes to flip through outside views: the system's sun – small compared to how ours had looked from Earth, big and burning in my Callistan eyes; the distant ochre disc of New Mars; and the paradoxical ellipse of the gate.

'Two minutes.'

She counted down the last minute. As she said 'Two!' I saw, in one of my screens, something moving against the stars: the first comet, seen with – not quite – the naked eye.

'One!'

'Ze –'

Cherenkov backwash flooded all our sight.

The other fragments followed with less than a second between them. Blue light strobed. Ten cometary masses, each of them weighing in at hundreds of thousands of tonnes. Four passed through the Gate, adding their mass to our side of it – and subtracting it from the other.

'We must be into negative mass, now,' Malley said. 'I wish I could see what it's like.'

We were in free fall, but we all stayed in our couches, too exhausted to move, and perhaps afraid to. We had nothing to do but wait, and watch the process by which we hoped to accomplish the destruction of a world. I knew, now – now that I too was a copied mind running in smart-matter – that the Jovians were not flatlines;

that they were, indeed, a superior species not just in the reach of their power, but in the depth of their minds. They, like us, had infinite space within, subjective worlds; they were not just entities, but beings.

And at this moment – no, at another moment, ten thousand years in the past – our first shots at them were crashing down, smashing those subjective worlds; our crude rocks were bashing in thinner skulls and deeper minds than ours. If, that is, we had succeeded in our aim.

It came to me, then, that what we *were doing* now had *already been done*, that the interactions of the Gate and the comet fragments in our immediate future had consequences in the far past – that, in some sense, the battle was already over. The universe within ten thousand light years of the Sun was already being colonized by our descendants, or theirs. There was no way of telling, of course – they, or we, might 'already' have near-lightspeed Malley Drive ships, dragging new wormhole gates, but if they 'had' penetrated further than New Mars, they wouldn't arrive until so many years in our future. The thought gave me an odd, fatalistic reassurance, when it wasn't twisting my mind in knots that only Malley, perhaps, could have unravelled.

I lay there and waited. What would be would be.

The Gate was still open; still hurtling along the orbital path of the other incoming comets, ready to intersect the next stream – as it did, half an hour later. These were larger, less shaped, but still small enough to go through. As was the next stream, and the next, until finally, ten hours and countless cometary fragments later, we reached the limit of the wormhole structure's capacity to sustain a negative mass.

Malley grunted, as if some calculation had been confirmed.

'Now we know,' he said.

The remaining fragments we encountered passed through where the Gate had been.

No longer held together by the tension of the Gate, its rim broke up into sections: dull arcs that drifted apart and then, very slowly, together, under the attraction of the enormous, invisible mass of some exotic matter which was all that remained of the warped space they had contained. It continued to move outwards, against the infalling stream of comets, out towards their source.

11

Looking Forward

M OVE OR COPY?
     The suit's query could, for me, have only one answer. I
had no wish to leave a second self hanging around in the suit's
circuitry. Nevertheless, my second self had second thoughts. Was I
– the real me, existing now, at this moment, about to die? About to
commit suicide, for the sake of another person, who would wake
with my memories, back in the presently unconscious meat? Or was
I – the copy – about to murder *my real self*, who would otherwise
awaken, with no memory of what had transpired between the loss of
her consciousness and its recovery?

Once you start thinking like that, I realized, there is no end to it.

'Move,' I said.

Something happened then, in that brief, eternal moment when I
sparked across the gap between the suit and the skull. I saw a
hundred billion stars, as they might be after a hundred thousand
years. It was, of course, a vision, a hallucination; or an intention, a
programme, a plan; but what I do not know to this day is whether it
was mine: whence it came, and to whom it was vouchsafed.

I saw a galaxy of green and gold, its starlight filtered through
endless, countless habitats; the federation of our dreams. And
behind it all, in the walls of all our worlds, an immense but finite
benevolence, a great engine of protection and survival; a god on *our*
side, a terror to our enemies and a friend to us, worlds without end.

A god who smiled, its work to see; and who now smiled on mine.

Someone was shaking me. I struggled, in too-solid flesh.

'Ellen!' Boris was asking. 'Are you all right?'

I opened my eyes and cracked an awful smile (I know, because
I've seen the recording that Boris's eye made).

'I'm fine,' I said. 'I just . . . passed out for a moment.'

* * *

'Situation report,' said Andrea, briskly. 'We're almost out of reaction-mass, although of course we can still get all the power we need from the drive. We're in an orbital couple with the dark matter, or whatever, where the Gate was, and heading rapidly outwards towards the local comet–cloud. We don't know if New Mars has fallen to any final transmissions from the *Running Dog*, and we don't know if our bombardment did in the Jovians. It was a lot weaker, after all, than the massive comet-strike we had set up in the Solar System.' She paused, gazing at the star-speckled forward view. 'And now the Gate is gone, we'll never find out.'

'Until the first Malley Drive ships turn up,' I said, grimly. 'Ours or theirs.'

'Why ships?' Malley asked. He seemed amused.

I stared at him. 'Well,' I began, 'assuming somebody can re-invent the virtual-mass drive you postulated, and which the first fast folk built for their probe, it can travel at close to lightspeed, and we're ten thousand light years away but ten thousand years in the future, so –'

I stopped, suddenly feeling stupid, as everybody got the point at the same time, and laughed.

That ten thousand years was time enough for any radio signals from the Solar System to reach us; signals that originated immediately after we left.

'It won't be easy to pick up,' said Yeng. 'I'll have to build a radio *telescope*.'

'How long will that take?' I asked.

Yeng frowned. 'Some time,' she said. 'I'd have to dig out our last parachute, which is of course not much use to us now, and rejig some hull-maintenance robots to paint it with a monomolecular foil mesh. It's half a mile across, so it should be sensitive enough, especially as we know where to point it.' She mentally calculated. 'It'll take several hours, at least.'

'*That* long?' snorted Malley. 'Good grief, woman, I thought you were talking about *years*.'

I'd been reckoning on months, but I didn't say it. I smiled at Yeng and said:

'OK, that's great. But I think the *first* thing we have to find out is if New Mars is all right. Because if it isn't, we could be in real trouble, real soon.'

Despite protests – somehow, the thought of waiting was even more intolerable, now that we knew we could find out – we went ahead and re-ran the procedure to check the New-Martian radio traffic. Yeng worked her way through her entire armoury of defences, and found them all clear, relaying the same insistent and wholly human commerce as she had found before. The incidents of the past hours were being analysed by many loud and conflicting voices. Nobody knew we were still in the system, and we had no intention, just yet, of telling them.

New Mars, at least, was safe. We left the radio on, in celebration. The New Martians' old music, with its perverse celebration of strange sad yearnings and desperate desires, began again to infiltrate our own minds like a viral meme. It formed the soundtrack as we all pitched in to help Yeng deploy and adapt the bubble-thin parachute, a process we called our STI project – the search for terrestrial intelligence.

It was a nervous joke. We didn't know what we'd find. We didn't speak of our fear that what we'd find would be the incomprehensible – or all too comprehensible – voices that told us that our exile, and our great proud crime, had been for naught.

When the telescope was completed, we all hung in the air around Yeng, on the command deck. Every sound was loud: the air conditioning, the murmur of the ship to itself, the ping of the radar, our breathing. Yeng ignored them all, working through the first faint signals her great dish aerial had picked up. She ran them through every check, through her hardware and software, the analyser fixels flickering in their game of life. For long minutes, she studied them, then without a word, without looking around, she flicked the speakers on and rotated a dial.

The command deck filled with the sounds of human beings from the far past: talking, singing, arguing, squabbling, claiming and disputing – a sound immediately redoubled by ourselves, doing much the same, but louder. Then we stopped yelling, and listened again. Most of the broadcasting was still being done by non-cos, and there was – just as on New Mars – a lot of ill-informed speculation, but it was obvious that our strike had been a success. The Division's internal messages were, as we could have expected, narrow-beamed, and nothing so far had leaked in our direction.

We drank a lot of alcohol that shift.

Some time later I found I'd eaten a pizza topped with synthesized anchovies, olives, banana and pineapple. I had never eaten such a revolting combination before, and I vaguely wondered about it as I licked a final ice cream before falling asleep. I slept for hours, longer than anyone else. I woke up among them all, still on the command deck, and was promptly and quite publicly sick.

Suze looked at me with a funny, speculative grin.

'Comrades,' I said, 'I have something to tell you.'

It was a month or so later that Yeng's telescope picked up the first signal directed at us: a television signal, open and unencrypted. The call sign had us all leaving whatever we were doing, literally in midair, and rushing to the nearest screen. Tatsuro's face appeared. He was sitting in a virtual conference-space, with some of the Command Committee members, a group of people in New-Martian commercial uniforms, and, to my surprise, Jonathan Wilde. (The copy of . . . but I'd stopped thinking that way. I had reformed.)

'I feel very strange saying this,' Tatsuro began. 'This message is to be sent by the most powerful transmitter we currently have, and will be repeated, on more powerful transmitters as they become available, for at least some years to come. It will not, of course, reach its intended recipients for ten thousand years. If you're receiving this, you know how strange the circumstances are. But I have to assume that you're there, in the future, and that to you this message seems almost immediate. So –

'To the crew of *Terrible Beauty*, we all send our thanks. Your comet-strike was just sufficient to disrupt the Jovian post-humans. To the best of our knowledge, they are extinct, not only from your actions, and ours, but also from fighting amongst themselves. You need not worry that you destroyed entities which might have been friendly to us – any that were, I'm afraid, were destroyed by other Jovians, who were in the process of a frantic race to upload copies of themselves into anything they could reach. Strangely enough, the target of their outbreak was the New-Martian trading ships rather than ourselves. Our computers were almost impervious to the Jovian viruses, whereas theirs were, ah, rather more vulnerable, as it turned out. Our latest investigations and reconstructions show that the Jovians were aiming for the Malley Mile, from which they could have mastered the entire span of the wormhole, and with it a large part of the universe. You saved more than you knew.

'Whether you saved the humans and post-humans of New Mars, we don't know. If you have not, or if this message is being received by our enemies, I hope the destruction of the Jovians is a sufficient warning of the terrible acts of which our species is capable. For we are going to build new virtual-mass quantum-fluctuation drive ships, and new wormhole gates, as soon as we have the capacity. We will re-establish contact with New Mars. And now, I'll wish you well, and pass the transmission to the survivors of the New-Martian trading expedition, who have messages of their own.'

One by one, the New-Martian men and women came up, each speaking a heartfelt, and heart-rending, personal message – some, in a way that struck me as strange, addressed to their own copies as well as to friends and relations. One of them finished by saying:

'This is just a general message to all of you out there. We'll do our best to maintain one-way communication – we'll keep in touch, until they build the ships. Of course, unless they build another gate as well, the ships will be one-way, too, as far as getting back to this place and time is concerned – but we're coming home. And you don't need to worry about how the Solar Union people will treat us – Wilde here has lived off their hospitality for years, according to his needs, as they say. But what most of us want is to do some business, with the non-cooperators if no one else – but I think we'll find more trading partners than that. There are a lot of energetic people on Earth, and now they can use electronics as they please, they are going to *boil off*. Things are going to change around here. We *will* see you again.'

Wilde had learned from the traders about the survival of his other self and his resurrected wife. He had messages for them, and for me.

'Ellen May,' he said, 'I thought you could defeat the Outwarders without finding the way to New Mars. Well, I was mistaken, and you've done both. You know what I feared – that your people would invade New Mars, a place for which I have . . . a certain affection. Now, looking around me, I wonder just who has invaded whom. Life may surprise us.'

He shrugged. 'That's all. Good luck.'

I'm looking out of what we still, from habit, call the forward view.

The sun of New Mars is a tiny, distant disc, barely noticeable against the other stars. We are in the thick of the comet-cloud, but this thickness is only visible in simulations, not in reality. All around us is what looks like empty space, apart from our very own comet, surrounded by the frail-seeming, diamond-strong structures we've built from its material; and the strange ruin of the Gate.

Exotic matter is useful stuff to have around. It pulled us into a close orbit with an even bigger chunk of normal matter: cometary matter, hundreds of millions of tonnes of it, rock and ice and organics. It took us five years, give or take, to get out to the cometary cloud, so by that time we were ready to appreciate our gain. These days, the remnant of the Gate has begun to acquire its own accretion disc. It is, as Malley once put it, an attractive feature.

Every home should have one.

Home . . . is here, in one sense. In another, it's ten thousand light years away – and ten thousand years in the past. (Although I still find myself thinking that *we* are ten thousand years in the future.)

The solar sources grew and multiplied – at the time we first heard them, they increased by the day and the hour. Within months they were detectable by much less sensitive receivers than ours, including those on and around New Mars.

The transmissions tell the ongoing tale of the struggle which that New-Martian trader foresaw, and whose conclusion no one can foresee: between the Union's common ownership and the unstoppable appropriation of the Solar System's resources by individuals and groups; a story intently followed by ourselves and by the New Martians. It has the immediacy of daily news, and the poignancy of ancient history, which nothing we can do will alter and whose ultimate outcome, if any, was settled millennia ago. It's already the subject of numerous documentaries, frequent debates, and several completely fictitious and laughably imaginative New-Martian drama serials.

The comet-cloud is vast, and we are used to communicating by narrow, cryptic channels, by winks of laser in the void. Around us the broader, more open signals of the New Martians and their robot comet-miners fill the spectrum. We know all that they do, and they know we're here, but little more. We keep contact to a minimum. We're happy with that, for now: we want to build a world of our own out here, out of rock and ice and carbon-compounds and weak sunlight, before we venture back to a world owned by others.

One day the Solar Union, or whatever replaces it, will have built its own near-lightspeed Malley Drive ships. And ten thousand years later, which could be any day now, they'll turn up here, perhaps dragging a new wormhole. I don't much mind if the people who arrive don't share our views. They certainly won't share our property. We may, by then, have the beginnings of our own little galactic empire quietly accreted around us, out here in the depths of the comet-cloud. When we have enough mass processed, we'll start growing people and animals and machines from the seeds in our stores, and we can grow a long way before anyone even thinks to stop us.

I'm scanning the analyser readings of a new lode, frowning over the sparse traces of metal, when a small body cannons into me and a voice says, 'Ellen, they're talking about you!'

Stef is four years old, lanky and bright. He looks a bit like his father, the photographer I met on Graciosa, but he'll grow taller than his father: my genes, and his microgravity environment, will see to that. It's a struggle getting him to keep up his induction isotonics, in addition to all the usual fights about brushing teeth and washing hair. He claims his suit takes care of all that, and it does, but that's not good enough.

'Back home?' I ask eagerly.

Stef shakes his head, impatiently. To him, the Solar Union is almost unreal, a mythical past, a tale we tell him of our Heliocene days. New Mars is, in every sense, more immediate and vivid.

'In the *world*,' he tells me.

'OK,' I say. 'Patch it through.'

Stef sticks his hand inside the open front of his suit, and tugs and twists the smart-matter fabric in exactly the careless, undocumented way I've always tried to argue him out of. To no avail, so far. He regards the suit as something between an imaginary friend and an intelligent stuffed toy, and treats any attempt to impose a system on their private language as just that, an imposition.

The image on my screen dissolves and is replaced by one of those late-night discussion programmes that New-Martian television stations put out for the slenderest of minority audiences, the sort of people who probably work in or around the media themselves and affect to despise the rubbish they put out for everybody else.

The format is utterly conventional, with a young presenter – a teenager, and thus more mature than most local newscasters – and a few older heads discoursing earnestly around a table. I recognize the bishop, who is probably, whether she realizes it or not, by now the Pope; the rabbi; a Reformed Humanist spokesperson; a couple of Post-Resurrectionist clerics – and David Reid.

'– calling it *justifiable genocide* is, shall we say, uncalled for,' one of the clerics is saying. 'I understand your need to be provocative, of course.' A quick, we're-all-in-this-together smile to the presenter. 'But I think we need to consider it in more, ah, morally neutral terms. We are, after all, talking about *machinery*.'

Reid leans forward, as usual establishing his priority to speak with a wavy trail of smoke. The presenter, knowing her limitations, wearily nods.

'Rubbish,' Reid says. 'If you want to talk about morality, you can't leave out machinery. We *are* machinery. The point is, I doubt if anyone could have done what *had* to be done to the Jovians without having a pretty hard attitude to the sufferings of machines. Mind you, the Outwarders had a pretty low empathy with the sufferings of humans, and the Jovians inherited that flaw, so –'

'Original sin?' interupts the bishop. 'I'm surprised at you!'

The two Calvinist clergmen smirk politely. Reid shakes his head.

'They showed it by their actions,' he says. 'By what they did to our ships.'

'Ah, but was that enough to condemn an entire . . . species?' the Reformed Humanist asks. 'I suspect Ellen May Ngwethu and her crew acted precipitately, but with a degree of premeditation, a refusal to consider alternatives, which in itself –'

'We live in a tough world,' says the rabbi. 'As my people have traditionally put it, life is short and shit happens.'

A few minutes of free-for-all follows.

'What everybody here seems to be forgetting,' says the presenter, trying to get a word in edgeways, 'is the evidence from the Solar System, which at least suggests that the Jovian outbreak was *no threat whatsoever* to the people in the Solar Union. So, in effect, whatever we think of what the crew of the *Terrible Beauty* did, it was to our benefit.'

'And to that of the new societies emerging in the Solar System,' one of the clerics adds. 'They wouldn't exist without the ending of the Jovian threat, which, whether we approve of it or not, the Cassini Division accomplished.'

The Reformed Humanist nods gravely. 'At some cost, moral and material, to themselves.'

The next comment, if any, is drowned out by Reid's cynical guffaw, and then he says: 'What *else* are communists *for?*'

The complacent laughter of all the good liberals around the table lightens the tone of the rest of the discussion, to which I pay not the slightest attention. I'm hugging the kid to my side and looking at the cheerful, chatting faces, and thinking, *Just you wait, you bankers! Just you wait!*

Our day will come, again.

THE STAR FRACTION

Ken MacLeod

In a newer world order where the peace process is deadlier than the wars …

Moh Kohn's a security mercenary with a smart gun, reflexes to die for and memories he doesn't want to reach.

Janis Taine's a scientist with a new line in memory drugs, anti-tech terrorists on her case and the STASIS cops on her trail.

Jordan Brown's a teenage atheist with a guilty conscience, a wad of illicit cash and an urgent need to get a life.

Between them they've started the countdown to the final confrontation, as the cryptic Star Fraction assembles its codes, the Army of the New Republic prepares its offensive and Space Defense lines up its laser weapons for the hour of the Watchmaker …

'Formidably intelligent and extraordinarily original'
New York Review of Science Fiction

THE STONE CANAL

Ken MacLeod

Jonathan Wilde is dead. His memory is immortal.

The young man who walks into Ship City remembers all of Wilde's life and death. That 21st-century anarchist agitator took some of his secrets to the grave, and beyond. His clone is back and looking for the man who sent him to a cold and lonely death.

Dee Model is beautiful and sophisticated. She knows she's just a machine, but she's felt like a human being for at least two days. And being a rich man's toy isn't her idea of fun any more. She's looking for people who know that information wants to be free.

David Reid never died. He lived through wars and revolutions, and through the AIs' catastrophic transcendence. Out of that disaster he built New Mars, and he isn't going to let the dead and the fast folk – the AIs – come back and take it away.

Only the construction machine knows the answers, and they're where identity and memory, self and story meet: at the end of the Stone Canal.

INVERSIONS

Iain M. Banks

In the winter palace, the King's new physician has more enemies than she at first realises. But then she also has more remedies to hand than those who wish her ill can know about.

In another palace across the mountains, in the service of the regicidal Protector General, the chief bodyguard too has his enemies. But his enemies strike more swiftly, and his means of combating them are more traditional.

Spirallling round a central core of secrecy, deceit, love and betrayal, INVERSIONS is a spectacular work of science fiction, brilliantly told and widly imaginative, from an author who has set genre fiction alight.

'A fantastic, awe-inspiring book … I can't imagine anyone not being won over by this deeply entertaining, thought-provoking and humane story'
The Express

Also by Iain M. Banks

CONSIDER PHLEBAS
THE PLAYER OF GAMES
USE OF WEAPONS
THE STATE OF THE ART
AGAINST A DARK BACKGROUND
FEERSUM ENDJINN
EXCESSION

Available from Orbit

Orbit titles available by post:

☐ The Stone Canal	Ken MacLeod	£5.99
☐ The Star Fraction	Ken MacLeod	£6.99
☐ Consider Phlebas	Iain M. Banks	£6.99
☐ The Player of Games	Iain M. Banks	£6.99
☐ Use of Weapons	Iain M. Banks	£6.99
☐ The State of the Art	Iain M. Banks	£6.99
☐ Against a Dark Background	Iain M. Banks	£7.99
☐ Feersum Endjinn	Iain M. Banks	£6.99
☐ Excession	Iain M. Banks	£6.99
☐ Inversions	Iain M. Banks	£16.99

The prices shown above are correct at time of going to press. However, the publishers reserve the right to increase prices on covers from those previously advertised without prior notice.

ORBIT

ORBIT BOOKS
Cash Sales Department, P.O. Box 11, Falmouth, Cornwall, TR10 9EN
Tel: +44 (0) 1326 372400, Fax: +44 (0) 1326 374888
Email: books@barni.avel.co.uk.

POST AND PACKING:
Payments can be made as follows: cheque, postal order (payable to Orbit Books) or by credit cards. Do not send cash or currency.
U.K. Orders under £10   £1.50
U.K. Orders over £10   **FREE OF CHARGE**
E.E.C. & Overseas   25% of order value

Name (Block Letters) _____

Address_____

_____

Post/zip code:_____

☐ Please keep me in touch with future Orbit publications

☐ I enclose my remittance £_____

☐ I wish to pay by Visa/Access/Mastercard/Eurocard

Card Expiry Date

_____